FALLEN RIBBON

Fallen Ribbon

The Dark Nursery Diaries

Book 1

Tiara J Vasquez

Edited by Bethany Berry
Cover Design by Stephanie Wilcinksi
Cover Photography from Shutterstock.com

ISBN: 979-8-9937789-2-1
Printed In USA
2nd Edition

Published by Tiara J. Vasquez 2025
Massachusetts USA
Tiaravasquez.com

Acknowledgements

To Mom and Grandma, who supported my love of vampires at an early age and encouraged me to read and write whatever I want.

To Claire, my first friend in Boston. It's easy to have a great idea, it's hard to follow through with a great idea, but I did it thanks to your support.

To Stephanie, for designing a beautiful cover I couldn't have done without you, and your endless patience for my indecisiveness.

To Nicole, for being the first to read the book. Your empathy and our shared love of reading and writing will always mean the world to me.

To Cailin, my longest treasured friend and the first to hear of the story concept fifteen years ago.

To my Launch Team: Kendall, Riley, and Beth, your participation and support through this process brought me to this point. Your feedback helped get this book on its feet. Let's see if it will spread its wings.

Part 1
The Mortal Realm

CHAPTER 1

GEORDIE
FALL

The heat of the sun beat down on Geordie mercilessly as she ran down the pathways of the Boston Commons. Her skin sweltered under the intense summer heat, and the humidity weighed her body down. The intensity of it all slowed her to a stop as she caught her breath. The air then shifted to a chill that pierced her skin. Clouds began to loom overhead as the winter angel, Frost, approached.

Geordie stumbled to her feet, running once more to get away from her longtime pursuer. She had to get away from Frost if she were to live. From the point she was born, angels were constantly trying to kill her, and she had to run if she were to save her own life.

Geordie tripped face first into a bright clearing of trees of the commons. Blood tasted like burning copper in her mouth as the scrapes on her hands and knees healed quickly, and only the dried blood remained. An icy cold hand whipped her around and blasted her full of ice, throwing her back. Geordie recovered in time to see Frost approaching menacingly.

"It's been a while, Half-Breed. Six months to be exact?" Frost cooed as she knelt at Geordie's eye level. "Why don't you come with me like a good little girl and stop resisting?"

"Not while I still breathe!" Geordie spat in Frost's face. This resulted in Frost lifting Geordie by the neck, strangling her with a grip that seeped ice.

"You know I'm not allowed to kill you in *this* world. Be a dear and come quietly. You know humans cannot see us, and no one will come to your aid."

Abruptly a male voice came from afar, interrupting the quarrel. Geordie could barely process anything over the sound of her lungs gasping for air. Geordie was flung across the commons into a large fountain in the common's center and spat up blood violently.

"You're not making this very easy for me…" Frost hissed. "People who try to help you end up dead. Spare me the headache."

"It's okay! You're going to be okay; I've got you." Frost was gone, and a young man rushed to her, saying something she couldn't process. Her head throbbed as blood poured down her face from the collision and everything went black.

MATT

The last days of summer were being enjoyed by Matt and his friends as they strolled the Boston Commons smoking weed out in the open. So many people did it regularly that the authorities couldn't be bothered to try to stop anyone anymore since it was decriminalized. He wasn't sure if it was because he was high, but he thought he saw a radiantly beautiful girl being nearly strangled by another woman with blue hair who looked like a beautiful force to be reckoned with. It wasn't until his friends got quiet, also staring at the girl choked, that he knew she was real.   She was being strangled by an older woman whose body was perfectly toned.

Before he knew it, Matt yelled in a feeble attempt to distract them. The older woman tossed the young girl into the giant fountain and ran across the street to a dark alley. When Matt approached the girl, her breathing was faint. The beautiful girl's hair was long and black, and her skin cream white like marble. It shone brightly in the summer sun and burnt to the touch. Where his hand touched her skin, a red-hot mark blistered. Matt pulled a hooded jacket out of his bag and quickly wrapped her in it. Looking around, his friends disappeared, and he was alone.

"You're going to be okay; I've got you." Matt picked her up, avoiding touching her skin. As he headed back to his car and was no longer covered by the shade of the trees, her face began to sunburn and blister. He carefully pulled the hood over her face to conceal it. "Look, it's going to be all right, I'm going to take you to the hospital."

"No, no hospitals, I can't go to a hospital." The girl's hoarse voice was barely audible.

Hesitantly, he took her to his apartment off Newbury Street where he knew she would be safe. She woke up along the way but didn't say much.

"What's your name?" He asked, but she only looked out

the window. "I'm Matt, you know, the guy that saved you? Are you from around here?"

No response. He knew she had to say something eventually, so he kept talking until she had no choice but to respond. "You know I need *something* from you, I can't just have some mystery girl in the backseat of my car."

"Then let me go." She whispered. "I need to leave; I've already spent too much time here."

"I can't do that, or you'll die of blood loss. I need to help you." Matt felt heroic as he said it. "Look, just go up to my apartment and let me patch you up. Then you can go wherever you want."

"You don't know what you're talking about."

When they pulled into the parking lot, Matt noticed she looked paler than when he first found her. Before he could help her out of the car, she was already a few paces ahead, walking towards the building. He wondered how she managed to move so quickly. "You move fast for someone who's injured.

"It's not as bad as you think." He tried his best to help her as they went up the staircase to the fourth floor of his building.

"Are you alright? You seem… sad." He examined her face. Her eyes were a piercing grey, and her hair was like a black waterfall cascading down her back. She was extremely

petite, almost gaunt, but curved as well. He unlocked the door
to the apartment, revealing a small living room, tossing his
keys on an end table nearby. "Would you like to come in?"

"I'm fine. I just need –" She stopped, mid-sentence,
looking around anxiously.

GEORDIE

When Geordie walked into his apartment, the first thing she
noticed were all the mirrors. It was like being watched from
all angles; there were at least four or five of them. She rushed
around the apartment, flipping them over. Matt could only
stare at her in awe, slowly following her around, mesmerized
by her craziness. She didn't care; she wasn't taking any
chances of being seen by an angel. When she finished, she
began to feel dizzy. She could still feel a bit of Frost's magic
lingering inside her body.

"May I please bandage you up before there's nothing left of
you?" He moved her over to a bed and sat down near her feet.
She looked at him in disbelief. She couldn't believe he was
willing to invite her into his apartment when they barely knew
each other.

"Why are you doing this?"

"Well… I want to help you as best I can. Plus, I already
want to get to know you. You seem like an interesting person.
Is that a good enough reason?" Their eyes met, and for the
first time, she noticed how beautiful his facial structure was.

It was unreal how beautiful it was. His face was slender and complete with chocolate brown eyes and short, dark brown hair and perfectly golden, honey skin. Geordie broke the gaze between them by placing her head on a pillow.

"Sure, fine, whatever. Do what you want to do, just don't kill me." Geordie closed her eyes for a moment and listened to Matt chuckle. It surprised her to hear someone laugh at one of her jokes.

"Okay. Uh, hold on, I need to get my First Aid Kit." He left the room for a long moment. Geordie carefully analyzed the cluttered room; there were various posters that lined the walls representing a wide range of bands. Next to the foot of the bed were two desktop computers and one laptop sharing one incredibly messy desk littered with energy drink cans. Closest to Geordie's head was a drum set, a bass guitar, and a keyboard. The clutter began to bother Geordie and she hoped that Matt would come back soon. Within a few moments, he came back in with a glass of water, a First Aid Kit, and a washcloth in hand.

"What's the cloth for?" Geordie eyed it carefully with a skeptical look.

"It's so that way you can bite down on it to get through the pain." Geordie furrowed her brows as he handed her the rag; there was no reason why she needed it but Matt didn't need to know that. "So shall we get through this?"

"Sure."

"Well, would you be willing to take off the tights? I need to get to the wounds better to clean them." His cheeks turned a flush red, and Geordie almost couldn't help but smile.

"Yeah, that's fine." She got up and removed her tights.

"I'll be just outside!" Matt quickly left the room, leaving Geordie with the impression that he was embarrassed of her.

As she took them off, she realized that the tights were a lot bloodier than she expected so she threw them in the waste basket beside her. Once removed, Geordie called Matt back in, and he immediately began cleaning up Geordie's wounds. The time passed quickly as Geordie watched him handle his human medical supplies. He was very careful with her, so she decided it best not to disturb his concentration. When he finished cleaning off the blood, Matt looked astounded at the sight of her where her wounds were supposed to be. "That's not possible... I saw there were scrapes there..."

"It's nothing to be concerned about... thank you for the help." She pulled her bare legs away slightly. "I must leave, *now*. I've already spent too much time here as it is."

She started to get up, but he pushed her back down onto the bed. His force was gentle, but also strong. Geordie flinched at his touch, demanding harshly, "What are you doing?"

"A little rest would not hurt. I will wake you up in a few hours." His deep brown eyes stared intensely into hers and suddenly she felt compelled to do as he said. After that he left and didn't return. She paced the room impatiently, waiting for something to happen. A headache started forming and she felt completely unprepared for it. She got back on the bed and fell asleep almost instantly.

SAM

Walking through the Boston Commons, Sam's worst nightmare came to life as Matt's attention was suddenly diverted to the attention of two angels out in the open fighting. Humans couldn't see angels, so he wasn't concerned about the mortals, but Matt's sudden focus on them was more concerning than anything else Sam had dealt with in his life. Matt shouldn't be able to see the angels as a human.

The rest of their group was also transfixed by the display of violence in the clearing of the common's trees, and Matt's sudden shouting at the quarrel. Out of nowhere, Matt took off running toward the fight faster than Sam was prepared for, "Matt, no!"

He was already on the other side of the commons by the time Sam tried to reach out to grab him. One of their friends, a fellow vampire, quickly grabbed Sam by the arm, stopping him from pursuing Matt and shaking her head. Sam looked back to Matt who was helping the younger of the two angels while the other took off across the street. It took every ounce of his being to not go after Matt right then and there.

"Let's go. I will find him later." Sam grumbled quietly and they all returned to the comforts of Andvari's Trove.

Not long after being stationed in Boston, Sam opened a club with the intention of providing a safe space for supernatural creatures to spend their free time. It resulted in being treated as a haven for the various species. Violence wasn't permitted in the club and that one rule was respected among the patrons unanimously. In time, after introducing Matt to the club, it became the one place Sam could count on that Matt would be safe in, no matter what.

As the staff prepared to open for the shift, Sam slumped his thin body into one of the elevated booths closest to the entrance as soon as they got back. He couldn't erase the image of two angels fighting out in the open from his mind. He wondered what got into them, that they would take their quarrel to the Mortal Realm. It was common knowledge that the angels had been threatening war on the vampires for years, but he had never heard of them having any infighting.

"Your thinking face is on." Lizzie slid into the booth with Sam, his fingers intertwined with hers as he pulled her into his arms, and she laid her head on his shoulder gently. To him, Lizzie was *his* beautiful guardian angel.

For over two hundred years they had been together since she turned him. Every day he looked at her, Lizzie's mysterious beauty astounded him. Her resemblance was more reminiscent of being an angel than a vampire, but he knew for a fact she was a vampire since she was the one who turned him. She did, in fact, share an uncanny resemblance to the angel with the black hair in the commons. Running his fingers through her long hair as she looked up at him with the same green eyes he possessed. From what Sam could remember of the girl's face in the commons, they could've been sisters.

"We ran into a couple of angels in the Boston Commons today."

Lizzie's eyes furrowed slightly in concern, "You saw an angel?"

"Two of them actually… they were fighting. It was strange to see. I've never heard of angels fighting each other before." Sam leaned his head back against the booth seat, looking up at the ceiling, lost in thought.

"What did they look like? Was it a man and a woman?" Lizzie sat up, leaning closer to him causing Sam to look down at her curiously.

"No, it was two women. One was wearing all blue with blue hair and she was using ice magic. The other was significantly younger and looked a lot like you. Do you know something about this?"

Sam knew there was much knowledge he didn't know about that Lizzie had from before their time together and he never questioned that, nor did he question her about it. He trusted that if whatever she learned throughout her life from before they met became relevant, she would share it with him. Lizzie just shook her head and reassured him, "I don't know much, except the blue one is Frost if she was emitting powers of ice. She's known as the Winter Angel and for being incredibly deadly. She's not known for taking people alive, let alone vampires. The other one, I'm not sure."

Without another word, Sam got up immediately to head to Matt's apartment. He couldn't believe he was so foolish to not recognize the Winter Angel when he saw her. What Lizzie said made absolute sense. Everyone knew about Frostbite Isaz. She took pride in killing vampires in the name of Ezra Daron, but everyone knew she only did it for fun.

Matt was in danger, even if he didn't recognize it, and Sam knew he would regret it if he didn't go out to at least help his mortal friend.

"Where are you going?" Lizzie called out behind him as he flung himself out of the booth.

"Matt saw those two angels and went after them. I must go find him. If he comes in here, warn him to stay away from them. His life could be in danger if he continues to meddle in the affairs of immortals." He then pulled his gloves on and his hood over his head before heading out to the hot setting sun.

MATT

The door shut silently behind Matt as he returned to the living room. He intended on calling his best friend, Sam, to apologize for what happened earlier, but he was already sitting in Matt's recliner in front of him. Just from his visage, Matt could tell that Sam had something smug to say. He always had something smug to say because that's just the way he was.

"Don't look at me like that." Matt collapsed onto the couch, sprawling out and stretching his muscles. He gave

Sam a side glance. There was an interesting resemblance
between Sam and the girl sleeping in his bedroom. They both
shared the same pale skin and gaunt look, as if they hadn't
eaten in weeks.

"Look at you in *what* way?" he asked, pretending to not
know what Matt was talking about. "I was just wondering
why you decided to run away from your friends, and never
bothered to give anyone a call to let us know where you were,
or if you were okay."

"I had to help someone out. She was in trouble with –"

"I've never known you to be so irresponsible, Matt." He
cut him off curtly, and quickly stood up, heading toward
Matt's room. By the time Matt asked him what he was doing,
Sam was opening the door. "I'm going to see this girl whom
you've just saved. I may know her."

"No!" Matt blocked Sam from entering. He gave Matt a
strange look and attempted to enter Matt's room. They
twisted and turned against each other. This kept up for a few
moments until Sam finally stopped impatiently and looked at
Matt sternly.

"Either you move out of my way, or I move you myself."
They both composed themselves, staring at the other. "I've
never known you to hide anything from me... This is big."

"I just… *really* don't want you to scare her… She needs
rest and is very eager to leave." Matt thought about how he

longed for her to stay. He didn't understand why. It was as though he *needed* the girl to stay there with him.

"Trust me; she'll never even know I existed." Sam then opened the door and glided over to the bed in complete silence where the mysterious girl lay asleep. He pulled down the covers only enough to reveal her small, pale face. "This is her?" His voice trembled as he looked down upon her with vicious green eyes.

"Yeah, that's her."

"Do you know who this is?"

"No… why, is there something wrong?"

"Get rid of her." He strode out before Matt had a chance to say anything else. Matt demanded to know what was wrong, but Sam was already gone, slamming the door behind him. Matt ran over to the main hallway of the apartment building to pursue Sam, but there was no one in sight.

Sunlight blazed down into the building from the vine covered skylights, in various patterns of light. Matt could see the dust and heat in the air as a fan outside a nearby apartment pathetically blew warm air towards the balcony. Out of the corner of his eye, a black shadow passed behind him without a sound. He turned around only to see his own reflection in the mirror next to his front door.

No one was around, so Matt checked on the girl in his

bedroom. He tried to find the right words to say to her once she woke up, but nothing proper came to mind. He thought maybe he could offer her some refreshments and some lunch to get her out of the apartment. Maybe he could finally learn her name. When he got to his bedroom, the bed was completely made and empty. Her tights were in the trash and there was a note on the pillow that read, *Thank You*.

CHAPTER 2

SAM

There was no doubt about it. The smell and the family resemblance: Sam had found the long-lost Vollner daughter who was the angelic vampire hybrid. After her father's disappearance along with his family's, they were written off as dead and the vampire communities stopped caring about her existence. But Sam had found her, in Matt's apartment. Better yet, Matt had found her.

Before Matt could come after Sam, he used his vampiric speed to round the corner of a shaded alley nearby the apartment. Pulling his hood safely over his head, he took in the sight of the fading sun over the cityscape. The sun was at a low point casting wide enough shadows to traverse Newbury safely without a hood, but there were still many rays peeking through the cracks between the buildings making it difficult navigate without at least some exposure to the sun.

Avoiding the main street, Sam went down the dark alley, taking the longer route to Andvari's Trove from Matt's apartment. He didn't love traversing the streets during the daytime, but it was the price he paid to protect his charge. As of now, Sam was unsure of how to properly protect Matt from the danger he found himself in.

Sam knew of the existence of an angelic vampire from decades ago, but he never thought he would meet the creature…

"No, not creature…" He sighed, "I never thought I would meet the *girl*."

Despite what he may have heard about her, she was still a person, a dangerous person who brought death and destruction around her everywhere she went, but a person regardless.

Sam stopped in his tracks, turning back to the entry of the alley from where he came. He should've killed her the minute he saw her and taken Matt far away. But where would they go? And how would he explain it all to Matt? Why couldn't he bring himself to go back there and finish her off? He had no problems with killing others in the past, so this time shouldn't be any different.

He would have to explain it to Matt later, one way or another, one day, but he had hoped to put it off for as long as possible, if not his entire life. All Sam ever wanted was to let Matt live out a normal human life under the radar, never having to worry about supernatural politics. Now that Matt had found himself in the mess that was the hybrid, keeping him out of it was no longer a possibility, and Matt was an adult now, which meant he had to learn to clean up his own messes.

Sam continued towards the club, by the time he got there, the club was open and beginning to fill up with mostly faeries and other mortal supernatural creatures. The evening's local band pick was still setting up and Lizzie was helping the bartender continue to set up by cutting fruit. When she saw him pull a seat at the bar, she poured Sam a shot of tequila and slid it over. "So, what happened?"

"Matt has found the angelic hybrid girl, the daughter of Lapetus Vollner." Sam took the shot in one swig, setting the small glass on the bar top as he stared through the empty glass with his head on the counter.

"Lapetus' daughter? I thought they were all dead…" Lizzie took the shot glass back, putting it in the dishwasher.

"So did the rest of the world, I guess…" Sam continued to mindlessly watch Lizzie prep. "None of that bothers me so much as Matt seeing the angels and going after them does."

"It's probably time to tell him about his heritage, before he finds out from someone else." Lizzie cut the perfect wedges from a ripe orange as she spoke without looking up. Her focus was intense.

"His mother made me promise not to tell him. She doesn't want to get him involved in supernatural affairs."

Lizzie slammed the orange she was slicing onto the cutting board, waving her chef's knife at him, "That woman is all the way across the country teaching her classes and doing God knows what. Her son is already involved whether you or her or anyone else has anything to say about it. Do him a favor, and do yourself a favor, tell him what he needs to know, before one of you gets hurt because of it. You're his guardian. It's your duty to protect him, and keeping this world from him as he is acutely aware of its existence, even if he doesn't truly realize it, is only going to put him directly in harm's way. You're protecting no one by hiding him from a world that would use his ignorance as a means of killing him."

"Jeeze, alright, you don't need to swing a knife at me to make your point." Sam leaned away from her cautiously. She made a point: hiding the world from him was only going to make him an easier target to kill.

"Don't be such a drama queen. You know you're far more skilled with a knife than I am." She smiled as she went back to her cutting, tossing the orange she had squished with her free hand.

Sam smiled back. "You're right, if you had a rifle, I'd be in real trouble."

"See, you're fine." Lizzie grinned. "Why don't you do a bit of research on the fallen during my next doctor's appointment. Maybe Fiona can send you in the right direction while she does my check up."

"The fallen? Where did you come up with that?"

Lizzie's six-month checkup was coming up and they would need to go to the coven house within the next couple of days. Fiona was the vampire elder who spearheaded the research development on vampires and other supernatural creatures.

"I'm not sure to be honest…" Lizzie set her knife and fruit down with a puzzled look as if she were trying to remember something. "The term just seemed… correct… like I had heard it before."

A long time ago, after an incident during a job, Lizzie suffered from chunks of her memory being lost and her abilities were never the same. Since then, the coven they were a part of, the Massachusetts State Coven, ordered her to come in for regular check ups to try to restore her to full strength, but she never recovered. She used to be one of the strongest vampires Sam had ever met. Now she had the barely above average strength of a human but the immortality of a vampire, and all her extra abilities were gone.

Sam was never sure why, but the coven was always hellbent on restoring Lizzie to her former glory. They poured a lot of time and resources into researching her ailments but never could find a solution. It irritated Sam because he was never permitted to be with her during these checkups and they didn't seem to go anywhere, and often she seemed to be worse afterwards. The coven always reassured him, however, that as long as he continued to protect her, time was infinite for vampires and they would eventually find a cure for Lizzie, they just had to be patient. Sam couldn't help but feel as though he was losing that patience.

"I like it, regardless, it makes sense in a way. I will go make the arrangements upstairs for your appointment." With that he leaned over the bar and kissed Lizzie on the cheek before taking the back stairs up to his loft above the club. Lizzie was right, if anyone had information about the fallen, it would be the coven house.

FROST

Humans passed for hours, completely unaware of her as

Frost stared at the fountain in which she threw Geordie. Humans weren't supposed to be able to see supernatural creatures, so why did this pitiful human break that unspoken rule? She wondered where the half-breed was at this point. Frost's distracted mind kept flashing back to the human who noticed Geordie and Frost. She couldn't focus on the more important task at hand, apprehending Geordie Vollner.

The thought of a human helping a filthy little half-breed enraged Frost. A weak human with no knowledge of the world showed too much compassion towards the girl. The human boy was bound to get himself killed if he continued to hang around the fallen, and for once Frost didn't want that. Enough blood had been shed over the decades because of Vollner. Frost was lucky she didn't always need to sully her hands in the blood of mortals over the past few decades, it was Gabriel who often volunteered to do so… Often enough to get himself in trouble.

As all good things came to an end, it seemed like her luck was running out. Geordie's presence in Boston meant that she was looking for a vampire coven for sanctuary, Frost knew that now for certain. If she received aid from anyone, that would be the end of the hunt and Ezra wouldn't get the girl's power. Failing Ezra was not an option.

As Frost tried to focus on Geordie's location, she felt a throbbing pain in her head as her vision was blocked. Mirrors were the field of vision between the Mortal and Immortal Realms. To find someone in the Mortal Realm, all an angel had to do was search her mind and if her target was within a mirror's sight, she would find them. After a few attempts, Frost was able to find Geordie.

She was leaving an apartment building, with sun-soaked skylights. In the sunlight, the girl hid from the human that had saved her earlier. She passed by unnoticed and left the building. Frost knew she could get information from the boy, so she stepped out from the alley and headed to the apartment she saw.

Upon Frost's arrival, she grasped the doorknob tightly; crushing it under her fist, watching it shatter in tiny frozen pieces. Under normal circumstances, in the Mortal Realm Frost had to hold back her normal strength to not destroy everything in her path, but in that instance, Frost wanted the human's attention, and from the look on his face, she certainly got it. But something else got Frost's attention as well.

A reeking smell of the undead lingered all over the small apartment. It made Frost's stomach churn violently, but she remained composed. A vampire that wasn't Geordie Vollner had been there previously not long before. The scent was still as fresh as flowers. For a moment, Frost thought he was the vampire, but the scent was not coming from him. His humanity sweat off him in pools of fear.

"Where is she?" Frost demanded, slamming him against the wall.

"I don't know who you're talking about!" He strained, gasping for air. Frost loosened her grip on the boy since she wasn't ready to kill him.

"I'm talking about the girl that you were with when you left the commons earlier. I know you saw me, and I know she was here, I can smell it!" Frost stared at him straight in the eye. "Where was she going when she left here?"

"I didn't see her leave, I swear!" The boy cried, clinging to Frost's grip desperately. She could not feel pain or pity for the human; he was a lower being than herself. "Please, let me go! You're killing me!"

Frost dropped him instantly. That was the last thing she wanted. Making sure to keep him within arm's reach, Frost ushered the human to a couch and sat across from him. "What is your name?"

"Matt… My name is Matt Hallow." Frost gave him a peculiar look. The boy's name sounded vaguely familiar.

"Tell me everything that happened with her. Tell me everything that was said." Frost paused for a moment then added, "I have no intentions of killing you, yet. I'm exhausted of unnecessary bloodshed. If you speak the truth, no harm shall come to you. I will guarantee that."

MATT

Matt tried to recall everything that happened when he met the mysterious girl. He didn't want to tell the intruder all the exact details, but he would tell her just enough to believe him. All she did was nod and listen to Matt's story all the way through without interruption. There was a long silence once Matt finished and suddenly the intruder stood up in front of Matt. The height difference between them was astounding.

The slender young man barely stood up to the finely built woman.

"Matt, I am willing to make a deal with you. If you help me find this girl, I will let you keep your pathetic human life. You can either come with me or you can stay here. Either way, you will tell me where she might be." The woman then began to pace Matt's living room until Matt finally spoke.

"How do I know I can trust you to not kill me?" Matt was frustrated at this point. There was no way he was going to unleash this monster on that girl, but if he didn't tell her something, then she would most likely kill him. "I don't even know your name."

"My name is irrelevant, but I give you my word, I will protect you from anything that tries to kill you. And there are no other options."

"Can you protect me from yourself?" Matt stared curiously in the eyes of the woman whom he knew nothing about.

"I can." Her eyes narrowed and her chest heaved a deep sigh. "Frostbite Isaz, but just call me Frost, please."

"Thank you, Frost, I will tell you where I think she might be, but you have to promise to stay here. I will bring her to you." Matt skeptically watched the woman as he proposed his idea.

"Fine. You have twenty-four hours. I will be watching

you, so I don't have to worry about you not coming back."
She then sat down at Matt's dining room table and stared at
him blankly. "I will wait for you right here, human, and I
shall not move until you retrieve the girl for me."

Matt nodded slightly and left without a word. His first
thought was to go to Andvari's Trove, the underground club
where most of his friends hung out for most of the daytime
hours. He hoped no one he knew was going to be there,
especially Sam.

Pulling out the wristwatch from his pocket, Matt took note
that a band would be playing by the time he got there. It was a
Friday evening so there was bound to be a lot of people at the
club. There weren't many college kids who *didn't* go to
Andvari's Trove after dusk. It was a place to escape.
Everyone just naturally wandered there like vagabonds with a
thirst for rebellion and release.

After moving to the east coast, Matt's life became
somewhat simplistic. During the daylight hours of the week,
he studied his notes and was a grad student. Once the night
came, it was time for an all-night smoke at the club. During
the holiday season when it was time to come home, he stopped
smoking, packed up, and went home. This hadn't happened in
years, so Matt's club and smoking routines gradually
increased over time. This life was fine for Matt, and remained
undisturbed until he saved a beautiful girl and made a deal
with an assassin.

CHAPTER 3

FROST

Uncertainty piqued Frost's mind as she wondered why she let Matt go. Frost felt the need to check on the boy, to see if he had abandoned his task. She focused all her energy on finding the boy but didn't have much success until the mirror finally revealed a large grungy club. Matt had just walked in through a crowd of supernatural creatures that seemed to gravitate towards him. Frost could see some of them in their true forms of fae, others were vampires, but almost none were human. There was something odd about this human. He showed no signs of supernatural knowledge or traits, yet the creatures were drawn to him.

Frost broadened her focus to the other angels. She wondered if anyone kept up with the hunt anymore besides herself. She hadn't any interactions with the other angels in years. She remembered the first meeting launching the hunt vividly. It was April 1949; with no warning the High Council called the most powerful angels for a top-secret meeting. The home of the council was a great cathedral where Frost had found her once friend, Gabriel, and told him to report with her to the leader of the angel's office, Ezra Daron. Gabriel was a messenger angel and one of Ezra's assassins.

In Ezra's office, all the council members were already accounted for including Orpheus, her right-hand man. Around her, Frost gave a nod to the other angels. Sat directly in front of Ezra's desk was the youngest of the angelic assassins, Pyre. His father was Council Member Pyralis and their whole family could manipulate fire, but Pyre was the only one born with the power of a phoenix.

There was also the mysterious dark angel, Corál who was the only angel with raven black wings. The only being with any information on him was Ezra who refused to answer any questions about Corál. All anyone knew was that he was powerful and was one of the few angels naturally born.

The members of the council began the discussion and everyone in the room silenced immediately, taking their seats before them. Orpheus began, "Our seers caught a glimpse of our future… A major threat has risen that will lead to the destruction of our realm."

"I'm not sure how to put this..." Ezra sighed heavily. "Recently a watcher angel has procreated with her subject, a vampire, during the last solar eclipse in the Mortal Realm." A noise of harsh whispering erupted within the room.

"What? Who is this traitor?" Frost screamed in outrage.

"Fine, let's kill them now!" Pyre stood up from his chair and was on fire.

"Silence yourselves!" Someone yelled out but the uproar dominated everything. Frost caught Corál's eyes, and he nodded towards Ezra who looked frustrated and stressed out.

"Everyone sit down and be quiet now!" Orpheus's powerful voice thundered, shaking the entire room. Without a word of protest, everyone sat down and waited for Ezra to continue.

"Before you all decide to get hectic again, please try to contain yourselves moving forward." Ezra rested her hands delicately on the sheets of paper sprawled over her desk. "The fact that someone has procreated with a vampire is not the problem. The problem is the creature our seers have predetermined will bring the destruction of our world."

"Your orders are to kill the parents on sight after the birth. There will be no negotiating on this." Orpheus continued in his commanding voice. "Following the birth of the child, you are to bring it here to be sacrificed for its power."

"Who is this angel?" Gabriel asked Orpheus. Why would someone dare break the rules, and breed with one of *them?*

"The angel is Elizabeth Nicholas. She has gone off the radar, but we think that Gabriel may be able to track her the fastest." Pyralis answered. "We expect the most of all of you, and let's hope that this problem will end soon. You are all dismissed."

MATT

All eyes were upon Matt the moment he walked in the door of Andvari's Trove. He wasn't expecting everyone he knew to be there. He pushed through the crowd of his friends, dismissing them as he passed, he headed toward the bar until he was stopped by Lizzie, Sam's girlfriend.

She leapt down from one of the platform booths like a bird and when she spoke, her voice chimed in a singsong; cornering him like a piece of meat, "Well, if it isn't Matt! What do I owe this pleasure?"

An uncomfortable stirring made Matt feel nauseous. Matt tried to focus on other things, like the terrible punk band playing, or the neon lights. It was always clear to both of them that neither of them liked one another, so the less that was said between them, the better. Matt didn't understand what he saw in Lizzie, but they had been together for as long as he had known Sam, and no one else seemed to have any issues with Lizzie, so Matt stayed silent about it.

"Sam told me you ran away over a girl. From what I've heard…" She leaned in closer seductively, "a very special girl."

As she pulled away, a smirk lingered over her thin pink lips. She knew something he didn't, but he wasn't sure if he wanted to find out what. Getting information from Lizzie usually came with a cost.

"What does it matter to you? It's honestly none of your business…" Matt leaned over the bar trying to look interested in what was behind the glowing mass of plastic. He could tell she wasn't buying what he was selling; therefore, he was trying very hard not to make eye contact with her.

"Actually, it is my business since Sam is *my* boyfriend and you are just a friend he picked up in a bar. When you tell him things, you tell me things. So, the next time you want to bring a strange girl, whom you know nothing about, into your apartment, I would suggest rethinking that heroic notion. It would be in your best interest to stay away from unsavory company." Without another word Lizzie sauntered off.

Turning his back to her, Matt tried calling Sam, but it went to voicemail. Sam was ignoring him; he didn't need Lizzie to tell him that. Matt hunched over the bar even further and called for a drink. This was very typical of Sam. Any time they had a disagreement about anything, Sam disappeared for stretches of time until it blew over.

The one time Matt called him out on it, they had just had their biggest fight. Matt was tired of only seeing Sam in the context of clubbing after dark and wondered why he constantly declined to make plans during the daytime. Years of not doing daytime activities had built up anger inside Matt and one day, he blew up at Sam in the club. When he finally stopped yelling at Sam in front of all his patrons, Sam still spoke in the calm yet stern demeanor he always carried with Matt.

"You're right, it's true. I do avoid conflict with you, and I don't commit to plans during the daytime. I cannot tell you the reasoning for the latter, but I can promise I can make adjustments to occasionally join you once in a while. Not as a regular thing though." Sam placed a hand on Matt's shoulder, trying to make amends. "As far as the avoidance you speak of, I would rather not say something to you we both will regret in the future, therefore I walk away from our conflicts to blow off steam. I don't want to hurt you in any way."

That was the last they ever spoke of it, and Matt knew that Sam genuinely tried to be a better friend, but he couldn't help but think there was something Sam was avoiding regarding Matt. The fear of Sam keeping secrets from him and lying about something was what fueled his frustration more than anything else.

GEORDIE

A thin, cold hand pulled back the blanket slightly, revealing Geordie's head. She fought to keep her eyes closed and not panic, but as soon as it appeared, it vanished. Two voices started arguing in hushed whispers, one of them was Matt's. The unidentifiable voice sounded shallow, short, and as cold as the hand it belonged to, a vampire.

The moment the vampire was gone, she immediately left the apartment. She checked her wounds quickly in the reflection of the window. Geordie was always amazed at how quickly she healed. They wouldn't be the last wounds she healed from. Geordie quickly scribbled down a note and left it on a pillow before running out of the apartment.

Despite the sun fading from the late summer day, the thick humidity beat down over her shoulders painfully. She was not used to the east coast heat compared to her homeland out west in Daron Forest. The weather there was perfect and crisp all year long. There were no freezing cold winters or boiling hot summers. It was always cool out. The thick clusters of trees that were the forest she grew up in made it perfect for any vampire to live safely from the sun, whether born or turned.

Although the sun was never truly a problem for Geordie, she did not prefer it. She didn't burst into fire like vampires, but she did blister, and her skin sunburned easily if she stayed out in it for too long. The constant downside of always being on the run was also never knowing where to go. She still had about an hour or two to go before the sun finally set and it was safe for her to roam comfortably.

If there was a coven in Boston, the vampire was likely to tell their elders and Geordie worried if they would send an army of guardians to slaughter her like the angels did. She had no way of knowing, but she needed to at least find somewhere safe to be before she could find out. Geordie knew that she was entirely unprepared to go against a fully trained guardian. Her father taught her that only the best in combat could become guardians. They had to be versatile in fighting various types of supernatural creatures, including angels and other vampires.

Before she could find out what it would be like to fight a guardian, she needed to find sanctuary somewhere. Nearby, she spotted two faeries headed toward her: a male and a female. They were beautiful and tall with matching golden tan skin and green hair. They both had tufts of brown fur on parts of their faces and bodies especially so down their legs which turned into dark hooves.

"Excuse me." She stopped them. They both stared at her with empty black eyes. "Is there a place for sanctuary nearby until dark?"

"Andvari's Trove. No violence is permitted there, even for

a hybrid such as yourself." One of the faeries spoke quickly before continuing past her without another word. Faeries were not creatures prone to associating outside of their normal circles.

"Where is it?" Geordie called out in a panic before they could get too far. This time it was the female who called back.

"It's the only club on a public alley, about six city blocks from here. You'll know it by the sign only one of us can see."

Confused by the faeries' words, it took Geordie almost an hour to find the club. It was hidden in the back of an alleyway with a sign to the mortal eyes that looked broken down and long abandoned, but to Geordie, it was an intricately carved hanging sign with glowing Viking runes Geordie assumed to spell Andvari's Trove.

The alleyway was too small for any cars to come down. The main entrance to the club was a garage door that had a large lever next to it. When Geordie pulled it, the garage door flew up quickly with a loud clanking and sliding noise that was hard to ignore. Looking back, there was no one coming down the alley or stopping to look for the source of the noise, so she entered without further thought.

She entered an old elevator shaft with an identical lever that once pulled, shut the garage door and Geordie could hear the elevator engines kick on and she began to descend into darkness. At the bottom, a door behind Geordie slid open, revealing a small entryway with two vampire guards in tight black t-shirts standing in front of a set of double doors with a black metal frame and bubbled textured glass that obstructed any view into the club. All Geordie could make out were the dancing colorful lights coming from inside and the slapping of a bass guitar over the sound of heavy drums.

As she approached, Geordie watched the security guards' nostrils flare up quickly in response to her smell and without a word they opened the doors to the club revealing a long bar directly to her left and an elevated platform seating area to her right.

Geordie found Matt sitting at the bar, drinking a dark cocktail while deep in thought. Before he could take notice of her, Geordie took a moment to try to read his thoughts. It was difficult for her to get a sense of what he was thinking; she couldn't get much of a reading except that he was worried his vampire friend was avoiding him.

She approached him warily as she felt Matt's emotions and mind screaming in anger and frustration. They were so strong, and intense, it was impossible to ignore the pain Matt's emotions were sending through her head. She couldn't help but hurt from his hurting.

"It's probably because you met me." Geordie answered Matt's thoughts as she approached the bar. She felt as though she shouldn't have approached him. It was wrong. She could get him hurt by interacting with him, but for unknown reasons, she felt magnetized to Matt.

The moment Geordie sat next to him; Matt's emotions were silent. Geordie had never met anyone whose emotions suddenly became completely nonexistent to her. She couldn't feel anything emanating from Matt. He gave Geordie a solemn look. "What are you doing here?"

She wondered what happened to Matt as she signaled for a drink from the bartender. "Oh, please, don't start that silent crap on me again! I've had enough of people's bullshit today! I would like to know a little more about you, like your life or why that psycho, Frost, is after you!"

Geordie's head flew up in shock at Frost's name. She must have gotten to Matt. There was no other way to explain it. She had to find out in some way, but Frost could be watching for all she knew. Geordie had no way of sensing other angels when they were listening in on her conversations.

"You really want to know all of that?" She asked him, looking at him dead in the eyes. Matt nodded silently. "You might not believe me, but it may do you some good since you dragged yourself into this mess."

"How did I drag myself into this?" Matt gave Geordie an appalled look.

"You did so by saving me. That was enough." Geordie stood up quickly, "Look if we are going to talk about this, we have to go somewhere private."

She looked around the room carefully and spotted her target. Signaling Matt to follow, Geordie headed towards one of the V.I.P rooms that were occupied. There was a couple making out when she opened the door. They tore away from each other like teenagers caught in the act. Geordie could smell the blood rushing to their cheeks as they blushed.

The male she approached first, sliding her hand down his thigh slightly, just close enough to get his attention. His eyes were a bright hazel as she stared into them, catching his undivided attention. "You and your girlfriend decided it would be better to go on the dance floor."

The man carried a lingering glazed look after Geordie focused on the girl. When she looked at the girl in the eyes, Geordie cupped the girl's cheeks in her hands gently. "You want to take your boyfriend out to the dance floor and offered me the V.I.P room. You got to meet the band, so you're satisfied. They were really nice to you."

Within a few seconds, they got up and did exactly as Geordie told them to do. Matt looked amazed as the girl got her purse and left to go dancing. Geordie pulled the curtains over the glass door and sat down, patting the red velvet cushion next to her, "Where shall I start?"

"You might want to start by finally giving me your name." Matt refrained from laughing.

"That would be helpful, wouldn't it?" Geordie collected herself. "My name is Geordie Vollner; I am the only half vampire and angel in the world."

Chapter 4

Matt

"You and I are from two different worlds." Geordie's words confused him. He looked at her wildly, wondering what she meant by that.

"How are we from two different worlds? What, are you from a different planet or something?" He laughed to himself awkwardly but stopped immediately at Geordie's serious look.

"I'm not talking about different planets. It's different, in a way that you may not understand." She swirled her finger over the rim of the drink abandoned on the small coffee table. It was a long moment before Geordie said anything else. "Matt, before I dive into this, I must ask, what do you know about vampires and angels?"

"Only that they are both dead, and that vampires only come out at night because they burn in the sun. And angels guide people to heaven."

"Well then, you don't know anything about either one." Geordie cringed, leaning back with a sigh. "Vampires and angels are very real, and they hate each other. They walk the earth in everyday life avoiding each other as much as possible."

"Alright, so what makes them different from how I described them?" Nothing Geordie said made any sense to

Matt. "If they're real, why can't I see them?"

"It seems as though you *can* see them… The whole thing about only being able to come out during the night is half a lie. The sun is only lethal to turned vampires, not bred vampires. Bred vampires can burn but they won't die from being in the sun. Even though they are independent creatures, they have covens and a government that monitors them as well as other creatures to protect themselves from exposure."

"Like an underground society?" Matt considered jokingly. *Why would vampires need a government? All they do is feed off humans.*

"It's a lot more complicated than that. Their government keeps them in order, because one little mistake, and they could get exposed by the humans and hunted."

"How did you do that?" Matt asked. He was having a hard time keeping up with her. "Did you just read my mind?"

"I can't control it, but I have an ability to read certain creatures' thoughts. It comes from my angelic side." Geordie gave Matt a sad look as she explained to him her heritage. He suddenly felt very sorry for her. "Vampires cannot read minds, only angels can, but only certain minds at that. Your thoughts sort of come and go."

"Whose minds can they read?"

"I'm not sure about the angels' abilities, but I know I can

only hear the thoughts of mortal creatures like humans and some faeries. I cannot hear immortals such as angels, vampires, and lygoids."

"What are lygoids?"

Geordie watched him carefully, "Lygoids are a demonic manifestation of the corrupted soul. They are the product of when the dark essence of someone's soul is forcibly ripped away from their body. Their minds are corrupted, and they become a dark, parasitic spirit. They are a step away from becoming a full demon. They'll do anything to get a chance to take over your body."

Matt stared in horror; how could they take over someone's body? "That's life; their power is fueled by emotions and souls, so they need bodies to feed off. From what my parents told me, they are commonly created from angels and vampires."

"So, what happens if *you* become a lygoid?" Matt's voice quivered.

"I don't know, but it doesn't matter; I have no intentions of becoming a lygoid." Geordie laughed. "I've been on the run for over sixty years from the angels, I can easily avoid the lygoids."

"That doesn't make sense to me… you said you've been on the run for sixty years, how old are you?"

Geordie burst out laughing suddenly. He stared at her, offended since he was being serious, and she was laughing at him!

"Haven't you learned to never ask a girl her age? Let's just leave it as I am the equivalent to being in my early twenties. In mortal years, I am much older."

"So, if you're on the run, what is your end goal? I feel like running to live isn't much of a life." Matt asked, processing the idea of angels and vampires being real.

"I'm on the lookout for a vampire coven that will take me in, but it's very difficult to do that when I have an angel on my ass, and I have you to worry about now." She leaned back on the sofa. Matt suspected that Geordie wasn't telling him everything.

"Which speaking of which, I have something to tell you."

GEORDIE

"I've been trying to figure out where you would be, because Frost sent me out to collect you." As Matt finally admitted what he'd been wanting to tell her, Geordie scooted away from him slightly. He must have noticed this because he quickly added, "But you must understand that even if you didn't tell me your situation, I still wouldn't have handed you over to Frost. She's insane and threatened to kill me!"

"That's nice and all, but you do realize, there's no way you were going to be able to force me to come with you. Your strength cannot even be compared to mine. You're only human." At the word *human*, Matt gave a solemn look. Geordie paid no attention to it. "How much time do you have to collect me?"

"She gave me a day."

Geordie stood up and held the door open for Matt. "We are going to confront her as soon as possible, and then I am going to leave Massachusetts. You won't have to deal with me ever again."

"Excuse me? I'm going to stick with you until all of this is over." Matt shut the door and pushed Geordie back down onto the couch, giving her a look she didn't appreciate. "You're right! I did drag myself into this, and you can't dismiss me that easily! I am going to help you, and we are going to get through this one way or another."

There was a long silence and the chatter of voices outside the room muted from Geordie's ears so it was only her and Matt's individual breaths she could hear. Geordie could feel intense emotions growing inside Matt as she clenched the couch beneath her closed fists. She knew she wasn't going to be able to get rid of Matt easily. Geordie would have to protect him, and she didn't want to do that. It was hard enough for her to protect herself. What if she got him killed?

"I can accept that." Geordie told herself and answered Matt. "You'll need to learn how to protect yourself, because I cannot protect you by myself."

"But you *can* teach me how to protect myself, and I can teach you how to protect yourself. We will work together." He offered Geordie a hand. She choked back a laugh. What did she have to learn from this frail human?

"Alright. As soon as this is done, we are done, I will go my own way and move on with my life, and so will you." She shook his hand and stood with him. "First lesson: avoid all mirrors. They are the gateways to an angel's sight."

"*Thanks!* I would have appreciated that information a while ago! Anything else you would like to tell me?" Matt laughed and opened the door for Geordie.

"Thank you." She headed towards the exit of the club as she spoke, "Learn how to recognize when someone's using you."

"What do you mean?" Matt stopped behind her on the dance floor.

"Frost was going to kill you no matter what you did. Even if you brought me back to her successfully, she would have killed you because you know too much. To her, you're just a means to an end." It was the truth. She'd been chased by the angels long enough to pick up on their habits and ways of thinking. It wasn't hard.

"Look, Matt, you don't understand what you're getting

yourself into, but you will. Just stick close to me and you will understand more later." What she said didn't seem to reassure him. Walking back over to him, she placed a hand on his shoulder and smiled, but he pushed it off.

"Geordie, if she tries to kill me when we go back to the apartment, can you guarantee that you will protect me from her for as long as possible?" Matt stared her right in the eyes, trying to hold back tears. Geordie could smell the fear on his back and neck. There was nothing she could do to assure him. All she could give him was the truth.

"For as long as I can." Geordie turned to leave the club, breaking out into the cool summer night. Matt followed behind her.

For the rest of the evening, they walked in silence in the direction of Matt's apartment. Occasionally they would say something to the other, but for the most part, they each enjoyed the cool air on their backs. As the night became darker, the streets became quieter. Eventually they approached his building; dark and beautiful, vines crept up the walls intertwining together. Geordie stared up at it in awe, mesmerized by its beauty she hadn't noticed before.

Chapter 5

Matt

Moonlight broke through the horizon as Matt and Geordie stared at his building from across the street. After hours of contemplation, Matt finally decided that he and Geordie could be becoming friends. She didn't seem as fearful of him as before and now he knew his purpose in life was to protect her. Matt knew as the moonlight shone down on them that they were meant to be together.

In some ways he felt as if Geordie was a creature of great significance, much greater than himself, and he was the one person she needed. She didn't need the other humans; they didn't have what Matt could offer her. Geordie needed someone who could help her; he knew in his heart that no one else could do that except for him. Geordie was the best thing that ever happened to him, and he needed her to feel the same way about him.

"Hey, Geordie, may I ask you something?" He asked quietly as they slowly approached the building

"Sure, I guess. What is it?"

"What was your family like?" Matt wasn't sure where the question came from, it was just something that suddenly came to mind.

"Well… they were great…" She looked over at Matt

sternly. "Why?"

"I was just wondering. I'm sorry." He wanted to know more about her. It was the perfect time to learn about her, let her trust Matt. "I have another question."

"I might have another answer." She smiled at him. She had such a beautiful smile; Matt longed to see it more often. He just wanted to see her happy.

"Were you close to your parents?" Matt stopped walking, thinking about his own parents.

"We were very close." Geordie gave him a confused look. "Why do you ask all of this? Are you close to your parents?"

"I don't know who my father is, he was never around, and my mother has always been distant from me. I'm as close as I can get to my brother, Nick." Matt thought about his little brother on the west coast. He missed him very much.

"I'm sure he misses you." Geordie smiled. Matt heaved a deep sigh as he knew what was waiting inside. All he wanted to do now was take Geordie's hand and run away forever. "Why don't I go inside first? It's me she wants."

"No. It will be too easy for her. Give me a minute head start and then when you see the door open, come in."

"I guess I can do that. Just don't get killed."

"No problem, I'm sure it won't be an issue." He grinned at her confidently, opening the front doors for her.

They walked in together and he left her at the base of the stone spiral staircase. His small apartment was on the second floor. The mirror outside his door reminded Matt that Frost probably already knew he was outside. He had bags under his eyes. He hadn't gotten any sleep over the past couple days.

Matt wasn't sure what to expect from the person behind his door. The doorknob was still shattered on the floor in front of him and all that was left of the lock was the metal rod the glass doorknob used to be a part of. It took him about five seconds to realize that he was walking into his own death. He wanted so desperately to whisk Geordie away and abandon all thought of confronting the wretched creature.

GEORDIE

Geordie waited impatiently on the ground floor, holding her breath as if it would stop time from progressing. Each moment she did, she hoped that no other angel would find her at this moment. What was taking him so long? She just needed to see the door open and then everything would be under her control. Panic began to take over. Geordie felt it resonating within herself and she could feel it sweating off Matt.

She wasn't even a few steps up the stairs before an icy chill set through the entire building and the world turned grey as Frost materialized on the landing leering down at Geordie. She knew she wouldn't be able to protect Matt against Frost.

Frost slammed her fist into Geordie's stomach and smiled with a sickly grin. The grin made Geordie's gut wrench more than the punch and the angel gracefully lunged her body like a lioness at Geordie, ready to take down her prey. Geordie slid out of the way as fast as possible and ran past Frost until Matt was in full sight. "Matt! Get out of here! Run away now!"

Frost's long nails yanked Geordie's hair as they dug into her scalp and threw her back against the railing of the landing. A searing pain and the smell of blood erupted as the back of Geordie's head hit the metal bar of the stair rail. For a moment her vision blurred, as her head seared with cold pain while Frost dug her nails into Geordie's scalp. "How do you like that, Miss Vollner? Is that cold enough for you?"

"Why don't you have a taste of your own medicine and find out?" Geordie groaned, snatching Frost's ice dagger from its holster, and swinging it across Frost's chest. Frost lunged back screaming in pain, causing Geordie to flip over the railing. She gasped for air as her back slammed into the ground floor. Rolling over in pain, she clutched her stomach tightly.

As Frost screamed, Geordie tried to regain herself while still clutching the dagger. Matt rushed downstairs, helping her up. Geordie flung the dagger at Frost as she leapt over the balcony watching as it plunged deep into her chest.

For the first time, Geordie managed to beat Frost. For the first time ever, Geordie was able to simply walk away from Frost as she lay there pinned to the ground by her own weapon, writhing in pain. "Matt, let's go."

The moment they got out of Matt's building, they bolted for the nearest alley without hesitation. After a few minutes of walking, Geordie noticed Matt with a pensive look of worry. There was now an angel after them both.

"That was Frost in all her glory?" He broke the silence finally.

"Yeah, that's her, but that's not even a fraction of her power."

"I definitely got that vibe from her." Matt looked as though he were about to say something more, but he remained silent until he added, "She's beautiful in a terrifying way."

Geordie and Matt both laughed loudly. She didn't see how Frost was beautiful, but she wasn't surprised that Matt would think so. He was *only* human after all, she told herself, but somehow wasn't convinced.

Something about Matt was very much not human. Geordie desperately wanted to figure out what was so strange about him but was afraid to. What if she didn't like what she found? Would she have to kill him?

"Where do we go from here?"

"I was planning on going into hiding. I need to lay low for a while. You're free to come with me if you want. Once Frost finds you, she *will* try to kill you."

"Why do you care if she tries to kill me?" A silly grin grew over his face from ear to ear. "Do you care about me?"

Stupid boy, of course I care about you. Geordie rolled her eyes. "What I think of you doesn't really matter. What matters is that I cannot tell you where I am going. Just follow me and I will tell you as soon as we are in a secure location."

"Alright, I trust you." Matt took Geordie's hand in his. She couldn't help but pull away uncomfortably. He was already gaining feelings for her that she could not control. She didn't want him to become attached to her. That was the last thing she wanted or needed. What she *needed* was to find the person who would help her get to Daron Forest.

There was supposed to be a man who sheltered supernatural creatures from being found by their enemies. He could take Geordie in for a fee, a fee she didn't mind paying since it ultimately, but temporarily, kept the angels off her back. This man supposedly had more than one face to him, so visibly recognizing the guy was almost impossible. Only a certain type of creature would be able to see the true face of this man. *I need to find him… the ever-changing man.*

The only type of creature capable of seeing this person were the dark faeries. Something about the dark essence inside them allowed them to see the true faces of anyone. Thankfully, plenty of dark faeries roamed the mortal plane so Geordie could easily pick one out in a crowd.

There was one invisible, across the street, following a young child eerily toward a nearby park. The moment the faery took sight of Geordie, he stopped cold in his tracks and stared at her with his huge, dark, glossy eyes. The fear she sensed emanating from the faery told her not to approach him too quickly; the faery was liable to attack her.

"I'm not going to hurt you. I just have a question." She took a slight step toward him, ignoring Matt's confused look since he couldn't see whom she was talking to.

"State your business, half-breed." He growled deeply at Geordie, his grey skin turning into a deep grayish purple. His voice sounded hard but blurred. It was like he was speaking through a thick glass.

"Where is the man with the ever-changing face?" she asked as nicely as possible, ignoring the hostility in the faery's voice. Geordie could tell the faery was looking through her aura, seeing if he could trust her. She didn't care whether he *could* trust her; she needed to get to Daron Forest.

As they crossed the street to get closer to the faery, it turned to Matt, searching his aura. It looked Matt up and down with a confused look, its head clicking as it rotated to the side like a clock.

"I'll tell you where to find him, but you must give me a little incentive." The faery's grin sent chills through Geordie's back. Her mind searched for what it was the faery wanted, but all the doors to his mind were shut tight. "Invading my thoughts won't get you any closer to what you want, angel."

"Alright, then what is it that you want?" Geordie now growled under her breath. It was very common for dark faeries to look for some personal gain.

"I want a taste of your friend." The dark faery stared longingly at Matt, licking his lips with a forked tongue. Geordie could then see the true form of the faery, his eyes golden with black slits for pupils, and his tongue long and pointed. Thorns sprouted from his cheek bones as if piercing his skin from within. Geordie became defensive over Matt, not wanting to give the faery what he wanted.

"Why do you want a taste of him?"

"Does one need a reason to taste something as peculiar and irregular as that creature over there?" *What did he mean by that?* Confusion filled Geordie's head with questions she did not know how to find the answers to. Was there something truly irregular about Matt?

"Fine." She pulled Matt over to the faery, pierced his thumb with her nail and held it up to the snake-like dark faery. Matt tried to pull away and yelled in protest but Geordie ignored him, letting the faery reveal himself to Matt and slither his tongue all over Matt's thumb. The moment he finished licking up Matt's blood the wound healed, and a look of utter ecstasy lingered over the faery's face.

"You… who *are* you?" He gazed up into Matt's eyes affectionately. "I have never felt so rejuvenated by someone's emotions before. What is your name?"

"Matt... Hallow." Matt trembled giving the faery a weird look as he glanced over to Geordie questioningly.

"Hallow?" The dark faery jumped back in shock, kneeling respectfully. "Impossible… they were said to be wiped out…"

He then muttered something to himself that not even Geordie could hear. Her patience was being tried by the faery. "Give me the information I asked for!"

"Go to the Pit! And ask for Jeremiah!" He then took off, running over to a tree filled with some other faeries, whispering something to them while staring at Matt.

Geordie and Matt backed away slowly, heading for the nearest train station. It was late but there were still a few trains left running for the night before they closed. Once they got off the train, Geordie breathed a sigh of relief. She didn't like the looks of the dark faeries, especially the one who got a taste of Matt's aura and emotions through his blood. He now knew everything about Matt and his heritage, something Geordie had yet to figure out.

All she wanted was to find the man that would help, Jeremiah. Going to this… shifter was difficult for Geordie. She had a hard time believing that the one person who could help her was someone who could easily disguise himself as anyone in the world he so desired. How would she know him when she saw him? Would she sense his aura? There were endless possibilities to how she could possibly know that the man she looked for would be the one she needed.

"We're here." Matt tapped Geordie's shoulder, yanking her out of the mental numbness she had built around herself over the course of the last hour. She wondered how he managed to break through the mental and emotional barriers that she put up to protect herself. A sigh of relief escaped her cold lips. She felt safer being away from the dark faery.

They climbed out of the train station, up two sets of escalators to Cambridge where the entire area known as the Pit was infested with faeries, lygoids, and shapeshifters, but no vampires. One tall slender female faery ran over to a scraggly old looking man, hugging and squeezing him affectionately, "Jeremiah! I missed you so much! Where have you been, you silly man, you?"

"I have had business in the desert with some *other* shifters." He smiled at her innocently. Something told Geordie *this* was the man she had been looking for. He could provide her with temporary sanctuary.

The two people chatted together, giggling and smiling close together as if they were an item. "Excuse me." The man named Jeremiah looked at Geordie with narrow eyes for a moment; he studied her soul, her aura, and her emotions all at once. She could feel his soul searching hers. It felt discomforting. After a while the man lightened up, but the girl by his side gave her a skeptical look.

"Well, hello, young lady! What can I do for you?"

"I have been searching for a man of many faces. Some call him Jeremiah, but I hear he has other names." Her heartbeat nervously as she faced this man that could very well not be the person she was looking for. "Are you that person?"

"Many call me of many names, however, most refer to me as Jeremiah." He pulled a small brown book out of his largely filled green duffle bag and started writing something down. "Now tell me, young lady, why did you find me? You clearly have your protection with you already, why drag me into this?"

For a moment Jeremiah studied Matt with a curious look in his eyes, and Geordie knew he was implying something she knew nothing about. Geordie forced an answer out as if suddenly life put her brain in slow motion, "I need you to make me disappear, temporarily at least, to Daron Forest."

"No, you don't." Jeremiah chuckled lightly and stood up, pulling his duffle bag over his shoulder. The man seemed very strong for such an old body. Matt and Geordie stood there watching him walk away. Her way to get home was walking away from her. This was a first. "You coming?"

"Oh. Yes." Geordie blushed and they caught up to him in surprise. "I thought you said I don't need you to protect me?"

"You don't!" Jeremiah smiled slightly. "But you do need me to provide you with a place to stay."

"Thank you very much. I appreciate you taking me to the forest."

"Don't thank me yet. You're not going to Daron yet." The three of them got into his dirty, mud-ridden car just a few blocks away. "I can put you up until the first snow in my estate; from there you'll be forced to visit other options. Whatever you're running from will catch you one day, but for now, you will stay at my place

CHAPTER 6

FROST

With a throbbing pain in her chest, Frost yanked the dagger out, gasping harshly. She had been left to rot, soaking in her own blood. Everything after was a blur, except a face. The last face Frost remembered seeing was Corál's. The mysterious dark angel saved her. She wanted to know why. She felt nauseous and dizzy.

Frostbite, you are safe in the council building of Cinereo Civitatum." A familiar voice answered one of her questions but not the rest.

"Is she waking up? Is the magic wearing off?"

"The sedation magic is wearing off; her thoughts are coming in more clearly." The voice wandered off, but Frost still couldn't see where or who it was.

"Frost, you're not dead, it's only been a few hours since you were found in the Mortal Realm." A warm hand lightly touched her forehead, sending heat through her cold skin. Only Pyre would touch her affectionately with that kind of heat. He was presently her only friend.

"Corál is here; he brought you back from the Mortal Realm seriously injured." The warmth went away as Pyre removed his hand. "When will she be able to see?"

"Remove the cloth from her eyes." Corál spoke with a deep voice.

Pyre lifted the cloth from Frost's eyes. The blazing light constricted her pupils as they were exposed to everything all at once. Slowly, Frost peeled her eyes open; everything was clear and crisp. She could focus on the smallest things on the ceiling and notice every tiny detail around her.

Pyre was different from the last time she saw him. His body radiated with a fiery brightness and his hair was no longer silver with orange highlights. Instead, it took in various reds and oranges with small hints of silver. His smile showed maturity and wisdom. He even donned himself with a new pendant of a black phoenix.

Corál and Pyre both stared at Frost intensely. "What am I doing here?"

"I brought you in here after I found you in an apartment in Boston." Corál sat in a chair in a corner, his voice full of judgment.

"We tried contacting Gabriel, but he's nowhere to be found, and he's blocking anyone from getting inside his head." Pyre approached Frost, watching her carefully. He placed a hand over her arm affectionately. "Do you know what happened to him?"

"I have no idea... I haven't seen him in months. This was Geordie Vollner's doing."

Both angels stared blankly at Frost. Neither of them believed what she said. She tried sitting up, but Pyre stopped her. "Frost, you are not ready to be up again."

Pyre pushed Frost back down and started pacing the room. "If the fallen, Geordie Vollner, managed to best you, then it could mean she is growing more powerful. And Gabriel's disappearance doesn't come as a surprise to us. There are allegations behind the deaths of our fellow comrades."

"What do you mean? This isn't the first time Gabriel has disappeared?" This could benefit her greatly. She just had to figure out how to prove to Ezra that she could handle finding him and bringing him in.

"Back when Hasdiel mysteriously died and all that evidence showed up against him that he was helping Elizabeth Nicholas and Lapetus Vollner, Gabriel disappeared for a long time without any notice. Then, when more of our comrades died, Gabriel disappeared again shortly after the massacre we caused in Daron Forest. Ezra has become suspicious of these disappearances."

"What is she going to do about it?" Ezra wasn't usually the one to strike against her own kind.

"She doesn't know yet. She's said she wants to talk to you herself." A small ember lit up in Pyre's palm and a phoenix formed from the heart of it. "And you are awake now, so I have no issues with bringing her here."

The phoenix flew off and disappeared through the low ceiling. Moments later Ezra and Orpheus showed up. As usual, Ezra cut right to the chase without even asking how Frost was doing. "Tell me everything you know about Gabriel's most recent actions in the human world. Include any information you know about the fallen."

Although she was a small woman, Ezra commanded a large presence whenever she entered a room. She enjoyed fashioning herself in opalescent hues of whites, ivories, and soft pinks that matched her short blond hair. Her frame was short and petite as Frost towered over her.

As Frost told her side of the story, she could feel the anger inside her growing as she realized how much of the information added up to Gabriel being a traitor. Ezra probably knew this too, but she didn't show it. Frost hoped that Ezra would understand her side of it. Even after Frost finished, Ezra stood in silence pensively. Orpheus, Pyre, Corál, and Frost all stared at Ezra, waiting for a reaction.

"All I can make a judgment with is your story, Frostbite, and that is not nearly enough evidence to take any kind of action in the Mortal Realm." Ezra fiddled with a pair of scissors on a nearby table as she spoke quietly.

"What will you do, Mistress?" Orpheus approached Ezra cautiously, but Ezra did not stir.

"Nothing. I will remain immobile. You, however," She turned suddenly to Frost making her heart leap, "will return to the Mortal Realm. Council Member Pyre will return with you, and you will collect Gabriel *and* Geordie Vollner."

"*Council Member Pyre?*" Frost nearly burst out laughing at the thought of Pyre being of a higher rank than her.

"Yes, do you have any issues with that?" Ezra's glare pulled Frost back into composure. "Pyre, your orders are to not interfere with the affairs of Frost capturing Gabriel *and* Geordie Vollner. You are to speculate from afar and report back to me with updates. If I see no progress being made, I will send someone else out to slaughter all of you on the spot. I am tired of this continuing! It must end now!"

"Yes, Mistress." Pyre bowed to Ezra quickly without any recognition of emotion.

She was about to leave when she let Orpheus pass and then added, "Oh, also Frostbite, I'm removing your ranking until I see results."

Panic struck Frost like a bolt of lightning, "*What*? No! Please Ezra, you can't do this!"

"I *can*, and I *will*!" Frost could feel her power that came with being a high-ranking angel drain from her body. "You seem to be losing sight of who you are, so maybe I shall remind you!"

Pain pierced Frost like the knife that she once drove through the flesh of her enemies. All the pain, all the grief she had caused in one lifetime came back as vividly as she could

touch the cold cushion under her. The deaths of those victims
came back, and she couldn't help but watch her victims die all
over again, only this time it was different from the first time.
The first time she enjoyed their pain. This time she could feel
their pain. For the first time ever, Frost felt sorry for the
deaths she caused.

"Do not forget your place in the Immortal Realm! Bring
back Geordie Vollner, or I will destroy you!" Without another
word, Ezra left Frost in her own pain.

She could feel Pyre's presence looming beside her. He
didn't say anything. He didn't have to. Frost knew that he felt
sorry for her, even though he shouldn't. It wasn't the way of
the angels to feel remorse for anything. Frost stood up for the
first time since she had been awake. Her legs felt like rubber.

"Will you be okay?" Even Pyre's voice felt warm. She
wanted his warmth to envelope her body. It was an insane
desire, but she wanted it, nonetheless.

"I'll be fine. I'm going to return to Massachusetts and try
to track Gabriel and Vollner. You're free to join me if you
wish." Frost watched him out of the corner of her eye as she
got the clothing that was laid out for her. Pyre looked as
though he wasn't sure what to do.

"I'm not allowed to help you." The conflicted look Pyre
gave her almost made her laugh.

"Just because you're not allowed to give me clues, doesn't

mean you're not allowed to watch me up close." Frost watched him turn around as she pulled off the white medical gown, revealing her slender yet muscular naked body.

"You're right, and you may end up needing my help. Ezra did not explicitly deny me to help you out entirely."

"I understand." Frost finished dressing. Together, they headed toward the center of the city. There, the gateway was open, always welcoming new spirits who pass from the physical plane to the spiritual plane, Aquavitas. She was the spirit of the fountain of all life and death; the neutral essence that guided both dark and light essences.

In the reflection of the water, she saw Gabriel was at an abandoned warehouse on the outskirts of Boston Harbor. He was alone but not for long. He was expecting company. However, Gabriel felt Frost within the Immortal Realm watching him. Frost exposed her essence to him and suddenly she felt his essence push hers back forcefully like a pounding migraine piercing her between the eyes.

Frost immediately stepped out of the connection. Gabriel's weakness was obvious. He couldn't block her from a different realm, which meant he wouldn't be able to block Ezra for long.

"He's taking shelter somewhere." Frost grinned wickedly. Pyre gave her a weird look and she dove into Aquavitas, swimming through the gateway of the Immortal Realm and the Mortal Realm.

Down by the docks of Boston Harbor, Frost found a gathering of various creatures in an abandoned factory where Gabriel remained hidden from her prying eyes, but she could sense him. He was nearby, somewhere in the warehouse, she just had to go look. "Do you feel it?"

"The darkness looming over that place?" Pyre asked. Frost nodded and he continued, "There must be dozens of dark creatures in there. It's clouding my ability to sense Gabriel, but I can feel it faintly."

"So can I. I don't care how many mortals I must kill to get to him, especially if he puts on a fight." She stared at the docks distantly.

"What if they're protecting him?"

"Why would dark creatures protect an angel, a creature of light?" Frost turned to Pyre quizzically, but he didn't answer.

"Whatever is going on down there, it probably has something to do with why he keeps disappearing." Pyre continued to watch the warehouse carefully. "We should greet our renegade."

"Yes." Frost smiled. Together they leapt across the buildings until they were finally on the roof of the warehouse itself. The roof was riddled with many cracked and dusty skylights that overlooked an open factory space. Down below, various dark supernatural creatures paced the room, conversing here and there. She couldn't find Gabriel anywhere. It was as if the essences of the dark creatures were blocking him from Frost's senses. "This is ridiculous. I'm going down there."

Frost jumped through one of the open skylights, landing hard on the concrete inside. She quickly caught the attention of all the creatures around. Dozens of werewolves surrounded her menacingly, along with dark faeries, some shapeshifters, and witches. There were no vampires in sight. Only lower mortal creatures.

"GABRIEL! COME OUT YOU COWARDLY TRAITOR!" Frost called out as Pyre landed beside her, flames ready and open. She withdrew her dagger, preparing herself. "You going to send these poor mortal creatures up against *me*? It's a fool's errand trying to resist… especially when I only want you…"

For a moment there was silence, and Frost could see the other creatures hesitate. Normally she would've taken that moment's hesitation as an opportunity to slaughter them all, but she was on a clear mission: apprehend Gabriel and bring him back to the Immortal Realm. Regardless she remained on guard, and so did Pyre.

"You're right." Gabriel called out, entering the circle from amongst the creatures surrounding them. "There doesn't need to be any unnecessary slaughter. But if you think you're going to whisk me away to the Immortal Realm, you're sorely mistaken."

"It's been a while." Frost finally relaxed after Gabriel

signaled the other creatures to fall back.

His long dark hair fell over his broad shoulders as he towered over the other creatures in both height and mass. Every inch of him appeared carved out of stone, chiseled to perfection. He was designed to be as beautiful as he was dangerous, like Frost.

"At least a human year." He shrugged. "What do you want, Frost? It clearly didn't take much effort to find me. You could've done so all this time, why now?"

"Ezra wishes to speak with you… we have reason to believe you've betrayed us. And from the looks of things, you have." Frost glanced around at all the creatures of darkness around her. It disgusted her to see him keep such filth for company.

"It would appear that way, wouldn't it?" Gabriel smiled at the group around him. "This is for my protection, nothing more. Just a means to an end."

"Oh? Why don't you explain this one to me? How are these wretched creatures a 'means to an end'? Is it an end to the task we were given?"

"I've abandoned that mission. I've discovered new information that could benefit the angels that will end all our problems with this realm. If you want to know that information, follow me." He turned away and beckoned her to follow him. For a moment she hesitated to go anywhere with him, but looking back at Pyre, she knew this was the only way she was going to get to Gabriel.

She reluctantly followed Gabriel to an office enclosed by metal and glass where she could clearly see Pyre still with the dark creatures. When Gabriel closed the door, she quickly told him to get on with it. "What is this all about, Gabriel?"

"So impatient, Frost. First off, have you ever heard of the First King Essence?"

"It's an essence, which only a creature of true darkness can bear. So what?" She shrugged.

"It's going to be the way we wipe out all the creatures of darkness all at once. Whoever has it can link with the dark factions, and their lives will all be tied together. Vampires, faeries, humans, lygoids, all of them can be dead from just killing one person, including the fallen."

"And how do you intend on finding the person who bears the First King Essence?" Frost rolled her eyes. All of it sounded like a fairy tale too good to be true.

"Rumor has it that under normal circumstances it is passed down through the bloodline of the person who first created the magic, but otherwise it can also be acquired by a person who kills the person already wielding it. As long as one person from one faction kills three other people from the other three factions, they can hold the First King. All these people here are followers of the longest living person with the potential to hold the First King, and they want to see that person become the ruler of their factions." Gabriel smiled.

"Okay, so what does that have to do with us angels, creatures of light?" Frost crossed her arms as she listened. She was beginning to lose her patience with him. Helping those wretched creatures get their long lost king back was not on her list of things to do.

"Well from what I have learned, the descendant of the person who created the essence is a local. If a descendant lives, the First King will always fall automatically with that person, all others must forcibly take it." A wide eerie grin crept across Gabriel's face, and Frost realized that the roles were suddenly reversed. "We could help the longest living Potential take the First King by force, and then kill them once they complete the link, killing all of the creatures of darkness!"

On his own, Gabriel was weaker than Frost. It was widely known for many years. There was no way he could best her in a one-on-one combat, but hand him an army, and he might have a chance. Frost looked outside the window of the office he brought her to. Outside, Pyre was fighting off a group of werewolves while a circle of witches chanted. Gabriel wasn't trying to keep Frost away from him, he wanted her there. He wanted to confirm that she knew what he spoke of. He wanted to prove his hunch correct.

"No!" She jumped back as he tried to lunge at her, his massive body crashing violently into the glass, but remained unscathed. In one swift movement, Frost withdrew her ice blade again and plunged it deep into Gabriel's back while he still tried to regain himself.

Still holding onto the hilt of her dagger, she swung him around quickly and yanked her dagger, stabbing him in the front this time. Repeatedly she swung at him mercilessly until he dropped to his knees. Blood poured out everywhere from the many cuts and stab wounds in his body. Frost's eyes narrowed on him as he breathed heavily on his hands and knees, and with a swift kick of her boot, she sent him to the floor on his back.

She swung a leg over him, straddling his waist and dragged her long icy nails down his chest digging deep into his flesh. She could feel the ice entering his wounds and festering into a cold chill he wouldn't be able to remove. "You are nothing compared to me. You could never best me, even on your best day. You're a disgrace to all angels. And those creatures around us? They were all stupid to follow you. It is a fruitless endeavor to try to revive the demon faction. You could never complete such an arduous task! They're too chaotic!"

"They're not following me." Gabriel laughed, coughing up blood. "I'm just following an order that was given to me by the one true king of dark creatures. He is the one they follow. You could join me and help me destroy all of them."

Something clicked in Frosts head; she stopped tearing at Gabriel's chest instantly, clinging onto it with a fierce intensity burning inside her. As she clung onto Gabriel's flesh, she wanted to rip him apart, but she knew she needed to deliver him alive. Breathing deeply, Frost stood up slowly,

not taking her eyes off Gabriel for a single moment. "What
are you doing?"

"I'm going to clean you up. Don't move; you're too weak.
You used up most of your energy source trying to fight against
me." Frost mopped up some chunks of blood that were left on
Gabriel's lower belly with a rag she found nearby on a table
beside them. Gabriel's perfectly shaped abdomen had no
flaws except the new cuts Frost provided him.

"Stop!" Gabriel groaned as he grabbed Frost's wrist
tightly, staring at her with a menacing look. There was a time,
theoretically, that Gabriel could kill Frost with a snap of her
neck, he had that sort of strength, but the chances of that were
destroyed the moment he lost sight of his mission.

"You know, I *was* going to give you a perfect bill of health
before I started torturing you," Frost slapped the bloodied rag
onto the table, "but you're just an ungrateful son of a bitch."

Her graceful fingers rooted themselves, nails first, into
Gabriel's chest. A loud scream emitted from him as she dug
her nails deeper into Gabriel's beautifully carved chest.
Flipping Gabriel onto his stomach, she then sliced the
shoulder blades where his wings lay hidden from human eyes.
He groaned and winced violently in her arms as she sliced
delicately over his wings, making sure to pull them out
without damaging them.

"Are you going to clip my wings?" He lifted his head,
shaking slightly in fear. Frost smiled, feeling a ping of
disappointment as she told him she wasn't going to clip his

wings. *I don't have the authority to do that.*

"You know what I am going to do, Gabriel?" She laid him down on the table, spreading his sparkling silver wings from shoulder to shoulder. All the feathers were beautifully intact, for now. Gabriel groaned painfully, coughing up ice and blood at once. She knew her powers were making it difficult for him to heal. This was good.

"I'm going to show you what it's like to betray someone, *truly.*" She leaned over, staring into his big brown eyes as she dragged her icy nails down his back. "And for every question you answer correctly, you get to keep a feather of your *precious* wings."

Frost put the knife she used to slice open Gabriel's back on the table in front of his face and tied down his hands to the table legs. She then pulled up a chair directly beside him so he could see her and sat down in complete silence.

"What… what… do you want from me Frost?" He spat out blood as he stuttered. She just smiled at him.

Behind Frost, she noticed the army of witches and werewolves slowly creeping up to her after subduing Pyre. Frost smiled at the thought of mere mortals trying to take her on, even in a group setting. "First, call off your little army or I will tear them to shreds."

Gabriel nodded for them all to back off. Slowly they backed away but watched very carefully. Frost patted his head like a little pup and grabbed a knife from the table and smiled. She circled around him observing his beaten body, continuing, he was too beaten up to argue with her, "Shall we continue? I will ask you a series of questions. Each time you answer me with a lie, or if you refuse to answer me, you will get a feather cut off. And sweetie," She leaned in close to him, whispering, "our feathers don't grow back."

"What do you want?" Gabriel coughed more ice and blood.

She grabbed Gabriel by the hair pulling his head back, and pressing her lips seductively to his neck, "What is your connection with the deaths of our comrades?"

He breathed deeply and coughed up more blood before responding to Frosts crazed behavior towards him. She loved the way he reacted to her. It made her feel crazy and alive. "We aren't connected at all. I don't know how they died."

Frost pouted at him cutely, she then began to laugh and smile at him asking Gabriel if he was sure in a cute way. "Are you positive?" Gabriel nodded; Frost burst out laughing. "Liar! You're a liar! You're lying to me!"

She then began to cut off a feather as Gabriel begged her not to. In return for his begging, Frost slapped Gabriel in the back of the head. She then cut off two more feathers, "I won't tolerate any begging! But I will ask you again, Gabriel, how connected are you with those deaths?"

Gabriel began to scream as the blood oozed from where the missing feathers were. Frost cackled at Gabriel's agony as she slid her knife across his shoulder blades, watching him be antagonized by her. "Fine! I was the one who killed Adriel, Hasdiel, and Cassiel! They had all betrayed us!"

"Oh, how silly of me! I forgot you're doing this for the good of the angels! You are spared a feather… for now. How did they betray us? And how is their betrayal any different from yours?"

Gabriel continued to cough up blood, trying to answer Frost's questions, "Hasdiel was going let his sister get away from us permanently and we never would have found her. I killed Adriel at the time that she found out I had discovered information about the dark factions. The only way for us to win this war is to allow them to restore their kingdom to full power. They need to link their lives to a king–"

"That doesn't make sense of how it would help us win the war!" Frost screamed in frustration. Then she heard his voice, *we need to assassinate the king to destroy the dark faction entirely. If the king dies, they all die. But they need to be linked.* "That's impossible…"

She couldn't believe it. She refused to believe it. There was no way defeating all the creatures of darkness could possibly be that easy. The last time a king of the dark factions was assassinated, the creatures didn't all die. Only he died. So, how was this possible to link all dark creatures to a new king? These were all questions she had to ask Ezra.

Frost realized that Gabriel gradually was losing consciousness, and she needed to re-strategize. "Well… looks like I have to heal you up a bit before we continue."

She untied Gabriel's arms, wiping away any spare blood she could find. To heal him she would have to hand Gabriel over to the Council of Angels because unauthorized healing was not permitted, even if you had the ability. Frost swung Gabriel over her shoulder, carrying him in the direction of the nearest mirror.

"Where are you taking me?" Gabriel's voice was quiet and raspy, and wavered as Frost walked over to a nearby full-length mirror.

"I won't be able to question you entirely myself, you're losing blood too fast. We are going back to the Immortal Realm, but you're too weak to teleport yourself." Frost carried Gabriels body back out to the crowd of dark creatures that still surrounded Pyre threateningly.

"Your angelic leader has lied to you all! There is no one coming to unite you all! Get it out of your heads *now*!" Frost announced to the large group of dark supernatural creatures. "This angel, Gabriel, is a fugitive, and he has been using you and your abilities to shroud himself behind your darkness to evade capture. He's had no intentions of helping your kind ever, nor would any angel in their right mind do so. Find your rightful leader, a creature of true darkness, in someone else!"

"What?"

"LIES!"

"How can she say this?"

Many voices erupted amongst the crowd, but Frost didn't care what they thought. She had no choice but to speak the truth of the lies Gabriel had built. As more people processed her words, the crowd grew violent and turned on her, preparing for an attack.

"Go ahead and try! I took him down with ease. I have no issues with killing the lot of you! And even if you were come at me, I still have my fiery comrade behind." Frost signaled over to Pyre who was still ready to release a blast of fire even though he'd been brutally attacked. "Spare yourselves and let me pass."

A long pause stopped the crowd, but momentarily a path to Pyre opened and she proceeded through. At that point Gabriel was unconscious. Hand in hand, Frost and Pyre used their powers to send themselves back to the Immortal Realm, where they would bring Gabriel before the council to be judged.

SAM

Two days later, Sam miraculously managed to get a last-minute appointment with Fiona for Lizzie. The coven house was located on a large estate out in a thickly settled forest about three hours west in the middle of nowhere. The vampire covens enjoyed their solitude in forests where humans and other mortals were unlikely to find them.

It was in the middle of the night when they arrived, and Fiona greeted them with open arms. "Welcome, Sam and Lizzie! It has been some time since we've seen your lively presence."

"Thank you, Fiona." Sam nervously cleared his throat and allowed her to pull him into a gentle hug. She always smelled of flowers and wore the traditional silk wrap dresses of the vampire motherland, Daron Island, like the queens and its many inhabitants. Sam was never fond of the style, but the queens enjoyed keeping tradition, so most vampires wore the cultural clothing to please them.

Fiona was sired from the youngest vampire queen's line, Anyanke Daron, and wore various hues of green most often as a homage to the family line colors. Each family line from the vampire queens had their own colors. The eldest queen Kathleena Daron's line dressed in purple, most often found in lilac. The family line of the middle queen Melandria's adorned themselves with various shades of blue.

Sam thought it was a silly tradition to try to make a distinction between the different vampire lines through the colors of a person's clothing. He barely liked the idea of being a part of a coven to begin with, he didn't want to be known for which vampire line he hailed from. He wanted to be known for who he was and what he accomplished for himself, not for the accomplishments of others.

"I have all your sleeping arrangements for the next two days set up. If there's anything you need from me during your stay, please don't hesitate to ask, Sam." Fiona wrapped an arm around Lizzie and Sam as she ushered them into the castle doors across the yard. "Lizzie, my dear, how are we feeling today? Any headaches or anything?"

Looking at her, Sam realized he never knew which line he and Lizzie hailed from. No one knew who turned her including herself. "No, ma'am. I've been okay recently."

"That's great! Let's see what we can do with you this time!" Fiona grinned wildly at Lizzie which made her and Sam visibly uncomfortable. Visiting the coven house was always an overall uncomfortable experience.

The Massachusetts State Coven was filled with lunatic vampire scientists who enjoyed experimenting with vampire genetics and using advanced technology to further scientific discovery in vampire blood. Their experiments were borderline morally questionable, but they also had one of the world's leading blood donation companies and medical facilities in the world. Having this large of a company under their control meant not having to needlessly murder humans. They were also the only company capable of treating Lizzie's illness.

"I actually do have a request for you, ideally keeping discretion in mind." Sam took Fiona's free hand in his as he looked into her eyes deeply.

"Oh, Sam, stop!" She giggled, visibly blushing. "You know I would do anything for you, and discretion goes without saying."

"Good." He smiled as he pulled his hands away from her. "I need to see the archives regarding the angelic vampire hybrid girl who's been on the run for some time now. I think she was a part of the Vollner family."

"The Vollners… That's quite a prominent family to be looking into, especially given their connection to–"

"Yes, I am aware of who they are connected to, but between us, I would rather investigate an unbiased resource such as the texts than go to their sire directly. I'm sure he's busy anyway." Sam cut her off quickly. There was no way he wanted *him* to know he was looking into the Vollner family just yet. Sam knew if word got out that another Vollner was out there, not affiliated with any coven, the Massachusetts State Coven would easily come to collect her.

"Of course, Sam. I completely understand. Thankfully, our leader isn't even here right now, so you don't have to worry." Fiona smiled at him.

"Oh? Where is he?"

"Daron Island, appealing to the queens for some of our research. He's left me in charge." Sam found that relieving. He didn't have to worry about researching the Vollners while being under scrutiny. "Would you like to go to the archives now and I will take Lizzie to her checkup?"

"I would appreciate that. Thank you, Fiona." Down in the basement of the castle was a vast underground library filled with historical records detailing the events of the vampires and their lineages. He hadn't been to the record room in quite some time but was all too familiar with it as he spent a lot of his earlier years in the coven studying the history of it to get an idea of what it was like.

There was one guardian always maintaining the record room in different shifts. When Fiona brought Sam to the front desk, he quickly hugged Lizzie and they left, leaving him alone with the clearly bored and lonely vampire guardian. "I would like to see the records of the Vollner family."

Without a word the guardian motioned for Sam to follow him, and they went toward the section titled Family Lineages. The guardian pulled a large dusty book out in the V section, but it wasn't the Vollner family he handed Sam. Instead, it read Victoire. Sam handed the book back to the vampire, "No, *Vollner.* I need to see the *Vollner* records."

The vampire sighed and took the book back, and brought it to a nearby table, flipping it open lazily. "There are six books of records in the Family Lineages section of this record room: Victoire, Drakon, Levington, Alexander, Kingsley, and Collins. Any vampires turned under those family lines will be in their first sire's book. The Vollner brothers were turned by a Victoire, so they are in the Victoire book."

The guardian flipped the book to a page towards the end that displayed large calligraphic letters spelling Vollner and walked away. Everything it had to say about them everyone already knew, it was public knowledge. Lapetus never turned anyone, despite being the elder brother, but his daughter was unknown. They never brought her into the vampire society, but they did register her birth records. She was born in their family home in Daron Forest, under the name, Geordie Vollner in 1949. She was registered officially as a fallen as her species.

It was public record that Lapetus Vollner was murdered and a verified fact that angels were involved in his death. However, due to the lack of magical reach from the vampires to the Immortal Realm, the angels were never able to be held accountable. Why the record never stated the angels' involvement confused Sam as everyone knew that Lapetus' family was on the run due to his involvement with the angels. No one knew why until Geordie's birth records appeared out of nowhere in the Northern California State Coven, and because all birth records were considered public coven information, they were forced to share it with the other covens.

Sam wondered what they hoped to gain from registering Geordie's birth. Did her parents hope a coven would take her in? Registered coven members were considered untouchable by the angels, and any child born from a coven member had a birth given right to choose to join the coven their parents were also a part of.

Sam closed the dusty old book and leaned back in his chair, closing his eyes as he thought. Geordie's parents probably died before they could tell her that fact. It would explain why she never joined a coven off the bat. She might have also been too young to join at the time of their deaths.

Between Matt's family line and now Geordie's connections, Sam was uncertain how to guarantee Matt's safety. Anyone who discovered Geordie's connections to the vampire government would no doubt try to use Matt to leverage any of her political power. Her mere existence was becoming increasingly problematic for Sam regarding successfully protecting Matt.

Bringing the book back to the front desk, Sam slid it across the equally dusty desk, "I would like to see your records of the fallen."

"I can't do that, sir." The guardian shook his head, taking the first book back.

"What do you mean, you *can't*?" Sam gave him a slight quizzical look.

The guardian came around the desk and headed toward the shelf he pulled the book from initially, barely looking back at Sam, "There are no records on file of the fallen."

"*How* are there *no* records on file of the fallen?" Sam followed him relentlessly. "There must be some sort of record of it, otherwise logically there's no way that a vampire with a *birth record* would have been officially registered as it! It makes no sense!"

The guardian shrugged at Sam as he put the book away. "I don't know, ask our queens that. I just keep track of all the information on where it is in this building. Maybe the information you're looking for is lost information."

"That's impossible. The information is less than a century old." Sam turned back toward the entrance as he started to leave in frustration.

"That we're all aware of."

FROST

"*Gabriel*! Let's *go*!" Moments later, in the middle of Cinereo Civitatum, Frost yelled at Gabriel as he sat in Aquavitas with a blank, dark expression. He looked up quickly at Frost who was staring at him with utter annoyance.

"Are there any creatures that live in the bridge between the two realms?" He climbed out of the fountain and faced Frost.

"No. There are just spirits traveling from one gateway to another." She started walking away so Gabriel and Pyre followed suit. There was no point in trying to hide or run away at this point. He couldn't get out of this world even if he wanted to. He was too weak and if Ezra didn't want him to leave, then that was it. That was the lovely thing about Ezra's powers, if she didn't want someone to leave the Immortal Realm then they couldn't. No one's power superseded hers.

There were wards set up around the inner city of the world that kept people from leaving whom Ezra did not want to leave. The only exit or entrance from the world was

Aquavitas, the water spirit that worked for Ezra; she was the fountain gate that led every spirit in and out of the Immortal Realm. Each droplet of water coming out of her was a spirit coming into this world. When the water stopped flowing, then people stopped dying.

The three angels walked in silence to the upper half of the city in the northern corner. Soon the expansive cathedral building where the council of angels resided came into full view, and they headed into the Harmony Angelic Council. There was a large crowd of creatures all over the main entrance hall of the building once they got to the check point.

In a dark corner there were a group of lygoids conversing with one another. There was one who was rallying them up and for some reason he was the only one who had a body. Out of all of them there was one female whom Frost could tell was once an angel. She looked as though she were once very beautiful but had long since lost that beauty. The one rallying the lygoids up was a male who was once a vampire. He had that ugly, unclean, and unwanted look about him. It disgusted Frost.

"These are for our protection." A guard snapped handcuffs onto Gabriel's wrists when Frost brought him up to security. The essence of light set the cuffs to blue flames, burning through Gabriel's flesh. He looked up suddenly in surprise at the group before him. Frost stared at the handcuffs in shock, along with the guards around. Gabriel's soul was lost in darkness. He was becoming a creature of darkness. "Get the chains! NOW! WE HAVE A LIVE DARK ANGEL IN HERE!"

A group of guards swarmed around Frost, Pyre, and Gabriel, wrapping Gabriel in more chains. They too lit in blue flames as they coursed around his skin. He fell to his knees screaming in pain as the guards assaulted him. Frost quickly dragged Gabriel up the stairs soon after to Ezra's office.

When they got inside, Frost threw Gabriel down to the floor at the feet of the entire council. Ezra stared at him completely unfazed behind her desk. Frost took a seat next to Pyre, who had a smug look on his face. Ezra's third in command, Riana, leaned down towards Gabriel and pinched his face between her index finger and thumb. Her long nails dug into his skin, making him bleed.

"Oh dear, Gabriel, your soul is *so* dirty. What happened to make you betray your race?" Her purple eyes stared deeply into his deep brown eyes.

"I never betrayed my race. I merely made the wisest decision for the moment." He then looked over to Frost and continued, "If anyone's soul is dirty, you might want to consider looking at Frost's."

"*Please*, he is lying! He just wants to distract you from his treachery, so you'll let him go." Frost pleaded with Ezra, but it was Orpheus who responded.

"Frostbite, silence yourself!" Orpheus looked down at Frost with a fury that terrified her. The look of anger was instantaneous. As soon as it was there, it was gone. It almost hurt her to see the council look so lowly at her. "Gabriel, is there anything you would like to say for yourself against your accused acts of treason and discord?"

"Yes. I will share what little information I can share."
Everyone's attention was on Gabriel now. "The fallen we
were meant to kill, Geordie Vollner, there's an easier way to
kill her that will allow us to kill off all of the dark supernatural
creatures. Just ask Jeremiah, the faery shifter."

Ezra's head snapped up at Gabriel's words. Although,
Frost did not understand the significance of this information,
and she knew Ezra would not tell her anything. "Everybody,
get out. *Now*!"

"But Madame, we need to-

"GET OUT!" Ezra cut Pyre off mid-sentence and pointed
furiously at the door. Everyone began to leave except Frost.
"That includes you, Frost."

Everyone in the room left Ezra with Gabriel without further
question. Something didn't bode well with Frost. She wanted
to know more. She wanted to know the significance behind
the dark supernatural creatures. From the way Gabriel made it
sound, there was going to be an uprising of dark creatures.
That could mean the end of the reign of the creatures of light.
And how did Gabriel know Jeremiah? Very few knew his real
name.

"Let's go pay this faery shifter a visit." Frost turned to
Pyre as they stood outside Ezra's office.

"What good will that do?" He asked.

"I want information, Ezra's not likely to give it, so I must find the source. Let's go."

CHAPTER 7

SAM

Once Sam and Lizzie returned from the coven house, it didn't take much effort for Sam to use his resources to find Matt when he discovered his apartment was destroyed with investigators traipsing all over the place. He could smell remnants of both angels and other vampires in the apartment. He wasn't the only one to discover the wreckage. This meant someone knew of Matt and the company he was keeping. Which also meant his life could be in danger… all because of the girl… the fallen.

As fast as he could, Sam rushed over to the cabin owned by the fae named Jeremiah. It was a couple of hours north outside Boston hidden amongst large, beautiful trees where faeries could roam about freely without being noticed. It was the ultimate sanctuary for anyone to hide from their enemies. Thankfully for Sam, he was not an enemy. Instead, he was a guardian, tasked with protecting Matt with his life. It was his job and duty to always find Matt no matter how far he went.

He reached the cabin by midafternoon and could already smell the sweet scent of fae behind its stone walls. Before getting out of the car, he made sure every part of his skin was shielded by his long black hooded trench coat. Today was not the day he wanted to get roasted by the sunlight, but he still had to get this done as soon as possible.

Despite the blinding sunlight, the cabin was beautiful. Large stone walls with a dark wooden porch enclosed the two-story house. Shades of amber and red trees surrounded the area, lining the large driveway in front of the house while the leaves covered the slowly yellowing lawn, crunching underneath Sam's feet as he strode across it to the front porch. Before he could even get to the door itself, a man he did not recognize came out, blocking him from the entrance.

"What do you want, Samuel Williams?" The man crossed his arms with a stern look.

"Who are you?" Sam gave him a weird look.

"I am the owner of this house, and you're not getting invited inside without my say so. So, I ask, what do you want?"

"I have reason to believe one of my charges is behind your walls. Matt Hallow. He's in the company of someone I also believe is a dangerous creature you should not have invited into your home."

"I will be the judge of that." The man took a step toward Sam, forcing him to take a step back down the stairs. For a moment Sam could feel the heat of the sun creep up against him. He could feel himself involuntarily tug on his sleeves to hide his skin. "As far as I'm aware, you're the threat right now. You're a vampire trespassing onto my territory uninvited, *and* you're a guardian of the Massachusetts coven."

"What does my guardianship to the coven have anything to do with the current situation?"

"Those are some dangerous people you work for, shady people, who conspired against the family of the very person I am currently protecting."

It finally hit Sam suddenly. He knew the name Jeremiah sounded oddly familiar. "Ah… I see… You're the *original* Jeremiah. One of the trusted advisors to the Shadow Kingdom."

"I am… you still haven't stated your business however, vampire." Jeremiah growled quietly. A look of mild disappointment had crept over his face slowly as Sam had figured out his identity.

"I'm looking for my charge, Matt Hallow. I've come to take him home." Sam shrugged simply.

"What if I don't want to come home?" Behind Sam, Matt came up the path of the driveway with the fallen by his side. There was something different about him. She changed something about Matt that Sam couldn't pinpoint.

"I'm afraid you don't have much of a choice in the matter."

GEORDIE

It had been a few weeks since Geordie and Matt had arrived at Jeremiah's beautiful home in the middle of the woods in Northern Massachusetts. In such a short time, the leaves had begun to change color to hues of yellow gold and red. It was too peaceful to be true. The faeries that lingered on the property were very accepting of Matt but were hesitant to approach Geordie.

The rumors of death that followed Geordie around like a looming shadow had to have passed around the faerie communities, and the vampire communities as well. It was only natural they wanted to stay away from her, for fear of their own lives. Regardless, Geordie enjoyed the sanctuary with Matt, even if it meant feeling alienated from everything. She remained grateful that she at least had Matt, and that he cared about her. Geordie didn't understand why, but something told her to just trust and accept it.

For now, nothing could dampen how she felt about Matt's company, until his vampire friend showed up at the property arguing with Jeremiah. Geordie and Matt had just come from a walk around the lake that overlooked the property, watching water faeries play peacefully. The peace and tranquility were easily forgotten when they approached the path and saw a vampire standing at the bottom of the porch with his back to them. He was completely covered head to toe in a hooded coat with black gloves and boots.

"I'm looking for my charge, Matt Hallow. I've come to take him home." He shrugged.

"What if I don't want to come home?" Matt called out from the path of the driveway with Geordie. Matt exuded a level of confidence Geordie was unfamiliar with. It was as if when he was around other supernatural creatures, he felt more confident and comfortable with speaking to them than he did with humans, and sometimes even Geordie.

"I'm afraid you don't have much of a choice in the matter." The vampire turned toward them, staring Geordie down with his catlike bright green eyes, scrutinizing her from head to toe, but giving a look of relief when he saw Matt.

"And why is that, Sam?" Matt asked, crossing his arms impatiently.

"That girl is a danger to you and those around you. I've already seen the aftermath of her presence being near you with that apartment. It's completely destroyed, and the humans are investigating the damage. I had to clean up the mess myself, and I am not planning on continuing to clean up anymore messes caused by her!" Sam yelled angrily at Matt.

"Do not yell at him like that! This is not his fault!" Geordie jumped in suddenly, feeling the need to defend Matt.

"You're right! This is *your* fault! If he had not saved you, he would still be safe and hidden! I would still be able to properly protect him! But you've thrown him into the radar of our enemies and now they will likely try to kill him because of *you*!" Sam turned on her next, looking down at her in hatred.

"What are you talking about, 'our enemies'? Are you one of them? Someone like Geordie?" Matt asked, trying to intervene. Sam's only response was a slight eye roll, but he didn't turn away from Geordie.

"No, he's not like me. He's a vampire, one that works for someone very important, from what I can tell of his persistence of taking you with him." Geordie stared menacingly right back at Sam without taking her eyes off him.

"How were you able to tell that? Did you read his mind?" Matt asked quizzically.

"No. I can't read vampire minds. I can tell by his smell and the fact that guardians are only as persistent as he is. And he is completely covered from the rays of the sun with his cloak."

"A what?" Matt then turned back to Sam with a look of expecting some sort of explanation.

"You're a smart girl; I have to give you that." Sam gave a short smile. "I guess the cat's out of the bag. Yes, I am a vampire guardian. Guardians are tasked with protecting someone very important, usually a royal or a high political figure. In this case, I was tasked with protecting you by your mother. I have been watching you your entire life."

"Why would my mother hire you to protect me? And why did you never tell me you're a vampire? Did you think I couldn't handle it?" Matt got flustered, pacing back and forth in frustration. Geordie wanted to do something to ease his mind, but she didn't know what to do. All she could do was stand there awkwardly in silence.

"I was sworn to secrecy, Matt. Plus, you're human.

Humans aren't supposed to know about this world, for their own safety. There was no way I would've been allowed to tell you, especially where your mother is involved." Geordie noticed Sam was no longer making eye contact with Matt and looked down in defeat.

"That's no excuse! You're supposed to be my best friend! You should've told me regardless of the repercussions. It doesn't matter what my mom wants…" Matt turned to walk away.

"Where are you going? You still have to come with me!" Sam yelled at Matt, but no response came. He then tried to speed over to Matt, making a motion to grab him by the arm, but Geordie stopped him before Matt could notice.

"You will *not* touch him." Geordie yanked Sam aside, slamming him against his fancy black car.

"Try that again, and I will end you." Sam maneuvered out of her grip and shoved her across the field. Baring his fangs at Geordie, he hissed, "This is *your* fault."

"I'm not the one who lied to him his whole life." Geordie retorted.

"No, but you haven't been there his whole life. You could never understand the level of danger you put him in by exposing him to this world. Every moment he gets closer to you, the more he is at risk."

"At risk from what?"

"I cannot say. All I can say is that there are people out there who would try to kill him if they found out who his family is." Sam paused, giving her a strange look. "Speaking of which, where is yours by the way?"

"What are you talking about? My family is dead. I had my mother and my father; they both died when I was thirteen. I have no family."

Sam laughed, rolling his head back against the hood of the car. "You really think they were your *only* family? Geordie *Vollner.*"

The way Sam let her surname roll off his tongue made her uncomfortable, as if he knew something she didn't. It also piqued her curiosity. What was he hiding?

"My parents never mentioned anyone else in our family." Geordie tried to rethink any time her parents may have mentioned other family members. Nothing came to mind.

"Maybe someone else in your family had a secret to hide as well. Nonetheless you will never find out if you're in Matt's life."

"What do you mean?" Geordie asked. Now that she knew she had family out there in the world, she needed to know who they were and where they were.

There was a long silence between the two of them. Sam was probably deciding his words carefully. "I knew your father's side of your family. If you choose to stay in Matt's life, you will never find out who they were. If you separate yourself from him, I will gladly inform you of your vampire heritage."

He then climbed into the driver's seat of his car and unrolled the deeply tinted window slightly. "I'll give you some time to think about it. I'm sure it won't be an easy decision if you truly care about Matt."

Sam chuckled lightly as Geordie watched him start the engine. It was probably one of the perks to being a guardian, getting nice cars and the power to manipulate others. She almost hated him for it, forcing her to choose between the first person to truly care about her and the family she never knew. He was right, it wasn't an easy decision. It was nearly impossible.

Geordie went to find Matt inside Jeremiah's cabin after watching Sam drive off when she was approached by Jeremiah in a rush. He was hurriedly pulling his dark green army jacket on when she had gotten back inside. "Where are you going?"

"There's something that's come up at my place in the city, and it needs to be taken care of *now*." Jeremiah fumbled around for his things before finally finding his keys and pocketing them quickly. "I don't know how long I'll be gone for. Everyone is already inside, including Matt. Don't answer the door for anyone, and most certainly do *not* leave the house at all until I come back."

"Why? What's wrong?" Geordie asked, panic stricken.

"I cannot say, but worse comes to worse, call that guardian fellow back to help you out." Just like that he left, slamming the door behind him and locking it up. Behind her, the faeries of the house also stared at the door in shock. No one knew what was going on, and it had Geordie worried.

FROST

Finding the faery shifter known as Jeremiah in the human world turned out to be a lot easier for Frost to do than she had initially thought. Although she hadn't seen or heard of him in quite some time, she remembered his old hiding place. A small, quaint apartment in the middle of the city. He lived alone, hidden amongst humans to cloak himself from unwanted enemies. But Frost always knew where to find him, no matter how hard he tried.

When she arrived, she mentally prepared herself for anything to come. He had a habit of shape shifting himself and creating illusions of the area around him; tricking the mind to seeing something that wasn't there. Frost hadn't seen this man in many years, so she wasn't sure what to expect.

Before Frost could knock on the door, it swung open with a fierce intensity that startled her, by an old man completely unfamiliar to her. Frost quickly recollected herself and took in the look that Jeremiah was sporting. "Is this a new body for you?"

"Maybe in your eyes. I've worn this face for years." He stepped aside allowing Frost to enter the apartment. It was completely different from the last time she was there; another one of his many illusions. Frost hated that his powers worked on angels.

"Do you honestly feel the need to change so often, old *friend*?" She looked around the living room and finally settled her cold blue eyes on Jeremiah.

"I only do it for my own protection." He handed her a glass of wine and poured another for himself. "What can I do for you?"

Frost smiled mysteriously at him. She could tell he was hiding something from her, and he was trying to get her on her way. She just didn't know what it was he was hiding. She could also tell that he feared talking to her. "I have a few questions for you."

"Yes?" He sipped his wine nervously, not taking his eyes off her.

"Where have you been the past couple months? You don't normally go off the radar so quickly before the winter." She gave him a daring look, wondering if he had the guts to lie to her.

"I've been helping some people out. Been giving them shelter until they can find better accommodations."

"Oh really? Now that's quite… generous of you…" Frost winced slightly. "I've heard some interesting rumors about you recently, or rather about something you may know. Someone's name dropped you about having some knowledge about a connection being made between all the shadow creatures and being able to wipe them out with one person. Is this true?"

There was a long pause as Frost watched Jeremiah think about her query. After a while he stood up and wandered over to one of the many packed bookcases. Without much effort, he plucked a large book out and handed it to Frost. "That holds the information you seek."

Frost slowly flipped it open, thumbing through the old pages carefully. There was a lot she did not understand. Repeatedly it mentioned something about a Shadow Kingdom, the First King Essence, and dark factions. None of it made any kind of sense. "What is all of this?"

"The only detailed record of the Shadow Kingdom alone. What you're wondering about is in reference to the First King Essence." Jeremiah nodded at the book in her lap.

"What is the First King Essence, *exactly*? My understanding is that it's something on its own from dark or light essences."

"It was an essence link a young king named Kearan Hallow created to bind the souls of humans, vampires, dark fae, and lygoids to him. From it rose four powerful beings called Potentials. Each one hailed from one of the species. They were called Potentials because they carried the potential to embody the essence he created and become king. He wanted to make his subjects stronger using his power and unite them."

"So, what does this have to do with the information I was given?" Frost asked, feeling herself getting increasingly irritated. Without realizing it, she froze the wine in her glass. Before doing any further damage, she set the frozen glass down on the table next to her.

"The information you received was only partially correct, but mostly wrong. The First King Essence does link all creatures of the four *factions* to the king, but it does not link their lives, only their powers are linked. And not just anyone can kill the king." Jeremiah got up and flipped the book to a page showing four men. "To link the lives of a mass population, you'd have to find a way to hijack the essence with a binding spell, which should not be possible."

Each man was of a different race. One a human, another a vampire, and the last two of faery and lygoid. From what she read, the idea Gabriel had to kill off the dark creatures was not so easily done and was false information. "Only a Potential can kill the king or another Potential."

"Exactly. And it only kills the link to their power, not all the creatures. There's no loophole to the ideas that your previous sources gave you." Jeremiah smiled shortly. He was still hiding something. Frost could feel it.

"What are you trying to keep from me, old man?" Frost asked simply. Sometimes she found it easier to just look for the answers through interrogation rather than torture.

"Who says I'm hiding anything?" He cocked his head to the side.

"All your muscles are tense, and you're trying not to sweat, even though you're failing." She studied his every movement as he sat across from her lying through his teeth. "So why don't you tell me now, so this doesn't have to get ugly."

Ice slowly crept across the room from Frost's fingertips room over to Jeremiah. When it started to inch towards his feet he winced, pulling them away quickly. "Okay."

The ice stopped, and she patiently waited for him to tell her what she wanted to know. She could see the strain in his entire body as he wanted not to tell her the information she sought. Eventually, he gave in.

"Of the four Potentials, I'm harboring one in my home safe from harm's way. He doesn't know he's a Potential, but I know, and someone else knows as well."

"Who? Who is this person you're protecting?" Frost nearly jumped out of her seat.

"He unknowingly goes by the same name as the first king. Hallow. His name is Matt Hallow. He not only is a Potential, but he is also the direct grandson of the first king, Kearan Hallow."

"Where are they?" This time Frost did jump out of her seat. She knew exactly what she needed to know to accomplish her goal.

"They? I don't recall a 'they'…"

"Don't play coy with me, faery," Frost snapped, glaring down at him. "I know the fallen is with Matt Hallow. Knowing the location of the fallen and withholding that information is in direct violation of angelic law. She is not being protected by any kingdom, coven, or order; therefore, any information must be given on her whereabouts. I can kill you for prohibiting me from doing my job."

"Even if that job means killing an innocent girl who's done you no wrong?" For a moment Jeremiah just stared up at her with no fear in his eyes. "Just so you're aware, this is in direct violation of a job I was given by the king himself. No matter what, I could die for my actions."

"Your king is dead. You can choose how you want to die. Either by my hand, or a lesser being. I personally don't care, but I will find the fallen one way or another." She didn't understand his lack of fear, but it didn't stop her from staring right back at him.

"They're in my cottage near the border of New Hampshire. It's right off Merrimack River."

GEORDIE

It wasn't until after the other residents had gone to bed that Geordie finally decided to approach Matt. She wasn't sure if he was ready to talk, but she wasn't going to give him a choice in the matter. "Penny for your thoughts?"

She slid a penny across the kitchen counter toward him where he sat eating a bowl of cereal. He smiled at her wit. When he finally managed to swallow his mouthful of food, he responded, "I don't know what I'm thinking really."

"May I inquire as to why?" She sat down on the barstool next to him, staring at him with concern.

"My whole world managed to change in such a short time. I moved here and met Sam when I came to college and now, I have learned everything I knew about him was untrue. He's been in my life since I was born? And he's a vampire? How old does that make him? How could he hide that he was a vampire to me?"

"I don't have the answers to those questions, I'm sorry. Maybe that's something you should ask him. Give him the benefit of the doubt."

"I don't know if I want to give him that much. He's lied to me about so much." Matt slowly laid his head down on the counter. "At least I have you to be completely honest with me."

"Hmm…" She chuckled. "Let me ask you this at least: why can you accept me telling you about all this but not

Sam?"

He had to think about it for a moment. "Because you didn't lie to me about who you were."

CHAPTER 8

FROST

In the weeks since her discovery of Matt Hallow's origins, Frost was ordered suddenly to return to the Immortal Realm until the first snowfall in the Mortal Realm. Ezra wanted her to prepare for apprehending the heir to the Shadow Kingdom and the fallen. They were to use the brute force of the weather in the Mortal Realm against the fallen. Frost begrudgingly agreed but wanted to attack Geordie Vollner head on and end the hunt.

In the outlands, far from the main city, Frost sat in meditation focusing her power and energy. Everything passed through her senses from the approaching flower storm to the flow of energy that resonated from Ezra in the heart of the world. Once the storm arrived, she used it to take control of the winds and moisture around her. She spun around and froze everything around her. In an instant Frost was able to turn the entire area as cold as winter. She found something wrong with it, however. It didn't feel as perfect as it should've been.

"You hesitated." An old woman's voice came from behind. Her skin was wrinkled and her whole body was spectral flickering. Thin, silvery hair fell down her back like lifeless violin strings.

"How are you not frozen?" Frost stared at the woman in amazement. "I changed the outlands from warm to cold and brought the deep abyss of winter. You should be frozen."

"Oh please, honey, you and I both know that only Ezra controls this world." The woman laughed at Frost, but she could only continue to stare in amazement. "I was created before this world even came into existence. Your magic has no effect on me."

"Are you a ghost?" She was spectral, but that could've meant anything.

"No, I am not. I am neither dead nor alive. My body is somewhere in the Mortal Realm, but my conscience is here. My life is tethered to something unknown that I'm sure would kill me if disconnected." She frowned as she looked down at her hands, as if examining the truth of her previous statement. Frost realized she had never seen this woman inside the city and there was no way of knowing what kind of power she held.

"What did you mean when you said I hesitated?" Frost folded her arms together.

"You may have trained for a long time, but you're still young. You're going against your nature to be different from the other angels. You want acceptance in Ezra's heart, but you also fear rejection."

"How could you possibly know any of this?" Frost snapped.

"I have the ability to not only read what lies within the mind but also in the heart. My name is Carola."

"Carola… why did Ezra create you? Especially so far from the others? Does anyone else know of your existence?"

"Ezra did not create me. I am not sure why I am here. I lost sight of that reason long ago. She refuses to acknowledge my presence in her world." Carola fell silent so Frost moved on from talking about Ezra.

"Who is your creator?" Frost tried to touch Carola's shoulder, but her hand went right through.

Carola just shook her head. "I was not created, I was born."

"Do you have any powers?" Frost sat down in the snow, crossing her pale long legs.

"I can see the auras, essences, and futures of the people around me if they are in focus." She was an intriguing creature. It was odd that she had those powers but wasn't of fae lineage. Frost wondered if she should report this creature to Ezra.

"Have you ever been inside the city, Carola?" Frost asked politely. Maybe if Frost lured her into the city Ezra would feel her presence and demand that Carola be brought to her.

"It is impossible for me to step foot inside the city."

"Why? I'm sure no one would have an issue with you."

Frost gave Carola a fake reassuring look. She couldn't believe she was trying to lure a creature into the city.

"Mystical veils around Cinereo Civitatum protect it from select creatures entering. That is how Ezra intended it to be when she first created the world." She paused, staring pensively towards the city. "Do you go into the city often?"

"Yes, I live there, why do you ask?"

"Someone I care about lives there; he's a lygoid."

"There are many lygoids in the city. Ezra allows them to live in this world since they cause too much chaos in the Mortal Realm. She closed the doors to the Mortal Realm for the lygoids long ago."

"Oh really? That is a new establishment…" She looked over to Frost slowly. "Will you send a message to someone for me?"

Frost wasn't sure how to respond. It wasn't in her nature to do anyone favors. Maybe if she did this for Carola, she could get information about the person the message was being sent to. Maybe they could tell Frost what Carola's existence was for. "Alright, what is it? Who does this message need to go to?"

"Do you know where the prison is?" She pointed towards Cinereo Civitatum, and Frost nodded skeptically. There was only one prison in the realm, and only a select few people were there whom Ezra saw as real threats to her. They were prisoners who could potentially throw the realm out of balance and overrule Ezra's authority. "There's someone there who has been unjustly imprisoned for many years. I need to send him something."

Carola grabbed Frost suddenly, wrapping her arm around Frost's waist, and pressing her free hand to her chest. For the first time, Frost could feel Carola's touch, and it hurt immensely. A surge of darkness filled Frost's heart electrocuting her entire body. The darkness clouded her mind, making her head throb painfully, as she screamed in agony.

"What are you doing to me? Stop!" Frost cried out, and Carola finally released her. Frost dropped to the ground, relieved the surge of dark energy ended, but the pain still resided.

"If you didn't already have some darkness inside you, I wouldn't have been able to forcibly enhance it. That pain you feel can go away if you fulfill my wish. If you do not go to the person I told you about, the pain will never go away, and you'll be consumed and lost forever. Not even Ezra would be able to help you."

Frost turned into her full angelic form with dark sapphire blue wings unfurling with a silvery shimmer before she flew off. She was not going to let the darkness reside in her and cost her life working for Ezra. She was tainted somehow, and there was no way she would let Ezra see her like this. She wondered if Ezra already knew. Darkness couldn't just be pulled from nothing, so she had to have had it beforehand.

When she got to the city, it was just before sundown and the streets were void of spirits or creatures. In the Immortal Realm, no one wanted to get trapped in the darkness. After sunset, lygoids came out of hiding to possess living wanderers. This was an attempt at escaping the Immortal Realm.

It was completely dark by the time Frost got to the prison, and she realized that Carola never mentioned who she was supposed to deliver the message to or what the message was. It was too late to turn back now. Dark clouds and a thick fog surrounded the area for miles. If it weren't for the light at the end of the street, she wouldn't know where to enter the prison.

Inside, everything was a blinding bright ivory and white. Even the security guard uniforms were white. The receptionist looked Frost up and down for a moment and then jumped up ecstatically, stumbling over her feet and her words, "Miss Frostbite, we were not expecting you!"

"I need to see one of the prisoners." Frost headed toward the double doors on the other side of the reception desk. The young Lucis faery followed Frost, asking pointless questions that she didn't bother to answer.

"Which prisoner would you like to see?" She stopped in her tracks as Frost turned on her and revealed a menacing icy hand.

"Give me your keys." Frost demanded quietly. The faery whimpered and unclipped her keys from her belt. For a moment she hesitated to give them to Frost but handed them over upon seeing a ball of ice form. "Leave these halls now and take the guards with you. You will get your keys back when I am finished."

"Yes, ma'am." The faery signaled all the guards to follow her out of the room.

"Do not let anyone enter here until I leave this building." Frost read the faery's thoughts, checking to see if she was going to tell anyone what happened. It seemed like she was too scared to rat Frost out, which was a good thing.

"Yes, mistress. I will not tell anyone." Frost loved how her power put fear into the minds of the lower beings. The faeries needed fear. The only reason they were permitted to be in the Immortal Realm was because the angels *let* them be there.

"You may go now." Frost dismissed her and watched the faery and guards leave, closing the doors behind them.

Most of the cells were empty except for a few. One of the prisoners was a worn down looking vampire whose skin was tinted grey and his veins were varicose. He looked drained of energy, unmoving and separated from the world.

There was a large creature in another cell beating on the plastic, and from what Frost could gather was screaming something inaudible. Frost steered away quickly seeing his singular eye and razor-sharp black teeth covered in ink black saliva, giving him a grotesque look.

In the third cell, a thin creature Frost could not get a read on looked angelic, but demonic as well. His skin was pale and dead looking which made his dark jet-black hair contrast brightly looking almost blue. He looked a lot like Geordie Vollner, but not nearly as healthy and alive. She found it very peculiar.

"You, child, come to me." A quiet voice came from inside Frost's mind. The very last cell at the end of the hall was a rawboned lygoid with only a few dirty rags to barely cover his pale, malnourished body. He also had long black hair that covered his face and went past his waist.

"I'm supposed to deliver a message to someone in here; I'm not sure to whom though." For once, Frost felt fear rising in her chest. Something about this particular lygoid made her uncomfortable and frightened. She thought it was perhaps due to him having a body. She had never seen a lygoid with a body before.

"You smell of angel, but you are dripping with darkness… and, oh god, you smell *so* good." He sat up a bit, sniffing the air and after a moment relaxed again in the corner of the wall. "You carry a familiar scent that does not belong to you. Where did you just come from?"

"The outlands, a woman named Carola sent me here."

"*Who?*" The lygoid appeared in front of Frost, pressing his body to the plastic wall, baring his teeth at Frost. "Why do you smell so delectably of darkness?"

The lygoid reached his hand through the plastic and gently placed his hand on Frost's chest in the same place Carola did. He was much gentler than she was, but Frost still felt pain searing through her body as the darkness was pulled out of her. The more pain she felt the more it seemed like the lygoid was in ecstasy. She began to feel as though she were going to die until the lygoid finally pulled away and was back in his corner again, holding a dark glowing blue orb in his hand. Her body felt lighter now, as if a weight had been lifted, but it still felt as though there was darkness inside her.

"What did you do to me?" Frost gasped, leaning against the wall of an empty cell, barely able to move. "How were you able to reach through the wall like that? They're supposed to be spelled to prevent that."

"You were carrying a piece of an essence that belonged to someone I was led to believe was dead. With that essence there was a message within it for me." The lygoid's mouth unhinged like a snake, eating the orb whole and looking around his padded cell walls before continuing. "To answer your other question, I hold more power than Ezra gives me credit for. Her prison cannot hold me hostage, but her gateway rules still apply to me, if you catch my drift."

"So, because you cannot escape this world you don't bother leaving this prison?" He nodded. "Can you take the darkness out of me entirely?"

"I cannot. You were made by Ezra taking a piece of her essence and placing it inside you. That mistake will cost her for the fact that she tried to create something perfectly pure of light. Ezra is not a creature of pure light, she has darkness inside her she desperately wishes to ignore, and therefore cannot create anything of pure light. If you join me and my cause, I will give you the freedom you desire to learn more about yourself as well as what you want most."

"And what is that? You don't even know me." Frost gave the lygoid a skeptical look. It was true, she wanted more from life. She didn't want to be blindly taking orders anymore. She wanted to be the one giving the orders.

"You want to kill the last fallen in the Mortal Realm. You don't want to apprehend her for Ezra." With those words, he had her undivided attention.

"The *last* fallen?" He only grinned at her. She couldn't believe the deal she was about to make. "Who are you?"

He then stood up and gave a short half bow half curtsy and introduced himself as, "Quinncey DeLavonte, but you, my dear, may call me Quinn."

"Quinn… What do I have to do to capture the fallen?"

"It's simple really," Quinn giggled manically. "Just bring the thing she cares about the most here to the Immortal Realm. She will follow."

"But she's alone in this world. She has nothing she cares about." Frost was confused. She couldn't think of anything she could bring over to the Immortal Realm that Geordie

Vollner would care about.

"Not according to my outside sources." Quinn shrugged with eyes closed. "Ah, yes, I can see her. My followers have recently reported that she has the company of a human she cares about deeply. For the life of me, I cannot see them whatsoever, but I can sense from her that there is someone she cares about deeply. A few someones, in fact. They recently told me the Vollner line continues, and there is nothing more important than *family*."

"How do you know all of this?" Frost was baffled at his knowledge of things in the outside world, things she didn't even know. "How do I know you're not lying?"

"It's not in my nature to lie, and I have a lot of resources around me, many people who would gladly die for me." He smiled. "I've been around for thousands of years, watching from afar, and waiting for this opportune moment. If you can get her family here, she will come to save them."

"Where am I supposed to find her family? I know nothing of vampire families." Finding vampires was out of her expertise, as well as forbidden since almost all vampires were a part of a coven that protected them from prosecution from the angels. It was an impossible task.

"Not all families are tied by blood, there are some bonds created that are stronger because we choose them." Quinn sang cheerfully. He then leaned in closely, "Ask Ezra about the Vollner line. Tell a tall tale to get the information you want. She will have much knowledge to give you; feed her the right lies and she will tell you anything."

"And how do I know I can trust you to help me with all of this?" Frost stood up, watching Quinn skeptically.

"You can't for now. But here's a little something that might help you. Go to Ezra, ask her about her fourth sister and see if she tells you anything. Come back to me later."

On her way out, Frost returned the keys to the frightened receptionist and headed immediately to Ezra's office to confront her. By now it was the middle of the night when Frost found herself banging on the door of Ezra's office. She refused to leave until she got answers. There was too much left unsaid that made Frost question whether she should continue to obey Ezra.

When she finally answered the door, Frost was greeted by a sleepy Ezra in a short white nightgown with an opalescent robe with pink feathers around the trim. "Frost, why are you here?"

"I need answers, and I am not going to leave until you provide me with some valid reason of why I should continue following you blindly." Frost shoved her way past Ezra. The office was no longer in the form of an office. It was dark, barely lit by one candle by her bedside. Ezra readjusted her robe, wrapping herself up as she sat down on her giant four poster bed with sheer curtains.

"What do you want to know, Frostbite?" Ezra sighed,

swinging her long legs up onto the bed and patting the space beside her for Frost to join her. Frost hesitantly joined her on the bed.

Choosing her words carefully, Frost asked, "Does Geordie Vollner have any other family besides her dead parents?"

"What are you asking of me? You know information about vampires is forbidden from being shared. It is a law the queens and I wrote that not even I am exempt from." Ezra watched her carefully.

"Were there any close family members that aren't vampire?"

They were both silent for a while. Frost was unsure how to proceed. Maybe she wasn't asking the correct questions. Maybe she had to rephrase. Reading Frost's thoughts, Ezra answered, "No, your questions work. There is one who is not vampire. Her name is Breena. She's of faery descent. She may not be of vampire descent, but she has many allies and people who would protect her because of who her husband is. That aside, she is a very powerful woman and can hold her own against an angel seeing as she has lived in the Immortal Realm for a portion of her life."

"Maybe if I can get to her, I can get to Geordie…" Frost thought out loud, but Ezra took her by the shoulders and shook her slightly.

"Frost do not go looking for a fight you cannot win.

Breena is not a woman to be trifled with. She knows the ways of angels and is not naïve. She has great power and is willing to fight any angel who threatens her. That being said, if you kill her, this war between us and the vampires will bleed out to the faeries, and we do not want them as an enemy. Do not go creating enemies for the angels and causing chaos." Ezra spoke sternly, shaking Frost once again. "Do you understand me?"

"Yes ma'am." Frost then remembered the other thing she needed to ask Ezra. "I just have one last question to ask of you."

"Yes, Frost, what is it?" Ezra nodded.

"Do you have a fourth sister?" Frost asked simply.

Ezra stared at Frost nervously. Silence loomed between them for a long time until Ezra swallowed nervously and finally spoke, "I do not have any sisters. You should know that by now."

She was clearly lying. For as long as Frost had been alive, she was always told and convinced that Ezra was the first and only angel with no family. She never put any thought into it until Quinn said something about it. She never even thought to question the truth. But now, here she was, questioning everything she was taught throughout her existence. Did Ezra have any sisters? Did she have three sisters other people knew about and a fourth that was a secret? Were all the sisters supposed to be a secret?

She arrived wanting answers to her questions, but Frost found herself with more questions and no answers. Whatever it was, Ezra was hiding something, and Frost had every intention of finding out what. Even if this meant Ezra wouldn't tell Frost herself.

"I think it is time for you to go. Let me sleep, Frostbite. You have plenty of work to do." Ezra pulled the covers over her legs and laid her head on the fluffy, white pillows. Frost took her leave and returned to the prison immediately to speak with Quinn. She wanted answers and she was unwilling to wait.

"Is Ezra a mortal being?" Frost asked Quinn impatiently. Once again, she terrified the guards and the receptionist into giving her the keys and privacy. Quinn started laughing immediately the moment Frost asked her question.

"She is indeed a mortal being, what makes you ask that?" Quinn laughed.

"You told me to ask her about a fourth sister. She claims she has no sisters! I've always known her to not have any sisters, and you want to try telling me she has *four*?" Frost couldn't believe the words that were coming out of her mouth. They went against everything she was ever taught.

"I'm not *trying* to tell you; I simply stating it as an irrefutable fact." Quinn approached the plastic, clear wall that separated them. This time his tone was serious and dark. "Ezra has four sisters. She was born an angel, but her sisters were different. Three of them were born vampires, they grew up to become the queens of the vampires. The last one and the littlest of them all was born a faery who would later create the Dark Order. The last sister was my mother, whom I was ripped away from when I was but a mere baby. Their names were Ezra Daron, Kathleena Daron, Melandria Daron, Anyanke Daron, and Carola Daron. They were the original five sisters, the first born of their kind. Ezra is by no means immortal."

GEORDIE

It had been a month since Jeremiah had come back to the cabin. It constantly worried Geordie with every passing day. As winter approached, it grew colder, and Jeremiah's power over the house began to fade. It was only a matter of time before Frost came for her. Geordie constantly worried about how it would eventually affect Matt. The longer Frost pursued them, the more likely Matt was going to get hurt. Geordie never gave Sam an answer the following time he returned, therefore he left again and never returned.

"What are you thinking about?" Matt's voice came from behind as Geordie stared pensively out a bay window overlooking the fall-colored back yard. She couldn't help but smile when he came over to sit in the window with her.

"Thinking about you, mostly." Geordie heaved a deep sigh, straining to smile as she continued to watch the trees.

The forest grew quiet, the air was still, and it slowly began to snow. For a while nothing happened except the silent snowfall that quickly piled up on the dead grass. At first

Geordie thought it was a product of Frost's powers, but soon realized this was nothing like her powers. This was the first real snowfall of the season. Not long, what used to be a dark forest laid out beyond the house was now blanketed in white. Jeremiah had mentioned multiple times before he disappeared that they would be gone by the end of the first snowfall. Geordie wondered what the circumstances would be that they would leave. One of the faery girls approached Geordie and Matt, staring at the snow as well, her eyes expressionless.

"Jeremiah mentioned many things to us regarding your stay." She paused. She then turned to Geordie, "You know, some have said that Jeremiah might've been clairvoyant. You don't get many faeries in the Mortal Realm who can get glimpses into the future. Most of them get taken by the angels and sent to the Immortal Realm to live out their days. From what I understand, they're treated like gods over there."

Suddenly gusts of wind whipped up from a quiet snowfall to a blusterous, bone chilling wind that felt too sudden to be normal. Distracted by the sudden ruckus of the weather, Geordie pulled away slowly, trying to listen to what was approaching.

"Geordie…" Matt breathed heavily. Matt couldn't sense what Geordie could from such a distance. "What is it?"

Geordie ignored him, continuing to listen. She had an eerie feeling she already knew who was out there, but she pleaded with herself to not let it be true. If she was wrong, she didn't want to falsely alarm the house for no reason. However, something didn't feel right. The weather shifted again.

Distantly, Geordie could feel the forest become smoldering hot. Then she could smell it, the fire. Wild embers blazed through the trees, headed straight for the cabin. Geordie quickly pulled away from Matt and headed to the back porch to see in the distance how close the angels were. Their powers were too familiar to not recognize. It had to be Frost and Pyre, the ice and fire angels.

Geordie then fled back inside the cabin and called for everyone's attention including Matt's. "Everyone I need you to get as far away from the cabin as possible! There are two angels approaching! If given the chance, they will kill you without hesitation!"

Panic rose amongst the faeries gathered around. One of them approached Geordie, "What about Jeremiah? Is this because he's gone?"

"Are they able to come to the property because the protection spell is weakening?"

"Did he abandon us?"

So many questions Geordie didn't have the answers to. She didn't even know where to begin or what to believe. All she could do was provide them the truth. "I don't know what happened with him, but I do know that they have the power to break through his magic, and they're after only me. So please, spare yourselves from the bloodshed."

Everyone in the house immediately fled the property until it was just Geordie and Matt. "Matt, I will treasure you until the end, but right now you need to get out of here."

"I'm not leaving you alone." Matt took Geordie's hand in his and they headed to the backyard to await the end. It took all her willpower not to pull away.

"She's here. She's come to kill me." Geordie nodded off in the distance where snow had begun to fall again. Ice formed on the porch railing. Somewhere beyond the forest, fire went ablaze, burning everything in its path relentlessly. Together Frost and Pyre signed their destructive signatures into the earth as a preemptive warning of their approach.

"Geordie Vollner!" Frost jumped from the shelter of the trees and released a blast of ice upon Geordie which she narrowly dodged, pulling Matt out of the way as well. "Your end has come!"

The winter angel landed on the porch with a hard thud that iced over the area where she stood. Geordie backed away slowly, nudging Matt behind her. "What do you want, Frost?"

"Isn't it obvious?" Frost smiled wickedly. "I want to take everything you hold dear, starting with him!"

She grabbed Matt, yanking him out from behind Geordie, and slammed him against the wall of the cabin. It froze behind him as he let out a loud groan of protest.

"Let him be, Frost!" Geordie begged. At this Frost's

expression shifted to a flare of anger. "He has no quarrel with your kind."

"She's right. He doesn't have any quarrel with our kind." Pyre slowly approached the cabin, letting wild flames dance around him.

"But, *Pyre!*" Frost shrieked childishly.

"Oh, Frostbite, you didn't let me finish." Pyre gave her a smile that suggested more familiarity than they let on. "The boy may not have any direct quarrels with our kind, but if what you told me is true, then he is our natural enemy that must be taken into custody."

Fire rose rapidly, covering the entire porch in untouchable flames that could kill them. Memories of her parents' deaths flashed back as she tried to save Matt. As quickly as possible, Geordie pushed Matt off the porch behind Pyre, letting him land on the dead grass. Geordie tried to follow, but more flames undoubtedly blocked her path. The one time she wished flames weren't harmful to vampires was then. Amongst the fire, Geordie could hear Frost's laughter of joy. Pyre's powers were growing stronger by the minute.

"Matt, you have to get out of here!" Geordie called out to him from beyond the flames.

Frost approached from behind, leaving a trail of ice behind her and extinguishing the fire. On one side she had Frost pursuing her, clearing a path to the inside of the house, but on the other side she had Pyre hidden amongst his flames nowhere to be found. For the first time since her parents died, Geordie felt trapped. Even worse, she could lose another innocent life. The night her parents died flashed before her as Matt's life and her own were in danger.

In a cabin much like Jeremiah's but far northwest in the Daron Forest of California, Geordie and her parents had once lived in the home of a faery family that gave them a sanctuary away from the angels. Everyone in the house feared angels. These fears were brought to life when the angels arrived with the fire of the phoenix angel, Pyre. All Geordie knew was that he could manipulate flames and turn into a phoenix.

Flames swirled around him and the other angels, burning anything in their path as they approached the cabin. Shadows emitted from another angel taking the form of wolves racing towards the house; this angel was Gabriel. The moment the wolves hit the cabin, the ground began to rumble violently.

"Elizabeth, get Geordie out of here!" Her father yelled as Geordie hid behind her mother. Everything happened so fast. One moment, the angels were approaching, flaunting their powers, and the next, Geordie felt someone snatch her from her mother. Gabriel grabbed her by the arm, squeezing tightly as Geordie screamed in pain.

Over by a couch, Geordie saw Frost pinning her mother down as she dragged her ice blade over her mother's back, digging out her wings and clipping them, making her mother mortal.

"It's sad that you can't enjoy the smell of fear and pain as much as I do, little girl." She caressed Elizabeth on the cheek gently before lifting her blood-stained blade into the air, stabbing her violently. Geordie tried to turn her head away, but Gabriel stopped her, so she closed her eyes as a deafening scream emitted from her mother. Tears slowly emerged as she listened to her mother die. Eventually Gabriel dropped her to the floor as she burst into tears.

When Geordie finally opened her eyes, she saw her father in the arms of another angel in the same way that she had been with Gabriel. They spoke something to her father that she could not make out. Slowly her father dropped down to the ground as he saw Geordie, crawling towards her urgently. Before they could embrace, a stake tore through his heart from above Geordie by Gabriel's hand.

Geordie's parents were dead, and the rest of the household was nowhere to be seen. Geordie felt more alone than ever at that moment. Everyone she ever met died because of her, including her parents. Relief washed over Geordie. The running was over now, she was about to die.

A scream broke out, piercing through the chaos, but Geordie didn't see what happened. Someone yanked her up from the bloodied floorboards and swept her elsewhere. It was probably one of the angels, taking her away.

"It's okay Geordie, I'm here. You're safe now." The matron of the household, Lily Perkin's soothing voice carried Geordie away from the chaos. She found comfort in the feeling of Lily's protective embrace. The affection in her voice reminded Geordie of her mother.

Although Lily saved her that dreadful night, Geordie never saw her again in the days following. It was in everyone's best interest that Geordie left. She no longer wanted to endanger anyone else. And now that was exactly what she was doing with Matt, endangering him, just as Sam had predicted. She truly was a monster.

Chapter 9

Frost

Frost froze the large porch while Pyre sent his flames flying in a fiery tornado, trapping Geordie in a cage of ice and fire. There was no way she would get away this time. It was magnificent. The embers of chaos and destruction engulfed the cabin, trapping Geordie on the porch where she could be captured and killed. Whatever could she do? The boy was already on the lawn, trying to recover himself. Pyre noticed this as well and went after him.

"I think I will enjoy the warmth somewhere else." Pyre stepped down from the porch and walked into the blazing grass.

"There's nowhere for you to run little girl." Frost turned back to Geordie, watching the panic overtake her as she tried to find a way of escape. It almost made Frost laugh at how pathetic she looked.

"You should really adapt to your environment. Let me show you the true power of angels."

Beside her, Frost summoned a white wolf made of ice and it leapt into the air, planting its long sharp claws into Geordie's chest as it tore her flesh with ease. Geordie screamed violently. As she watched Geordie writhe in agony, Frost could feel Pyre's fire burning the entire forest. Looking back, the boy was gone and from the way the house felt, it was going to collapse at any moment.

While Pyre pursued the human, creating flames with every step he took, she tried reading the boy's thoughts but they were completely silent to her.

Pyre, I can't hear him.

I know. Neither can I.

What should we do?

I will kill him. And you take the girl back to Ezra.

Frost turned back to Geordie who was being guarded by the snarling wolf. She laid there unconscious and bleeding out. Harsh cracks erupted from the house in protest to Frost's footsteps; the deck was going to cave in soon.

The place is about to collapse, Pyre!

Get out of there now!

"No!" A voice boomed as the cabin began to crumble quickly. The voice sounded familiar. It came from the boy, but it wasn't his voice. His face was dark and invisible to her, as if covered by a shroud. "I will not let you take her!"

The human boy stood up to the two angels, black shadows crawling all over his skin like the smoke in the forest. Frost sent her wolf after him, teeth snarling, ready to tear his flesh out. Pyre followed suit by sending wild flames toward the boy at full speed. All their attacks he easily deflected. He grabbed the wolf by the throat, crushing it to pieces in one tight choke hold, then shoved Pyre aside going after Frost.

"I do not care if I cannot kill you! Give up Geordie Vollner, *now!*" An explosion of emotion surrounded him, knocking Frost off her feet. She could feel everything: anger, hatred, lust, all aspects of a dark creature. Along with it a force of dark energy hit Frost even harder than before. She fell to the ground, paralyzed and unable to move. Moving past her, he lifted Geordie into his arms.

Something was not right about him. A mere human caused so much devastation, more than two angels. Where his powers landed, dark fire spread like a disease. Instead of burning to ash, the trees withered and died. The grass disintegrated along with the leaves. Stone turned to dust and blew away with the wind. Eventually the cabin exploded but Pyre's flames continued to grow.

As soon as the dark currents dissipated, Frost she got up and ran over to Pyre, who was on his back staring at the human in awe. "Get up and put these flames out! Your powers are getting out of control!"

For a second Pyre glared at Frost but looked back at the flames and without a single movement or blink of the eye, the fire slowly died out. When the flames were finally gone, Pyre gave her a furious look, "What is your problem, Frost? When will you stop showing off and start doing things efficiently?"

"That human blasted me with the strongest dark power I

have ever felt. For a Potential, let alone a human one, he was incredibly powerful.” Frost stared at the spot where Matt Hallow left as Pyre continued to glare at her.

“I know. This is why we must kill him.” He paused for a moment, “I can guarantee his presence will become problematic in the future.”

“Understandable,” Frost glanced over to Pyre as he finally sat up. “He *did* manage to defeat you.”

“That is *not* my point. He showed a resemblance almost identical to Kearan Hallow. He’s not just a descendent or a Potential; he has the essence within him.”

“Oh… right…” Frost played with the dirt around her.

“The Shadow Kingdom is weak; it would be in our best interest if it stayed that way. If it were to rise again, they would have the ability to wipe out all creatures of light, if they so choose, theoretically.”

“But that is only a theory, correct?” Frost looked up at Pyre and he took her by the hand, pulling her to her feet.

“It’s a theory Ezra would not want to take chances on.”

“Does it really matter what Ezra wants at this point?” Frost asked, thinking about everything Quinn had told her so far. Shortly after her confrontation with Ezra and Quinn, Frost told

Pyre about her experience. At first, he didn't want to hear anything of it. Questioning Ezra meant betraying the angels; neither of them felt ready to take that on.

"What do you mean, does it matter? She is our leader! She created all of us!" Pyre exclaimed. She could see the look of betrayal in his eyes. He still couldn't accept what she had told him.

Frost thought about it. It didn't make sense why Ezra would want to hide vital information about the origins of the angels from them. If she herself had darkness in her, that meant she was a hypocrite. "Look she has four other sisters, all of them are not angels which means she lied about her heritage. She's not a creature of pure light, which means none of us are either. Everything we've known has been a lie."

"If that's the case, then where do we come off from judging the dark creatures. We are dark." What Pyre pointed out was something Frost had been in denial about since she met Quinn. Is anyone truly either light or dark? Was there a point in having the two factions of essence? "Maybe we should join allegiances with someone who will actually tell the truth to us and not hide from the truth. And if that is the case, where do we go from here?"

"We do what Quinn said. If he's correct, then Ezra is no better than the vampires she has forsaken, therefore we will align ourselves with Quinn. We will go to Los Angeles and find the other Vollners. From there we will bring one over to the Immortal Realm. He wants to meet Geordie Vollner, and that is the only way to guarantee we will get her there."

"Very well, but just know, we are about to kidnap one of the most powerful fae alive. That is not going to be an easy thing to pull off. Do you have a plan?" Pyre asked as they began to leave the decimated forest.

"Don't worry, Quinn gave me a way of defeating any fae no matter how strong they are."

SAM

Hours after the club opened, Sam felt a strong explosion of darkness awaken suddenly. As suddenly as it appeared, it disappeared moments after. He could tell quite a few of the local creatures felt it as well as he watched numerous people stop to experience the dark wave of energy. It was as if they relished in the feeling it gave them. What worried Sam was that it felt all too familiar. Matt's powers had finally awakened.

Rushing upstairs to his loft, Sam grabbed his phone and called the only person he knew would have knowledge of that kind of power. "Michael? Hello?"

"Sam? I felt a strong darkness appear from your neck of the woods. Do you know what it was?"

"Sort of, not really. Where are you?"

"Donor Compliant Corporation."

"You might want to come with me for this, I think I know who it came from."

A few minutes later, Sam's old teacher, Michael Anderson picked him up and they sped over to the cabin where Matt and Geordie were staying. A few hours later at the cabin, everything was in black flames that were slowly dying down, and it was completely vacant and destroyed. They decided not to test their luck, so they went around the property to the back. After a while of searching, they finally found Matt and Geordie unconscious a few miles from the house near a creek. Lifting her into his arms, Sam noticed Geordie was colder than a normal vampire, and upon closer inspection there were shards of ice festering from her abdomen. They were both covered in blood, and he could hear their heartbeats slowly fading. Sam had no other choice but to take them to the worst place in the world, Donor Compliant Corporation.

He wasn't going to risk losing more people he cared about. Even seeing Geordie in her condition made him remember when Lizzie came down with her sickness. It pained him severely to see Lizzie constantly hurting, and it happened when they were still with Vexus, the vampire who took care of them and whom Sam dearly missed, along with Vexus' progeny, Triana.

Travelling with Vexus, Triana, and Lizzie was Sam's entire life at the time. It had been a constant danger, but the last mission turned out to be the worst of all of them. Normally, they had collected ancient artifacts, dealing with countless types of creatures all over the world, but not once had Sam ever dealt with a werewolf. Eventually, the war on faery half-breeds brought them to Germany due to Vexus' desire to end the war for his wife, whom he could not be with due to the war. Sam felt lucky to be able to see Lizzie every day because she was his sire. Vexus rarely got to see his wife.

It was back in the nineties; Lizzie had sat down with him one evening in the courtyard of Vexus' home in Germany. "Are you nervous? I know you've never dealt with werewolves before; they can be tricky."

"I am a bit, but I've dealt with numerous other things before too. What's a werewolf at this point?"

"A creature almost as fast as us but can kill us with one bite or scratch." She spoke with a serious tone.

"What do you mean?"

"Their fangs and claws are lethal to us if they manage to draw blood. Even if you get scratched it will be the most agonizing and painful death you can imagine. That's why Vexus wants us to be faster and more cunning than those *dogs*. For our own safety."

The evening passed slowly as they prepared for their mission. They were given a minimal amount of information and simple orders: kill as many of the werewolves as possible and drive them out of the caverns of a mountain while Vexus and Triana retrieved a magical stone . Silver was lethal to them along with wolfsbane, so Vexus equipped them with a full arsenal. Sam could feel the fear and nervousness crawling up his insides like a million tiny little bugs as he geared up.

Everyone else was too focused to notice his nervousness.

Before they left, Vexus approached Sam personally, which he did not do often. His demeanor was serious as always, "Sam, there are a few things you must know about werewolves before I send you out there alone with Lizzie."

Vexus was pacing the living room with a serious tone while Sam sat in an armchair in front of him. Lizzie and Triana sat on a loveseat off to the side, spectating as if they were watching a comedy. Triana was the only vampire Vexus had ever turned and he always kept her near him. He did the same with Lizzie as well, but he was not her maker. No one knew who made Lizzie into a vampire and no one knew his reasoning for keeping her so close.

"What is it, Vexus?" Sam didn't think killing werewolves was very complicated, but then again, he had never encountered one before.

"Werewolves may be slightly slower than us, but they are still faster than most other creatures. They also match our strength easily. They like to fool people."

"How so?" This astonished Sam since Lizzie mentioned they were stupid.

"Werewolves are completely identical to normal wolves; they tend to run with real wolves to deceive hunters, and if you slip up, it could be the end of you." Vexus showed him pages in a book that showed the diagrams of werewolves next to normal animals. "I wouldn't recommend your usual sword and gun combo. Stick to the rifle; keep them at a distance at all costs."

"Sir, what if I end up killing the real wolves?" Sam thought about it. He wasn't sure how he felt about killing innocent animals. He liked wolves for the most part. They didn't deserve to be slaughtered as cannon fodder.

"I don't see what difference it makes in a life or death situation. Do what you need to do to complete the mission and survive." Vexus stood up and they continued to prepare for their mission. The goal for the evening was to clear out a den of werewolves and retrieve a very special piece of stone for Daron Academy. No other information was given except to reduce the likelihood of more deaths for the vampires, it was deemed a two-person mission.

When Sam and Lizzie got to their post near a cavern in the mountains, something unexpected waited for them there. They were stationed at the bottom of a winding mountain that had a zigzagging path traveling up and around the side. A hidden cavern lay at the bottom, slightly overflowing from the river running through it. The water levels had been slightly higher because of a storm that had hit the previous evening.

Seeing the environment, the odds didn't seem like they were in Sam and Lizzie's favor. All they had to do was wait on a large rock at the entrance of the cavern for the wolves to come out for their run. The intensity of the wait made it impossible to talk. All they could hear were the echoes of dripping water, until a roar erupted from the forest behind them. Without a word, they both leapt off the rock and slowly headed towards the forest. More roars and howls erupted from within the cave as well, the vibrations of the roars reverberating throughout Sam's entire body.

Sam swung back toward the cave, waiting for something to emerge. Lizzie and Sam both readied their weapons, Lizzie pointing her gun toward the entrance and Sam watching the dark depths of the cavern. The growling began to emit from all directions. From the darkness, wolves emerged from every direction surrounding Sam and Lizzie and closing in on them. Sam aimed his rifle carefully at the wolves, ready to fire the moment one of them tried to make a move.

As soon as one leapt at them, they began firing their guns at any wolf that got too close. At some point, Sam realized that Lizzie was no longer by his side. She wasn't anywhere to be seen in the cavern. Finding her became Sam's top priority. Sam threw off any werewolf that got in his line of path as he tried to make his way to the outside of the cavern. She wasn't anywhere in the forest down the path.

Sam headed outside to check if Lizzie had escaped, but her scent didn't linger anywhere outside the cave. She was still trapped inside somewhere. Behind him the cavern wall collapsed from the loud echoing sounds of gunfire, growls, and screams. There was no way he was going to get back in through the front entrance again.

Sam rounded the side of the mountain, balancing on the narrow cliff while holding onto a tree branch hanging over the cliff. At the end of the cliff there was another entrance going into the mountain. Sam followed the tunnel all the way from the back entrance to the level they had initially started at. Inside there wasn't anyone around, but Sam could still hear gunfire and the werewolves' vicious snarls. He headed down the tunnel in a rush towards the noise. The water levels reached up to his knees, making it hard to run at full speed.

"Lizzie? Lizzie, where are you?" Sam called out but there was no response. Amidst the roars, he could hear screaming, as if someone was being mauled. The closer Sam got to Lizzie the more he sensed her fear. He found her fighting off dozens of werewolves at once. It looked as though they were trying to contain her instead of trying to kill her.

"We were set up!" She spun around and shot a were-wolf in the head. The body turned immediately back to a human girl. Her body was completely broken, and her face blown off from the gunshot.

"Why would Vexus set us up?" Sam yelled as he shot one of them.

"Not by Vexus! The man who hired Vexus for the job did this!" Sam tried to remember the man who hired them. Then he realized, it wasn't a man, in fact, it was a boy. A three-hundred-year-old vampire in the body of a teenager named Harrison hired them.

Harrison appeared and blasted her with a shock of dark energy. Purple waves of darkness that faintly resembled shadows crawled over her body as she collapsed. "Lizzie!"

Sam screamed out for her as the entire cavern began shaking and rumbling. The entire wall next to Sam collapsed sending rocks and dirt flying everywhere.

"Give up! You're surrounded!" Harrison yelled at Sam. He was right, looking around, there was no way Sam could get Lizzie *and* get out of there.

"Harrison! Under Daron Authority, I hereby arrest you for treason and plotting against the royal family!" Vexus busted through the crumbling wall with Triana. Instead of complying, Harrison sent all the werewolves after them. The way Vexus moved made killing the werewolves look like a light exercise. Meanwhile, Harrison was escaping through a dark tunnel. Vexus paused, retrieving Lizzie first and brought her to Sam.

"Sam, take Lizzie and get out of this cave… you need to take Lizzie back to Daron Island with you and report this situation." He gave Sam a pleading look, slightly shaking him by the shoulders. "I have to apprehend Harrison, but I trust you, Sam!"

"But how do I get to Daron Island? I've never been there before!" Sam yelled at Vexus as he ran off with Triana. Harrison blasted more shadows at Vexus and Triana. Vexus fell back allowing Sam time to run up to them.

"Everything is already set up for you. Just get Lizzie outside!" It was a heavy ordeal, but it had to be done and Vexus didn't give him an opportunity to argue. "Don't fail me, Sam!"

That was the last Sam ever saw of Vexus. From what Sam heard, Vexus eventually managed to return to the Ancient Artifacts Library, but he often disappeared during his missions for months at a time. After the events of that night, Sam swore to never let anyone disappear or get hurt ever again.

It was a long drive to Donor Compliant Corporation, and Sam thought it best to inform Matt's mother what had happened. He knew he wasn't going to hear the end of it, but she deserved to know.

"Hello?" A tiny feminine voice picked up the phone at the fourth ring as Sam was beginning to lose hope.

"Naómi? It's Sam. I need to tell you something regarding Matt." He breathed carefully. Sam always felt on edge talking to her. Naómi was the only witch he knew, and he didn't want to say the wrong thing. Even though she hired him to watch over her eldest son, she made it very clear how she felt about vampires, and it made it even weirder to deal with her as a vampire.

"What's wrong with Matt? Is he getting behind in his studies?" Her voice sounded like a mixture of irritated and worried at the same time. Sam almost regretted calling her. Her worry wouldn't wane until she heard from Matt, if he decided to call her.

"It's not about school. I don't know what's wrong with him right now. I found him at Jeremiah the shifter's cabin. I think his powers have awakened as a Potential because the forest surrounding the cabin was on fire. It was black fire,

Naómi. He sent off a strong pulse of dark energy right before I found him too.”

“What do you mean? What happened to my son, Samuel?” Her voice trembled.

“He and a girl he has been with were attacked by angels. It appears they fought them off and the experience woke his powers. I am bringing him to Donor Compliant Corporation now to tend to his wounds.”

“How dare you! I told you to never bring my son into that building! If they lay a finger on him, I will personally curse all of them including you! And who’s this girl he was with? Was she the reason why his power was awakened? You’re not telling me everything, Samuel!” She shrieked into the phone. Sam was surprised that her voice didn’t wake up Matt and Geordie in the car.

“She is no one, Naómi. She’s just a hybrid.”

“A hybrid of *what*?” Naómi demanded. Sam could hear her heartbeat quicken.

With a long sigh he revealed Geordie’s nature, “She’s the fallen…”

“That is impossible.” She hissed.

“I know. Do you want me to arrange for you to fly out here

so you can oversee Matt's recovery?" Sam hoped that she would say no but was certain she would say yes.

"No, I want you near him around the clock at all times. I cannot go out there. Have him call me."

"Alright." He sighed. "I will have him call you as soon as he is well enough."

"Watch yourself, Samuel! If you push me, I will shove back. You have him call me as soon as he wakes up." She had a dark tone to her voice that had a menacing underlay to it. It made Sam seriously rethink his previous statement.

"We'll see about that." He hung up, leaving Naómi a challenge, which was probably a mistake, but that was a problem for the future.

A part of Sam was starting to believe that Naómi didn't understand the full weight of Matt's potential. There were too many possibilities to her thinking. She either didn't understand it genuinely, she was in denial about it, or she stopped believing in the possibility. He hoped none of those possibilities were true. If she stopped believing, then it would be difficult to convince him of his true heritage.

To guarantee Matt's inheritance, Sam wished he had more information about Matt's father, but according to Naómi there was no record of him. There had to be a record somewhere of Matt's family tree. If he could find one that showed Matt's father's lineage, then Sam would be able to prove that Matt could bring back the Shadow Kingdom.

There was only one place where every family tree was kept: Daron Island. Every record of vampire and faery history was kept on the invisible ever moving island. The only problem was that people needed authorization to go to the island, and Sam only knew of one person who had that authority.

Nick Hallow, Matt's younger brother, had a good connection with the queens at Daron Island. Even though he was born a vampire, the queens felt as though he had great potential to be guardian. He was lucky because most guardians were only turned vampires and shapeshifters. But Nick was not only close friends with the royal family, but he went to school with the successors to the throne.

As soon as Michael and Sam got Geordie and Matt admitted into the medical center that was the Donor Compliant Corporation, he let the healers do what they needed to do and made a call to Nick Hallow. As the phone rang, Sam watched the healers tend to Matt, and he could feel Matt's dark energy calming down, and his wounds began to heal.

"Sam, what's up? It's great to hear from you!" He answered delightedly. Sam could hear the smile in Nick's voice. In the background, Sam could hear Nick's girlfriend sigh and move away from him.

"Is this a bad time?"

"Huh? No! Not at all! Valerie just got here five minutes ago is all."

"Okay, well I need your help with something." Sam took a deep breath before continuing, "I need to get to Daron Island, and I know you can get me the proper authorization."

"Hmm... why do you need to go over there at this time of year?"

"I need to do research on a family tree and speak with Queen Anyanke." There was a very long pause and some whispering until Nick came back to the speaker.

"Alright, Sam. It just so happens that I have been called in, so I'll take you with me when I go. You'll just have to make your own appointments."

"That is fine. When will you be leaving?" Sam got a pen and paper ready.

"Sunday at four in the morning. Meet me at pier twenty-nine in San Fransisco at three." Sam wrote the information down and tucked it into his pocket so he wouldn't forget. He then turned to Michael who was talking to a doctor nearby about Matt.

"It looks as though Matt will recover just fine. Geordie has some leftover ice inside of her from the angel's magic that we cannot get rid of. It appears it can only be healed by angelic magic." Michael looked over to Geordie who was being worked on by healing faeries. Sam felt some kind of concern for her, but he wasn't sure how to help her since her heritage was unknown to him.

"What am I supposed to do about her?" Sam asked shortly.

"Honestly, the only thing that can heal her is angelic magic. I don't know if we *can* help her."

"So, what is going to happen to Geordie?" Matt came out to the hallway in a hospital gown and a wheelchair. A nurse wheeled him out from one of the patient rooms.

"Matt…" Sam groaned but Matt ignored him.

"What is going to *happen* to Geordie?" Matt repeated angrily. Not once did he look at Sam. He only watched Michael for answers.

"We don't know. The most logical explanation would be that if the ice is not controlled in her body, then it will spread, continuing to lower her temperature. Thus, from there her heart rate will slow and she will simply fall asleep." Michael told Matt, but Matt didn't seem very satisfied with this answer. Now he watched the doctors work on Geordie, staring at her longingly. "We've tried transfusing blood to her in hopes of her vampire side accepting it and healing, but it doesn't last nearly as long because of the ice. It heals her a little, but not enough to make a lasting effect."

MATT

Matt ignored Frost as he walked away from the flaming catastrophe that was their last place of consolation. He didn't know where they were supposed to go from there. Matt swore he was going to protect Geordie with everything he had. With his determination to protect her, something awakened inside Matt and he did not know where came from. It had to be a part of what Sam was hiding from him for most of his life.

Unsure of how far they had gotten from the wreckage, Matt stopped with a jolt. He felt as though he might drop Geordie out of exhaustion. He couldn't feel his legs anymore, and they refused to move any further as well.

Just keep moving. Keep moving.

As much as he tried to motivate himself, no movement came except the swiftness of his body collapsing underneath him into the snow. Geordie fell out of his arms and rolled down the hill, but he wasn't sure where she ended up.

Get up. Keep moving. Get Geordie to safety!

All the thoughts in the world couldn't get his body to move and rescue Geordie. He could feel himself losing consciousness. Nighttime darkness turned into sheer darkness.

As his vision faded of the black fire and falling snow, what felt like a long-forgotten memory pushed its way to Matt's mind. He could see Sam at a distance, following at a slow pace behind as Matt ran forward, weaving between large rocks and tree roots. He was in a forest and looking behind him, Sam was grinning with his hands in his pockets as he followed the young and ever running Matt.

"Keep your eyes on the road! You don't want to fall!" Sam laughed as he continued to pursue Matt. Something was off, Sam wasn't wearing his normal black hooded long sleeve and dark jeans, concealing all his skin. He wore a tight t-shirt with his arms and face exposed. It had been so long since Matt saw Sam during daylight, he forgot how similar they looked. They could've been brothers. Matt was starting to remember; this was the forest his mother's school was in. The trees were tightly clustered together, never allowing direct sunlight through their branches.

"I'm not going to fall–" Before Matt could finish his sentence, he tripped over a tree branch, scraping his exposed little legs. This was when he was seven. Tears started rolling down his cheeks in large streams and before he knew it, Sam was by his side.

"Sam how did you do that? You were so far away." Young Matt sniffled as Sam held him, inspecting the damage to Matt's knees, tears still going.

He smiled quietly and pulled a band aid out of Matt's backpack he'd been carrying. "Everything in the eyes of a little one like yourself looks so much bigger than they really are. I am never that far from you truly."

"Will you always be there for me, Sam?" Matt looked up into the green eyes he had become familiar with growing up.

"Of course, Little One. I will always be there to protect you." Sam lifted Matt onto his feet, brushing the dirt off his shorts before wiping the tears from his eyes. "I may have to go away sometimes, but I'll never be far, and I'll always come back."

"How do I know you won't leave me?" Matt pouted. By this point his mother was already spending less and less time with him and spent sometimes days at a time at the school she never brought him to.

"You see this bracelet, Matt?" Sam showed him the charm bracelet on his left wrist. Matt always loved looking at the different pendants; he thought they were so pretty. Matt nodded quietly, still sniffling. "This means that I am a protector. I protect those who are very special and those who cannot protect themselves. You are both very special and right now you cannot protect yourself, and as long as I have this bracelet, I will always be there to protect you in some form or another. Sometimes you'll have to forget me for a little while, but understand, I will *never* leave you."

"Thanks, Sam. You're the best big brother ever." Matt smiled, wrapping his arms around Sam's neck as he could feel Sam wrap his arms around his little frame. After a moment, Matt pulled out of the hug and instead pulled Sam's wrist back to look at the bracelet once more. "When can I get one of those? I want to become a protector for someone, just like you!"

"Not for a very long time, my young friend." Sam laughed, pulling his arm up slightly, and allowing the bracelet to slide onto Matt's tiny wrist. "One day, you will become everyone's protector and you won't need one of these because everyone will know you and they will love you."

"Like a king?" Matt beamed at him excitedly. Sam lifted Matt into his arms, holding him against his side.

"Exactly like a king." Sam smiled, allowing Matt to slide the bracelet back onto his wrist before looking into his eyes. "But for now, you must forget our time together until our next meeting. You see, I don't grow old, and we can't exactly have you finding out about this world until you're ready. I hope one day when you remember this, you'll understand."

The last Matt remembered was resting his head on the shoulder of a stranger who found him in the woods, lost and alone. Was that how that memory went? How long had Matt known Sam for? He knew now that he was a vampire, but how long had Sam been lying to Matt about their history? Was that a dream? It felt so real.

Matt briefly managed to wake up long enough to try to crawl over to Geordie. Her skin had turned blue and was colder than normal. She was completely unconscious, and Matt soon fell unconscious again.

Eventually, footsteps approached accompanied by two male voices. All Matt could think about was fighting anyone who would try to harm Geordie. Every muscle in Matt's body ached; he felt drained in every way. In the single moment that Matt unleashed all that power, he felt every emotion and aura of every creature in the forest for miles. None of them were distinguishable from another, however, nearby, Matt felt Geordie's emotions and aura waning. She was weak, her body was slowly dying.

Then something warm enveloped Matt's skin. His body felt lighter and better. It was as if he were being rejuvenated. Matt finally was able to summon the energy to open his eyes. Multiple girls surrounded him wearing grey long sleeved coats on top of a wrap sort of dress. One of them acknowledge Matt waking up, "Good, you have finally awakened."

"Where am I? Where is Geordie?" Matt groaned, still feeling some soreness in his body as it slowly dissipated.

"You are at a medical facility known as Donor Compliant Corporation. It is controlled by the Massachusetts State Coven. We are the Lucis faeries assigned to assist in your healing process while you are here, Mr. Hallow." Matt wasn't sure what a Lucis faery was, but it didn't matter. "Ms.Vollner is still in surgery being treated for her wounds. Her injuries were beyond our capabilities."

"Let me see her."

The faeries helped Matt get dressed and settled in a wheelchair and the woman who spoke to him rolled him out to a hallway. Sam was standing in the hallway speaking to someone Matt had never met before. They were discussing Geordie's condition.

"Are you a doctor?" Matt asked, finally looking back at the man and Sam.

"No, my name is Michael Anderson." Michael chuckled. "I am basically the errand dog of the covens. I do a lot of travelling around and facilitating projects. I am old friends with Sam, and he called upon me for help. It is nice to see you have regained full consciousness with no memory loss or any other side effects."

"Thank you, I appreciate all that you have done for me and Geordie. Is there someone I can talk to who would know more about her condition?" Matt tried to smile, but it was too difficult. He needed to know she was going to be okay.

"The doctor who has been working closely with Geordie should be wrapping up shortly with her. It was very lucky. I happened to be visiting the D.C.C. with Doctor Lee at the time Sam had called me, so she was able to help you both once we returned to the facility. She's one of the best vampire doctors our government has ever seen. Geordie is in good hands."

"Thank you, Michael. What is it do you do exactly?"

"I document and record the vampire history, laws, and any information I find that could be considered useful knowledge for the progression of our species. Although I do have some personal assistants, I am the only one in my profession, so my work does keep me away from home a lot of the time." Michael laughed.

"It must be pretty hefty having to be the only person to record everything for an entire species." Matt wasn't even sure how many vampires there were out there. And for one person to be doing it all by himself was extensive.

"Not really. I have plenty of assistants who help me with the organizational parts of it and bookkeeping. I'm just the person who writes it all down. I've been at it for a very long time."

"Ah, Michael, you're here." A woman in scrubs came out of the operating room where Geordie lay. The doctor was wiping her hands with a paper towel and disposing of it in a nearby trash bin before shaking Michael's hand. She then turned to Matt as well, introducing herself, "My name is Michelle Lee, I am the head of the Department of Medical Treatments for Vampires. I am the doctor who will be facilitating Geordie's treatment while she heals. You must be Matt Hallow; I've heard much about you."

"Is Geordie really going to heal? Are you going to be able to fix her?"

"I am doing my best to ensure that she does, but it is a difficult task to do. I am unfamiliar with angelic magic; therefore, my resources are limited. I have something that might help her contain the ice inside her chest, but I have yet to test it on a person of her caliber. I don't want to say anything that might get your hopes up, so please bear with me these next few steps." Doctor Lee tried reassuring him. "The only thing I can definitely guarantee is that the best way to guarantee her healing process is to have an angel remove the ice."

"I understand. Do you know when she will be awake?
When will I be able to visit her?" Matt had to fight hard to not
start crying. If a solid solution was not found, Geordie could
fall into a permanent coma.

"She is awake now; you may go visit her if you wish."
Doctor Lee then grabbed him by the shoulder quickly as he
turned to head into Geordie's room. "Word of caution, try not
to stimulate her. We need her calm for her treatments to
continue to work."

Matt nodded and headed inside immediately. In the middle
of the room, Geordie lay in a hospital bed staring up at the
ceiling. Tears quietly rolled down her cheeks. "Geordie, are
you okay?"

"I failed, Matt. I'm never going to get protection from a
vampire coven now." Her voice whimpered quietly as she
sniffled.

"Don't say that!" Matt stroked her hair out of her face and
wiped away the tears. "I'm sure we can find a coven."

"You don't understand…" Geordie cried, turning onto her
side with her back to him. "I can feel it. The ice festering
inside me. I'm so tired already. It's going to cause me to fall
asleep and at that point I might as well be dead because no
angel will heal me."

Matt didn't know how to help her. He knew what she said was true and there was nothing he could do about it. He was just a pathetic useless human, and he hated himself for it. Matt wished there was something he could do to help her but all he could do was sit there by her side as he held her hand. He could tell she was trying not to be vocal about her crying, but he could hear the quiet sobs regardless. A moment later, Sam, Michael, and Doctor Lee came in to check on them.

"Ms. Vollner, if you don't mind, Mr. Anderson has a few questions he would like to ask you while I change your blood bag and check your wounds." Doctor Lee came over to the bed, giving Geordie a concerned look as she sat up with swollen red eyes from crying. "Do you want us to come back at a later time?"

"No." She shook her head, wiping away the tears. "I don't know how long I will be able to stay up for, so I'd like to answer any questions you have now, rather than later."

"We greatly appreciate that, Ms. Vollner." Michael pulled up a chair in front of Geordie's bed where he would stay out of the way while Doctor Lee worked. Sam stood off to a corner watching them.

"We intravenously administered human blood while you were asleep. If you'd like we can continue that method, or I can just give you a bag to drink from directly. It's your choice." Doctor Lee brought over an assortment of medical gear including what looked to be heat pads.

"I can just drink from it." Geordie took the blood bag from the doctor, and Doctor Lee began to undo Geordie's bandages.

"Ms. Vollner, I'm just going to ask you a few questions for research purposes. Anything we discover could help us figure out a way to help you." Michael pulled out a book and began writing. Geordie nodded and so he continued, "How is it during your time alive you managed to go unnoticed by the government?"

"It's not that they didn't notice me… None of the covens want anything to do with me."

"I see." Michael continued writing. "And who are your parents?"

"Lapetus Vollner and Elizabeth Nicholas. My mother was an angel tasked with watching my father."

"Interesting. Are you aware of your father's personal history from before you were born?" Michael looked up at her curiously for the first time since he started writing.

"He was an elder of a coven."

"He wasn't just any elder, my child. He was a highly regarded elder who was turned during the same human lifetime as his maker which was shortly after The Great Rise. Your family name is widely known amongst the vampire community."

"What do you mean? What is The Great Rise?" Geordie winced as Doctor Lee activated a heat pack and pressed it firmly to Geordie's chest.

"The Great Rise was a period during our history when the vampire race exploded into existence thanks to the queens and the first men of our kind. There were six strong humans, champions, given the honor of being chosen to be the first of the turned species. During two different generations, about a century apart, they each bore children with the queens and therefore began the six family lines of vampire royals. Of course, with no government or regulations in place, these newly turned vampires also went on a killing spree and decimated a large portion of humanity. But where some casualties were made, others turned into vampires, and thus began the long chain of turned vampires.

"Amongst the newly turned vampires, your father and his brother were also turned by the first chosen champion who is also the strongest of our kind. What makes your family so special outside the royals is that this champion never turned any other human into a vampire aside from your uncle and your father. Your father himself never turned any human, and to our knowledge, your uncle has only turned one person to this day. Something you must understand Geordie, is that the bloodlines of parents to children is very different from the bloodlines between a vampire and its maker. It's a connection of energy, power, and strength. When a vampire turns another, they share their essence and strength with that person, and therefore are connected for all time. They could be on opposite sides of the planet and if the one sired were in danger, the maker would feel it. It is a connection only breakable through death.

"Therefore, when your family comes into topic, I find this very interesting because your father never turned anyone into a vampire, but he did have one child, you. And although his brother only turned one person, he also bore one child, a son. All of this is very interesting to me, and I would like to investigate both of your bloodlines. Neither of you are half human half vampire. Both of you have an unorthodox mix not normally seen. Something tells me both of you are very special, and we just need to find out why."

"Why is any of this such a big deal? Ms. Victoire has angel in her as well, and no one is making a fuss about her." Doctor Lee placed a hand on Geordie's shoulder, giving Michael an impatient look.

"Ms. Victoire is a completely different circumstance, and you know that. We have come to an understanding regarding her situation. But with Geordie, she's very different and I don't know why. I must learn everything I can, especially given the nature of the men in her family." Michael grew impatient with Doctor Lee.

"What do you mean by that?" Sam finally spoke for the first time since Matt came into Geordie's room.

"Well, think about it. Both have always been aware of the connection that is shared between a maker and its progeny. Why do you think they would opt out of making any more vampires? Could it have anything to do with who made them? I find it curious that both Lapetus and Vexus Vollner, after spending centuries with their maker, would not only refrain from repopulating the vampire species through turning, but would also distance themselves from their maker for the rest of time?" Michael turned to Sam, and it seemed like something clicked in his brain that Matt wasn't sure what was. "To add, why would both Vexus and Lapetus choose to have children rather than just creating a vampire? You were his student as a human, Sam, so why would he have Lizzie turn you but not himself? Curious don't you think?"

"I have never known the answer to that question, nor have I questioned him on it. I'm sure he had his reasons." Sam frowned, thinking about all the secrets Vexus must have been keeping for years. "That bastard… I'm *sure* there's a reason given who turned them."

"Who turned my father into a vampire? And who is Vexus Vollner?" Geordie asked quietly. She looked over to Sam, who looked unsure of what to say.

Michael closed the book that he was writing in. "I apologize, Geordie, the person who turned your father does not wish to have his identity shared. As for your uncle, Vexus is an elder of the Southern Californian State Coven, although he is not there most of the time, and no one has seen him in many years."

"Vexus was my mentor and taught me everything I knew. I never met your father, but from what I understand, both were great men. Your father's death saddened the entire community when we heard of the news." Sam bowed his head solemnly. "I apologize for how I treated you in the past, I am a guardian, and my first duty is to protect my charge. I thought your involvement in Matt's life would endanger him.

As it turns out, he was the one who protected you. I underestimated you both, and for that you have my sincerest apologies."

"Alright, Geordie needs her rest now." Doctor Lee stood up impatiently. "Everyone, out! Now! Matt you can come back and visit her in the morning. I will ensure she wakes up."

"Get some rest, Geordie!" Michael called out as he was being ushered out of the room. "In the meantime, I will go to my office and do some more research about your family. Maybe next time I see you, I will have more answers!"

Before Michael could get another word in, Doctor Lee shut the door behind everyone. Sam, Michael, and Matt all stood there in silence awkwardly.   Moments later, Doctor Lee came out and turned against Michael. "You are playing a dangerous game, you are!"

"What do you mean, Michelle?" Michael backed into the wall of the hallway with a nervous smile.

"You know exactly what I mean! You're looking too deep into information that is not yours to know! If *he* finds out that you are looking into him, he could have all your research burnt to a crisp! And you risk taking these two kids down with you! If Sam's not careful, he will go down too!"

"Michelle, all the activity coming from this coven doesn't add up, and the history of the Vollner family doesn't either. If

I don't investigate this, no one will, and I am in the best possible position to do so without getting caught. I am being careful."

"You better be! And Matt and Geordie better not suffer for your actions!" Doctor Lee sauntered off without another word, leaving Matt with Sam and Michael.

"I have to go do some research in my office, but I will let both of you know when I find any further information." Michael spoke quickly as if he were in a rush to go do something.

"Where is your office? Maybe I can help you? I used to be a teacher's assistant during my undergrad." Matt offered help since there was nothing he could do for Geordie.

"That won't be necessary, my boy. My office is all the way in California. I am going to take an overnight jet back. You are better staying here where you can be near Ms. Vollner." Michael gathered his bags and paperwork, then turned to Sam before taking his leave. "Sam, it was great seeing you. Continue to watch over the two of them. They're going to need all the help they can get. Make sure you support each other."

"Yes, Sir." Sam nodded before turning to Matt and facing him with a serious tone, "Speaking of supporting each other, you would do well to contact your mother and let her know you're alive."

"Why would I do that? She's never cared about what went on in my life." Matt felt appalled Sam would suggest such a thing. He knew what Matt's relationship was like with his mother, yet Sam would suggest he call the one person he knew Matt didn't get along with.

"You've always known my standpoint on the issues between you and your mother. You don't understand the position she's in and why she would have to distance herself from you." Sam sighed, rubbing his eyes with a hand. "Just give her a call. I already told her the situation you got yourself in. You should give her the decency and just call her."

"Fine. Whatever." Matt dismissed Sam. Whatever her reasoning was, Matt hated her for it.

"I don't understand how you can be so selfish, but okay." Sam started walking away in the same direction Michael left in.

"Where are you going?" Matt called after him.

"There are only a couple hours until dawn; I need sleep." Sam called back waving a hand dismissively. "Everything is set up for you to stay here for the next couple days until the doctor says you can leave. I see no further reason to be here."

CHAPTER 10

MATT

The next evening, Matt and Geordie were permitted thirty-minute walks around the medical center's campus outside as long as they had a supervisor and Geordie remained bundled up with heat strapped to her chest. Little did Matt realize that the supervisor was going to be Doctor Lee herself, which slightly annoyed him. He had wanted some alone time with Geordie to perk up her spirits, but she said very little, and only spoke in one word sentences the entire time.

It was as if she had lost all hope and personality the moment she realized she might not complete her goals. Her mind was constantly elsewhere and behind them Doctor Lee scribbled vigorously in her notebook, barely paying attention to her surroundings. Matt was left alone with his thoughts and the sound of crunching snow underneath their feet. There wasn't much snow on the ground, but it was cold enough to where it crystallized and crunched with every step like glass.

Matt constantly wondered what Doctor Lee was always writing in that notebook of hers. Earlier in the day, she asked him permission to do blood tests because she wanted to learn more about his powers. Matt obliged figuring the more she learned, the more he learned. Sam still wasn't talking to him, and Matt still had not called his mother like he said he would. There was too much negative history between him and his mother where she paid more attention to his younger brother, Nick, than she did to Matt, and he resented her for it. He never resented Nick for it because Nick was the only person who ever stuck by him through everything. He always tried to reassure Matt that she had a good reason for not getting close to Matt. To make up for her faults, Nick would always try to spend excessive amounts of time with Matt to make him not feel lonely, but Matt always told him to go play with kids his own age. He didn't want Nick to be held down by his own issues with their mother. It wasn't fair.

Eventually it began to snow, and he could see his breath as the air grew colder. Ahead of him, Geordie wandered the courtyard circling the columns that stood around the perimeter. Doctor Lee sat down at a sheltered table bench and continued to write her notes down, occasionally glancing up at Geordie, but ignoring Matt. He breathed slowly, letting steam leave his mouth through the scarf that had been given to him by Doctor Lee.

Near one of the columns, Matt heard a thud in the snow from a distance. Whirling around quickly, he saw that Geordie had collapsed without any warning. Both he and Doctor Lee rushed over to her. "Geordie!" Matt scooped her into his arms, feeling her body shake heavily. Her eyes looked exhausted, and her skin was paler than normal.

"Geordie, are you okay? Talk to me, what can I do?"

Doctor Lee started to undo Geordie's tops, starting with her jacket and ending with the gauze wraps that covered her healing wounds. Only her wounds weren't healing. Shards of ice poked out from the scars, causing her chest to turn purple and cold. "We need to get her back inside."

"Okay..." Matt breathed, carefully lifting Geordie into his

arms. The walk back to the facility was slower than before.
He was worried now. Matt knew that Frost's attack on
Geordie took a lot out of her, but he didn't think it was this
bad.

Once they got back inside, Doctor Lee instructed Matt to
turn on all the space heaters she had placed in the room after
he laid Geordie in her hospital bed. As he started the heaters,
Doctor Lee hooked up Geordie to a blood bag after putting her
into a hospital gown. She then cleaned the wounds with a hot
washcloth, but neither the washcloth nor blood seemed to be
working. Geordie was getting colder by the minute. Her skin
was a light shade of purple, and more ice festered over her
wounds. After a couple of hours with no improvement,
Doctor Lee finally said, "Your tests will have to wait, she
needs to be transferred to ICU immediately."

Within minutes Matt and Doctor Lee were wheeling
Geordie down the hall to a different room that turned out to
have significantly more equipment in it than Geordie's
original room. On the way there, many doctors came to join
them, asking Doctor Lee many questions Matt did not
understand. Soon they came to a large room with lots of
bright lamps and tools surrounding an operating bed. Doctor
Lee swiftly transferred Geordie to one of the beds and then
called one of the other doctors to her side.

"What's going on, Doctor?" The woman barely glanced at
Matt as she came in. Instead, she went right over to Geordie
and examined her wounds, horrified at what she discovered.

"This is Geordie Vollner, half angel half vampire. She was

attacked by a frost angel a day and a half ago. Her wounds since then have only progressively gotten worse." Doctor Lee started hooking up another blood bag to Geordie as she spoke.

"And who's the human?" The younger doctor started putting plugs all over Geordie's body and then turned on a large screen that showed a bunch of images of the inside of Geordie's body.

"He is Matt Hallow. He's her human companion." Doctor Lee turned and started swiping at the screen till it showed Geordie's internal organs. "Boy, you need to get out of here now, and let us work.

Without even giving him time to protest, Doctor Lee shoved Matt out of the room, shutting the door behind her. To his surprise, Sam was walking down the hallway towards him as Matt slumped down on the floor in defeat. He felt as though Sam was about to say something snarky, but it never came.

"What happened here?" Sam looked confused at the situation.

Matt pulled his knees into his arms and rested his head on them. He then responded with a defeated voice, "Geordie got worse, and now Doctor Lee and a team of doctors are operating on her. She might not make it."

Sam sat down next to him, also pulling his knees up to his chest. "I'm sorry to hear that."

It was weird, no matter how many times they fought, Matt knew Sam would always be there for him. He laughed, "You know, you can be a real jerk sometimes. Like… a *real* asshole."

Sam laughed as well, "I know, but I'll always be here to protect you. Regardless of how you feel about me."

"I know." Matt chuckled. "So why are you here?"

Sam sighed deeply. "I'm here because unfortunately I must leave. I need to tend to some official vampire business, and I won't be around for a while."

"Before you go, I need to speak with you." Michael came whizzing down the hall in a hurry. "I need to speak with all of you!"

SAM

"Michael, what is going on? Geordie is in surgery." Matt and Sam simultaneously stood up at Michael's approach.

"Sam, do you remember Breena Vollner?"

"Vexus's wife, sure. What about her?" Sam nodded, "I haven't heard anything about Vexus or Breena's whereabouts in many years."

Michael pulled them both around a corner of the hallway as people passed. "I just got news that there was a break in at Ancient Artifacts Library. There was a commotion. That angel who attacked you and Geordie, she attacked Breena. Now she's missing, and no one can find her."

"What?" Sam stared at Michael wide eyed. Sam wasn't expecting the angels to move so fast. It couldn't have been a coincidence they attacked Geordie and Matt right before attacking Breena Vollner. "How is it possible they can be in multiple places so quickly?"

"I don't know, but if I know any better, I would say the moment word reaches Vexus, he will drop anything he is doing to find her. As an elder, I cannot allow this to happen." Michael leaned in closer to Sam and Matt. Now he began to whisper manically, "I am telling you both this because this greatly affects Geordie, and you were close to Vexus, Sam. This is no coincidence. They are trying to lure Geordie out. Two attacks on the Vollner name–it's heresy."

"What do you want me to do?" Sam readied himself for anything Michael might tell him.

"Nothing. Your job is to protect Matt, and now Geordie. I want you to do nothing." Michael pulled them around another dark corner with his arms around each of their shoulders.

"Michael, I don't need protection, they are not after me!" Matt whined.

"How can you expect me to do nothing? I am a guardian!"
Sam tried to control his voice to a whisper, but it came out in a
sort of shriek. He was struggling to contain his anger. He
swore he would never let anything happen to Vexus, and that
extended out to Breena as well. They were his family, his
chosen family.

"As an elder of the Northern California coven, I am
ordering you to do nothing!" Michael whispered harshly. It
was the first time Sam ever saw Michael get short with him.
He was almost hurt by it. "Vexus going after those angels will
be the death of him. He taught you everything you know.
You are like a son to him, without the connection of an
essence. If he catches wind that you are going after something
in the name of his wife, he will jump to the worse possible
conclusion and risk getting himself, you, and Breena all
killed."

"But this is the worst possible situation! What are you
going to do, nothing?" Sam couldn't believe what he was
hearing.

"No, no, not at all! I am going to send someone he will
never see coming or even sense. Someone he has never met."

"Who could that possibly be? You don't honestly think
this is a good idea, do you?" Matt asked with a concerned
voice.

"Oh, but I do!" Michael finally stopped pacing in the
hallway. "I am going to send Seth Vollner. He's very good at
staying under the radar, he's part faery, and it's his mother

he's saving. He won't say no. He can't."

"You clearly don't know Seth very well." Sam grumbled.
About an hour later of silence, Doctor Lee greeted them with
solemn eyes. Matt immediately stood up and asked her how
Geordie was.

"She will be fine for now. I surgically administered this gel
into her chest after successfully removing a lot of the ice from
her body." Doctor Lee handed a clear tube of blue gel that
resembled toothpaste over to Matt. "There is bad news,
however: I could not remove the magic itself, so it will
continue to grow. You're going to need to constantly reapply
that heating gel to her wounds at least five times a day
minimum. More if it seems her body temperature is dropping
too much. Just inject her right in the chest using a syringe.
Sam, make sure she only feeds on blood that is at least 97.2
degrees. Blood bags will probably suffice on the short term,
but you're better off finding her a live donor."

"What does she mean, a live donor?" Matt turned to Sam.

"She means a human who is willing to feed Geordie their
blood." He answered.

"She will never truly get better as long as she doesn't get
the real help that she needs." Doctor Lee handed a bag full of
medical instruments to Matt. "Hopefully you can help her in
the meantime."

"Frost wants Geordie dead; I think healing her will be the

last thing she wants to do." Matt growled under his breath as he sifted through the bag full of medical supplies.

"Well, thank you for helping them both out." Michael shook hands with Doctor Lee.

"Yes, thank you, Doctor, for helping Geordie. I don't know how I could ever repay you." Matt smiled.

"You may call me Michelle for one. And you can give me that blood sample to study. If I can help you at all to understand your powers and heritage, I would like to." She paused for a moment and hummed in consideration. "If it's alright with you, I'd like to get that done before you leave the medical facility."

"That can wait until at least tomorrow, Michelle." Michael interjected before Matt had an opportunity to respond. Sam breathed a sigh of relief. He didn't want Matt to give that blood sample. The less people knew about his heritage, the safer he would be. "Is Geordie awake yet? I would much like to speak with her about something that is rather time sensitive."

"Yes, right this way, Michael." Doctor Lee directed them all toward the room where they were keeping Geordie.

GEORDIE

A searing pain in her chest woke Geordie suddenly, and it

took her a moment to gain her bearings. The room smelled of blood, chemicals, and sterilized rubber. White, fluorescent lamps hurt Geordie's eyes and for a moment she wondered if she was in a human hospital. In panic, Geordie fought with the hospital gown she was in and quietly kicked off the heated blue blankets covering her. She was about to tear off the gown in frustration when Matt and Sam barged in with Doctor Lee and Michael.

"Geordie, what are you doing? Get back into bed!" Matt barked at her but gently pried her hands away from the neckline of the stupid hospital gown. Seeing Matt immediately calmed her down and she complied.

"Where am I? What happened?" Geordie asked looking over to Sam and the company he had behind him. "Last thing I remember was being in the snow and feeling faint."

"You collapsed in the courtyard a few hours ago. We rushed you back inside and had to transfer you to ICU for surgery because the ice was festering too quickly to let it be." Doctor Lee answered quickly.

"There has been some news that you need to know regarding your family." Sam took a step further into the room from the doorway. From there Michael took over.

"We have reason to believe the angels that are after you recently kidnapped the wife of your uncle. A woman named Breena Vollner who is considered fae royalty has gone missing after an angel broke into her place of work and confronted her."

"Wait, what?" Geordie didn't know she had an aunt by marriage.

Before anyone had a chance to continue, someone knocked on the door, and Michael answered. An abnormally tall, somewhat muscularly framed man entered. His skin was golden, deep and rich like honey, but his hair was dark with specks of white and gold in it. "I'm sorry to interrupt, I was told you would be in here Michael. Good evening, Michelle. I'm sorry it has taken me so long to get over here, I drove from Maine."

"Not to worry, come right in." Michael ushered the newcomer inside. "Geordie, this is Seth Vollner. He is the only son of Breena and Vexus Vollner. He is also your only cousin."

"So, this is the person you mentioned the other day who is like me? Sort of?" Geordie asked, "You're a half breed with vampire and faery?"

"Yes, there aren't many who share my heritage, but I was one of the first as far as I am aware." Seth nodded. "You are the half vampire half angel."

"That is correct."

"Have you ever met Vexus? Or Breena?" Seth asked politely. He seemed puzzled about something that Geordie couldn't pinpoint. She tried reading his mind, but it didn't work. "I've never met either of my parents."

"No, I haven't. I only knew my father and mother. They never even mentioned that they had other family members. How is it you've never met your parents?" Geordie felt genuinely guilty for asking, but she couldn't fathom the idea of not knowing her parents.

"Seth's parents conceived him during a war on faeries in the early nineties. At that point half breeds were hunted by werewolves, so they thought it was better to send him to a safer home amongst the humans. They hid his essence from the world so that no one would try to hunt him for his powers." Michael explained to everyone.

Beside her, Matt had his face hidden amongst his now long dark hair, staying silent. Seth's expression was completely blank. Geordie could not tell how he truly felt about the situation. She wished she could read his mind. It would help her to figure out how she truly felt but all she had were more questions.

"Why are you telling me all of this now?" Geordie turned back to Sam with tears in her eyes.

Sam shook his head, "As the only reachable Vollners, it is up to you two to figure out what you want to do about the targets that are on your backs."

"There is no target on my back. This is not my fight." Seth stood up and started heading toward the door. "I don't even know these people. Why should I risk my life for someone who abandoned me at birth over a crusade? I will see myself out. I do not want to listen to any more of this. Next time, call me for something that actually affects me."

"Seth!" Michael called out, grabbing him by the arm. "This is your mother we are talking about! If she's truly missing, we must find her! She's your family!"

Seth effortlessly pulled his arm out of Michael's grip, "They are no family of mine. They *abandoned* me at birth! My mother is the person who raised me, Michelle Lee!"

Seth took notice of Michael's quick glance over to Geordie who was watching intently. She couldn't help but relate on some level with him. Before she knew of Seth and his parents' existence, she believed she had no family, and she was fine with that. She wasn't sure if she could change her mind about that.

For a long moment, Seth and Geordie locked eyes as if they were trying to read one another. "I'm sorry, Geordie. I've spent much of my life alone and have grown content with it. I wish you the best of luck in your endeavors. I am glad to have met someone of my own blood whom I could connect with. If *you* are ever in need of help, I will try my best to help you."

"Thank you." Geordie whispered barely able to get the words to come out. Seth nodded and left without another word. No one had ever truly resonated with her that deeply before on an instantaneous level. She felt as though Seth truly understood where Geordie came from, and they didn't have to speak about it. They both just knew. They grew up alone, they didn't have anyone they could rely on, and getting involved with other people's affairs only lead to death and more heartache.

After Seth left, Michael turned back to Geordie in frustration, "So what would *you* like to do? Your family has gone missing, you're brutally injured, and I'm afraid that the medical teams we have here will not be able to continue to help you."

"What do you mean?" Matt asked. "I thought the blood and the gel were working."

"Both of those work to some extent, but they're not a permanent solution. She's going to have those wounds for the rest of her life. She needs to accept that. The ice will continue to fester, and she can have it removed surgically every so often, but the chill that it is causing her is also slowing her healing process. Continuing to give her surgeries every few days will be more detrimental than beneficial."

"Look at your chest, Geordie." Sam gestured toward her, and Matt helped her up to look at the mirror. There were numerous surgical scars all over her chest that were discolored blue and purple. They were also cold to the touch. "You were in surgery for the past few hours, and Doctor Lee removed as much of the ice as possible. It's still growing back at a rapid pace. No human would've been able to live through the surgery that you went through. It was too invasive. How many more of those do you think you can go through?"

Geordie ran a hand across her chest. It was the handiwork of Frost. It wouldn't be easy to heal her body. An angel had to heal her, but none would. It was hopeless.

Michael then broke through her thoughts, "Your best bet might be travelling to the Immortal Realm to get healed from an angel."

"Then maybe we should focus on that for now." Matt rubbed Geordie's back gently, but she pulled away quickly, wrapping herself back up in her robes.

"Even if we went with that option, I don't know how to use any of my angelic powers. And if we did get into the Immortal Realm, I don't think they would ever let me leave. It wouldn't be an easy endeavor." Geordie sat back down on the hospital bed, trying to hide the fact that every movement hurt excruciatingly. "I am deemed an enemy by the creatures who are capable of saving me. There's no way they would go for it."

"Maybe, maybe not." Sam shrugged. "We will figure it out one way or another."

"We?" Geordie laughed. She then winced in pain. It hurt to laugh. "Does this mean you're actively helping me now?"

Sam smiled, "Yeah, I guess it does. Maybe you're growing on me."

"Thanks, man. I appreciate it!" Matt smiled, slapping Sam on the back. Geordie was happy that they reconciled.

"In the meantime, you two can stay at my loft with me." Sam offered generously.

"Thank you. We appreciate it." Geordie smiled, thanking Sam. She hoped that nothing would get between Sam and Matt ever again, not even herself.

FROST

A few hours after leaving the decimated forest, Frost and Pyre appeared in the Ancient Artifacts Library where the vampires and faeries worked together to supposedly maintain balance and collect objects that would disturb that balance. Ever since it was founded, Frost was skeptical of the idea of vampires hoarding so many magical objects. It sounded like a set up for disaster. Vampires should never have so much power.

Even as she stood there in the artifacts building, hidden in plain sight, Frost still couldn't help but think about how much she hated all the vampires. She wished she could go to her home, the Immortal Realm, and never have to interact with such parasites. The only thing that could possibly lighten her mood was the sight of the setting sun through the skylights above. She knew what she had to do, but some parts of her didn't want to do it. Breena Vollner was a natural ally to the angels. She had committed no crimes, yet Frost was about to apprehend Breena Vollner for what seemed like an even greater cause.

Up in the highest tower of the building was the office of Breena Vollner, one of the last living relatives of Geordie Vollner, and the keeper of a very important book in the vampire government. It was known as the Anthropaemia Codex. It held every detailed account of the vampire history and Breena knew the contents of it. Frost and Pyre waited quietly in her office until dark before Breena finally arrived.

Mild shock flashed across her eyes as Breena entered her office, but she recovered quickly back to her normal unimpressed visage. "What are you doing here Frostbite?"

"I've come to inquire with you about a few things." Frost smiled and stood up; she offered the desk chair she previously occupied to Breena.

"And him?" Breena nodded toward Pyre, who was sulking in a corner, arms crossed. He wasn't thrilled with Frost's motives but chose not to speak against her.

"Added security." Frost briefly glanced at him. "This is Pyre, he's the angelic phoenix. I believe you two have only briefly met in passing."

"I see. If by passing you mean, he destroyed my late sister's cabin…" Breena stared skeptically at Pyre. "So why are you here, Frost? If Ezra wants something, she can request my presence herself."

Frost shook her head, "I am not working on Ezra's behalf. She has no idea I'm here."

"A rogue angel, huh? This could be dangerous." Breena laughed. "I'm sure she won't be thrilled to find out about that. How long has it been since you broke away from your chains?"

"Long enough. I don't see how that is your concern. My affiliations do not factor into my actions today. I am working independently."

"Fair enough. So, do you mind getting to your point? I am a busy woman; I have plenty of work to do. I'm sure you would understand as a newfound independent woman."

"I want you to return to the Immortal Realm, and I want you to hand over the Anthropaemia Codex." The two women stared at each other with a fierce intensity that could not be broken.

"Why would I do that? There's nothing in the Immortal Realm for me, this is my home, and the Anthropaemia Codex is a sacred text. I'm not allowed to just give it away." Breena refused to break the stare between her and Frost.

"If you don't, I will slaughter every living member of your family there is left. That includes your dear husband and Geordie Vollner." Frost knew that Breena was testing her. She wanted to see how unwavering Frost really was in her mission.

"If you touch them in any way, I will end you faster than you can retreat to the Immortal Realm." Breena took a step toward Frost, looming over her, staring down menacingly. Her long red hair fell down her shoulders like wildfire. She was the exact same height as Frost while Frost wore platforms. She would tower over Frost otherwise. Frost was not intimidated or afraid of Breena. However, seeing as she was immortal, and Breena was not, there was no way for Breena to follow through with her empty threat.

"Our kind may be natural allies, but your kind will always be inferior to us angels. The day one of you kill an angel will be the day the angels submit their dominance over all other species." Frost took a step closer to Breena, glaring up at her. "Give me what I want, or I will rain ice and fire down upon everything you hold dear. It will be just like that fateful night with your sister and her husband along with poor Geordie's parents. I'm sure you remember."

"How could I forget? You people destroyed my family's home." Breena sighed impatiently. She then went over to a table off to the side of the office and poured herself a glass of red wine. "I'm not coming back with you, Frost."

"That's fine. I don't want you specifically. I want you for Geordie. I want her in the Immortal Realm." Frost began to slowly approach Breena from behind.

"You think I'm going to help you kill her? I would never betray my family like that."

"She'll die regardless, even if she doesn't come." Frost took another step toward Breena as she had her back turned to Frost. "I wounded her internally. Besides, it's not my right to kill her. I'm only tasked with bringing her to the Immortal Realm. Remember, only an angel can heal angelic afflictions. If she stays here, she will die, slowly and agonizingly."

"She's never going to come to the Immortal Realm

willingly. She doesn't remember who I am." She shook her head solemnly, but Frost had an easy response.

"There are people who, I'm sure, will inform her of the unfortunate circumstance of her dear, long-lost auntie getting abducted." Frost knocked a glass statue off Breena's desk, and she whirled around in surprise. Looking down at the broken glass and back up at Frost, Breena rolled her eyes and sat back down behind her desk. "And if that doesn't motivate her, I have another plan in motion to give her a little more incentive."

"Excuse me?" Breena leaned back in her chair as Frost used her powers to knock a bunch of books off the nearby wall shelves while walking toward her. As soon as Frost was within arm's reach of Breena, she took the opportunity to slash Breena across the face with her icicle nails.

She immediately fell to the floor, gasping for breath as blood poured onto the black stone floor. She quickly got back up and lunged herself at Frost, summoning large vines around her body off her many tattoos on her arms. Whipping them at Frost, she in turn slashed Frosts skin but the wounds did not last long before healing. Behind them, still in his corner, Pyre set the vines on fire with a snap of his fingers, completely unmoving, and unhelpful. Lazily, he called out, "You are outnumbered and overpowered, Breena. Your Früx powers are no match for my fire!"

"Even so, I will not let you hurt any more people for this pointless mission! The balance does not hang in the brink!" Breena breathed heavily.

"You don't get to have a choice in the matter!" Frost sent ice flying at Breena, knocking her out. Together, Pyre and Frost went over her unconscious body, staring at it in silence before he latched iron cuffs onto her neck, wrists, and ankles. The moment they touched Breena's skin it seared, turning her skin slightly red.

Pyre then swung her over his shoulder and turned to Frost, "Ready to return home?"

"Yes. Yes, I am."

CHAPTER 11

SAM

As soon as Sam got Matt and Geordie settled in at the loft a few days later, he informed them he needed to make a trip out to Daron Island for a little while. Neither Geordie nor Lizzie were happy about it, but Lizzie assured Sam she would take care of Geordie and protect them no matter what. Sam had never seen Lizzie connect to someone like Geordie so deeply before.

Sam also tried to hire a blood donor for Geordie so she could get blood right from the vein, but she wouldn't hear of it. She would only drink from heated up blood bags. Lizzie promised Sam that she would keep Geordie regulated with lots of warmed up blood bags, so with that Sam settled in defeat and left for his trip to Daron Island.

The trip to Daron Island took a week by boat after flying out to California. Sam grew more anxious as the boat drew closer to its destination. He had exactly a month to figure out what Matt's family lineage was and couldn't tell Nick of his intentions since he was Matt's younger vampire brother. It would cause rivalry between them that could break their bond as brothers. If one of them ended up being the heir to the throne, then they both would need to be protected from others who would want to take that away from them.

In the Shadow Kingdom, an heir to the throne meant that three other potential people would be also awakened. For now, Matt and Nick were the only known two out of four people who were Potentials. Sam had no clue as to who the other two were, but he was sure that the queens would know something about the matter. The only problem was getting a chance to speak with them alone. If the wrong person heard this information, people would be hunting the Potentials down like animals. Sam did not want that on his conscience.

"Is something the matter?" Nick Hallow approached Sam, noticing his pensive trance over the passing sea. Sam stared at the icy waters that loomed underneath them, as if they carried secrets in their incessant waves. Nick had arrayed himself in traditional clothing of Daron Island consisting of black silk with a red wrap. Sam didn't care for the traditional clothing worn on the island, so he opted to stay in his own clothing underneath a heavy cloak.

"Just thinking..." Sam looked back at the sea, wondering if Nick could handle the idea of him or his brother being leader of a great kingdom. Could either of them handle not being chosen by the First King Essence?

"Okay, well the ship should be coming into port in about an hour. Be ready to dock when we get there." Nick left the hallway and when they finally did dock, Sam and Nick rode into the castle together by horse. Everything on the island was beautiful; an eternal summer bathed the area in warmth, sunlight, and constant green grass. From a distance, Sam could see young Früx faeries tending to the fields beyond the castle walls. Where some faeries were replenishing the life of the earth around them, others were soaking in the warmth of the sun and shifting into beautiful lively plants.

Coming back to the homeland had a downfall that only affected turned vampires. None of the faeries had to worry about this, and neither did the queens, but the rest of the vampires had to conceal themselves in thick robes that covered every inch of them during the daytime.

Nick noticed the faeries had caught Sam's eye and chuckled. "Vapid little things, aren't they?"

"Indeed, I would not touch one with a ten-foot pole." Sam rolled his eyes as one gave him a devious smile. "I don't trust Früx faeries."

"Neither do I!" Nick laughed as the female faery stalked off in disappointment.

Once they arrived at the gates, Sam said his goodbyes to Nick and headed off to the faery and vampire council. The council room was an octagonal shape with multiple tiered levels of seating with an open space in the center. The room was mostly dark with a center dome window over the top that barely let any light in, keeping the seating areas shrouded in shadow. There sat ten faery representatives with six vampire representatives, expecting to see Sam when he finally walked in. He had only stood before them once in his life to request permission to become a guardian. It felt intimidating, being there alone, with no one to vouch for him. They either had to take his word for the truth on his proposition, or simply deny it. He hoped that they would at least hear him out on what he had to say.

"Samuel Williams, you are here upon request of Nick Hallow who says that you wish to have an audience with the queens." An old man spoke first who was a vampire. He read from a scroll without looking at Sam.

"Yes, I am."

"And it says here that you have declined us a reason why you wish to have said audience." The old man peered down at Sam condescendingly through his small circular spectacles.

"I have reasons -

"And what would that be?" From the vampire's demeanor, Sam felt like he was being prosecuted.

"I wish to only share that with the queens." At Sam's words, the representatives shifted uncomfortably. The old vampire began to speak again, but a female faery cut him off.

"We have these rules and regulations in place for a reason, Mr. Williams. If we do not know your true intentions, how can we ensure the safety and protection of the Daron sisters?" The woman was the female representative of the Summus Order. She was soft spoken and beautiful.

The Summus Order was considered one of the oldest faery orders in history, their magic effectively the combination of all the other orders' magics and by extension surpassed their power. Fae of the Summus Order had an acute understanding of most forms of natural magic and their innate abilities allowed them to easily master most magical feats. Because of these natural abilities, they also considered themselves above the other orders. Their personalities were typically akin to what someone would find in an angel, and historically they were known to be allies frequently.

"I understand the reasoning for rules and regulations and wanting to know everything, but the impact of you not letting me proceed straight to the queens could mean the continuous decline in the Dark Order." Sam turned to the two representatives of the Dark Order. Next to them the Lucis Order representatives raised an eyebrow and whispered something to each other. "The Shadow Kingdom could be in jeopardy if I do not speak to the queens."

"The Shadow Kingdom has lacked power for ages, that has not changed in thousands of years and is not bound to change in another thousand. What does any of this have to do with our government? That kingdom has been long since lost in its dissension that it's near impossible to unite them as a whole!" A Früx faery laughed hysterically and the Lucis faeries joined in with him. The old vampire smiled, but looked as if he were seriously considering the idea of the Shadow Kingdom becoming united.

"That can change. I may have found two Potentials to the throne." Everyone went silent. Every person knew what that meant. If the Shadow Kingdom were united by a king again, then the peace treaties could be signed between the dark representatives and the light representatives. This also meant that the angels could no longer enter our realm without permission. They would have to either play nice, or permanently leave our realm and never return.

"Where's your proof of this? You didn't bring these said 'two Potentials' as proof, and we need four to unite the kingdom! Come back to us when you have proof and all four Potentials." Something didn't seem right to Sam. The only ones uncomfortable by Sam's words were the Lucis faeries. Did he have to worry about them? The worst-case scenario was that they report everything back to the angels. Sam hoped that wouldn't happen.

"No, we must decide as a unified congregation if this is vital enough to let you pass without knowledge of the subject. We will -

"I *really* don't think that will be necessary!" The doors to the council room flew open violently as Queen Melandria burst through unannounced. Everyone immediately bowed down to the second queen in command as if invisible hands bent everyone's back down.

"Queen Melandria, Your Majesty, what are you doing here?" The main vampire stuttered quickly while still bowing. Sam rolled his eyes quickly.

"I heard Sam was requesting an audience with me and my sisters, and I was wondering what was taking so long." She smiled at Sam and took his hand quickly, pulling him towards the giant double doors. "We will be talking in Kathleena's garden. Nobody disturb us!"

"But we haven't approved his appointment yet!" The old man was insistent to keep Sam from talking to the queens

privately. He tried to mask his furious anger from Melandria,
but she saw right through it.

"Sam, I approve of your appointment." She paused for a
moment and then tugged at him again. The man gave her a
weird look that she ignored. "Now let's get *going*."

Melandria pulled Sam through the doors, ending the
conversation as they made their way down many hallways to
come. As she strode, her long brunette hair flowed behind her
like a long cape. Her firm hand on Sam's wrist did not let up
until finally they rounded one last corner after many and
entered a giant glass house.

There was a beautiful patio surrounded by thousands of
flowers and plants that were being tended to. The patio was in
the center of the glass house with benches surrounding the
perimeter. The patio had heated stone flooring that was
desolate of any cracks or scratches. In the center was a white
wooden table with four matching chairs around it. Amongst
the flower beds, Früx and Oceanus faeries were feeding the
plants. On a bench on the opposite side, Kathleena and
Anyanke Daron were conversing quietly to themselves. When
Sam and Melandria entered, they both turned to them with
smiles and took their places at the small table.

"Sam, it's so good to see you." Kathleena grinned, taking
his hand in hers and squeezing tightly. Her eyes spoke of
enervation, but her smile spoke of genuine happiness. He
patted her hand and gently kissed it respectfully.

"As to you, Your Majesty." He smiled and turned to Anyanke, "You are blossoming today, Queen Anyanke."

"*Please*, she's always blossoming! You're too kind!" Kathleena teased Anyanke before she could say anything. She just smiled and accepted his kiss. Melandria rolled her eyes and took a seat next to Anyanke.

"Please, sit." Melandria gestured to the remaining empty seat.

"Thank you." Sam sat down, looking toward Kathleena for some sort of starting point.

"Sam, I hear you have some interesting ideas about the Shadow Kingdom." Kathleena spoke as she poured everyone tea. Sam quietly declined his tea, and she shrugged happily, moving on to sugar and milk.

"Not so much ideas as a rumor I heard. Michael Anderson told me that Nick and Matthew Hallow might be Potentials to hold The First King. I was hoping to look into their family lineage to see if it's true."

"Michael Anderson doesn't know anything! He'll believe anything that comes out of the Anthropaemia Codex." Kathleena threw back her head in triumph as if she beat Michael at some game they were playing. She then leaned toward him quickly, as if to share some dark secret. "Now, tell me, do you believe him?"

"It's like I said before, I'd like to look into the family lineage to justify or disprove it." Sam wasn't sure what the right answer was in this situation. What did Kathleena want him to say?

"It's so like Vexus to train you to tell people what they want to hear instead of what you *want* to say." She shook her head while still fashioning a triumphant grin, "I love that about the both of you. It makes having a conversation with you so... fun!"

"What makes you think we can't just give you the answers you seek? Right here, right now." Melandria huffed an impatient sigh, cutting in. She was always the one that went straight to the point. Kathleena like to draw things out and push her subjects to figure things out on their own. Anyanke was somewhere in the middle.

The youngest and the eldest sisters looked to Melandria as she spoke, respect glistening in their eyes. The three of them knew something that Sam didn't.

"Well, I never said that. I'm simply asking–"

"We know what you're asking." Anyanke cut him off. "But you're asking the wrong questions. Ask the right questions, and we can simply provide the answers."

Sam thought long and hard about what he wanted to know. It wasn't every day that someone got a last-minute unsupervised meeting with the queens. Sam was going to utilize this time with them as much as possible, and he was going to get as much information out of them as possible. He just hoped that he would be able to do something with the information given. Sam looked at all three of them and after a long moment, asked, "Are Matt Hallow and his brother descendants of King Kearan?"

"Yes, they are. They each have almost a little bit of every dark creature in them. Both have exceptions." Melandria was the one who told Sam what he wanted to hear. She took a sip out of her teacup without taking her eyes off Sam. He was sure they were hoping to see some sort of reaction, but he remained completely composed.

"Who are the other Potentials?"

"We don't know." Kathleena spoke quickly. A little too quickly.

"You don't know, or you don't want to tell me?" Sam was about to start getting frustrated if he didn't get some real answers.

"Both? Look, even if we did know who the other Potentials are, we couldn't tell you. It would break our contract with the first Potentials to never reveal them until they revealed themselves. And we are not above the law." Anyanke crossed her arms. "I'm sorry, but it's classified information."

"Do you know who *is* going to be king? Matt or Nick?"

"No, we don't know who is going to be king, but in the end, it doesn't matter. We can neither confirm nor deny that they both could be Potentials." Kathleena spoke softly. It didn't make any sense. They are both descendants of Kearan. If they don't become king, then that meant one of the other Potentials could kill one of them, or both.

"Just because they're both descendants does not make them both Potentials?" Sam asked Kathleena. She nodded silently, taking a sip out of her tea. Nick was a vampire and Matt was a human, but Naómi only hired one guardian to protect one of her sons, which meant she was only concerned about one of them. "Can you at least tell me who their father is?"

"Does it matter who the father is? The lineage is the same regardless, is it not? The boy is still a Hallow." Melandria stood up and her sisters did so too, ignoring his anger as if it were just his imagination. "Now if you excuse us, our time here is done."

"What? But you haven't told me anything!" Sam stood up quickly, blocking their path from leaving the green house. A few faeries stopped to stare, and a few guardians made their presence known in the garden. He had no idea that any guardians were there.

"Oh, but we have! We have told you everything we are at liberty to tell. Now go, go find the other answers you seek in the scrolls within the library. We are done here." Kathleena kissed him on the cheek and left with her sisters, single file.

After searching through the archives of family trees, Sam had no luck finding out who fathered Matt and Nick. He was beginning to lose hope. He did find out that Naómi's bloodline led to King Kearan. Kearan Hallow's line descended from creatures originally called the Lost, whatever that was, and eventually mated into dark witches. There was no mention of a father's line on Nick and Matt's side and there was no public record on the Lost. Sam began to feel desperate in his search for their father. If there was no way to validate their lineage, then there would be no proof that they could take the throne. Somehow, he knew that he would have to look elsewhere for information. The last place he could look for a real family tree would be in the Anthropaemia Codex. The only problem with that was getting permission from Breena Vollner to borrow it, who was missing.

By the end of his stay at Daron Island, January had come, and he had to return to Donor Compliant Corporation for the annual coven conferences. There would be no time to visit to Los Angeles. Instead, Sam made took a ship back to the mainland and was back on the east coast by the end of the month. The ship went from Daron Island in the middle of the Atlantic to New York. From there he took a short flight back to Boston. He was happy to finally be returning home after a month of being away.

Geordie
Winter

As the days grew colder, Geordie's wounds healed less and less. Geordie and Matt began to wonder whether they were going to find a cure for her without an angel, if it was even possible, but Sam assured them they would find a way. As time passed however, Geordie's confidence began to wane and the ice inside her began to take its toll. She felt slower, colder, and her thirst was harder to satiate. Sometimes the thirst was so bad that she craved vampire blood as well. Just being around Sam and Matt was difficult. All she wanted to do was rip them apart and feast on their blood but felt too tired to do so. It seemed like the only one whom she did not want to drain was Lizzie, Sam's girlfriend.

Something about her smelled off, as if her blood was familiar yet unappealing, but the way she treated Geordie as well was comforting. It was as if Lizzie understood what Geordie was going through. They didn't say much to each other, but Geordie could sense Lizzie was trying to help in her own way. She would help Geordie relax and get comfortable in the loft; she would make sure the blood bags were extra warm and help her around whenever she could. Geordie was grateful to have her.

Aside from the ice inside Geordie, Breena Vollner's whereabouts were still unknown. No one had heard anything more about her disappearance since they first got word. Geordie and Matt began to wonder if anyone was going to take any action in finding Breena. She wished she could do something, but all she could do was hope for someone to come up with a solution.

The best Sam was able to do so far was hire a druid to do a location spell on Breena, but they had no luck. The only thing the druid said was that Breena was no longer on this plane of existence. The best they could come up with was that she might be in the Immortal Realm, but there was no way to confirm that. They faced another dead end. What was even worse, the dark creatures in Massachusetts were becoming more anxious. Something dark had appeared in Boston, causing the appearance of lygoids, and even more were appearing day by day.

A large group of faeries and vampires were all gathered around something down the street like a crime scene. Geordie managed to push her way past the crowd to discover a creature she recognized turned into a dark transparent wisp that was neither dead nor alive. The creature used to be a dark faery that helped them find Jeremiah, but all that was left was a bodiless ghostly creature that would be eternally corrupted; a lygoid.

"We need to leave." Geordie squeezed Matt's arm gently. He nodded without a word, and they left. Once out of earshot, he finally asked her what happened to the creature. "It was a faery who helped us find Jeremiah. His body and soul were forcibly ripped apart from each other. If he consumes other people's souls or essences, he will become a demon."

"What is a lygoid specifically?" Matt asked her as they headed back to Sam's loft above the club.

"A lygoid is the beginning stages of creating a demon. This demon can only be created from lygoids when their soul is ripped from their body and corrupted. When this happens, the soul is forcibly removed. There is no willingly giving away your soul, you don't become a demon from that. It's the force that causes a lygoid to be created because in the process of ripping the soul away from the body, it corrupts the mind, essence, and body. Then they crave what they have lost.

"Lygoids spend the rest of their existence possessing people with souls and draining their life force away until there's nothing but an empty shell. Lygoids can only possess people who are currently alive." They turned down a street headed toward Andvari's Trove. After what they saw, talking to Sam was the top of Geordie's priorities.

"Oh god!" Matt winced harshly, collapsing to the ground while gripping his chest.

Geordie could sense a sharp pain emanating from his heart. Ever since the incident at Jeremiah's cabin, both Geordie and Matt seemed more connected now, she could feel his emotions more as well as any pain he was experiencing. She could tell he thought she didn't know about the pain in his chest. She didn't want to say anything about it because she knew he would tell her to be more concerned about her wounds that couldn't be healed, but she was more concerned about him. All of this happened when Matt unleashed a powerful wave of dark magic.

After Geordie pulled Matt aside to secluded place, she called the one person she thought might have some answers regarding Matt. Doctor Lee took blood samples from Matt right before they left the D.C.C. and mentioned she was going to investigate his biological chemistry. She was the only person she could think of who had any information about Matt's genetic makeup. Before they parted ways, Doctor Lee gave Geordie her contact information, telling Geordie to call her if she needed anything.

"Doctor Lee, this is Geordie, I'm using Matt's phone. I

have a few questions about Matt." She sat propped up against a dirty alley wall with Matt's unconscious head in her lap as he breathed heavily.

"What happened, Geordie?" Doctor Lee sounded worried.

"Matt just collapsed with a sharp pain in his chest, and I can sense a lot of dark energy built up inside him. Ever since we came out of that forest, Matt has been radiating with more dark energy than I've ever seen come out of a normal human!" She absentmindedly ran her fingers through his soft brown hair. "It's been getting gradually worse."

"That's interesting. I performed some tests on his blood recently, and I discovered that Matt is a mix of dark creatures: faery, vampire, lygoid, and human. Apparently, he possesses a restorative power of energy to each faction."

"What does that mean exactly?"

"Basically, Matt contains a bundle of dark energy inside him that builds over time. He has the ability to release that energy back into the creatures of each faction, giving them more power and thereby releasing energy from himself. If he does not do this regularly, the energy could cause him pain like a detonator within him."

"What do I do about this now? He's in pain!" Geordie watched Matt grip his chest in pain as she spoke to Michelle Lee over the phone.

"Until we have a better idea of how he can use his powers, there is nothing you can do." Michelle paused for a moment, "Just wait it out for now, and don't move him. It will pass with time. But in the future keep an eye on how often these episodes occur. It will be useful knowledge for the future."

"Thank you, Michelle, I greatly appreciate your input." Geordie hung up the phone, trying to hold back tears. On some level, the information Michelle gave her made no sense, but then again, if Matt was powerful enough to start a dark fire, then he was something more than human. This confirmed that Sam really was hiding vital information about Matt's true nature, and Geordie had every intention of finding out exactly what it was.

Ever since Sam made the ultimatum to Geordie, she had been wondering what the significance of Matt's family was and why he needed to be protected at all costs. She figured now it had something to do with the dark power that emanated from him. As Matt finally stirred awake, the dark power inside him calmed down and he looked up at her in confusion as she helped him to his feet. This wasn't the first time he collapsed from the surge of dark power, but it was the first time he fell unconscious from it. She knew he didn't want to discuss it, but it worried her, and it was difficult not to say anything. Therefore, she was going to say something to the next best person.

After a few minutes of walking in silence along the brick laden streets of Boston, they finally arrived at a back alley where Sam's nightclub was located, Andvari's Trove. Inside there were mostly faeries and shapeshifters on the dance floor with a few stragglers at the bar. It was decently empty because it was still light out and the vampires had not come out yet. It wouldn't be long until the pace picked up; there was less than an hour left before sundown.

At the back of the dance floor there were large booths on platforms. They were covered in a glittery dark red vinyl with black metal trimming. It almost resembled a retro diner style seating, and yet was slightly classier.

At one of the booths were Sam and Lizzie in the company of what looked to be a few faeries. Before anything else could happen, Geordie turned to Matt, pulling him close by the arm and whispering in his ear, "Why don't you meet me upstairs? I need to talk to Lizzie about something private. Girl stuff."

Matt looked slightly confused but headed up to the loft without argument. Looking back at Sam and Lizzie, Geordie begrudgingly headed in their direction. The moment Sam noticed her, he quickly dismissed his company except for Lizzie. "May I have a word?"

"Absolutely. We are long overdue for a private chat."

SAM

The night was ripe with lust and blood as the sun began to set and the vampires began to come out. Dancers of all kinds– vampires, faeries, and shifters alike–flowed like waves on the dance floor. Amongst them Geordie approached with a certain elegance of her own that she was seemingly unaware of. Sam figured it had to be the angelic mix in her.

Everything about her, he questioned. She reminded him so much of Lizzie and he couldn't understand why. They were so similar in personality as well as looks, they could have been twins.

To some degree, Sam already knew what Geordie wanted, but he was curious if there was something he could get out of her as well. The last time they had a one-on-one conversation, he gave her an ultimatum between information about her family and being with Matt. Given the new circumstances of Matt's situation, Sam wasn't entirely sure where he stood on that notion. On one hand, Geordie's existence posed a threat to Matt's life. On the other hand, she could be useful to helping Matt become stronger.

"What can I do for you?" Sam offered her a seat at his booth. Geordie quietly sat down and exchanged a quick smile with Lizzie.

"Ever since the attack from Frost and Pyre, dark energy has been building up in Matt and it's causing him pain to the point that he fell unconscious earlier. I'm worried that if something isn't done about this then he will end up hurt beyond repair. When we spoke before, you alluded that there was something special about Matt. What, exactly, is going on with him? I want you to tell me the truth."

Sam sighed, "Geordie, there's only so much I can tell you. Not because I don't want to, but because I am limited in what I know. Matt comes from a family line of royals by the name of Hallow. Once there was a kingdom created to unify the humans, faeries, vampires, and even lygoids, and the ruler of this kingdom is an ancestor of Matt's. In his bloodline, he carries the lineage of all four of those factions, and with that comes the ability to restore power to the factions using his own energy. I was tasked with protecting him at all costs because he is one of four people with the potential to become ruler of these unified factions known as the Shadow Kingdom."

"Wait what? What does all this mean?" Geordie looked confused. It didn't surprise Sam that she wouldn't know about any of this. Because it was a part of vampire history, many vampires were taught about the Shadow Kingdom from those who still remembered its existence. "How does this put him in danger if he has all this power?"

"There are people out there who would seek to prevent the Shadow Kingdom from being restored." Lizzie continued this time, equally aware of the situation as Sam. "Only the king has the power to restore the kingdom, but there are four people who have the potential to be king. Matt has proven that he has the power of a king by that display of dark energy he released, but it doesn't make him king if he doesn't have the power of all the bloodlines. If someone were to find out he's a Potential, his life could be at risk."

"For a while now, I have been trying to prove Matt's lineage, but I have had no such luck on finding any information about his father's bloodline. Without any tangible proof, I have nothing to go off." Sam explained his plan and what he had been trying to accomplish.

He was almost certain that Matt did have all four bloodlines just from what he had seen, but it wasn't enough. Between Matt and his brother, their mother only deemed it necessary for Matt to need a guardian and to be watched over.

To add, Matt's father's side was such a well-kept secret that it meant someone knew exactly what Matt was. "Ideally, I would like to find out who all four Potentials are so I may better help Matt ascend to the throne. Unfortunately, it is extremely difficult to find these people, especially because they might not know they are Potentials."

"How would this help Matt?" Geordie asked, clearly frustrated.

"If Matt were to ascend to the throne of the Shadow Kingdom, he wouldn't need protection from anyone. He would be able to master his abilities, and he would be stronger than anyone in any of the factions." Sam wondered to himself if he could somehow use Geordie to help Matt get stronger.

"Would that cease his pain from all the dark energy building up inside him? Is there a way we can fix that now rather than waiting for him to ascend or whatever?" She seemed like she was fighting the urge to cry. Her breathing was heavy, and her fists were clenched.

"There is nothing we can do about that. He must learn to control his powers in his own time. The energy will release itself when it's ready whether he likes it or not, just like what happened at that cabin in November." Sam spoke softly. He could see tears rolling down her pale cheeks. "You have to let him discover his power on his own and let him handle it accordingly."

"I just want to help him." Geordie whimpered, looking down at the table solemnly. "If something were to happen to him, I don't know what I would do with myself."

"You want to help him…" Sam scoffed, leaning against the back of the booth and wrapping an arm around Lizzie. "Just like you are able to help yourself?"

Underneath the table, Lizzie pinched Sam in the ribs so incredibly hard that it was nearly impossible to pretend nothing happened. "Look, be real, Geordie. You're dying; there's no way to heal you unless you somehow make it into the Immortal Realm and convince an angel to do so. How can you be of any help to Matt right now? I'm sorry but you're useless to me."

"There has to be something…"

Next to Sam, Lizzie made a low whimpering noise only intended for him to hear. She clenched his hand in hers tightly as she also clenched her chest with her free hand. When she looked into his eyes with a painful expression, her eyes were a near black with small fragments of color where the bright green was supposed to be.

"I'm sorry to cut this short, but I have some private business I must tend to with Lizzie." Sam began to get up but was quickly stopped by a hand pulling him back down, Geordie's hand.

"Wait! You're a part of an official coven, correct?" She asked urgently to which Sam nodded. "If I remember correctly, my father once told me that all the covens kept detailed records of vampiric ancestry and history in the coven houses. If we can get an audience with your coven, maybe there will be some information they can share with us about Matt's heritage?"

"The bottom line is, yes, I am a part of the official Massachusetts State Coven, but I'm just a guardian, and for an outsider to be granted permission to enter a coven house, you would have to be invited in by an elder. To be honest with you, there is absolutely no way to guarantee you'll receive an invitation."

"Couldn't you either ask them to grant us permission or even sneak us in?" Geordie stared straight into Sam's eye as he got up to put on his jacket.

"There are so many guards protecting the house, you'd barely make it through the gates alive if you tried to sneak in." Hand in hand, Sam and Lizzie began to step down from the platform. "Besides, did your father ever tell you anything about my coven?"

"Not really. He mentioned that some of the people there weren't to be trusted."

"Do yourself a favor, Geordie, don't trust any of the elders there. They are all shady and getting wrapped up in their ideals will only get you hurt. Don't bother trying to seek them out." Before she could speak another word, Sam and Lizzie left the nightclub

Chapter 12

Geordie

Geordie sat in silence for nearly half an hour, still at the booth where Sam and Lizzie left her. There was so much to process, but what she couldn't get out of her head was the unwavering truth behind Sam's words. She was useless. With a hand tracing the wound on her chest, she knew she didn't have much time left in this world. She wouldn't die from the ice inside her, but she would fall into a deep sleep that she would never wake up from. She might as well have been dead in that case. What neither Sam nor Matt knew was that the medicines Michelle Lee gave her were working less and less.

She could feel the ice festering inside her. With every passing day, it was harder to breathe, and it was even more difficult to stay awake. Geordie knew that it was only a matter of days until she was done, and yet she felt as though she had so much unfinished business. She wasn't ready to quit, especially not on Matt's account. He needed help discovering his true nature, and Geordie wasn't going to give up now. She still had a little time left.

"You don't have as much time as you'd like to believe." A gentle hand touched Geordie's shoulder and she looked up to see Lizzie covered in what smelled like blood but was black.

"Are you okay?" Geordie gave her an alarmed look.

"I'm fine now, but Sam is outside handling a situation." Lizzie winced suddenly and gripped her head tightly with one hand while steadying herself on the wall of the booth. "We should go upstairs though; more privacy, and I need to clean up."

"Are you sure you're going to be okay?" Even though it was painful, Geordie helped Lizzie up the stairs to the loft as best she could.

Hidden amongst metal columns and framing were the stairs to the loft. From them in the back of the club leading up to the loft, it was impossible to see anything on the dance floor. The platform booths acted as a wall partitioning the dance area from the service area and bathrooms, so very few guests were back there.

"My head is just pounding, don't worry about it." Lizzie groaned.

When they got upstairs, all the lights were off, and the apartment was eerily quiet. Geordie called out to Matt as Lizzie turned on some of the lights, but there was no response. "Maybe he's asleep?"

Lizzie shrugged in response as she grabbed blood bags from the fridge and began to heat them up.

The common areas of the loft looked the same as they did when they left earlier that morning, untouched and empty. The apartment itself had minimal furniture. There was a large six-person dining set that stretched across the length of the tinted glass wall that faced the city. The living room had a long black leather couch with a coffee table, and across from it was a floor to ceiling bookshelf completely packed with books. There were no kitchen appliances, and very little food in the fridge, strictly for Matt. No one else in the household needed food since they were all vampires except Matt.

Geordie checked the guest bedroom where she and Matt were staying, but when she turned the bedside lamp on, the bed was still neatly made from the morning. Matt was nowhere in the apartment. He never even made it inside the loft. Geordie didn't want to believe it, so she checked the bathroom and Sam's room as well, but they were in the same condition as well. Making her way back to the living room, Geordie gathered her shoes and jacket as fast as she could. "Where could he have gone?"

"Listen, Geordie, stop! Calm down." Lizzie grabbed Geordie's shoes from her gently. Matt was missing.

"I don't know where he is! It's not like him to not check in if he planned on going out." Geordie breathed heavily as she tried to keep herself from crying. It hurt her chest and she could barely breathe as she felt the ice fester while her heart pounded. "Something has happened to him."

"Look, we don't know that." Lizzie looked deeply into her eyes, trying to reassure Geordie. She then pulled her over to the couch and sat her down. "We just need to wait for Sam to come in and he will know what to do."

SAM

As they exited the club, Sam wasn't sure why he bothered to warn Geordie about the elders. He didn't particularly like her or her role in Matt's life. He also didn't like the elders. If he had any choice in the matter, the Massachusetts State Coven would've been one of his last choices of covens to join. He never met Lapetus Vollner, but he and his brother, Vexus, shared the same ideals and opinions about the coven. The elders were secretive and sinister. They committed shady practices and believed themselves above the law, and yet were considered the strongest and longest lasting covens in the country. *How can a coven so corrupt last so long?* Sam had been asking himself that question since the incident with Lizzie and Vexus in Germany.

Outside, the January cold would've been a shock to any human, but for Sam and Lizzie, it wasn't the cold that shocked them. A horrific stench emitted from the back end of his alleyway. It reeked worse than death. Lizzie didn't seem to share the same sentiment. She suddenly became extremely ravenous and went searching for the stench. Sam slowly followed, skeptical of what could've grabbed her attention so strongly. Against the back wall of the alley, a dirty little girl stood alone. Her skin was drained of color as if she were dead, and her eyes were dark. The moment Lizzie saw her, she lunged at the little girl and tore into her throat. Sam tried to grab her but, she was too strong, "Lizzie, don't!"

It was too late. Lizzie leapt on the girl, tearing her fangs through her neck. The girl let out no noise of protest. There was no ear-shattering scream or cry. No quiet moan of death. It was as if the girl was already dead to begin with. It was horrifying. There was nothing normal about the girl.

The girl lost blood rapidly, and from what Sam could see of it, it was black blood. Sam tried to pry Lizzie off the girl, but she was too strong. He wasn't sure if it was because she was over a century older than he was, or if it was because of hunger. Either way, she effortlessly shoved him away with one hand into a wall. He could feel bricks shattering underneath his back painfully.

When Lizzie finished feeding, she dropped the body like a rag doll. Her eyes went from the dark color to their normal bright green as she wiped away the blood from her mouth on her sleeve. She seemed completely unfazed by the idea of a nameless girl laying on the cold, frost-covered ground, lifeless like a mannequin.

"Do you know what that little girl was?" A young man approached Sam out of the shadows of the alley. The man was thin and tall like a rail. He carried himself with grace that only a vampire could pull off, and his eyes were bright red. Something was oddly familiar about this platinum blond vampire. Sam was sure he had met him before.

"No, I don't know what she was, but it doesn't matter now." Sam stared at the frail, lifeless corpse. *Could she have been a lygoid in a host body?* She smelled terrible to Sam, so there was the possibility the host was a werewolf.

"Pity... it always helps to know what you're killing. On the upside, at least you can guarantee that girl was not a human." The man pointed towards the girl. From behind Sam at the entrance to the alley way, another man approached them, only this one was a bit younger, and he carried a more innocent look to him.

"I could definitely tell you she used to be a werewolf!" The second male laughed.

"And how would you know that?" Sam stared at the strawberry blond skeptically. Something about this pair made him nervous. He didn't want Lizzie to be near them. "Lizzie, go up to the loft, now."

"But..." She protested quickly, but he shot her a stern look and she immediately backed off, leaving the alley way.

"What do you people want? Who are you?" Sam barked at them quickly. They both exchanged bemused looks and smiled wickedly.

"You mean you don't recognize us? I'm hurt, Sam, that you don't remember us." The blond vampire pouted. "The girl you were speaking to earlier in your club, we have a message for her." The blond handed Sam a black envelope with a maroon seal with the letter "Q" stamped on it.

"Make sure that ends up in the hands of Geordie Vollner, and nothing more will come of this." The other male took a step threateningly toward Sam, and he got a quick whiff of the mysterious boy's smell. He was half human and half vampire, one of those born vampires who were conceived during a mortal solar eclipse. Sam assumed that was the same case for the blond, but as he approached to pull his friend away, Sam noticed he was just a turned vampire.

"Why should I give this to her? Who the hell are you anyway?" Sam threw the eerie envelope back at the blond who suddenly looked very agitated.

"Because if you don't, our master will kill everything you the love most! Don't get any further involved than you already are if you want what's best." The blond threw the envelope back at Sam impatiently. He wasn't sure whether to call this man's bluff or not. He wasn't going to risk it.

"Fine, but you have to tell me your names." Sam tucked the envelope in his inside jacket pocket.

"We don't have to tell you anything! We're the ones in charge here!" The mortal vampire yelled at Sam, becoming irrationally angry. This made it clear to Sam who was in charge and calling the shots. The blond had more composure and control over the situation than his friend did. His friend was too emotional to have control over a ransom of sorts.

"It's fine, our names don't mean anything." The blond touched his friend lightly, signaling him to back off. "My name is Jason Anderson, and this is James Lee."

So, that's who they were… members of the Northern California coven. Sam finally figured out why they looked so familiar to him. He met Jason briefly years ago; he was the only biological child of Michael Anderson. Sam and Lizzie met Michael briefly during the wolf war when they were sent out to destroy a clan of werewolves in their immediate area. They only saw Michael's son from afar, but the resemblance was uncanny. "Thank you."

"Now, you must deliver that envelope!" Jason pointed at Sam's chest where the message remained hidden in his jacket.

"Fine, but a word of advice: you will not approach me again if you value your lives. I have plenty of practice killing other vampires, born… or otherwise." Sam turned and left swiftly, heading back to the loft. He wondered if it was Michael who sent them. It didn't make any sense. He wouldn't be so dark or vague, and he wouldn't threaten other people's lives. The entire situation was too alarming for Sam to let it go unnoticed.

Inside the club, Sam ignored the bartender calling for his attention and went straight into the back office where he dealt with any business management. Locking the door behind him, he got on the phone with Michael in hopes of clearing up any lost details.

Michael was just as shocked as Sam was, maybe more. Sam could tell that Michael didn't want to believe that his son was working for someone unknown. "But then again, I don't really know my son at all. He's like a complete stranger to me."

"Come on, Michael, I'm sure that's not true." Sam pleaded with him.

"No, it completely is true. Ever since Jason turned, he's secluded himself from Layla and me, never talking to us. He was always shunning us. For all I know, he could be completely capable of planning something insidious." He sighed deeply on the other end of the line.

"What do you want to do?"

"Well, if all of this is true and my son has suddenly appeared in Massachusetts, then this is most likely no coincidence. Something is going on, and I intend to find out what." Sam could hear some background talking, but he wasn't sure what was being said.

"Michael? What's going on?"

"I'm sending Seth Vollner, who's still nearby, to sort this out." There was a sudden spark of hope and triumph in Michael's voice as he said this, which piqued Sam's curiosity. "As a part of the Northern California State Coven, he will have no choice but to obey my order and investigate the situation. This is now a coven matter."

GEORDIE

As Lizzie tried to comfort Geordie while they waited, Sam finally came back to the loft. Something about him was off. He looked as though he had seen a ghost. "What is going on?"

"Matt is missing."

With a deep and heavy sigh, Sam pulled out an envelope and handed it to Geordie. "This is for you. I was told explicitly to give it to you."

She stared at it blankly, not opening it. Was it from Matt? "What is this?"

"I honestly don't know. Do you know somebody named Jason Anderson or James Lee?" Sam crossed his arms as he also stared at the envelope.

"No. Should I?" Geordie began to tear it open.

"They are a part of the Northern California State Coven. Jason is Michael Anderson's biological son and James is Michelle Lee's nephew. They ordered me to give you that."

She pulled out a letter from the envelope addressed to her and read aloud, "By the time you read this we'll have captured your human, Matt Hallow. If you want any chance of finding him alive, come to the abandoned factory on the outskirts of Boston harbor. Come alone."

Whoever they were, they didn't realize what they had started if they really did have Matt. There was no way Geordie would allow them to kill Matt. Geordie started to leave, but Sam blocked her way quickly. "Where do you think you're going?"

"Where do you *think* I'm going? They have *Matt*! I'm going to get him!" She tried to push past Sam, but he was stronger than her and remained immobile.

"Don't be stupid! You don't know what you're getting yourself into!"

"They are going to *kill* him, Sam! Did you not hear me when I read the note?" Geordie seethed, breathing harshly through her teeth.

"I *did* hear you, and they are *not* going to kill him." Sam motioned for her to sit at the couch, but she would not move.

"Do you really want to take that chance that they might be bluffing?" Geordie screamed at Sam, appalled by his lax demeanor and attitude toward the situation. She thought he would've been right behind her on the situation already.

"No, I know for a fact they're not bluffing, but they don't know they can't kill him." Sam urged her toward the couch, "But you need to calm down for a moment so we can discuss this before jumping into a situation we're in the dark about."

Geordie huffed impatiently, plopping herself onto the couch. "Fine, but I don't agree with sitting here to talk about the situation."

Sam rolled his eyes at her and took a seat across from her. "Only the Potentials can kill Matt. Matt's half-brother, Nick, is a vampire. They share the same Hallow bloodline, so I have a theory he is the vampire Potential of the four Potentials. Matt is the human Potential. If I am correct about Nick, it would be impossible for James and Jason to be Potentials since, they are also vampires. That would only leave one lygoid, and one faery. Matt is likely safe in their hands, and they don't even know it."

"You don't even know for sure if Nick *is* a Potential! How can you bet on Matt's life like that?' Geordie could not begin to fathom how Sam could be so careless with his friend's life.

"Look, I'm not betting on anyone's life, especially Matt's. If it will make you feel any better, Seth is on his way here right now to sort this whole situation out. Michael thinks that Jason's demands might have something to do with Breena's disappearance, so he sent Seth to figure it out. I suggest we don't take any action until he gets here."

"Alright, that's nice and all but do you know how long until he arrives?" Geordie sat up straight, focusing on Sam fully now.

"No."

"Okay, well then where is he coming from?"

"I don't know."

"Do you have any way to call him?" Geordie didn't see this conversation going anywhere. She probably could've found Matt by now if it weren't for Sam's stalling.

"No, I don't."

"So how do you even know he's coming?" Geordie screamed at Sam in frustration. She found herself questioning Sam's competence.

"Because I'm already here." Seth let himself into the apartment, stunning Geordie and Sam into silence. "Michael said you were in some sort of trouble again, Geordie. I came as soon as I heard. Do you have any new information about Breena's whereabouts?"

Sam shook his head slowly, answering for Geordie. "No, we have no new news. Where did you come from?"

"I was already in Boston by the time Michael called. My previous assignment was in Maine, and I decided it best to stick around in case you all ended up in trouble again. I guess I was right." Seth sat in one of the dining chairs with the back of the chair pressed to his large chest. His head rested on his forearms as he fiddled with a ring on his thumb. "What is going on?"

"This is what's going on." Geordie tossed the note to Seth who caught it flawlessly. "I thought faeries couldn't touch metal."

Seth looked at his jewelry in curiosity. "That's just iron. I only wear silver. It helps ward against werewolves."

"Sounds expensive."

"Not really when you make it yourself." Seth sat up straight, rereading the note over again. "James Lee wrote this?"

"You know him? He was with Michael's son, Jason Anderson." Sam groaned, leaning his head back.

"He's my girlfriend's brother. We all went to school together at Daron Academy." Seth rubbed his temples as he attempted to process the situation. "James and Jason have been best friends for most of our lives. They are a few years older than me, so I never really got to know them, but they've always been joined at the hip… to think they would betray the coven like this… if we catch them, they will have their guardian titles stripped for sure."

"Yeah, I know…" Sam groaned again.

"Geordie, I don't think you should meet them alone. When we were all in school together, Jason was at the top of his class and James wasn't too far behind him. They are exceptionally smart and fast learners. We don't know what they have up their sleeves, and it's not a safe idea to go in there alone and uninformed." Seth handed the letter back to Geordie who was rather irritated with both Sam and Seth.

"You two don't seem to understand! I don't *care* what they might do to me, I must save Matt!"

"Trust me, Geordie, I *do* understand. I know what it's like to lose a loved one and not know if you're going to get them back! But that doesn't mean you go charging in there not knowing what to expect or what waits for you! That's how you get more people killed!" Sam yelled at her as she got up again to leave. "I know that factory, Geordie. There's nothing but werewolves and lygoids there. Both of which have the potential to kill you if the magic inside your wound doesn't first! And you're no good to Matt if you're dead before you can even get a glimpse at him."

"I don't care if I get killed if I manage to save Matt. If I get him back to safety, nothing else matters. I must go after him!" Geordie got close to Sam as he pressed himself to the door once more, blocking her way to leave the apartment. "Step aside, Sam."

"Look, Geordie, I'm not saying don't go. Do what you believe is right. But do *not* go in there alone without a plan unless you're willing to face the repercussions of having other's blood on your hands when we come after you." Seth approached Geordie as well, and they both stared at her with serious eyes.

A part of her hoped he would try to make another attempt to keep her there, but it didn't happen. After a while, he let out a long, heavy sigh and moved slowly out of the way, letting her pass and face Sam.

"I must go there alone. That's the safest way to get Matt back. Please, don't follow me." She pleaded with Seth. "Understand this is the best way for me to prevent you from getting hurt and saving Matt."

"If you go out there with no knowledge what you're getting into, you *will* regret it." Sam made no attempts to dissuade her or try to keep her in the loft. He only gave her the final warning before turning back to Seth, "Is there any way you can try to sense Matt and the other dark essences?"

"I can, but it will be more difficult than usual since I've never seen the place. But I am a fae of the Dark Order, so I should be able to sense any dark presences regardless." Seth closed his eyes, taking a deep breath. His hands gripped the sides of the chair as he concentrated.

He was completely motionless for a for a long moment until Geordie sighed impatiently. He furrowed his brow in frustration. "You said Jason *and* James kidnapped Matt?"

"Yeah, why?" Sam watched him carefully along with Lizzie.

"I could only sense Jason and the other creatures that are there. I can't sense Matt or James." Seth frowned, "It doesn't make any sense why I wouldn't be able to see them... Maybe they're not there."

"We'll see, but I'm unwilling to bet on it." Geordie slammed the door behind her as she left. The feeling of guilt sunk into the pit of her stomach. She felt bad Seth came all this way for nothing, but it was something she *had* to do alone. She didn't have any other choice.

Using her vampire speed for the first time in a long time to run down the cold streets of Boston proved treacherous. The icy paths of the winding sidewalks betrayed her feet, causing her to slip at almost every corner, and the ice in her chest made it difficult to use her powers to their full extent. It was after dark, and all the creatures of darkness were out stealing glances at her as she ran past them. The more she ran, the weaker she felt her body become.

The factory was just on the outskirts of the city, on the harbor. It was near a bunch of fishing docks and construction zones that were only populated in the early morning or daytime. No human would be found anywhere near the site this late in the evening. As Geordie approached, she could sense a lot of dark activity going on in the factory. It seemed like Sam was right. Geordie could smell the werewolves, and she could sense the lygoids. Retrieving Matt was going to prove dangerous if they were aligned with Jason and James.

Geordie looked up at the night sky. The moon was barely visible behind the clouds, but the light still managed to seep through into the night. Tonight was a full moon. Even in their human forms, the werewolves would be rampant and wild, ready to tear anything apart that was vampire. Geordie regretted not accepting Seth and Sam's help.

As quietly as possible, Geordie weaved between the dilapidated brick buildings of the old factory where a bunch of storage and shipment containers lay abandoned. At the front of the factory there was no one who stood guard outside the large double wooden doors. Looking through the musty glass panels of the front doors, Geordie couldn't see anyone inside the factory either except a few stragglers that looked to be werewolves pacing around in their human form frantically. Off to the side of the building, towards the back, Geordie found a small side entrance that was a singular metal door down a wooden ramp that met the docks.

The side entrance was thankfully unlocked, and Geordie managed to get into a dark storage room full of various sized boxes that smelled as musty as it looked. The small storage room led to the main open factory room where a crowd of lygoids, dark fae, and werewolves were shuffling about. Some were conversing while others were moving boxes from one place to another. Closer to the open side of the factory that met the docks, two vampires stood at a distance from the crowd, talking quietly. A few feet in front of them, closer to Geordie's direction, was Matt, completely bound and tied and lying on the floor.

She could smell blood coming from him and spotted a small pool of blood near his head. Geordie quickly dove behind another pile of boxes, getting increasingly closer to Matt as he began to stir. Geordie couldn't see much as Matt's feet were directly facing her from the new angle she was at. He slowly turned from laying on his stomach face down to his side and wiggled a bit as he realized he was tied up.

Matt's squirming against the ropes that kept him bound captured the attention of a nearby ginger vampire who was talking quietly to a large burly werewolf. He quickly approached Matt and sprayed him with something in a plastic canister. "I'm sorry, but we can't have you knowing our location."

"What's going on?" Matt called out frantically.

"Shut up!" The vampire kicked Matt in the stomach so hard he flipped over to his other side. Matt groaned painfully, coughing up blood. Watching Matt get beaten made Geordie wince for him, but she stood her ground. She knew it would cost him his life if she didn't properly assess the situation first now that she got herself into the predicament.

"Who's there?" Matt whispered as a beautiful woman with bright blonde hair crawled over to him with lustful dark eyes.

"My name is Lilian. I'm a lygoid." The woman whispered to Matt as she pushed some of his hair off his face.

"What do you want?"

"I want to know why it is that when I'm near you, I feel stronger." Geordie watched as her lips pressed his cheek and slowly met his as he turned his head toward her.

"Hey! Get away from him!" The ginger yelled and suddenly dragged Matt away. The lygoid woman shrieked and hissed as the werewolf struggled to pull her away as well.

After a few moments everything went silent, and a second vampire leapt down from a nearby skylight, his feet thudding to the ground. "It's almost dark out, you'd think she would've come to collect her human by now."

"Maybe she thinks we're bluffing." Matt's two captors referred to Geordie.

"Well, once the moon reaches its apex, his carcass will be proof enough that we are serious." The blond paced around Matt's body. "James, get the wolves ready. I want everyone here to see exactly how serious I am."

"Exactly how serious about what?" Geordie had had enough and emerged from the stack of boxes she hid behind. She wasn't going to allow wolves to eat Matt.

"Geordie! Where are you?" Matt called out as Geordie ran up to him, embracing him tightly.

"I'm here, Matt! I would never leave you!" She stood him up, but his legs gave out and he fell back to the floor again. "What's wrong with you? What did they do?"

"They sprayed my eyes with something, and I don't know why I can't move." Matt leaned his head on Geordie's shoulder as she held onto him, but the ginger vampire known as James yanked him out of her arms.

"What are you doing?" Geordie cried as her fingers strained to grasp onto him.

"That's enough! If you do not do what we want, we *will* kill him!" James screamed back at Geordie.

"Fine, what do you want?"

"I want you to take us to the Immortal Realm. Bring it!" The entire area went silent as the blond waved a hand forward and a couple of werewolves brought forth a wide full-length mirror.

"And what makes you think I can take you there?" She felt unsure of herself; she'd never used her angelic powers before, and she knew she was weak.

"Because you have angelic blood, you have the power to go between worlds."

"Well, I'm sorry to break the news to you, but I've never travelled between worlds before, and I don't know how. You're out of luck."

"No! That cannot be! You have to take us there!" James squeezed Matt's neck tightly, digging his nails into the side of his neck. "You're the only angel in the human world!

"I can't!" Geordie screamed back furiously. "I'm telling you the truth!"

"Fine, then. I guess you don't mind these werewolves making him their dinner tonight!" The blond was the more composed and leader of the two vampires. Laughter erupted from every direction. The wolves were now crowding around them excitedly. There were too many for Geordie to take on by herself.

"You said if I didn't *come* you would kill him!" Geordie tried to approach Matt, but the blond quickly stopped her, grabbing her from behind by the arms tightly. "Get off me! Matt!"

"Enough!" The vampire pushed Geordie toward the mirror, nearly pressing her face to the glass. "Take us to the Immortal Realm, or I will let them tear your friend apart!"

"Geordie, you don't have to do anything! I don't know what these people want, but if they're willing to go to these lengths to get there, then it's not worth it!" Matt called out to Geordie.

"Shut up, you!" James yanked on the rope holding Matt, throwing him to the ground again.

"Matt, if I don't do it, they'll kill you!" Geordie groaned as the blond pressed her against the mirror with his full strength. She was no match against a turned vampire.

"Do it now!" He yelled at Geordie. "The moon is almost to its apex, and if you don't get a move on, nothing here will stop these beasts from killing him."

"Please don't! I don't know if I can!" Geordie cried out, trying to find the power inside her. Behind her, she could hear clothes ripping, bones cracking, and groans of pain erupting from the surrounding crowd. The transformation was about to begin. They had maybe a minute left, at most.

"Do it!" The vampire screamed again as fur exploded everywhere and yowling erupted into vicious roars. Geordie's head snapped up as someone else's voice called out to them.

"James! Jason!" Seth's voice roared amongst the sounds of men moaning and wailing as their bodies turned to beasts and their moans became snarls. "You will remove your hands from him!"

Behind them Seth was fighting off numerous werewolves without much effort, making his way over to Matt who was being held by the neck by James. Further behind him, Geordie could see Sam also fighting off werewolves at the entrance of the factory.

As Seth threw a wolf across the factory, he charged James swiftly, landing a solid punch to James' jaw. James tried to knock Seth away while still maintaining a hold onto Matt, but they lost balance and collided into each other like bowling pins.

Without realizing what she was doing, Geordie began to faintly glow along with the mirror that Jason held her against. The werewolves began to back away nervously but continued to snarl and bare their teeth at the quarrel.

Seth continued to struggle against James, pulling a knife out and cutting Matt free. Blinded by the light, Jason let Geordie slip through his grasp as he shielded his eyes. They all stumbled into each other as Geordie and the mirror grew brighter and Seth tried to pry James off Matt.

Geordie briefly managed to find her balance on something smooth that seared to the touch, realizing quickly it was the mirror and she could no longer remove her hands from the surface. Before she knew it, she was falling into the mirror with Matt's hand in hers and the other's bodies fell into hers, pushing them further into the mirror through a vortex of light and darkness.

Part 2
The Immortal Realm

CHAPTER 13

GEORDIE
THE IMMORTAL REALM

As the blinding light engulfed them all and they fell into the mirror Jason had brought out, Geordie felt a tightness over her body as if someone was squeezing every organ in her body. On one side she could feel Seth and James pulling on her arm and on the other side were Matt and Jason clinging desperately onto her as they tumbled into each other. All five of them held desperately onto each other as a vortex of darkness and light sucked them between worlds. It was as if they were being pulled through a tight ventilation shaft with little room to breathe.

Geordie lost her grip on Seth and James, watching as they disappeared into darkness. Realizing this, she wrapped her arm tightly around Matt as she began to panic. With her free hand she got a better grip on Jason, not letting him go, even though she wanted to rip his throat out for threatening Matt. She refused to lose anyone else that she dragged into whatever hell they were about to face.

The falling sensation came to a gradual stop, and it felt as though Geordie's lungs were filling up with water. She tried desperately to find air but the next thing she knew, she emerged to the surface of the water to see a giant fountain before her.

Geordie found herself sitting two feet deep inside it as Matt and Jason also emerged from the surface on either side of her.

She looked around eagerly trying to make some sort of sense of the occurrence, but there were no doors, holes, or tunnels that they could've come through. It was as if the portal *was* water.

"Oh my god, I can finally see!" Geordie turned to see Matt rubbing his eyes and taking in his surroundings. The entire area was grey as far as the eye could see.

Small cottages surrounded the square with the fountain at the center with only two main streets to take in either direction. Each of the cottages looked as though they were carbon copied from one another, but there were two larger buildings that were completely different from the rest. Down one street there was a cathedral with bright, beautiful clouds surrounding it. In the opposite direction was a dark street that led to a building that disappeared into storm-filled dark clouds. The dark end of the city sent a chill down Geordie's spine.

Geordie stepped out of the fountain thinking about exactly how they came to be there. She then turned back to Jason shoving him back into the fountain as he climbed out. He crashed back into the fountain, causing him to become soaking more than he was before. He then exclaimed angrily, "What was that for?"

"*You're* the one who got us into this mess! Where is Seth? You and your friend did this on purpose; you wanted casualties!"

"Excuse me, but I've never had anything against Seth Vollner in the years that I've known him. I never even expected him to get involved! But *he's* the one who blindly jumped into the fray, with no regard for the consequences! So maybe you should think about that for a moment! And, if you haven't noticed, my best friend is just as much of a 'casualty' as Seth is, so nobody leaves my side until I find James!" Jason pulled a large parchment out of his jacket and unrolled it to reveal a map of the whole area.

"You can't actually believe we're going to stick by you, do you?" Matt waded through the fountain, climbing out and turning to Jason.

Jason used his vampire speed and wrapped an arm around Matt's neck from behind, pulled his head to the side and bared his fangs down over Matt's skin. "You will if you want to live. Remember this next time you two decide to threaten me; you are a human, Matt Hallow, and I'm a vampire. I could end your life with the snap of your neck, or I can just tear out your carotid artery with my teeth."

"Well, I'm part angel, which makes this place an advantage for me, and *we*," she indicated herself and Matt with pursed lips, "outnumber you."

He then threw Matt from his embrace, glaring at Geordie. "You can't use a place you know nothing about to your advantage. It doesn't work that way."

"Jason!" James called out from the dark street behind them. Behind him, Seth was trailing behind slowly. James ran up to Jason and briefly hugged him until Jason pried him off with a serious look.

"Looks like we don't need to play tag along anymore." Matt sighed and patted Seth on the shoulder as he approached.

"Actually, I think it might be a good idea to stick with them since they have the only map of the place." Geordie stared at the map that would hopefully show them a way to get home. Jason noticed this and chortled loudly.

"Oh, I'm sorry, but I no longer need you now that I have what I need. But one more thing, to remember me by," He then turned to Seth quickly and bit his neck, holding a vial underneath the wound. Seth groaned painfully and pulled away, breathing heavily as Jason held on without issue. Once Jason got the blood he wanted, he pushed Seth into Matt. He then strode over to the dark street that went towards the eerie building shrouded in dark clouds and withdrew a lighter.

"What are you doing?" Seth groaned, cupping his wound painfully. Geordie tried to yank away the lighter, but Jason was too fast for her.

"We *have* to stick together if we are to ever get out of here!"

"I'm sure you three will do just fine on your own, but we have a date with the strongest lygoid alive." Jason grinned as he drew a line over the start of the street between two cottages using a bit of Seth's blood. He then flicked open the lighter and burnt the map. When the embers of the map blew towards the line, they exploded into a giant wall of fire. "So that way you nor anyone else can follow us until sunset."

Geordie, Matt, and Seth watched in dismay as the two vampires ran off into the darkness. It would take a miracle to get out without finding any angels or lygoids on the way, let alone Frost.

"Where do we go from here?" Seth groaned, sliding down to the ground, sitting with his knees propped up. He looked to Geordie for the answer, but she could not find one.

"I don't know." She whispered. Matt tried to wrap his arms around her, but she pulled away. "Please don't."

"We'll figure something out." Matt whispered in her ear.

"While you guys do that, I think I need some help over here." Seth bowed his head in between his knees. Geordie placed a hand over his forehead. He was sweating bullets and running a fever. "We should probably head towards the cathedral looking building."

"That's not a good idea. We don't know how many angels are in there." Geordie stared hesitantly at the cathedral.

"Well, if we don't find a cure, I won't be able to protect either of you." Seth slowly uncovered his wound. It wasn't healing. "I probably only have a day until it festers and kills me."

"Wait, vampire bites kill faeries?" Matt exclaimed, kneeling to Seth's level as well.

"Yeah. It's not information we like having spread around." Seth barely chuckled. He then pointed towards the cathedral, "Look, our best bet is to go to the place we can actually access."

"Maybe if we come across anyone along the way, they can tell us if Breena is here." Geordie stared up at the cathedral ahead of them apprehensively. She could feel the ice in her body growing rapidly. It felt as if Frost's power inside her grew the moment Geordie wound up in the Immortal Realm.

"Maybe we should prioritize getting both of you healed." Matt watched Geordie, and Seth silently agreed. Together, they all headed toward what could be their doom or their salvation.

Ahead of them was a building full of angels that most likely wanted to kill Geordie on sight. The opposite way, Jason and James were headed towards a dark eerie end of the city that looked like it could be the home of a bunch of lygoids, none of which would be their allies either. Geordie honestly thought they should try to pursue Jason because if he knew how to get into this world, it meant he might know how to get out. At the same time, she didn't want to risk Seth's life on a hunch that could lead to a dead end.

"We are heading into the den of our enemies in the hopes of finding a cure for the both of you. I feel like this will be the end of us." Matt spoke as he helped Seth down the street.

"On some level you're right. This is the Immortal Realm. It houses mostly angels and lygoids as the primary occupants, but we might have one thing that helps us." Geordie paused and both Seth and Matt looked at her, pausing. "Faeries also reside here. There might be someone who would side with Seth who might know of a cure for a vampire bite. Plus, with no other paths to take, it's not like we have a choice." Geordie found herself agreeing with Seth's plan as the words spilled out.

"Let's try to find a cure for both of us and try to find Breena." Seth groaned painfully as they continued down the street. They managed to deduce that Breena was not in the Mortal Realm before they came here, the only viable option was that she had to be in the Immortal Realm. It was just a matter of finding her.

FROST

Frost knew her new master's task had been completed when she felt the energy of the fallen arrive in the Immortal Realm. Sirens in the council building also announced that Geordie wasn't the only one to arrive. Trespassers made their way through the gates of the water spirit Aquavitas. The next step was simple. All she had to do was ensure that Geordie Vollner made her way to Ezra who waited in her office for the half breed.

"Miss Frostbite, we've detected two intruders and a faery in the city square. What should we do?" A guard showed Frost an image on the security mainframe displaying three people walking toward the council building. It was Geordie Vollner, as predicted, Matt Hallow, and another half breed, a faery vampire.

"That's interesting…" Frost focused in on the faery. He was of vampire heritage, but his fae blood made him a guest in the Immortal Realm. Something seemed familiar about him. It piqued her curiosity. He was also injured and bleeding out profusely. "Escort the girl and the faery to Ezra's office. Arrest the human and send him to the prison. Make sure you have back up when you bring them in."

Frost left the security room without waiting for a response from the guards. On the way to Ezra's office, Pyre met up with her and gave an update on his latest task. "I've hidden Breena Vollner like you told me to. There's no way they will be able to get to her unless they can read my mind."

"Well, you better get out of here then, because Geordie is on her way to Ezra's office right now. I don't know if Geordie Vollner can read angelic minds or not, but I am not going to risk our leverage on her in the case she can." Frost paused for a moment. "And I *can* read your mind so scamper off somewhere hidden until all of this is over. We don't need someone finding Breena unless we *want* them to."

"I understand, ma'am. I will return to the Mortal Realm."

"Good idea, now *go!*" Frost snapped and pushed him farther down the hallway as she approached Ezra's office. As soon as Pyre was out of sight, the office door swung open, and Ezra beckoned Frost in.

Today Ezra was adorned in a tight white dress with a large, beaded necklace around her frail neck. She matched the office décor perfectly in her many shades of white. It was all a little too bright for Frost's liking, but she dealt with it. "Congratulations, you were correct. She did figure out how to get here. Now, you said she'll be looking for Breena Vollner."

"That is correct. It also appears that someone else is with them. A faery hybrid, ma'am." Frost nodded as they both watched a flickering image of the three intruders on Ezra's desk. Upon closer inspection, Ezra's eyes widened, and she started laughing.

"That would be Seth Vollner, the only living heir of Breena Vollner and Vexus Vollner. He's a half faery half vampire from the Summus and Dark Orders." Frost watched Ezra play with the holographic images of Seth, Geordie, and Matt. She seemed entranced with Seth for reasons that Frost couldn't possibly fathom. "What is wrong with his neck? Why are they practically carrying him?"

"I don't know, ma'am, but he's not supposed to be here." Frost shut the image off to get Ezra's full attention.

"Oh, posh! That's neither here nor there. Plenty of fae have wound up here by some means and plenty others have wound up in the Mortal Realm. I could send the intelligence order to figure out how it keeps happening, but I really don't mind the presence of the faeries. They are pleasant in their own rights, but my point is, he would've wound up here somehow anyway so why try to prevent it?" Ezra smiled at

Frost, her perfect, straight teeth showing through her thin rosy lips.

Frost scrutinized Ezra's peppy physique "You seem very relaxed for someone who's going to execute someone very soon."

"I'm excited! I finally get to rid the Mortal Realm of a pest that shouldn't have been born in the first place. But I must admit, I am also excited to meet her for the first time ever!"

"Well try to calm your demeanor, ma'am. I can sense them approaching the building now. It will be less than five minutes before the fallen and Seth Vollner arrives."

"Yes, you're right, Frostbite." Ezra tried to conceal her glee, but it was practically impossible. Frost rolled her eyes and continued watching the door like a guard dog. Letting someone else force Geordie to use her powers to come to the Immortal Realm was something Frost had never thought of. It seemed easier than trying to incapacitate the stupid girl unconscious and dragging her to the Immortal Realm.

It was thanks to Quinn that it was possible to capture Geordie. He told Frost where to find his most faithful follower, a woman named Lilian who proceeded to gather the rest of his followers and lure Geordie Vollner out of hiding. All Frost had to do was wait for a signal from Quinn. In the meantime, she had to play as the faithful dog to Ezra, even though Ezra had betrayed everything Frost stood for.

Frost checked the door again for Geordie and Seth. They were approaching from the west hall with two guards. They each looked irritated and defeated. Frost felt powerful and righteous; she wanted to be sure Geordie suffered for every year she spent running from Frost before Ezra executed her.

As they entered the office, Frost and Geordie exchanged a brief look of hatred before Frost joined Ezra's side and the intruders were released from their shackles. Ezra stared at Geordie in amazement as they finally came face to face. She took a long moment to study Geordie up and down before finally settling on Seth, who was cupping a bleeding wound on his neck. He looked faint and pale with pools of sweat as he bled out.

"What happened to him?" Ezra asked Geordie quickly, going over to Seth's side and examining him with a closer look.

"He was bitten by a vampire who made us come to the Immortal Realm." Geordie mumbled quietly. Ezra looked back at Seth's wound, gently removing his hand. The wound looked infected and dark, covered in dried and wet blood.

She stood back up and returned to her desk, dismissing the wound. "That's impossible. My detectors only found you and your comrades invading my world."

"Is it? Is there a way you would not have detected them? How do you explain a vampire bite killing a faery?" Geordie continued to stare down at the floor, speaking very quietly.

"Look at me." Ezra snapped, and Geordie slowly looked
up at Ezra, staring her up and down with apathy. "Do you
even know who I am?"

"No."

"I am the one who put in the order for your death alongside
your parents'. You are both angel and vampire. What makes
you think I can't just assume you bit your friend here? It
wouldn't be the first time a vampire betrayed its own kind."
Geordie showed no mark of astonishment or emotion of any
kind, so Ezra continued. "You must understand, this is nothing
personal against you. I just have to follow certain guidelines
and expectations I set for the balance of light and dark. You
living between worlds will throw off the balance, therefore
you must die. And seeing how you trespassed on sacred
ground, that is also an offense punishable by death."

"But we didn't come here intentionally! We were coerced
here by two vampires who bit me! If we don't find a cure, I
will die! And seeing as how the Immortal Realm is supposed
to be sanctuary for *all* faeries, if you let a fae die under your
authority, you *will* have the Summus *and* Dark Orders to
answer to!"

"Speak when you're spoken to!" Frost barked at Seth,
glaring at him, and he shot her an equally dark look.

"Intent is not a factor in this world. We have strict
guidelines in Cinereo Civitatum, but I must admit, you do
have me there. I cannot allow you to die so easily in my
world, so I will give you the cure to a vampire bite, but I want

something in exchange for it." Ezra leapt over her desk, leaning in close to Seth's face. "You see, Geordie over there still has committed a crime by coming here. Only angels, fair folk, and lygoids may enter this world alive. Everyone else may only enter once their spirit has left the Mortal Realm."

"What do you mean by that? What is it do you want?" Seth growled, making Frost chuckle quietly to herself. She wondered what Ezra had in store for these two.

"What she means is that this place is the afterlife for all other creatures like vampires." Geordie clarified for the faery boy in a dull tone. "But I have rights seeing as I am *part* angel."

"Well, no. You don't have any rights here, darling. You've been declared an enemy of the realm." Ezra smiled.

"Well, if you've been waiting this long to kill me, then just do it!" She snapped finally.

"There's only one problem with that, caused by forces beyond my will. You see, I am willing to heal poor Seth over here," She leaned her head on Seth's shoulder, and he shuddered in disgust. "But I want you to sign a contract with me. I don't know *exactly* how to kill you, but I am in the process of finding out. So, until then, you are free to live in this world, as long as when you *do* die, you sacrifice your powers and essence to the Immortal Realm. You won't be murdered or touched by any of my angels here, including Frostbite."

Frost couldn't believe Ezra was making a deal with that creature! She also couldn't believe that Ezra would have the audacity to include her in a deal. In the Immortal Realm, pacts were binding for angels. The moment a deal was struck, all parties in the deal were eternally bound to it until the person writing the pact decided to call it off. In this case, Ezra was the one writing it, and everyone else was affected by it. This meant that as long as Geordie Vollner remained in the Immortal Realm, no angel could touch her.

"If I sign your agreement, you will give the cure to Seth, and no one will try to kill me?" Geordie asked and Ezra nodded, passing the contract forward to Geordie. "What makes you think I'm going to sacrifice myself for you?"

"That is where I sweetened the deal for your friend here." Ezra nodded at Seth who was still bleeding out and fighting to stay conscious. She then offered a parchment with her terms written to Geordie, "I'm sure you already know that Frost has delivered to me Breena Vollner, and she is being held here as… leverage. Well, I, too, have been busy as of recently. One of my agents has also procured me Vexus Vollner, who was discovered trying to find a way to save his wife, Breena."

"You have my father as well?" Seth groaned as he switched hands covering his neck bite. At this point he was practically covered in blood and as pale as a corpse. He no longer had the radiating color of a fae in his skin.

"I figured it was time to end this whole charade your family has been playing for so long. Breeding with demons such as vampires. It is a disgusting business that needs to end. I want you to swear no matter what, that when you die, Geordie, my world will acquire your essence. In exchange, I will hand over *one* of the Vollners of your choosing, Seth."

Geordie took the parchment and read it aloud, "Miss Geordie Vollner is permitted to remain alive and protected in the Immortal Realm under the conditions that when a method of her death is discovered, she shall admit defeat and release her essence into the world. Under the terms of this agreement, Ezra Daron shall provide a cure to Seth Vollner's ailment of a vampire bite and release either Vexus or Breena Vollner under his custody."

Geordie continued to read the contract silently, her eyes scanning left to right. All the details were in the contract, but there was only one detail Frost worried about. If that contract was sealed, she wouldn't be able to harm Geordie Vollner while she remained in the Immortal Realm. Frost found herself pondering the ideas of how to get the girl back into the Mortal Realm without Ezra noticing. It seemed like an impossible task. She needed to find a way. Frost hoped that the girl wouldn't take the deal, but she seriously doubted that would happen. As long as she remained in the Immortal Realm, she had complete immunity. Frost wondered if Geordie realized this.

"So, you'll give Seth back one of his parents as long as I sacrifice my essence to you in this world?" Ezra nodded quietly, letting Geordie think about it further. "And what will happen to his other parent?"

"They will live out their days here imprisoned. They are to be made an example of. I can't have any more half breeds popping up as if it were allowed." Ezra shrugged.

"What difference does it make what creatures outside of the angels do in their own private lives?" Geordie screamed angrily. To a degree, Frost had to agree with Geordie. Ezra's methods didn't make any sense. Faeries were considered a neutral ally between the angels and vampires. What difference did it make to Ezra?

"It makes all the difference in both realms! I will not tolerate a higher power being born nor will I tolerate the vampires infecting the bloodlines of other species! They are a parasite that should be exterminated!" Ezra slammed her fist on the desk, seething through her teeth like a snake.

"No. Don't sign it, Geordie." Seth breathed heavily, leaning into Geordie as she tried to hold his large frame up. "It's not worth it. We will find another way to get my parents back."

"Actually, you will never find either of them if she doesn't sign the contract. No one in here knows the location of Breena, and the one person who does, left this realm shortly before you entered the building." Frost finally spoke up, driving that verbal knife into Geordie's back, making it harder to decide.

They were trapped now. The only options Ezra left for the two imbeciles were to rot here forever or sign a contract in which only one of them could leave. Either way, Frost succeeded in getting a hold of the little pest who calls herself an angel apparently. The girl knew what her options were. Frost just hoped she could make the wrong decision, for Frost's benefit.

"There isn't a better option, Seth. I'm sorry, but I have to do this. I need to save your life. If I can do that, maybe you can find a way to find both your parents." Geordie took the quill as Frost's heart sank and signed the contract in tiny cursive writing. Seth groaned as she signed the contract, and Ezra grabbed a knife from her desk.

She approached him cautiously. Both Seth and Geordie stared at Ezra in horror as she sliced a long, deep cut into her wrist and held it up to Seth's mouth. "Drink it. There may not be a cure for a werewolf bite in a vampire, but there is a cure for a vampire bite. Angelic blood is a pure, untainted form of vampire blood. Drink it and you will heal instantaneously. I am a woman of my word."

Seth stared at her wrist with disbelieving eyes but nodded and mumbled the words 'Thank you' and drank the blood. As Ezra predicted, Seth's bite wound healed instantly. The sweat went away, and the color came back to his skin. It was unbelievable. Frost wondered if what Ezra said was true, if there really wasn't a cure for a werewolf bite. When Seth finally finished, he let go of Ezra's wrist and wiped the blood off his lips. "Again, thank you."

She then turned to Geordie offering her wrist as well, "Drink it. I know you are wounded by Frost's powers. When you arrived in this world, your affliction worsened, but you will not die from it. It will be impossible for you to function and slow your body until finally you cannot use your own powers. At that point you will be useless to me. Drink it. Consider this an act of good faith."

Frost watched with disgust as Geordie begrudgingly took the offer from Ezra. In turn, Frost could feel the effects of her powers leave Geordie's body. Everything Ezra did made it difficult for Frost to complete her tasks. She wondered if Ezra knew of her betrayal.

"How do I explain this to Matt?" Geordie set the quill down quietly after signing the contract, not looking at Seth, Ezra, or even Frost. Her hair covered her face, making it difficult to see her expression. Her tone of voice said it all though. Regret dripped off it like a poison.

"Oh, you don't have to worry about that. He's going to be executed at sundown." Ezra folded up the contract and slid it into one of the drawers of her desk, locking it securely.

Geordie jumped out of her seat in astonishment. "What? Why?"

"Darling, I told you already. It is a crime punishable by death to trespass upon my world." Just then Ezra's office doors burst open by Orpheus who came in with an army of angels in a panic.

"Ezra! The prison! Two vampires slaughtered everyone there! The trespassers… unaccounted for… we were set up!

And we can't get back into the prison!" He ran back out in a hurry with his army.

"Frost, we must go!" Ezra threw on her coat and headed for the door until Frost stopped her.

"Ma'am, what about the two Vollners?" She pointed blankly at Geordie and Seth.

"*Now*, Frostbite! I will deal with them! Go with Orpheus to the prison!" Ezra snapped at Frost. She turned quickly to leave, but not before she saw Ezra put a locking spell on them.

MATT

When Matt and the others arrived at the cathedral it looked more like a corporate business building inside than a church. Before Matt could take it all in, Seth and Geordie were apprehended by two guards heavily covered in armor. Someone jumped him from behind and threw a cover over his head.

Sometime later he found himself in what was a blindingly bright padded cell. A large pane of plastic separated him from the hallway with rows of other identical padded cells. He had no idea what happened to Geordie and Seth and worried about their injuries. He hoped Geordie was trying to find a cure. If something happened to Geordie, and he managed to escape, he swore he would kill the angels himself.

Matt Hallow?

"Who's there?" Matt jumped, trying not to show that he was startled. He didn't find it normal to be hearing someone else's voice in his own head. A surprisingly attractive man approached Matt's cell slowly, examining him. Matt found it nearly impossible to look at this person full on. He was so beautiful and perfectly sculpted; it was impossible to believe. Geordie and this man looked nearly perfect in all the same ways. It was very peculiar to Matt. They both seemed to have a dark beauty around them based on the way they carried themselves. They also both had very pale skin and silvery eyes.

"I'm amazed. You are the descendent of Kearan Hallow, which makes you a *true* creature of darkness." The man waved his hand quickly and the plastic wall disappeared. "If you really were human, the sight of my true form would've killed you."

"Who are you?" Matt stepped into the hall, quickly taking note of the large raven black wings coming out of his back.

"My name is Corál." He politely gestured toward the hallway where a security guard lay on the front desk, unconscious. "Don't mind him. I had to put a sleeping spell on everyone who would've tried to stop me."

Matt carefully stepped over the sleeping female faeries as Corál held open the front door for him. They quickly exited the front hall to be greeted by a dark, foggy city before him.

Matt finally felt his eyes and head relax from the blinding light of the prison. "Why?"

Before he could get a response, Corál pulled Matt behind a smaller building and folded his dark wings over the two of them as two other people approached the prison. Matt slowly peered between the thick feathers to see Jason and James going up the front steps to the luminous building. Why would they willingly go in there?

"I put a spell on them and got you out of there because there doesn't need to be anymore unnecessary bloodshed. There is a breakout about to happen, and you don't need to need to get in the crossfire. You need to get to Geordie, find Breena and Vexus Vollner, and leave the Immortal Realm."

"What about Seth? He's dying, and how am I supposed to find a way to get out of here?" Matt looked up and down the dark streets as they jumped out from behind the building they were hiding behind.

"I will help you." Corál pulled Matt down the stone path faster than he could've kept up on his own, talking as he went. "Seth Vollner is being healed as we speak, and he can come and go as he pleases. Ezra has some sort of fascination with him that I do not understand and am unwilling to investigate. And if it means anything to you, Geordie is also being healed."

Knowing Geordie and Seth were being healed put Matt's mind at ease as Corál pulled him off to the side again as three angels crept over the stone path ahead of them. All three of them were alert and on guard for anything and Matt recognized one of them as Frost. She had her large dark blue wings fully expanded and wore light armor.

Eventually they disappeared into the dark fog, only to leave a faint luminescent glow in the distance. It didn't seem like there was going to be a breakout. The surrounding area was dead silent. There were no signs of life anywhere, no animal calls, no screaming, not even the sound of the angel's footsteps could break the silence of this dark and terrifying fog. Corál continued to pull Matt down the alleyway until finally they broke free of the fog, and it was daylight again.

"Why is that street so dark and foggy?" Matt shivered at the sight of it. Something about it didn't sit right with him, and he just wanted to focus on getting back to Geordie and Seth.

"The entire area of the city has a dark fog cast over it to protect the lygoids from the light. It's also where Ezra gets the lygoids who pose a threat over into the prison. You saw her earlier with Frost. She was the woman in white."

"Who was the man with them?"

"Orpheus. He's one of the council members directly under Ezra. He –" Corál stopped suddenly and grabbed his pocket in his army trench coat which was wiggling viciously.

"What is *that*?" Matt stared at the wiggling pocket in shock as it fought against Corál's hand.

"The key to getting you three to Seth's parents safely, but it won't sit still." Corál fumbled with the pocket until it settled down. "We need to get moving. We don't have much time until Ezra closes the portals."

"I thought only Breena Vollner was here. How is Seth's father is here as well?" Matt asked confused about the situation.

"I have been watching the Vollners' for quite some time, the moment word about Seth, Breena, and Geordie reached Vexus, he made it his mission to get his family back, but Pyre, the angelic phoenix caught him first. I sensed it the moment they entered the Immortal Realm."

They headed back to the cathedral building, only this time when they entered, no one was there to stop them. The place was completely desolate. Every step they took echoed down the empty halls, imitating Matt's pounding heart. He felt as though the hallways never ended and went on endlessly.

Eventually they stopped at a large ornate door but with no hinges or doorknobs. Corál gently placed a hand on a large emblem in the center of the door and a bright light shone through. A lock clicked open and so did the door. Standing there completely unharmed were Geordie and Seth.

"Geordie!" He ran up to her and squeezed her tightly. He was becoming exhausted of nearly losing her to their enemies. She returned the hug but pulled away quickly.

"Why is *he* with you?" She nodded toward Corál who was wrestling with his pocket again.

"This is Corál, he helped me escape the prison and brought me over here to you guys." Matt smiled at Corál who returned a silent nod. It was scary how stoic he was.

"He is one of the angels sent to kill me! You can't trust him, Matt!" She glared at Corál as she spoke to Matt. Corál's façade endured Geordie's strong accusations.

"What? But you helped me get out of that prison!" Matt stared at Corál in astonishment.

"If you haven't noticed, I've never been interested in pursuing you in the sixty years you've managed to avoid the other angels. I've always known where you are. I give you full props on that, by the way." Corál took a seat at the desk and started going through the drawers.

"It doesn't matter anyway; she can't be killed in this world now." Seth gave Geordie a look of disappointment. Matt was clearly missing something there.

"I am fully aware of the situation, sir. I am the one who suggested making the agreement." Corál spoke as he sifted through the drawers of the desk.

"What is going on? How is this even possible? We are in their world." Matt turned to Seth to give him the answers he sought.

"The faery is correct. Neither I nor any other angel can bring harm to Geordie while she is in the Immortal Realm." Corál directed his attention to Geordie who looked surprised about something. "Having Ezra make you sign that contract was the only way I could guarantee that you would be able to live through retrieving your family."

"Wait, what contract?" Matt was fuming now. That was when Matt finally noticed Seth. He was no longer sweating, and the bite wound on his neck was completely healed. "What did you *do*?"

"I signed a contract with Ezra saying that when I die, I must sacrifice myself and my powers to the Immortal Realm. In exchange for my sacrifice, she agreed to give Seth the cure to a vampire bite and heal me." Geordie fell to her knees in tears, sobbing quietly to herself. No one in the room approached her to comfort her. Seth stood at a distance, Corál stared pensively and patiently at her as she sobbed quietly, and Matt tried to process what was going on.

"Does that mean she can't leave here?" Matt looked to Corál as panic sank in his stomach like a large, heavy, painful pit.

"There was nothing written in the contract that said she could not leave. As long as you three hurry, you can escape this world with Seth's parents. But you only have until daybreak, then Ezra will permanently close the gates." Corál knelt to Geordie eye to eye. "The contract will be void in the Mortal Realm, so try not to end up here again, because if you do, Ezra will surely not let you go so easily next time."

"How will she let me go this time? She seems bent on keeping me here now. And what do you mean, Seth's parents?"

"She won't. She wants you to stay. The only difference between now and then is that she won't see it coming this time around. If there's a next time, she will know what to look for and will be on guard." Corál then turned to Seth, "Your father found out about you, Breena, and Geordie and tried to come after you but also got captured."

"Of course he did, why am I not surprised?" Seth pulled Geordie to her feet and wiped away her tears.

"Hopefully, I can stall the other parties involved, but you don't want to be in the city after night fall, which is why you must get moving *now*!" Corál ushered all three of them towards another door in the back of the office that no one noticed before. "Here, take this."

He rifled through his pockets and pulled a weasel out of the pocket that had been wiggling before. As he handed it to Geordie, it curled up comfortably in her arms, chirping affectionately at her. Corál continued to search his numerous pockets and eventually revealed a large spherical orb that was glowing.

"This will help you in the task at hand." They all exchanged worried looks. "You have until nightfall to find Breena and Vexus and get to the outlands outside the city. Once you get your family and light begins to appear, make your way toward the center of the city as fast as you can.

Once the Immortal Realm reaches full daybreak and Ezra has closed the gates, you'll be trapped."

Seth took the orb and examined it carefully as it shone brightly in his large hands. "How do you know when she'll close the gates?"

"I have seen it; I was blessed with seer magic when I was born." Corál pushed them through the back-office door that was actually a bookcase.

"What if we need your help?" Matt asked hurriedly.

"I'll know if you need assistance, no matter the distance; you just won't know it." His serious face was unhindered.

"Will I ever see you again?" Geordie finally turned back to Corál urgently. Seth proceeded through the bookcase's opening behind her.

"You will, one day, when it is time for you to truly know me. The real me." Satisfied with his answer, Geordie climbed through the doorway, and Matt followed her as Corál shut it behind them.

CHAPTER 14

SAM
MID WINTER

Where Sam stood useless, at the entrance of the factory, his eyes seared against the blinding light of the mirror and Geordie. As soon as the blinding light dissipated, they were all gone. Matt, Geordie, Seth, James and Jason were all gone, and all that remained were the filthy mongrels that were werewolves.

All of them were gone. There were no traces of bodies, or scorch marks where the lightning hit. There wasn't even a fire. It was like magic. Sam frantically ran over to the site where his friends once stood, trying to get some sort of semblance of hope that could tell him that his friends were still alive, but there was nothing. It was like they had never even been there in the first place.

"NO!" Sam cried out, slamming his fist into the concrete floor of the abandoned factory. He was left there, alone, to bask in his own stench of fear and failure. He'd failed everyone to keep Matt safe.

On top of it all, Seth being unable to sense Matt and James confirmed they were all Potentials. Three Potentials were gone, lost in the Immortal Realm. Sam wasn't sure if they were still alive, and there wasn't any way to find out for sure. He wasn't even sure how he'd explain it to the elders. He'd already broken the law by telling Geordie about the Potentials;

he couldn't imagine what they would do to him for knowing who the Potentials were in the first place.

For three weeks, Sam stayed in his loft, alone and afraid of what was next to come. At first Lizzie tried to reason with him, but nothing could console his dark thoughts. The one job he ever cared about, the only one that ever mattered, he supremely failed at. He had one job, to protect Matt, the heir to the Shadow Kingdom, at all costs, and he failed.

His thoughts traced back to his first meeting with Matt at the bequest of Naómi. It was the same day he received his guardian bracelet during the ceremony graduating new guardians. Michael approached Sam after the ceremony, congratulating him. "Sam, I have no doubt in my mind, you will do great things with the resources at your disposal. Now that you are a guardian, it is time for you to receive your assignment."

"Already? Hasn't it been only five minutes?" Sam laughed but gave Michael an odd look regardless.

"This is important.   You know Naómi Hallow, correct?"

Sam had not only remembered Naómi, but he had befriended her two years previous, "Yes, I met her during my studies throughout my training. She was one of my professors."

"Good. Come with me." Michael smiled at Sam, wrapping an arm around his shoulder as they left the campus of Daron Academy.

A short drive later, to the far eastern side of Daron Forest in the Kensington Hills Estate, Michael brought Sam to the home of Naómi Hallow. He had never been to the Kensington Hills Estate before; it was where the majority of professors and noble families resided between the school years.

It was a beautiful cluster of homes surrounded by large redwood trees. Naómi's home was one of the smallest by comparison to some of the mansion-like houses that Sam had been sure were home to some of the royal families, such as the Victoires and Levingtons.

When they had arrived at her front door, a faery greeted them, bringing Michael and Sam through to a cluttered dining room that had clearly been converted into a small library with wall-to-wall shelves. Sam and Michael sat waiting for maybe five minutes on a teal velvet loveseat before Naómi had entered the library from a set of white French doors. In her arms she carried a tiny bundle in a grey blanket that was a newborn baby. "Good evening, gentlemen."

"Wow." Sam stared in awe at the sight. "I never realized you were pregnant. Congratulations… How long has it been since I last saw you?"

"It's been over a year since you were in my class. A lot has happened, but this isn't my first child, to be perfectly honest."

Naómi smiled, tilting her newborn baby slightly for Sam to see. "His name is Nick Hallow."

"I see." Sam stared blankly at the soft sleeping face of the baby. "He's not your first?"

"No, I have an older son, named Matt." Naómi took a seat with her baby on a matching loveseat across from Sam and Michael. "Tell me, do you know anything about my family, the Hallows?"

"I don't think so." From that point, Naómi explained the family history of the Hallows and how they were descended from the first faeries and Kearan Hallow, the man who created the First King Essence. It was the first and only time Sam had ever heard the history of the Hallow family and he never forgot it. "So is my first assignment protecting you and your family?"

"No, that is unnecessary. I don't need the protection of vampires, thankfully. And my little baby will be mine to protect alone." She gave a soft smile to her newborn as she ran a finger down his cheek. "It's my son, Matt, who needs to be protected. I recently performed a spell to test his magical abilities, and as it turns out, he's host to the First King Essence."

"He holds the First King? How are you able to tell?"

"There's a spell that Kearan Hallow wrote to test our family members for signs of the essence. It gets performed on each of us while we are young by the current matriarch of our family. As the only living female member of the Hallow family I am the only one capable of performing this spell. It is without a doubt Matt who carries the First King Essence." Still holding her baby, Naómi had gotten down on the floor on her knees in front of Sam, looking up at him with vulnerable eyes. To date, it was the only time Sam had ever seen her be vulnerable with him and ask for help.

"Sam, you are one of my only friends and the only vampire I trust. Please, protect my son with your life. Provide him with the love and guidance that I, myself, cannot provide him. Be his teacher, be his friend, but most importantly, please be his guardian and equip him with the tools he needs to harness this power when he's ready."

No one had ever pleaded before him in the nearly two centuries he had been alive until then. Naómi had been the first and Sam had no idea how to process it. When his graduation ceremony day had finally arrived, all Sam could think about was getting back to Lizzie. He had waited for the day he could be reunited with her for years and was told he had to travel to the Massachusetts State Coven to do so. The thought of protecting a child hadn't crossed Sam's mind of possible assignments he could've received. He'd thought his assignment would've been Lizzie. It seemed like the obvious choice.

Without a word, Naómi carefully stood up and passed her baby over to the faery standing by the white French doors of the library. "Please go and retrieve him."

The faery nodded and disappeared through the white doors
with the baby. A moment later the faery returned, holding
hands with a toddler with dark hair and chocolate brown eyes
just like his mother's. Naómi stood at a distance, looking
visibly uncomfortable but never taking her eyes off the child.
Sam stood up quickly as the child and faery approached him
cautiously. "Sam, this is my son, Matthew Hallow."

Even as he stood before the child that held the First King
Essence, Sam could feel the immense power that emanated
from his little body. It was intense.

Sam fell to his knees in shock. This child was the most
beautiful thing he'd ever seen, and his power had been the
most intense he'd ever felt. He couldn't make any sense of it,
the feelings he got from being around the child. He wanted
more than anything to always be in its presence; he wanted to
love it more than anything else and protect it from anything.

"Naómi, what is this? Why do I suddenly feel so…" Sam
had stumbled over his words as he took in the sight of the
child.

"It's a side effect of possessing the essence… Creatures
who are of the dark essence, such as vampires, humans,
lygoids, and some faeries, are naturally attracted to the First
King Essence. You'll want to love him and be near him
instinctually. Here," Naómi approached Sam and touched him
on the back of his shoulder. Her hand radiated with an
unfamiliar warmth for a moment before she released it. "I
enchanted you with a spell that gives you immunity to the side

effects of Matt's essence. It will no longer affect you like it
does others, but you'll still feel its presence."

"Did you do this to yourself as well?" Sam looked up at
her from the floor, still on his knees.

"I did. I needed to know if what I felt for my son was real."
Naómi turned away from the group quickly. Michael
remained on the loveseat in a contemplative trance, seemingly
staring into nothing.

"Mommy?" The child reached a hand to her slowly with a
confused look.

"Matt, this is your new friend. His name is Sam. You will
be spending quite some time with him from here on out." Sam
could hear Naómi's voice tremble as she tried to hide her
tears. Watching her turn her back on her first-born son
compared to how she stared at her newborn sickened Sam.

Looking back at the confused child staring at his mother
with a matching longingness she once expressed for her baby,
Sam realized the meaning behind Naómi's plea. This child
needed to be loved, and she was not likely to provide that for
him. "Matt, I would like to spend some time with you, if you
don't mind."

He took the little boy's hand in his, pulling the attention of
the small child who held an intense amount of power for one
being to hold, let alone a child. Matt and Sam exchanged a

long look that made Sam realize that he was going to commit his life to the protection of this child.

The boy's voice trembled as he accepted Sam's hand and offer, "Okay…"

From that day onward, Sam committed his life to protecting Matt. He would be whatever Matt needed him to be, whether it was a friend, a brother, or even a teacher. It did not matter, whatever Matt needed, Sam would provide. When he lost Matt to the Immortal Realm, he knew he had failed.

Sam knew it was only a matter of time before the coven found out about his epic failure. So, it came as no surprise when Lizzie came in with the mail one evening, and there was a letter addressed from the coven elders. A dark royal purple envelope sealed with a lavender wax seal with the letter V for the head elder, Gerrold Victoire.

The summons was for the next evening, with all five of the elders, which meant that they had every intention of punishing him. It was not a trial. It was an execution, and Sam was ready for it. He not only failed at protecting Matt, but also lost him in the Immortal Realm where the angels were likely to kill him by any means possible. As far as Sam was concerned, Matt and Geordie were as good as dead. There was no way to save them without the help of an angel.

The next evening, the drive to the coven house was long and arduous. Even though he was prepared for the worst to come because he knew he deserved it, a part of him was scared for what the elders were about to do to him. They were not known for being merciful.

Inside the grand hall of House Nastrond, the home of the deadliest vampire coven in the country, stood five dark wooden thrones in an equally dark room. There were no windows for natural lighting and the room was dimly lit with candles like an old castle.

Across the room, on either side were a set of doors where the elders began to enter. There were three male elders and two female elders, all over hundreds of years old. The sound of their footsteps echoed on the granite floor like a stabbing in Sam's chest as they all approached their respective thrones. As the leader of the elders, Gerrold took his place in the very center.

Even after knowing him for nearly two hundred years, Gerrold's presence intimidated Sam greatly. He was the same age as the vampire queens, Kathleena turned him as a young human nobleman. He was the first human Kathleena ever turned. If Sam had to guess, Gerrold had been turned in his mid-thirties. His skin was fair and young, while his beard was as full and neatly trimmed like the rest of his hair, and it was a rich dark brown. He towered over Sam, giving him an even more intimidating presence. Everything about Gerrold was greater than Sam, and he knew this.

Without a word, he turned away from Sam and took his seat. Once he was seated the other four elders took their seats as well. Gerrold spoke with a booming voice, "Bring him in!"

Behind him, a guard opened the main doors of the grand hall where Sam had entered. In came two more guardians with Jeremiah the face shifter in iron chains. His wrists were burnt from the iron, but he made no efforts to resist. Confused by the situation, Sam thought he was supposed to be privately meeting with the elders.

"Gerrold, what is the meaning of this? We approved a meeting with Sam Williams, but what is this business with the shifter?" The Kenyan warrior, Feye, boomed angrily, turning on Gerrold.

Gerrold's response was calm and serene, with no hints of any anger at Feye's tone. "Word of a betrayal has reached our coven, and it must be addressed. That is why I have called Sam here."

Two of the elders, Saku and Fiona, exchanged a look of curiosity. Fiona was the youngest of the elders, but still quite a few centuries old. She was originally from Ireland before being assigned to be an elder in the states. Saku was one of the oldest vampires hailing from Japan.

Gerrold and Jeremiah stared each other down with looks of pure hatred for a long silent moment. Since the fall of the Shadow Kingdom, there had been turmoil between them, but they weren't the only ones. There were many people directly involved with the Shadow Kingdom at the time of its fall that took issue with each other. It was part of the reason the species factions became so disconnected and therefore the kingdom divided irreparably.

"Standing before you now is the accused, Jeremiah of the Shadow Kingdom, now fallen, and current member of the Dark Order." A guardian announced as everyone finally settled. Sam realized this meeting was not an execution for himself, but for Jeremiah.

"What is he accused of?" Feye asked.

"Committing treason against the Dark Order and Shadow Kingdom by leaking sacred information about the king's lineage to an angel with the intent of having them killed."

Sam stared at Jeremiah in shock. It all added up. Jeremiah's cabin was well protected even from angels. The only way they could've found Geordie and Matt back during the fall would be if someone had leaked the information to them directly. That someone had to be Jeremiah. Geordie had mentioned he disappeared before Frost showed up. There was no doubt about it. Jeremiah put the events in motion because it was that event that awakened Matt's powers.

"And how do you plead?" Feye began to write his notes.

"Not guilty." Jeremiah continued to stare only at Gerrold. His plea caught everyone's attention, especially Sam's.

"Do you deny giving up information about King Kearan's descendants?" Fiona's voice was soft spoken and showed empathy.

"No, I do not, ma'am."

"But you do know that giving anyone information about the heir to the throne is an act against Kearan's dying wish?" She continued, clearly making a point. This was something that every faery knew.

"I am completely aware of his decree." Jeremiah sighed impatiently. "Look is there a reason why I was beat the crap out of and pulled out o' my home?"

"I'm sorry, I don't understand. You *knowingly* gave up information about the heir of King Kearan to an angel?" Saku leaned in closely, trying to wrap his head around the concept.

"Yes, I did, and I don't regret it. See unlike you people, I lost my loyalty to the kingdom when the kingdom itself proved to be self-destructive, divided, and treacherous to its own subjects." He pointed to everyone in the room. "If I'm going to betray anyone, I'm going to do it rogue."

"If you truly felt that way, you would've *officially* left the kingdom when Kearan died." The other female elder, Lisica laughed looking highly amused. "You knew your actions were an act of betrayal. What was your intent by helping this angel?"

Quick witted, Lisica was a Slavic turned half vampire shapeshifter hybrid who was not much younger than Gerrold and was considered his secret keeper. It was known that she would use her shapeshifting abilities to gather information for Gerrold and keep him informed about everything that happened within the coven. Her favorite form to take was a black fox with a silver tail.

"I had no hidden agenda, I simply did not care of the repercussions." Jeremiah rolled his eyes and readjusted himself.

"And who was this angel you, so *willingly* gave sacred information to?" Gerrold took a turn asking the questions with a smug smile. He was up to something; Sam could sense it.

"Frostbite Isaz." Every elder except Gerrold and Lisica gasped in shock. Somehow, he didn't seem surprised by this. It was almost as if he already knew.

"Do you know the severity of your crime?" Feye's heavy voice thundered throughout the great hall. "You sent the strongest angel to ever come out of the Immortal Realm after the heir to the throne! This angel, might I add, is the same angel who has unwaveringly hunted the fallen for almost seventy years!"

"Once again, I am completely aware of what I have done, and hold no regrets."

"Are there any other confessions you would like to make before we reach a verdict?" Gerrold was smiling again, but before Jeremiah could respond, he then turned to Sam and finally addressed his presence. "Sam, you are called here today to witness this occasion and give your thoughts since it has recently come to our attention that under your jurisdiction you allowed the fallen and the heir to the Shadow Kingdom to be kidnapped into the Immortal Realm."

"Yes, sir. I am truly sorry for my complete failure–"

"Yes, yes, I am sure you truly are." Gerrold interrupted Sam, waving him silent with an indifferent hand. "I must ask, do you personally, with the knowledge you have now, think that your two friends would have wound up in the Immortal Realm, if they were not discovered in the accused's home?"

Sam looked over to Jeremiah. On some level he had always respected the position Jeremiah held between the vampires and faeries over the years. Although he was not a vampire himself, he once acted as an ambassador between the two species, contributing to the lasting peace they had with each other. He did not know Jeremiah well, and thought very little of him, but he respected him. That did not excuse the fact that Jeremiah knowingly betrayed Geordie and Matt, therefore causing a chain of events that inevitably led to their kidnapping.

"No, I believe they would still be as safe as they could be with me in the Mortal Realm had Jeremiah not interfered with their safety." Sam felt guilty for his response, but as a guardian, he was sworn to the truth.

"And do you recall this man's full list of abilities?" Gerrold asked, his eyes narrowing on Sam firmly.

He had to think about it for a moment. It was no secret; he did have many talents that most faeries did not. "He can change his appearance at will."

"Is that all?"

At that point Sam wasn't sure what the correct answer was. He felt as though he were missing something. "Yes?"

"I see." Gerrold spoke quietly as Fiona handed him a small pile of papers before continuing, "It might interest you to know, Jeremiah also possesses clairvoyant abilities much like his fellow Lucis faery kin but stronger. We have reason to believe that these psychic-like abilities contributed to his actions against your charge."

"Yes, I betrayed the Shadow Kingdom knowingly. I saw a vision of the angels' approach on the fallen and the heir to the throne. Within that vision I also foresaw the awakening of the truest Potential, along with the other three Potentials. With their awakenings, a great war will begin between the four Potentials spanning over many years. The downfall of our greatest enemy will finally come, but not before his greatest rise. The war will not end there. It will continue and with its end the Shadow Kingdom shall come to reform. We will all be saved, but not by the Shadow King.

"I am the one who brought the fallen to my cabin. I am also the one who told Frostbite about the Potentials. While, yes, I have committed these crimes, I am also the reason why that girl is still alive after the massacre turned countless creatures into lygoids upon the death of her parents. As far as you people are concerned, I have no intentions of helping a society that lies to its subjects while using them as sacrifices in its pointless wars and experiments. I will have no part in shunning an innocent girl from society just to spare some heartache from the angels. I may not agree with the idea of anyone joining your coven, but I'm not going to stop anyone from joining if it is their choice. If you all have issues with the angels interfering in *your* world, then you need to buck up, stop hiding behind your well-placed deceit, and do something about it! Don't use an innocent girl to keep your enemies at bay, and don't feed her to the wolves when she can't even defend herself!" Jeremiah yelled at the whole group of elders, leaving them all speechless and guilty looking, except Lisica and Gerrold. They were completely unfazed by his confessional monologue.

"But weren't *you* the one who 'fed her to the wolves' by telling her pursuer her location?" Gerrold tried to trap Jeremiah.

"I don't see how that was any relevance since it got both to awaken to their true powers in the end. The Potential now can harness his power, and the fallen can finally learn to defend herself with her angelic abilities." Gerrold's ruse didn't work.

"Well, if there's nothing more to be said, I think the elders will now come to a verdict." Gerrold wrote his decision on a piece of parchment and passed it around, leaving Lisica for last. "Lisica, call it. What is the verdict?"

"Kill him." She crumpled the paper in her fist and threw it at Jeremiah's face with a bored look.

Without hesitation, the guardians tore apart Jeremiah's body, limb from limb. Blood pooled everywhere over the marble floors from where his head and arms used to be.

Lisica was the first to leave, followed by Saku, Feye, and Fiona. Saku and Fiona looked mortified but said nothing. Feye was visibly filled with pure rage. Whether that was directed toward Jeremiah or Gerrold, Sam couldn't tell. Just as Feye passed Gerrold, he whispered something to Gerrold inaudible even to Sam's vampiric hearing.

The only ones left were Sam, Gerrold, and the torn apart limbs of the faery once known as Jeremiah. Even though the natural blood lust of a vampire was strong in Sam, he couldn't help but feel disgusted at what he had just witnessed. Was the coven more corrupt than Sam thought? "Sam, may I speak with you?"

Sam tore his eyes away from the massive pools of faery blood to look over to Gerrold who was watching him carefully in his perfectly pressed black and purple pinstripe suit. With both hands in either pocket, Gerrold approached Sam and gestured for him to follow, leaving the grand hall.

"I would like you to know that I do not fault you for the loss of your friends. From what my sources have informed me, they were coerced by a band of extremists who follow one of the vampires' greatest enemies. If I had to guess, they are hoping that they can somehow release their leader. I strongly believe this endeavor will end in failure."

"Sir, if you don't mind me asking, how do you know all of this?" Sam hoped Gerrold would admit that he had Lisica out spying on him.

"As the head elder of the Massachusetts State Vampire Coven, there isn't much that happens in this state that I am not aware of. I have many sources of intel." It was a roundabout way of saying he had Lisica spy for him.

Sam wished that Gerrold would reach his point so he could go home and sit with his self-loathing. He didn't want to play any of Gerrold's games, and he certainly wasn't expecting to walk out of the grand hall alive, so when he did, he suddenly had the strong urge to return home to be alone.

"I know you feel as though you failed your assignment to protect that human boy, but it may interest you to know he's not likely dead."

"There's no way to know that. And even if he is alive, it's not like there's any way to bring him back." Sam groaned impatiently, scratching his unkempt beard absentmindedly. Since Matt and Geordie's disappearance, all regards for personal hygiene had left Sam's thoughts. For the first time since he was turned, he had an unkempt scraggly beard.

"You might be surprised. Ezra Daron cannot personally kill him if he really is the heir to the Shadow Kingdom, and if she realizes that, then yes, she might try to hold him hostage, but we might be able to pave the way to rescuing your friends."

"You think you can negotiate with Ezra Daron, the leader of all the angels who hates vampires?" Sam laughed for the first time in weeks. He genuinely thought Gerrold was crazy.

"I've known her for many years; you'd be surprised at what I am capable of accomplishing." Gerrold smiled, his sharp blue eyes twinkling deviously. On some level, Sam fully believed Gerrold was capable of practically anything.

"And why would you help me with this task?" Sam asked suspiciously. "What's in it for you?"

"Let's just say, I have an invested interest in Geordie Vollner, and I feel as though it is time we finally met. I wouldn't mind also meeting your friend I've heard about as well. He might prove to be quite the ally in the not-so-distant future." Gerrold paused as a group of faeries turned down the hall towards them.

Sam realized they were slowly making their way back toward the front gates of the castle. "Sam, you have been a valuable asset to the coven for years now, and I am not a man who likes to easily throw away assets. I would like to help you with your problems, that includes the declining health of your sire, Lizzie Levington. Bring her in to be examined and we will do everything we can to help her under Fiona's care; and then while she does that, you and I will investigate our options for bringing your friends back to the Mortal Realm."

"And what do you want in return for your act of generosity?" Sam was baffled at Gerrold's selflessness especially because Gerrold was not a selfless person. He only did things that ultimately benefited him. Sam let it be clear that he was skeptical of the entire situation.

They were now in the front courtyard where the driver that escorted him to the coven house was still waiting beside the shiny Mercedes with black tinted windows. By this point it was nearly light out, all the vampires would be turning in for the day, and Sam still needed to get to shelter as well.

"I have a strong feeling Jeremiah's visions were not too far off from the truth, and I would like to prevent that future from happening. I believe Geordie Vollner and your friend are the keys to preventing such a future from happening.

"The upcoming anniversary of our coven will be this summer solstice in June. I would like you to bring them in for the celebrations as our guests. And I would like you to turn them as well. It would be nice to extend the coven's connection to potentially powerful beings." The last part confused Sam, but he wasn't in a position to refuse or question him especially because Gerrold was his superior.

"Fine. I will do it. But after them, I am not turning anyone else." Vexus had taught Sam that turning anyone into a vampire was considered sacred and intimate, and it was not something to be taken lightly. Sam had hoped that he could do it with someone very special to him, but he wasn't sure if there would be someone more special to him than Lizzie.

"Good, now go clean yourself up and get some sleep. You look like crap. I want you back here in two weeks refreshed and ready to get back to work." He then turned and went back into the castle, leaving Sam to contemplate his appearance before getting back into the company vehicle to head to the loft.

As planned, a couple weeks later Sam cleaned up and was ready for whatever Gerrold wanted to dish out for him to do. Sam half expected Gerrold to give him some sort of menial task but that didn't happen. The moment Sam was let into Gerrold's dimly lit office, he could tell that the elder was in quite a frenzy. "Were you aware that both Breena and Vexus Vollner have been captured and brought to the Immortal Realm by angels?"

Gerrold's voice was distressed, which Sam was not used to hearing. It made Sam uneasy seeing Gerrold like that, but not as uneasy knowing Vexus got captured. Sam couldn't help but feel personally attacked by the angels knowing everyone he cared about was trapped in the Immortal Realm against their will. "I knew about Breena, but I did not know about Vexus. He must have tried to go after her when he found out and got himself captured."

"And why didn't you share this information when *you* first learned of it?" Gerrold snapped slightly.

"I didn't think it was relevant since there was no way to guarantee her safe return while we have no way of getting over there." Sam's head was still reeling over the thought of Vexus taking matters into his own hands and getting captured over it. How could he be so stupid?

"Perhaps you're right. We will need to speak to someone on that side to gather a better idea of what is going on." Gerrold rubbed his chin pensively, but before he could say anything more, an angel walked into Gerrold's office unannounced.

"Well perhaps it is your lucky day, Gerrold Victoire."
Everything about the angel's appearance looked charred and
burnt. His hair was dark with grey streaks in it, his skin
equally as dark with eyes bright and fiery in contrast to the
rest of his appearance. The man had an intimidating flare to
his demeanor with the imperfect complexion he bore. The
thing that stood out about him the most was that he wore a
large pendant of a bird's eye with flames in the center.
Engulfed in the flames was a small black gemstone that
looked like a piece of coal burning. This was the pendant of
the angel of fire. Was this one of the angels who attacked
Geordie at Jeremiah's cabin?

"Why are you here, Pyralis?" Gerrold asked impatiently.
Sam found the number of times the angels appeared in the
Mortal Realm in such a short period of time alarming.

"Councilor Ezra wishes to speak with you… alone." The
man named Pyralis looked over at Sam with a disgusted look.

"Sam here is directly involved with my affairs right now;
he will be joining me regardless of how Ezra feels about it. If
she has any issues, she can bring it up with me." Gerrold
turned to leave his office as he spoke. "Come, both of you."

They headed over to the other side of the castle with the
angel closely by their side. At the highest point of the castle
there was a tower Sam had never before been permitted to
enter overlooking the courtyard. Inside, there was an
enchanted planetarium with an overwhelmingly large
rectangular stand with metal double doors in the center. As
they drew closer to the object, Sam felt a weight over his body

as if something was attempting to put him to his knees. The moment Gerrold opened the metal doors, a burst of energy flooded the room as though the earth's gravity suddenly slammed down on Sam. Alongside the energy, a thick eerie fog filled the room, making it impossible to see the surrounding walls of the room.

"That feeling you're getting, Sam, it is what happens when the dark and light essences mix to form a magical energy. This mirror is a gateway for communication between the Immortal Realm and the Mortal Realm. It is how I am able to speak to Ezra Daron, the leader of the angels." Gerrold finally explained what was going on to Sam. Eventually Sam managed to get over the weight of the magic and was able to get back on his feet, but it took all his energy to not let it overcome him.

Behind them, Pyralis closed the doors to the planetarium, briefly disappearing into the fog, and then reappearing once more after the sound of doors closing echoed throughout the room. Sam noticed that the mirror was double sided once opened. On one side were black stone etchings of what appeared to be demonic creatures and, on the side facing Pyralis and Gerrold were white stone etchings of angelic creatures. Pyralis began whispering something in an unknown language quietly and after a few seconds the mirror began to pulsate with a dim light, and a beautiful young woman appeared in the reflection of the mirror.

Ezra Daron was nothing like what Sam had imagined of the person who swore a lifelong hatred for the vampire race. He imagined a strong, intimidating, large woman with a similar demeanor to Melandria Daron. Instead, she resembled something like real life Daisy Buchanan. She had an opalescent vintage look about her.

"Gerrold, you look the same as ever. Demonic youth treats you well, I guess." Ezra greeted her audience without so much as a hello. She quickly turned to Sam, "And who is this?"

"This is Samuel Williams, he is a guardian who will be working alongside me for a while. I found his insight and perspective to be useful for what I am trying to accomplish. What is it that you want, Ezra?"

"I just wanted you to know that I have Geordie Vollner, alongside the rest of her family, here in the Immortal Realm." The fog pulsed with lights as she spoke, creating a luminous effect in the room.

"I am fully aware you are holding her, Breena and Vexus, alongside a human. Although I have been aware of this for quite some time, it's nice of you to just now let me know about this almost a month later."

"Oh, you know time works differently between the two realms. For me it has only been a couple of hours since they arrived." Ezra giggled slightly. "But it's not just Breena and Vexus, I have their son as well, but don't worry, I am treating him as a guest, not a prisoner."

"Excuse me?" Gerrold looked over to Sam out of the corner of his eye. Personally, Sam didn't care that much if

Seth was in the Immortal Realm. He knew that as a fae, Seth could easily walk out of the Immortal Realm any time he wanted. Sam was only concerned for Geordie and Matt, mostly Matt.

"Trust me, it's just as much of a shock to me as it is to you. It seems Pyralis' son Pyre caught Vexus Vollner by surprise. Frost and Pyre together caught Breena, and from what I have been told, Geordie and her companions were coerced here by two vampires. As it stands now, I possess the entirety of one of the most powerful vampire families to come after the Daron queens and that is not even the best part."

"Ezra, I demand that you send Geordie and her family back. They do not belong in your world!" Gerrold was furious with Ezra. Both of them knew something about the Vollners that neither of them were making clear, probably because of Sam's presence in their meeting.

"Ah but that's the thing, Geordie doesn't belong in your world either, does she? She doesn't belong with anyone, and she doesn't have a twin. As far as the rest of them are concerned. I have no quarrels with them."

"That remains to be seen, Ezra. Do you have a point in boasting that you have all these assets that rightfully belong to the vampires? What more do you want?"

Ezra burst out laughing hysterically. Sam couldn't help but think he was lost on the punch line of a private joke. It seemed like she was just toying with them.

"You really don't know, do you?" Her laughter slowly ceased as she took a long hard breath to stop. Between her sighs and smile, a few chuckles escaped her thin lips.

"Know *what*?" Gerrold asked impatiently. Sam was also growing impatient as the room continued to make him feel fatigued and sick to his stomach from the strong magical energy. He yearned to leave the room as soon as possible.

"That *boy*, the human who is a Potential with stronger levels of darkness in him for even human standards…"

"Yes? What is it, woman?" Gerrold barked harshly at her.

"The heir to the Shadow Kingdom is *your* son." She spoke with a snide smile. If Sam's heart hadn't stopped over a century ago, it would've stopped just then.

"That cannot be possible!" Gerrold growled.

"Oh, but it is! Maybe you should have a talk with the boy's mother, Naómi Hallow. He's the spitting image of you."

Sam couldn't take his eyes off Gerrold in horror. If this really was true, once they got Matt safely back to the Mortal Realm, there would be no protecting him from Gerrold's clutches. Gerrold would do everything in his power to get his hands on Matt and use him to his benefit. There was no way Sam could allow this to happen. He needed to figure out a way to keep Matt away from Gerrold.

"What does this have to do with anything?" Gerrold ignored Ezra's comment about Matt's mother.

"Well, I have all the Vollners, the heir to the Shadow Kingdom, who is also your son, and I have discovered the other Potentials are here as well. I'm honestly not sure how any of these people managed to get into the Immortal Realm undamaged, but we have more prevalent problems on both of our hands. Two vampires that are here are trying to break a dangerous lygoid out of this realm as we speak. All of them have managed to slip under my radar thanks to the lygoid shrouding the entire city in darkness. Gerrold, this is a problem that could affect both of our worlds."

"And the only person capable of stopping or controlling lygoids is the Shadow King, who is dead. We could face a lygoid epidemic of vast proportions." Gerrold processed the danger they all were faced with. If the lygoids escaped the Immortal Realm, it could flood both realms with darkness. This could result in the balance being tipped too far to fix.

"Exactly. If the boy met the lygoid now, he wouldn't stand a chance against such a supreme being. That lygoid could kill your boy with a single flick of his finger. I am thinking of sending him back to your world, so he can discover his lineage and give us a fighting chance of getting through the problems at hand."

"And what about Geordie?" Gerrold asked.

"She doesn't get to leave here."

"And why is that?" Gerrold's voice suddenly boomed throughout the whole room in an echo.

"She signed a contract with me. She can only be killed here in the Immortal Realm by her own hand. No one else can kill her so long as she's here, and I am sure as hell not going to send her back to the Mortal Realm where anyone can kill her. Take her family back, I don't want them anyway, but you can't have Geordie."

"Why are you doing this?" Gerrold growled deeply, gripping the mirror with a fierce expression of hatred even though touching the mirror was clearly causing him pain.

"It's simple, really. I want to harness her power as an angel and extract it. But I can only do that if she's willing. Until then, she stays, safe, in the Immortal Realm."

"That is *not* happening!" Gerrold finally snapped. Then turning to Pyralis, who was silent the entire time, Gerrold barked, "End this connection, and get out of my castle!"

Once the connection was severed, Pyralis disappeared, and the mirror's doors were closed. Without another word Gerrold stormed out of the no longer foggy planetarium, giving Sam no indication of a plan as they headed back down to the main part of the castle. It was almost difficult to keep up with Gerrold; his anger caused him to move at a speed faster than even Sam was capable of summoning after feeling drained of his energy.

"Gerrold, what is happening? Where are we going?" Sam
attempted to keep up with him as they sped down the halls.

"We are going to Daron Academy. I would like to speak to
the supposed mother of my child."

Two days later, Sam and Gerrold arrived in San Francisco
airport an hour after sundown. A specially ordered limousine
greeted them at the plane with at least ten guardians at
Gerrold's disposal. At first Sam was stunned at the level of
security for one elder, but he remembered that Gerrold wasn't
just an elder. He was also the founding member of the
Victoire royal clan. He was the most powerful vampire alive
next to Queen Kathleena.

"If you already have these guardians at your disposal, then
you don't really need me, do you?" Sam stared at the
guardians skeptically. He didn't recognize any of them.

"It's actually quite the opposite in many ways. They need
me more than I need them, and I need only need you for the
time being." Gerrold glanced quickly between Sam and the
other guardians. "It's just customary for them to send this
many guardians when they find out a royal family member is
visiting… such hospitality."

Sam watched Gerrold croon at the guardians as he slid his
narrow body gracefully into the limo. He then gestured
toward the guardians and told them to leave. He then
beckoned Sam over to the limo. Sam also climbed in, sitting
across from Gerrold. As soon as the doors were closed it was
completely dark. With the tinted windows, nearly no light

shone through. This was a customized feature for turned vampires who happen to need to travel during the daylight hours. For Sam and Gerrold, this was not the case due to it being after dark already.

"Can you finally tell me how you and Naómi Hallow know each other? How are you Matt's father? And just so you're aware, I haven't told her Matt is missing yet." Ever since he lost Matt, Sam dreaded the idea of facing Naómi. He didn't fear the idea of being hexed. He feared her anger and disappointment in Sam for losing her eldest son. He feared her resentment towards him for allowing herself to trust a vampire. "How is it possible for a vampire and a witch to reproduce a completely normal magicless human?"

None of it made any sense. Nick was born a vampire and Sam was always under the impression Matt and Nick shared different fathers. There were five years between Matt and Nick, so, it was possible for Gerrold to either be both their fathers or only Matt's and still not know regardless.

"About twenty-six years ago, I used Naómi so she would make me curses and potions to use on my enemies. I led her to believe that I loved her so she would do these things for me. And as I am sure you already know, male vampires do not require an eclipse to reproduce, so she eventually got pregnant. Afterwards she found out what I was up to with the curses and potions and told me she wanted nothing to do with me any longer. I was easily obliged and left her to deal with her destitute situation. I honestly haven't seen her since, but I did hear she eventually got a job teaching at Daron Academy."

"And since then, you had never bothered to inquire about her wellbeing?" Sam snapped. How could Gerrold be so selfish?

"You must realize, Sam, that I am over a thousand years old. There have been only two things I have ever cared about: my wife and my life. I have already reproduced the heirs to the Victoire clan, so for what reason would I possibly care if a produced bastard boy or two with no claim to my positions in life?" Gerrold paused, taking a long deep breath before he continued, "I can see now that I was wrong before to let Naómi raise Matt by herself. And I wish to rectify the situation."

"You do realize that no matter how much you try to redeem yourself, your *wife* will never let you back in her good graces. Nor will she ever let you set foot back on Daron Island." Sam pointed out.

"True." He shrugged. A slight smile curved on his lips as he reminisced about the past. "But I will always love her, no matter how she feels about me. And no matter how many other lovers she takes.

"I'm sure she has good reason to hate you." Sam spoke softly to himself, completely aware that Gerrold could still hear him.

"I have done a lot of things, most for the good of our kind. Many of those things Kathleena did not approve of. You see, unlike her, I do not let morality get in the way of what needs to be done. She is ruined by her morals, but it doesn't matter at the end of the day. What I do is to keep her, her sisters, and all other vampires safe, and I will always do what needs to be done, regardless of how many people's feelings I hurt." Gerrold's words barely influenced Sam.

They barely influenced anyone anymore. The queens, and all the vampires who knew of Gerrold's long history, were no longer surprised by his misdeeds or lack of morality. He simply had no regard for his behavior as a vampire. Sam hated it, because that sort of behavior was the reason the other species, especially the angels, hated the vampires.

Sam and Gerrold sat in silence as they left San Francisco and headed for the Kensington Hills. Sam grew fed up with the darkness of the limo and unrolled his window. The smell of the nighttime air amongst redwood trees greeted him blissfully. He could finally hear the crackle of rubber tire on rocks and dirt and the sonorousness of the forest animals communicating together. As they drove through the dirt paths of the forest, Sam caught glimpses of young mortal vampires and shape shifters running in the darkness of the night. They were students of Daron Academy. It would only be a few minutes now before they would arrive at the gates of the academy. After that it was another ten-minute ride to get past the dorm houses to the main educational buildings.

"Ah! We've arrived!" Gerrold spoke excitedly as they pulled through the gates and continued through the residential district of the campus. As they passed, students stopped left and right, staring at the limousine in curiosity.

Eventually the vehicle pulled over at the courtyard of the education district, and Sam climbed out of the limousine first, followed by Gerrold. Sam felt some nostalgia as he walked the campus stone paths to the humanities building.

The last time he stepped foot on campus was the day he was officially declared a guardian. His fingers met the cold metal around his wrist that was the charm bracelet they received after pledging loyalty to the queens. Every guardian had one so you could easily identify them by the bracelet. From what Sam could tell, there were guardians everywhere. No matter where he looked, there was a guardian standing nearby, and all of them were paired in teams of two. Daron Academy never used to have such high security detail.

"Gerrold, why are there so many guardians here?" Sam whispered. Gerrold looked just as surprised at the security measures as Sam was.

"I'm not sure to be honest. The Californian covens don't speak to the Massachusetts coven, so I do not know the ongoings over here." Gerrold turned to the main humanities building. Everything inside was the same as it was twenty years ago.

They were greeted by two grand staircases that curved toward a large archway that opened to another hallway on the ground floor. The building was beautifully designed with natural mahogany wood paneling and dark emerald green trimming. During the daytime hours, sunlight shone in adding a plentiful amount of natural lighting for the faeries and shape shifters. But with having vampires attend the academy as well, the school had to have a nocturnal schedule in addition to the diurnal schedule.

Up to the second floor they turned left into the department where Naómi taught in a classroom at the end of the hallway. Gerrold swiftly glided over to an abandoned bench, crossing his legs and folding his hands neatly over his knees. Sam took this as a sign that it was his job to announce their arrival. Taking a deep breath, Sam steadied himself, trying to compose his thoughts as he slowly gripped the door handle with his pale boney fingers. With his free hand, he knocked twice on the door and cracked it open so only his face peered through to see Naómi with her students. As soon as she realized it was Sam, her face hardened into a grimace.

She turned to her class and dismissed them as they all stared at Sam in curiosity. About thirty students quietly gathered their things and left. A few girls caught sight of Gerrold and stared at him with awe. Sam rolled his eyes at the thought of teenage girls clamoring at Gerrold's royal feet. He didn't understand what it was that women found so alluring about Gerrold. Sam found him repulsive in every way imaginable. It was probably because they didn't know what Sam knew. They were naïve to the truth behind Gerrold's dark past. It would explain why Naómi fell prey to Gerrold when she was so young.

As soon as every student had cleared the area, Gerrold stood up and joined Sam in entering Naómi's classroom. Inside, the walls were the same wood paneling as the hallways but featured a few pieces of artwork. At the front of the room there were three paintings of each of the queens. The wall across from the door had a large painting of the first elemental faeries with their dragons.

Sam took a deep breath and began nervously, "Naómi, I don't know if you remember this man, but his–"

"I remember you, *Gerrold Victoire*. Don't think that I don't." She spoke venomously, cutting off Sam and ignoring him for the time being. As she stared up at Gerrold, Sam could actually detect a hint of hesitation in her stature. He could tell that no matter how confident she felt around vampires, she was still untrusting of them.

"It's nice to see you again, Naómi. Mortality has treated you well over the years. You are just as beautiful as the last time I saw you." Gerrold smiled at her as he thumbed through her student's assignments.

"Naómi, I –

"Bite your tongue, *boy*. I will get to you in a moment!" Naómi snapped at Sam, cutting him off once more. This time he silently backed into a corner, far from her, and pretended to be interested in an essay project pinned up on the back wall.

Gerrold let a small chuckle escape for Sam to hear and apologized, "Oh, don't be mad at him, darling. I'm the one who brought him here. He's under strict orders to go where I go until I say otherwise."

"That's *not* what I am mad about." She truly had no problems with showing her anger when in front of a powerful vampire. "You don't honestly expect me to be stupid enough to believe that your arrival is purely coincidental, do you? I know you're here about my son. Who is stuck in the Immortal Realm!"

"Well, you're not the only one who has the right to be upset." Where Gerrold's voice was quiet and composed, Naómi's was filled with emotion. Sam felt safe in thinking it was a bad idea to come to see her before retrieving her son.

At least if they retrieved Matt beforehand, Sam could tell Naómi it was just a small mistake and leave out the details of the events. But Gerrold insisted on seeing her. "I know I disappointed you, Naómi. I did the one thing you told me to specifically not do when you entrusted the care of your son to me. But for one moment, I need you to look past your human emotions and help us find a way to get Matt back. For Matt's sake."

Naómi stared at Sam with furious eyes that planted a heavy lump in the back of his throat for a long time. The look she gave him was so menacing that he immediately regretted saying anything at all. He knew it wasn't much of an apology but on some level he didn't care. There were more important things to worry about than Naómi's feelings about the situation. For example, Matt and Geordie's safe return was the immediate problem at hand.

After a long moment of silence, Gerrold finally broke the ice, "Naómi we have unfinished business." He offered her one of the student chairs before sitting himself down in her large desk chair.

"You're right. We do." She took the seat Gerrold offered, facing him. "So, what do you want to know?"

"Are you the great descendent of Kearan Hallow, king of the Shadow Kingdom?" Naómi's expression was unfaltering as Gerrold broke the very last wish that Kearan Hallow decreed on his deathbed. No creature of shadow shall question nor speak of the identity of the king's heirs.

"Yes, I am." Naómi pursed her lips in satisfaction and crossed her legs, giving her a regal look.

"Why didn't you tell me when you found out you were pregnant with your first son, Matt? Did it not occur to you that he could be our hope for survival?"

"Your survival, Gerrold? Or the vampires?" Naómi made a shot at Gerrold. So, she *was* fully aware of who she was dealing with.

"You know what I mean." He growled as he crushed a pen in his fist. Ink exploded onto one of her folders. Naómi quickly threw a Kleenex box of tissues at him, and he began to mop up the spackles of dark ink from the manila folder.

"I hope you know: I don't care if you or the entire race of vampires dies out. At least this world will be rid of people with the likes of *you*!" Bitterness dripped off every word she spoke to Gerrold. Sam was amazed that she even dared to speak that way to a royal vampire, let alone Gerrold.

Gerrrold jumped at her menacingly, baring his fangs at her, "Woman, you better hope that neither I nor the rest of the vampires die out any time soon. You need us more than you think."

Naómi not once moved nor flinched at Gerrold's demeanor as he loomed threateningly over her. Her voice this time was soft spoken, but remained perfectly calm and serious, "I rather doubt that, Gerrold. I can handle almost anything."

"You arrogant little girl, you cannot even take care of your mortal son without the help of a vampire guardian." Gerrold indicated toward Sam. "I'd like to see how you'll do when an entire army of lygoids comes bearing down upon your pathetic little school you so desperately attempt to protect."

"That's impossible. Lygoids don't run in groups, let alone armies." Naómi spoke with such a disbelieving tone that it shocked Sam that she was not taking the conversation more seriously. She absolutely refused to heed any of Gerrold's well intended warnings.

"They do if they have a strong enough leader. Someone who can command the essence that dwells within them would easily control an army of lygoids." Gerrold sat back down in his chair, retracting his fangs finally. "According to Ezra Daron, the worst possible lygoid you'd ever want to escape the Immortal Realm is about to do just that. So, either get with the program, or turn me towards someone who *can* help me."

Naómi was unresponsive. In the past, Sam knew her only
by her reputation with battling lygoids. She hated them and
everything they stood for more than she hated most vampires.
She would unhesitatingly do anything to prevent them from
being united and having power.

"This lygoid's arrival… it means war is upon us, doesn't
it?" She looked up to Gerrold with a subtly lachrymose
expression.

"I'm afraid that is exactly what it means. This is why we
need your help." Gerrold handed her his handkerchief as he
began to pace the room impatiently. After a long droning
silence, Gerrold finally turned back to Sam this time, "We
need to find a way to get Matt, Geordie, and Seth back as soon
as possible. Who knows how long they've been there. If the
dangers Ezra warned me about come true, we will need Matt
to be at his fullest potential. Naómi, I must ask, why didn't
you tell me about our son?"

"Because I know you!" Naómi shoved the desk in front of
her violently out of the way as she suddenly forced herself in
Gerrold's face. Behind the unwavering anger in her dark eyes,
eyes like Matt's, Sam could see a glimmer of fear. It was
small, and barely noticeable, but it was there.

She was only twenty-two when he met Naómi. He had
known her for so long that it was next to impossible for her to
hide her true emotions from him. He could tell that the
immediate anger stemmed from the fact that Gerrold had the
audacity to bring this up after so much time had passed, but
the fear was for something else. The fear stemmed from the

questionable idea that Gerrold might try with all his willpower to have some sort of back curtain influence on Matt's life, maybe even Nick.

"If I had told you that I was the descendent of Kearan Hallow, you would have taken Matt away from me and raised him to be a war machine! I would never allow that for either of my sons."

"But they're Potentials; it's their destiny to lead the great factions of darkness." Sam spoke softly thinking about the first time he'd met Naómi. She was young and alone.

"Nick is *not* a Potential and thank *god* for that." Her voice quivered with fear as she spoke. "I don't know what I would do if they were both Potentials."

"What are you talking about? They're both from the same family!"

"I understand now…" Gerrold cut in, rubbing the stubble of his chin. "Being a Potential is not determined by your family line. Just because Matt and Nick share the same lineage doesn't mean they both share the marks of being a leader."

"He's right, Sam. To be a Potential, you must have the willpower or marks of a leader. That ability to lead gives the Potentials the ability to command the dark essence within dark creatures. To be king, the other Potentials must die or the king must have become the full embodiment of the great factions of darkness. The whole reason I didn't want Matt a part of this was because I didn't want to risk anyone trying to kill him, but I guess I have *you* to thank for all this happening." The look of pure hatred directed at Sam terrified him suddenly more than anything else in the world. The last thing he'd ever wanted was to get on the bad side of a witch, let alone Naómi.

"I think I know who two other Potentials are then." Sam tried to change the subject while being helpful, but Gerrold shook his head.

"Don't tell us. Guard that information with yourself, Sam. Our priority right now is to find a way to get Matt, Geordie, and Seth back to this world safely."

"There might be a way for us to get them back, but I don't know if it will work." Naómi gathered her coat as she spoke. "We're going to have to go underground for this."

"What is it?" Sam followed her eagerly, Gerrold taking his time behind them.

"You'll see."

As they left the humanities building of Daron Academy, Naómi took them behind the school into the mountains where they discovered a covered entrance to a large cave that sloped downhill to a tunnel gradually. Inside, a path of blue lights lined the walls of the cave showing them the way inside. Naómi led the way down the lit path that eventually turned into a pool of water. For a while it was just damp dirt until suddenly Sam took a plunge face first into ice cold water.

Splashing toward him quickly, Gerrold pulled Sam out of the water and straightened his clothing out violently. Gerrold mumbled, not truly paying attention to Sam, "Are you alright?"

Sam nodded silently knowing Gerrold wasn't looking nor cared about whether or not he was alright. He was focused on something else. Up ahead, Naómi was standing in front a large stone mirror with an arched top practically identical to the one in the planetarium of the coven house. Both she and Gerrold were completely unfazed by the bone chilling water as they stared at the mirror in awe. The water completely closed in around the mirror with only a small slab of stone separating it from the water.

"It's a mirror." Gerrold pointed out with a bored tone.

"You should know better than to just see things with your eyes, Gerrold." Naómi spoke without taking her eyes off the mirror.

Gerrold sighed and grumbled, "What *should* I be looking at?"

"Nothing at the moment." Naómi traced her hands over the mirror's frame slowly, making sure to touch every inch of it, top to bottom. "This mirror was once used as a gateway for travelling between the realms. It linked creatures of darkness to the Immortal Realm and the Mortal Realm, as well as the Shadow Kingdom."

"Wait, what are you talking about? I thought the Shadow Kingdom was already in the Mortal Realm." Sam approached the mirror, taking a closer look at it.

"You're right, it is in the Mortal Realm. But it isn't as well." Naómi took a seat on the small slab of stone, letting the tips of her boots touch the water ever so slightly. "The Shadow Kingdom was an underground city that only creatures of darkness could access. This mirror was once the doorway to it."

"What happened to it?" Gerrold asked, as he stared at a cracked hole in the frame. "It's missing a piece."

"The mirror was shattered after everyone left the kingdom and when someone tried to put it back together, there was a piece of the stone frame missing. No one has seen the piece since the mirror was destroyed." Naómi's fingers softly traced the large crack and gripped it tightly.

"If the mirror is broken, then what's the point of bringing us here?" Gerrold started heading back to the entrance of the cave. Naómi quickly got up and stopped him, grabbing him by the arm.

"If you stop for a minute and just think about it, you can understand. There was a time when you would listen to me for hours about our intertwining history. Just listen to me now…” Gerrold turned back to her slowly, staring into her dark eyes deeply.

Sam turned away quickly. Something told him Gerrold did care for her, and Naómi wanted it to be so. “If you somehow located the missing stone piece, and you reopened the gateway to the Immortal Realm, Matt will be able to come through.”

“And we could get Geordie and Seth back… because they’re all creatures of darkness.” Sam realized out loud.

“Exactly.”

“And how do we find it if no one has seen it in a long time?” Gerrold groaned.

“Ask Ezra Daron. Supposedly she knows what happened when the mirror got destroyed.” Naómi finally let go of Gerrold and headed back to the entrance of the cave.

Gerrold scoffed a mocking laugh, “And what are you going to do while Sam and I search for this missing stone piece?”

“I will try to find information that could help you in my down time when I’m not *working*! You two idiots better find a way to get my son back or I will have to take this up with your queens!”

“I’m sure we can avoid the hostilities and all agree to not let the situation get that far.” Gerrold pushed his way past

Naómi as she scowled at him. "Sam, I must return to Boston.
I want you to remain here with Naómi to ensure she acts on
her part accordingly. Since you are the guardian to her son, I
cannot think of anyone more appropriate than you."

CHAPTER 15

FROST
THE IMMORTAL REALM

When Frost, Orpheus and Ezra first entered the prison building, she immediately sensed a powerful magical presence that didn't belong to any lygoid or vampire. There was no way it belonged to anyone in their group, but it belonged to someone nearly as powerful. The magical presence came off the sleeping bodies that were the prison staff. Ezra and Orpheus stepped over the sleeping Lucis faeries without acknowledging them.

From the hall leading to the prison cells, a black fog seeped out from under the cracks of the door, a sign of Quinn's power getting ready to be unleashed. With a swift flick of her wrist, Ezra waved her hand and the door to the hall of the cells blew off their hinges sending them flying down the hallway. The hall was completely concealed in black fog with no light to illuminate the cells. Ezra muttered, "Come out, you monster."

"I am here auntie…" Quinn's voice quietly echoed in the fog as the sound of bare feet slowly slid across the stone floor.

"Show yourself." Ezra called a little louder. Just as she did, the fog lifted, but darkness still surrounded them. Where most of the lights were broken, there were a few that flickered, struggling to illuminate the area around.

Across the hall, Quinn approached slowly, his feet and arms covered in blood. Peeking around, all the other creatures from the other cells were slaughtered, still in their cages. *How did he do this?* Pools of blood stained the floor, seeping out from the cells of the massacred creatures. Some were lygoids like himself, others were dark fae, or even hybrids. None of them were Matt Hallow.

"You killed your followers?" Ezra looked around in mild shock. Frost could tell a part of her was surprised and disgusted and another side was not.

"Of course not. What kind of leader would I be if I killed the people sworn to serve me?" Quinn smiled. "I'd be no better than you, Auntie."

"Do not call me that." Ezra hissed. "You are no family of mine."

"Just like Carola was no sister of yours? Or how about Kathleena? Melandria? Anyanke? Does anyone matter to you other than yourself?" Quinn stared at his hands pensively, not once looking at Ezra. "My mother… you punished for falling in love with my father."

"Your mother was an abomination for all that we stood for once!"

"My mother did *nothing* to deserve her fate!" Quinn screamed, finally looking up at Ezra with deep red eyes. Just as quickly as the rage filled his eyes, it was gone, and he was completely composed again. "That doesn't matter. Your lack of initiative to defend your sister means nothing to me."

"What does that mean?"

"The ones I truly want punished, the ones who played a part in my lifelong sentence, my father's imprisonment, and my mother's demise, they shall be punished." Quinn's milky white, razor-sharp teeth shone as he grinned from ear to ear in a sinister smile. It creeped Frost out. "But before I can enact my vengeance, I must leave this place."

"And how will you do that?" Ezra asked quickly. Frost could hear the slight panic in her voice. "You're completely alone."

"Am I?"

Appearing from the darkness, a group of people emerged slowly from behind Quinn. Two living vampires Frost recognized from earlier, an angel she didn't recognize, and three lygoids. Two of the lygoids Frost recognized immediately. They were the lygoid couple she heard rallying the others when she had first brought Gabriel to Ezra. The woman was once an angel with the lingering beauty of one, and the man was once a vampire to which Frost could still sense the vampire life force inside him. The last lygoid was the woman Quinn sent Frost to find, Lilian.

"I see you have your most trusted followers to help you escape. Tell me, how was it you were able to get so many of your people into my world without me noticing?" Ezra's eyes scanned each person carefully, but Frost noticed her eyes linger on one person in particular. It was the angel Frost didn't recognize. His features were shrouded in darkness behind Quinn, and she could tell Quinn was actively using his powers to shield the man's identity. All Frost could see was that he was some sort of angel with black wings. *Could it be Corál? That traitor...* He was the only angel Frost knew of with black wings.

"It wasn't hard. I knew if someone as powerful as Geordie Vollner was entering your world, your sight would be solely focused on her. The rest of my faithful followers slipped right through your gates on their own. Lilian, here, coordinated the whole thing without any word from me." Quinn affectionately stroked the cheek of the shortest woman on their side with a bloodstained thumb. He looked over at Frost in the eye. "I also had the help of my newest follower ensuring that you remained distracted with the fallen and her friends."

"What?" Ezra looked behind her at Frost. Frost took that opportunity to stand by Quinn amongst the shroud of darkness he put forth. "Frostbite, what is this betrayal?"

"I should be asking you that, but I know that nothing that comes out of your mouth is ever the truth. All you ever tell me are lies." Frost's voice trembled. Despite standing in the dark, her true allegiances were brought to light as Ezra realized her world would come crumbling down around her. "You did this to yourself. If you had only told me the truth from the start, I would have stayed by your side. Instead, you chose to hide behind your deceptions over the entire angelic race!"

"Ezra you are severely outnumbered, even for your grand abilities. With the aid of my followers' presence, I have enough darkness surrounding me to shroud your entire world and allow me access to every corner of it. You may either step aside and let me pass or stand in my way and I will eliminate you just like the rest of these dead, pathetic creatures. The choice is yours. I have no quarrel with you despite you imprisoning me for over a millennium."

At his threat, Orpheus stepped in front of Ezra protectively, wielding a large sword in front of him, staring Quinn down. Ezra's voice trembled weakly, "What are you going to do?"

"I am going to slaughter the entire family of the person who persecuted my family. And then when it is only him left, I will finally end him slowly."

"There's no way I can stop you, can I?"

"No, you cannot, unfortunately."

Without a word, Ezra took Orpheus' free hand in hers and stepped aside, allowing Quinn and the rest of his followers to pass. Frost proceeded forward, and for a small solitary moment, she and Ezra locked eyes. Both had pain in their eyes but said nothing. As the entire group left, the darkness went with them, leaving Ezra in her light, but even then, it slowly dimmed as her world began crumbling around her.

Once they were safely outside, Frost watched as Quinn took a deep breath and stretched his body toward the sky. "Freedom smells as good as I imagined it to be! Now we must make our way to Aquavitas, the gateway that will take us back to the Mortal Realm. Unfortunately, it will be some time before I can get the gateway to open.”

“And what about us? Now that you are free, and we have finally met in person, will you turn us to lygoids now?” One of the vampires spoke impatiently.

“Jason, I presume?” Quinn asked, and the blond vampire nodded. “Your times as lygoids have not yet arrived. I have plans… for both of you. You see, before I turn anyone into a lygoid, I like to get as much use out of their current form as possible, as well as their allegiance first and foremost. So, for now, you remain the disgusting creatures you had the misfortune to be born as until I say otherwise.”

Without any further arguments, the group proceeded down the alleyway toward the center of the city. Quinn gave permission to the two vampires to search for lingering faeries to feed on. For the first time since she arrived at the prison, Frost found herself wondering how the guards ended up unconscious in the first place. “Sir, I was wondering–

“I know what you were wondering… Another traitor to Ezra, not one of us, cast a sleeping spell over the guards to rescue the Hallow boy not long before you arrived.” Frost could tell that Quinn was also contemplating the situation. Something about it wasn’t right… How did Ezra not notice something like that?

“And you didn’t think to tell me this?” Frost asked impatiently, and the rest of the lygoids burst out laughing.

"Let me get one thing straight here, Frost. You may have gotten used to barking orders at lowly angels and vampires, but you are my follower now which means you don't have shit compared to me. You will be taking orders from now on, and you will cease to question me."

For the first time ever, she was at a loss for words, and only bowed her head in silence. He was absolutely nothing like Ezra, but that was probably because he didn't show or express emotion. Ezra held on to her emotion. It was the most mortal thing about her, and probably why she never wiped out the vampires like she said she would. At least with Quinn, Frost could guarantee he was going to actively attempt to follow through with his threats.

"Frost, I want you to track the fallen. Do not harm her, it will prove useless. Just find out for me the state of the Vollners and the Hallow boy. Our escape is dependent on their survival. If they pass through the gateways alive, we will be able to safely travel through to the Mortal Realm. As for the rest of you, we will leave this prison forever."

"Yes, sir, but how do I find her? Only Pyre knows where the Vollners were hidden since he was the one who did so." Frost asked as they all began to clear out to their separate ways.

"I would suggest looking in the Room of Roots."

The Room of Roots was a hidden room in the far back end of the council building. It was the location of every family tree that spawned from the Daron sisters. Not many people were permitted to enter, and those who managed to get in never came out for some reason. Frost never knew why no one ever left the room, but she was willing to face whatever force Pyre managed to get through in the Room of Roots. It made sense why Pyre would hide the Vollners in there. Not many people would look to find anyone in there, not even Frost or Ezra.

When Frost left, Quinn and his followers took residence in the surrounding houses around the square. As Quinn's powers festered, storm clouds roared above the city, covering every piece of land except for the outlands. No one could control the outlands. The darkness allowed the lygoids to roam the city in secret, undetectable by any angel. With the darkness looming over the city, there was no angel in sight, and lygoids openly flooded the city like a giant ocean wave of darkness. She wondered if this truly was a small fraction of what Quinn was capable of.

He was the first being Frost had met who was able to alter the energy of the city. Since Ezra was the one to create the Immortal Realm, she alone was the only one who could control the balance of light and dark energy in the world. That changed the moment Quinn escaped from his cell.

GEORDIE

The corridors of the council building were long and dark. With every turn they made, a new hallway opened up to Geordie and the others, desolate and empty. There were no lights to guide them except the glowing ball Seth held that pulled them in the direction of Breena's location.

Inside her pocket, the weasel wiggled and writhed against the grip of Geordie's hand as she desperately tried to keep the creature from escaping. It even tried to nip her fingers which only caused her to grip the weasel tighter. It took a second bite out of her hand, causing Geordie to hiss in pain loudly.

In front of her, Seth and Matt stopped suddenly, causing Geordie to slam into them hard. As she stretched her arm outwards to gain her balance back, she caught a grip on a solid piece of wood in front of her that felt like a door. "Are we here?"

"I'm pretty certain this is the end of the hallway" Seth held the ball of light over their heads, revealing the wood frame to be a door as Geordie had initially thought. "I don't think this is the end of our journey though…"

"Breena might be behind this door." Matt traced his hands over the door and jiggled a doorknob and tried to open the door. "It's locked."

Seth handed the glowing orb to Geordie absentmindedly, examining the door closely. Geordie nearly let it slip out of her hands, not expecting him to hand it to her as she wrangled with the weasel. In the center of the door there were carvings in an unknown language going in a circle around a large indentation. Around the indent there were four square blocks jutting out that reminded Geordie of locks.

Without thinking, she placed the orb in the depressed space and the light in the orb went out. Out of nowhere a loud noise erupted from the door like wood grinding against wood. The entire door lit up in the scriptures, glowing like blue fire as it slowly opened.

A brightly lit, beautiful golden room opened to them with a large tree in the center. The roots of the tree went in all different directions across the floor and climbed up the walls to an unseeable ceiling. Dangling from the branches were scrolls of leaves of various sizes; some long while others were short. Geordie wondered what was inside the scrolls, but something told her not to touch any of them. There was something eerie about the room. It felt as though they were being watched closely.

All over the floor surrounding the tree were large golden eggs, with something large weaving and slithering in between them. At a first glance, Geordie thought it was the tail of a serpent, but then the head popped up, revealing a hissing chicken's head. Seth saw it as well and shoved Matt and Geordie behind him. He also reached into Geordie's jacket pocket and threw the weasel in the creature's direction.

"Stay close behind me and focus only on me. I will get us out of here." Seth took each of their hands and led them around the room in search of another door.

"What is that?" Matt whispered as he tried to get a look over Seth's shoulder.

"*Don't* try to look at it! It's a cockatrice. One look from its eyes will kill you instantly! The weasel will take care of it." Seth started walking towards the large tree and Geordie couldn't help but notice a large tattoo on his forearm. It was a black Celtic design of wings surrounding a dagger with a rose on the hilt. It looked vaguely familiar, but she couldn't place where she had seen it before. "There's a door behind the tree, but I haven't seen the beast in a while."

"Where could it have gone?" Matt looked around quickly and suddenly let out a gut-wrenching scream as something grabbed him and pulled him into the air.

Geordie turned to see what happened to Matt and found him dangling a foot off the ground as the creature held him by the beak. Geordie quickly grabbed onto Matt's arms, trying to pull him back down as Seth took off somewhere else in the room. "Seth, what are you *doing*?"

"Don't worry! Just get Matt away from the cockatrice! And don't look at it in the eyes!" Seth called back from the other side of the tree. Geordie could hear him wrestling with something as he knocked over the large golden eggs.

"Geordie, get me out of here!" Matt cried out as the cockatrice flung him across the room. Both Matt and Geordie crashed into a corner of the room, and she wrapped her arms over Matt's head, shielding him from the glare of the cockatrice's eyes as it approached them. Out of the corner of her eye, Geordie noticed a golden door to the left, directly behind the tree. She also noticed Seth swooping across the room with the weasel, behind the cockatrice. She was careful to keep her eyes set on Seth and not on the approaching monster.

At that moment, Geordie could hear her heart pounding frantically. As soon as he was close enough to the cockatrice, he released the weasel and motioned for Geordie to head towards the next door. Without hesitation, she swung Matt over her shoulder and bolted for the door.

Behind her, a loud shriek came from the creature as the weasel hissed and clawed at the cockatrice. Suddenly, she could feel the large creature collapse beneath her feet, tripping them inches away from the door. The cockatrice recovered rather quickly and turned its attention to Matt, biting down on his leg. Matt screamed, kicking the cockatrice's head urgently.

"MATT!" Geordie screamed, trying to look back at him to see what was going on, but Seth pulled her free arm towards the door and swung it open violently. All three of them clamored into the next room clumsily, one after another, where Seth collapsed onto the floor and kicked the door closed. The moment the door shut completely, darkness closed in around them as they all gasped for air, panting heavily. "Matt, are you okay?"

A low, painful grunt emitted from Matt as he breathed harshly, "Yeah, but I can't move or feel my body. And my heart feels like it's going jump out of my chest."

"Sounds like it." Seth dragged his exhausted body over to where they sat on the floor. "I can light our way."

Seth fiddled with something for a moment, and suddenly the charm bracelet he'd been wearing emitted a golden luminescent light. Each of the charms on the bracelet lit up brightly, illuminating the entire room.

It was a small room with nothing in it. There were no other visible doors that Geordie could see and there were no windows. A pungent smell of faery blood filled the air. On the other end of the room, it was dripping slowly, creating a large pool of blood.

Seth took a small step towards the blood, but hesitated for a second, "I can sense another presence here. Geordie, you need to come with me."

As they approached the source of the dripping blood, Seth's glow going with him, the light revealed an unconscious woman chained to the farthest wall by the wrists and ankles in cold iron. Everywhere the iron touched her skin, she bled and large red rashes festered. Her hands and feet were also pinned into the wall, her body hanging like a cross for display. Her face and body were beaten to a pulp, making her barely recognizable. Her dark, wet hair hung over her shoulders, also drenched in blood. Everything about the bloody scene had Frost's torturous habits written all over her. When Geordie looked up to Seth, his face was pale and frozen in terror. His voice barely uttered the name, "Breena."

MATT

Matt couldn't move or see anything that was going on as Geordie brought him over to Seth's light. All he could think about was the feeling of the crumpled scroll stuck hidden in his hand that he had stolen from the golden room. Something about it called him to take it. He didn't know why. He just knew needed to read it. It felt as though it knew something about himself.

"Oh my god…" Geordie gasped and dropped him on the floor. His body made a hard thud on the ground, rolling into something wet.

"What? What happened?" Matt groaned, spitting out whatever got into his mouth that he landed in. It tasted like blood, but it was sweet as well.

"Oh, Matt, I'm sorry!" He could feel her kneeling down close to him as she wiped his hair out of his face. She then pulled him aside and sat him up on a wall. "Here, let me get you out of this mess."

"What *happened*?"

"It's Breena." Seth's voice quivered slightly. "She's chained and pinned up to the wall by iron."

"Oh… How do we set her free?" Matt tried to look over to Seth, but all his muscles were completely unresponsive.

"I cannot touch the iron. They're extremely poisonous to faeries. Maybe you, Geordie, should use your vampire strength to break the chains." Seth kicked the bottom of the chains with his steel toed boots.

"Alright, do you want me to heal her too, while I am at it?"
Geordie went over to the chains, fiddling around with them.

"No. I don't want vampire blood running through her
veins. If for any reason she dies and has vampire blood in her
system, she will come back as a vampire. She will never
forgive us for that." Matt could feel irritation filling him as
Seth spoke, even though he didn't have a reason to be irritated.
He agreed with Seth for once. He made a valid point. But as
he thought about agreeing with Seth, it made him
unreasonably angry.

But Geordie pleaded against him anyway, "Do you even
realize what you're saying? If she *dies,* she will *never* come
back! You will never see your mother again!"

"And that's fine! That is what mortal creatures are meant
to do! We are born, we live, and then we die! Immortality is
only for those of your kind: vampires and angels. Faeries are
not meant to live forever. Granted, we have a longer lifespan
than humans, but we still must die eventually. It's a reality we
mortals must all face. I'm sorry, Geordie, but there's no way
you could understand the position I am in."

"But Seth…" Geordie's voice trembled. "She's losing a
lot of blood, and her heart is struggling to hold on. Even if I
remove the shackles and pins, she'd lose a tremendous amount
of more blood in the process."

"I can attempt to heal her with my own magic. I am one
third Summus fae; I do know *some* magic that won't taint her.
You just worry about getting those chains off."

Matt couldn't see their faces in the shadow of Seth's light, but he knew Geordie accepted her task. A loud jolting noise echoed from the chains as Geordie yanked them as hard as possible. After a few grunts and yanks from Geordie, the stone wall gave way, and the shackles came crashing to the floor with a loud bang. She then pulled all four pins out from the wall as well and they crashed to the floor. As the pins released her, Seth caught Breena in his arms and lowered her to the floor next to Matt, away from the pool of blood.

As he laid his mother down gently on the floor, Seth began to whisper something inaudible under his breath and his hands began to glow a golden orange color. He traced his hands all over Breena's body, and the wounds all began to heal slowly. All three of them watched Breena's body with a strong tension in the air as they waited for something to happen. Then, Breena's chest finally rose significantly as if taking her first breath in a long time. "Seth?"

"Shh… You're still very weak. I managed to get almost all the poison from the iron out of your system, but you're going to be weak from the blood loss for a while." Seth continued to heal her, and Geordie came over to Matt and pulled him into her arms.

"How are you feeling? Is the venom wearing off yet?" She whispered in Matt's ear. He wanted to shake his head but realized that he couldn't move at all.

"No… it's not. But don't worry about me. I'm not the one on the brink of death." Matt watched Seth's hands trace over the spots where Beena's wounds used to be.

"Geordie? How are you here?" Breena coughed violently and tried to sit up, but Seth stopped her, forcing her to lie back down.

"Both Jacob's and Michael's sons forced Geordie to take them to the Immortal Realm, and I ended up in the mix. James bit me, and we got captured by angels where they healed me. Jason and James went to go break someone out and Matt somehow escaped. We found ourselves being led down a dark path in the cathedral to find you and wound up in a golden room with a tree and a cockatrice, but we escaped with Matt only being bitten by the creature." Seth summed up their whole experience in the Immortal Realm so far as if it were nothing.

"Wow." Breena cleared her thoughts, "Sounds like you three have had quite a busy day."

Both Geordie and Seth gave a short laugh, and Matt wanted to laugh as well, but once again couldn't. Instead, he asked, "So, do any of you happen to know any cure for my paralysis?"

"You got bitten by a cockatrice?" Breena asked. "Basil might do the trick, but I don't have any on me."

"But you could grow some right? Aren't you a Früx faery?" Geordie asked impatiently. Matt saw Seth's head shift toward her, but he couldn't see his expression.

"Not in here. I need soil and fresh air. But before I can use my powers, I need to rejuvenate my body with the natural elements." Breena began to cough again and rolled over onto her side.

"The elements?" Matt asked.

"Fire, water, earth and air. Breena is a rare mix of Früx, Summus, and dark fae. Summus fae draw their energy from the elements and aspects of the other orders." Seth explained as he lifted Breena into his arms. "Breena, who brought you in here? And how did they leave? We can't go out the same way we came. The cockatrice is probably still lurking in the other room."

"Pyre did all of this and hid me in this dungeon. There's a trap door somewhere he escaped through that I assume only angels can unlock."

"That's your cue, Geordie." Seth groaned obnoxiously. If Matt had the willpower, he would've punched Seth in the face. He didn't understand why Seth was taking command of this whole situation. It should've been Matt left in charge to lead them out.

"Seth, give me a light." Geordie trailed the room for a long time, staring at the floor as she looked for a door no one else could see. "It's here!"

She stopped quickly and Seth ran over to her with Breena. Geordie then got on all fours and pulled at something invisible. Another dark, ominous tunnel opened to them, and they stared into a daunting hole beneath them. Geordie then ran back to Matt, smiling from ear to ear as she swung him over her back. "You ready?"

"Do I have a choice?" He managed to get a look down the dark hole and he felt a sudden chill crawl down his spine. Matt and heights did not mix well. There wasn't even a ladder for anyone to climb down.

Seth jumped down the hole with Breena in his arms and disappeared into darkness, the light he wore following down with him. Geordie followed, keeping a tight grip on Matt's body that almost hurt him, but he was thankful for it. He figured he'd much rather be hurt by Geordie's grip than to be hurt by the impact of his body hitting the floor beneath them, if there was a floor.

The drop to the bottom made Matt's stomach wretch. It was like sitting in a roller coaster waiting for it to drop down a tall curve at full speed. Regardless of the fact he had no idea how far they had fallen, Geordie landed on her feet flawlessly with the grace of a cat. He was grateful for Geordie as she protected him. He didn't want her to ever let him go, he just wanted her to hold tightly onto him and never leave him. But he couldn't find the courage to say those things to her. He needed to be strong for her. Geordie was the one who needed protection and support.

"I don't think we have much of a choice about where to go at this point. There's only one option." Geordie stared down the long, dark tunnel that opened to them.

"Let's go." Seth beckoned them to follow him. As they walked quietly down the tunnel, there wasn't even an echo as their footsteps made no noise. It felt like ages until they came to the end of the tunnel.

Once they reached the end, there was a single ladder that led up to a circular grate above them. No light shone through, but Matt could feel a low breeze coming through. Seth gently laid Breena down on the floor and climbed up the ladder. He tried to open the grate but when he touched it, his hands turned a bright red and steam shot out like a train engine. Seth suddenly erupted into a loud gut-wrenching wail as he dropped from the ladder and hit the ground, writhing in pain. Beneath him, the ground cracked where Seth hit it.

"Iron! The grate is made of iron!" Seth seethed as he nursed his hands between his arms and sides, curling up in a tight ball. "Geordie, open it!"

"I got it." She gently set Matt down, climbed up the ladder, and pushed open the grate. She then climbed back down to help Seth first, "Here, let me help you up."

"I got it. Just help Matt, I've got Breena." Seth snapped at her, shrugging off Geordie's helping hand. He turned to Breena with a gentle voice, "Hey, we're going to climb out of here. Can you move?"

"Yeah…" She nodded and wrapped an arm over Seth's shoulder as he helped her onto the ladder. Once she had gotten up the first few steps, Seth followed close behind and Geordie lifted Matt back up.

"Alright, Matt it's our turn." She slowly climbed up the ladder with one arm and held Matt with the other. "I'm going to get you out of here, and then we will cure you of this paralysis."

Once they got outside, Matt noticed that it was nearly sunset. On either side of them there were nothing but rows of small cottages, all completely identical to one another. Both paths were completely identical, and it didn't seem like either way led to a particular place. Geordie reconvened with Seth as he tended to Breena, "So now what?"

"We probably only have another half an hour before sundown." Breena coughed as she tried to speak. "We want to be out of the city by then."

"How? There's nowhere to go and we still haven't figured out where Vexus is." Seth slouched against one of the cottages, shaking his head slowly.

"Vexus is here? Curse him… that doesn't matter now, I guess. We are sitting in Cinereo Civitatum, Ezra's city within the Immortal Realm. Surrounding it is an area out of Ezra's control called the outlands. Almost no one leaves the city so no one will detect us, and by the time it's completely dark, the angels will be the least of our worries." Breena finally managed to find the strength to stand up. Seth tried to urge her to sit back down, but she shrugged him off before he could get a word out.

"So, how do we leave the city?" Seth tried to offer a hand to Breena again, but she impatiently flipped his hand away.

Matt wasn't sure if the stubbornness was a family trait or a faery thing.

"Just walk through the wall…" Breena groaned, leaning against one of the cottages.

"What?"

"Just *walk* through the *wall*!" She repeated, slightly snapping at her. Geordie hesitantly proceeded forward like Breena said, through what appeared to be the wall separating the city from the outlands. For a moment she hesitated until Breena reassured her, "Do you think this was the first time I have been in the Immortal Realm?"

Geordie picked Matt back up and walked through the wall. Matt expected them to slam into the wall, so when nothing happened and the entire city disappeared, he was surprised to see nothing but flower fields for miles. After a second, Seth and Breena joined them as well and Breena told them to go as far out as their feet would carry them.

They walked for miles in an unknown direction as the sun set, warning them of the very little time they had left to seek shelter. When they finally got to a stopping point, they hid behind a large hill that had a cave underneath the flower beds. Seth then laid Breena down in the light of the fading sun and her skin began to shine brilliantly whilst vines began to climb up her body.

Her body was gradually encased in various plant life like a cocoon. As she was nearly covered, the wind suddenly picked up and trickles of small water droplets crawled their way to Breena as well. The four elements surrounded Breena and rejuvenated her into a terrifyingly beautiful creature.

Once finished, Breena then turned to Matt and embraced him tightly as Geordie let him go. She laid him gently in the grass and basil leaves began to grow all over his body. In only a few seconds, Matt was briefly covered head to toe in basil and he could not see anything beyond them. With them came a refreshing feeling. It felt as though their properties were loosening up his muscles and sending a powerful surge of energy through him. When he finally sat up, the basil fell dead around him. Before he even realized it, Geordie rushed over to him and wrapped her arms around him. Her tears dampened his cheeks, and he wrapped his arms around her cool body, returning the hug and whispering, "Thank you."

Chapter 16

Sam
Early Spring

In the weeks since Sam and Gerrold parted ways, Sam tried his best to stay out of Naómi's way while she figured out the location of the missing stone piece from the travelling mirror. She set up sleeping accommodations for him amongst the nocturnal dorms, but Sam spent most of his days either in the library or underground studying the mirror.

In many attempts to understand the mirror's origins, Sam got to put his rusty artistic skills to use by sketching every detail he could of the foreign object. When he wasn't sketching the mirror, he stared at it for hours at a time, hoping to see Matt in its reflection similarly to how they saw Ezra when Gerrold spoke to her the previous month.

Both Gerrold and Naómi tried to reassure Sam that Matt was indeed alive, but he knew that there was no real way to know that unless they saw him. Even though everyone involved ordered Sam to continue to work towards getting Matt back, a part of him was inclined to believe that he was dead and there was no way to save him. Without any substantial proof of Matt's condition, there was just no real way to tell, and Sam was not one to believe in blind faith. If the mirror would just show him that Matt was alive, that would be enough. But every night, the mirror remained unchanged, always showing the dissatisfied look Sam carried when he realized again that he was nowhere near closer to figuring out where the missing stone piece was.

One evening, in another attempt to better understand the mirror, Naómi quietly approached him on the small rock island that held the source of all Sam's problems. "Staring at it isn't going to get you very far."

"You think I don't know that? I have sketched every inch of its surface to better understand it. I have studied every etching on it. I read every book available to me the Summus faeries would provide in the library, and I have only gotten as far as understanding how it was built, and nothing more. How am I supposed to save your son, if I have nothing to work with?" Sam looked at her with defeated eyes as he tossed his sketches in the air in frustration. In silence they watched the sketches fall all around them, some landing in the water, some landing on their quiet little island.

"There's someone here to see you." Naómi stood up, offering her hand to Sam.

"Is it Gerrold?" he asked skeptically.

"Do you think I would be this collected if it were?" She chuckled slightly. Sam took the hand she offered and hoisted himself to his feet.

In the library of the Daron Academy, the entire place was completely desolate save two people. One was the librarian, a Summus faery who couldn't seem to take her eyes off the second person. By herself at a table, in a beautiful, silky sky-blue dress, Melandria Daron read a hefty looking book that seemed to be too big for her. She sat quietly on top of a study table surrounded by other significantly smaller books, but the biggest one of them all held her attention the most.

For the first time, she seemed like a normal young girl, not the over thousand-year-old queen who was one of the strongest people in existence. Records of the queens' lives before becoming turned vampires was unknown to most, but based on their complexions, Sam would've guessed that they were turned at very young ages. Between Kathleena, Melandria, and Anyanke, they had to be early twenties in their human years. It was difficult to say since they were also triplets and yet looked vastly different.

"We are quintuplets, Sam. Not triplets. Don't forget, we share two other sisters." Melandria looked over to Sam with a wide smile. For some reason she was always genuinely happy to see him. "If you're going to think about me, I really wish you would do it quietly."

"How did you do that?" Sam asked, approaching slowly.

"Do what?" She smiled again, innocently.

"You know what."

"Oh, there really is no fooling you. That's why I like you so much." Melandria laughed. "You know Ezra is my sister, correct?"

"Yes, although I do not understand how."

"We were all born from the same parents, that's all you need to understand. But we all share the same abilities, it's just that some of us excel in certain abilities more than others. We all carry the ability to read the minds of others, but Ezra is the best at it."

"I see." Sam processed the idea of his thoughts not being private in front of the queens. "Your Grace, if you don't mind me asking, why are you here?"

"I heard you were looking for the stone to complete the Dark Reflection." Melandria held out an open hand toward Sam, waving it open and closed as an indication for him to approach.

"The what?"

"That mirror Naómi tells me you stare at all the time? Its name is Dark Reflection. When Ezra created the Immortal Realm, she realized we had no means of visiting her except through death, and so she participated in creating a series of mirrors that would let creatures travel through both realms without having to die."

Melandria flipped the book she was reading over to a page that showed two mirrors, one on each page. On the left page there was a tall black mirror completely identical to the one Sam had become so familiar with. On the opposite page across from it was a white mirror similarly identical. The sizes and shapes were similar, but the engravings were different.

Looking over the pages, Sam realized he did not recognize the book she was reading. He had never seen it in the library before. "And what of its access to the Shadow Kingdom? And what is this book? I asked the librarian for every book she had in here regarding those mirrors and this was not one of them."

"Oh, this old thing… this is one from my personal collection." Melandria hugged the book tightly before flipping it over to show Sam the title. The Anthropaemia Codex. "And the mirror didn't always grant access to Obscurum City. Kearan Hallow and his ingeniousness tampered with the mirror using his dark magic and created the secret passage to the city. Only a Potential can open the gateway, so don't worry about it right now."

"*How* do you have the Anthropaemia Codex? I thought Breena Vollner had it stored somewhere in the Ancient Artifacts Library?" Melandria let Sam thumb through the pages carefully. He could tell this was the real deal. The pages were old and crisp. A part of him feared tearing the pages, they felt incredibly delicate in his hands.

"Breena's copy is a counterfeit made for the faeries. This one is the original kept for our records. There is a copy for each major species, but this," Melandria stroked the book gently, "this one is the original my father began writing before I was born. When one version of the book is updated, so are the other two. They're all magically connected."

"So why did you bring it here?" Sam looked up at Melandria with worrisome eyes.

"I want to help you, Sam. Everything about this situation worries me, from Gerrold's involvement to the possibility of the escape of an extremely powerful lygoid. There are many things we need to prevent as well as accomplish, and if we want any semblance of hope to succeed, then you and I must work together."

"Yes, my queen." Sam bowed his head respectfully before taking a seat beside her.

"Now Sam, I have much I need to discuss with you, but before I do, I need to know how involved Gerrold is with this endeavor."

Sam told Melandria everything about Gerrold's involvement, from the deal he forced Sam to make regarding Lizzie, to wanting Geordie and Matt to be a part of the coven by the next summer solstice. As he voiced the events that led up to that moment, Melandria listened without interruption, only occasionally nodding in acknowledgement. Sam came to realize how trapped he really was in Gerrold's games, just like everyone else who met the horrific thousands-of-years-old man.

Even though Gerrold wasn't there to supervise him, he still had his influential grip on Sam's neck, forcing him to do his will until said otherwise. Perhaps with the help of Melandria, Sam could find a way to loosen that grip. She was older than Gerrold, not by much, but she and her sisters were the only ones stronger than Gerrold. He was as old as they were, if not a bit older in human years. They were all mortal at the same point of time to the point that Gerrold was the first human

Kathleena had ever turned. And Kathleena was the first to begin turning people into vampires as the eldest of the three vampire siblings.

At the end of his story, Melandria processed everything he told her quickly and moved on. "So, first of all, Sam, I am going to need you to go back on your promise to Gerrold."

"Which one?"

"All of them. Leaving Lizzie in his care is not advisable. I have a suspicion he is doing something illegal in that castle of his. I intend to find out what, but for now, your attention needs to be on the immediate problem involving the Vollners and Matt Hallow.

"They are all keys to helping us get rid of all our problems: Gerrold, the lygoids, and the upcoming war. We need to focus on getting them out of the Immortal Realm. I already spoke to my sister; she is willing to begrudgingly give all of them up, there's just one problem. The lygoid in question looking to escape has bathed the realm in darkness and Ezra has almost no influence over her world anymore. She doesn't know where any of our comrades are, and in her weakened state she cannot put up a fight against this lygoid."

"Who is this person that everyone is so frightened of?" This was not the first time that someone has mentioned one lygoid specifically escaping the Immortal Realm.

"I'm sure you've heard him mentioned before, but he is the most dangerous man to exist, more dangerous than Gerrold. He is also our biggest mistake as a nation. His name is Quinncey DeLavonte, he's the son of the first ever lygoid. Because Quinn was born and not created, he has a body he's managed to preserve for thousands of years but can still hop into other people's bodies using only his essence. No other lygoid has this ability, which is what makes him so dangerous. While he has been imprisoned in the Immortal Realm physically, that has not stopped his influence in the Mortal Realm and his ability to hop into other people's bodies to do his work. The likelihood of him escaping the Immortal Realm vastly increases day by day, especially with his closest followers at his side now. If we are to defeat him, we need Matt to meet his full potential and become the Shadow King, and we need Geordie to join a vampire coven, preferably one without Gerrold's influence."

"If this man is so dangerous, why haven't you killed him yet?" How was it that information on this guy managed to go unheard of with Sam for so long? How many people knew of him?

"We don't know how to kill him, and plus, he is my nephew. I cannot kill my own family."

Sam couldn't believe what he was hearing. If someone was posing a threat over the entire world, he would kill them without a second thought if he knew he were capable. *How could Melandria let the concept of family stop her from doing what was right?* "Because, Sam, it's because of Kathleena, Anyanke, and myself that Quinn hates us so. He is determined to see the end of the vampire race over what we did to him and his family. Even though he wants to see our end, I cannot bring myself to face him. I know what we did to him is wrong, but I still can't help but care for him because he is my family."

"Fine. I can't say I agree with your methods of dealing with this guy, but if it means preventing the end of the vampire race, then I will help in any way I can, especially if it means I get Matt and Geordie back. Nothing else matters."

"I'm glad you feel that way, and you are not obligated to agree with how I feel about Quinncey. I just want to protect my people, but someone else, not me or my sisters, needs to end Quinn, once and for all."

"Any idea of how we get Matt ready to face Quinn as the Shadow King?"

"Unfortunately, yes. I don't like our limited options, but Gerrold is the only person older than Quinn who can teach Matt the necessary skills to defeat him. I'm sure Gerrold would love that."

"Why do you think that?"

"Gerrold was the one who called for the persecution of Quinn and his family. Although he wanted to kill them all, Kathleena wouldn't allow it. Being our eldest and wisest sister, Anyanke and I agreed with her."

"So, our fate lies in the hands of someone we cannot trust to do the right thing for our species?"

It was a harsh reality that Sam and Melandria faced. The strongest of their race was the only person capable of taking down their strongest enemy. How they would accomplish saving them all without allowing Quinn through the gates had yet to be discovered. Sam felt it would be next to impossible to keep him from escaping the Immortal Realm if Quinn was as powerful as Melandria made him out to be.

CHAPTER 17

FROST
THE IMMORTAL REALM

It didn't take long for Frost to trail Geordie's scent along with her companions. The dark corridors carried the fallen's stench all the way to the room of golden scrolls. When she got to the room, she cautiously awaited an attack from the cockatrice, but it didn't happen. Instead, Frost found the cockatrice's body sprawled out with cuts and gashes in it beside a dead weasel. Someone was helping them. Frost knew that there was no way the fallen would've known how to get past a cockatrice on her own. She wasn't smart enough.

By the back corner of the room, near the exit, there was a scroll missing from a tree branch. All that was left on the edge of the branch was a golden inscription that read: Hallow. Frost felt a bit envious of Matt Hallow. He managed to find his family tree before she could get to it. Frost had originally wanted to investigate his family lineage, but she forgot all about it with everything going on.

She cut her losses and proceeded on to the next room. Inside it was completely pitch black. There was no way for her to see her surroundings. Frost could tell the room was the place where Pyre hid Breena Vollner and tortured her. The entire room wafted with the aroma of faery blood and iron, a deadly combination for any faery. Frost, for a moment, hoped Breena was too far gone to help Geordie.

She slowly paced the perimeter of the room, feeling out any kind of hidden door or latch. As she moved to the center of the room, the tip of her boot kicked something loose and made of metal. Kneeling, she felt around the floor for the object, confirming that she found a trap door. With a triumphant smile, Frost swung open the door to another dark tunnel. It didn't take long for her to reach the end and find the ladder that led up to the city.

Outside, the city was completely engulfed in shadows and dark, stormy clouds above. It was no longer the bright, vibrant city she had become accustomed to. It was as if it were an entirely different world. As Quinn predicted, his power exceeded Ezra's, rendering her control of the world useless.

Frost picked up pace as the smell of faery blood began to dissipate in the air. The trail finally ended at the perimeter of the city where there was a secret opening to the outlands, where the darkness had not yet reached. It was impossible for Frost to proceed forward. Something was blocking her from leaving the city.

"So, you managed to track Geordie Vollner all the way here as well?" Pyre appeared out of thin air, approaching Frost while trailing his fingers gently on the invisible border that prevented them from proceeding into the outlands.

"Why can't I leave the city? And where have you been? I needed you!" Frost pressed her hands on the border again. It wasn't long ago she used to train in the outlands, and now she wasn't permitted to leave the city.

"I have had some business to attend to, besides, you told me to make myself scarce… so I did." Pyre stared at her blankly. Frost found it impossible to read him.

"Business kidnapping Vexus Vollner?" She snapped. "That wasn't a part of the plan."

"He was starting to ask questions. Plus, I found out something interesting that might change your opinion on me acting on my own." He pulled her away from the border finally and sat her down on a nearby bench. "Don't bother. Someone is using magic to protect them that supersedes ours. There's no way we can go after them."

Frost sighed in defeat. She didn't want to let the fallen get too far away. "What did you find out, Pyre?"

"Geordie's family, the Vollners, they are one of the oldest families in existence after the Darons. Her father and uncle, Lapetus and Vexus, were the first ever turned vampires in existence by Gerrold Victoire who was husband to Kathleena Daron for many centuries. Not only are they the first two turned vampires after Gerrold, but they are also the *only* two vampires turned by Gerrold. I also learned that their allegiances are mostly with the faeries and they are within the good graces of the Summus Order due to Vexus' marriage to its hierarch, Breena."

"Why does this matter, Pyre? Lapetus is dead, and we have Vexus thanks to you." Frost shrugged off his panicked urgency.

"It matters because Vexus not only has the strength and capabilities to kill angels, but he has also done so in the past. But what's worse is that he has the power to spread this knowledge to his son and niece, who are headed in his very direction! We need to kill them while they are still in the Immortal Realm."

Pyre's words stopped Frost. Ezra had already decreed that Geordie would not be killed in the Immortal Realm, but now Pyre was talking about wiping out an entire family of vampires who were also hybrids. "This wasn't part of Quinn's plan…"

"Who cares about Quinn?" Pyre yelled, violently kicking the bench Frost sat on. He reminded her of a child when he lashed out. "Who even is this guy, Frost? Do you know anything about him?"

"He's a powerful lygoid who promised to take down all of the vampires and he's helping us end Ezra's tyranny!" For Frost, it was plain and simple to see. She didn't understand what more Pyre needed to hear to convince him to be by her side on this.

"Okay, but where did he come from? How does he have a body? Why is he so much more powerful than Ezra that he can shroud *her* world in darkness? And why does he care about the vampires so much?" Pyre began pacing the street impatiently.

"I don't know…" She realized she had never bothered to ask any of those questions.

"Frost, look, I understand how you feel about Ezra, but killing the Vollners would be for the good of the angels. This darkness," Pyre gestured toward the sky, which was still storming violently in dark clouds, "this is not good for the angels. They do not thrive in darkness. They need light."

"Did you forget already? I betrayed the angels. And I thrive in darkness." She spoke with a frustrated tone, crossing her arms. She couldn't believe what she was hearing.

"No! No, Frost…" Pyre pulled her arms out from her sides gently. He cupped her hands in his and spoke softly, "You didn't betray the angels. You did what needed to be done; you betrayed Ezra Daron and no one else. She is not the leader they need. They need someone who is not going to lie about our history and origins. Ezra did that. She lied to us all. She is not fit to lead us, even if she did create us…"

"But you betrayed her as well… you can't say that you didn't!" She didn't want to, but she knew that she was going to have to force Pyre to decide between her and Ezra for both their sakes.

"I didn't though! I didn't choose to follow darkness in this crusade you've joined. I want and always will want what's best for the angels first and foremost, and that happens to be the downfall of the vampires. If you believe your chosen leader can accomplish that better than Ezra, then I will stand by your side."

With fists clenched, Frost sat across from Pyre in silence, fighting the urge to burst into tears for the first time in her existence. She wanted to believe Pyre's words but somehow even he didn't sound too convinced by them. His apprehension towards Quinn worried Frost.

"Pyre, I need you to do something for me." Frost stared down at her knees, avoiding looking at Pyre at all costs.

"What is it?"

"I need you to choose."

"What?"

"You need to choose who you're going to stand by. Is it me or Ezra? You can't serve us both. I chose to follow the darkness to defeat the vampires. Now you must choose which side you will stand by to do the same thing. Me or Ezra."

Pyre's voice trembled slightly as he whispered, "Please Frost, don't do this. Don't make me choose."

"You must." She looked at him suddenly with eyes filled with tears. "If you truly care for me… if you love me, then you will be by my side and rally the angels against Ezra. Have them join our cause."

Another long silence between them and finally Pyre agreed. "Okay, I will stand by your side, and I will rally the angels to our cause."

His voice still trembled as if he were unsure about his decision. Frost decided it was best to leave it be at this point. She wanted to believe his words, so for now she decided that was what she would do. A small part of her hoped that the situation would not change, but she knew that his uncertainty could become problematic. Without another word, they went their separate ways.

Frost returned to the square where Quinn sat in a meditative trance surrounded by his various followers. When she approached, he gestured for her to also take a seat and so she did without question. Looking around she realized that she knew none of the names of any of his followers except Lilian, the other physical lygoid, and Jason, one of the vampires. The rest didn't seem so inclined to introduce themselves.

There was a wide assortment of them. Two vampires, three lygoids, and another angel. Or was he an angel? Something about this man remained a mystery to Frost. He reminded her of Geordie in some way, but his essence felt more chaotic and darker than hers. If Frost could say anything positive about Geordie, it would be that despite her dark vampire heritage, her essence was of the light.

"I think you made the right choice, giving him that ultimatum. I believe it put things into perspective for him." Quinn finally opened his eyes to look at Frost.

"Were you watching us?" Frost mumbled.

"I watch everything I am capable of seeing. It may interest you to know that Pyre will come through for us regarding the angels. We will need them in the war to come. We need everyone who will see the error in the vampires' ways. Their tyrannical reign needs to come to an end. They've been in power for too long."

"So, what is your plan for the vampires? Are you going to kill them? What about Matt Hallow and the Vollners? Are you going to do anything about them?" Frost's head was spinning from all the questions she had. She wanted to be sure she was aligning herself with the right group with the right motives.

"My plan will reveal itself in its fruition. All you need to know is that the Vollners and Matt Hallow are not to be touched while we are all in the Immortal Realm. They must make their way back to this point in the city to get back to the Mortal Realm."

"How are they supposed to get back here if there is a barrier blocking the outlands from the city?" Frost remembered the force that prevented her from entering the outlands. "What if they cannot get back in?"

"I'm not sure whose magic it is, but it does not concern me. Whoever is helping Geordie Vollner is guaranteeing her escape from the Immortal Realm. You may rest easy, Frostbite."

"And what about Ezra? What if she tries to keep us all here?" Worried by the idea of Ezra retaliating from Frost's betrayal, she wondered what was to stop them from escaping.

"Ezra no longer holds any power over this place. I am presently ensuring that. I've spent most of my imprisonment honing my powers to overcome hers." Quinn stepped down from his perch on Aquavitas and attempted to walk through the waterfall waypoint that would lead them to the Mortal Realm. After several moments of nothing happening, Quinn smiled, "It is not time yet. The mortals haven't found the key yet."

"What are you talking about, sir?" Jason asked as they all gathered around the fountain.

"A long time ago, I had a magical stone sent to the Mortal Realm in the hopes that one day the correct people would find it. Once it is reunited with the gateway mirror it belongs to, we will all be able to leave with no effort. I used all our essences to preset our destination once we come through to the Mortal Realm. All we must do is wait for the mortals on the other side to figure it out."

"So, now we wait for Ezra to realize your plan and come stop us?" Frost didn't like the sound of Quinn's plan but couldn't outright say anything about it.

"Oh darling, she may *try* to stop me, but she won't have much luck with that." Quinn laughed out righteously. "And once we leave, this world will come crumbling down, Ezra along with it."

GEORDIE

"Someone is blocking the waypoints." Breena spoke softly as she lit a fire in the cave they found in the flower fields. Geordie sat huddled next to Seth as they all tried to keep warm and plan their escape. Matt was the only one of the four of them that sat separately from the group. Geordie wondered if it was due to his paralysis; perhaps being attacked by the cockatrice alienated him, but she also felt she couldn't talk to him about it. Since they had been forced into a group with Seth, Matt grew gradually more distant.

"Is this a good thing or a bad thing?" Seth asked, breaking Geordie's thoughts.

"It is neither here nor there as long as we can get out." Breena stood up and grew three beds of soft flowers around the fire. "We need to focus on finding Vexus. There's no telling what we may be up against, and I refuse to let Vexus die in this place, so you all should rest for a few hours."

"If he's even alive…" Matt murmured under his breath. Geordie knew Breena couldn't hear him, but Matt's words caught Geordie and Seth's attention with their vampire hearing. Seth shot Matt an incredibly dark look that seethed with anger.

At that moment, Geordie wished she could read either Seth's or Matt's mind to figure out what was going on. It wasn't long after she met Matt and his powers awakened that she began to struggle to read his thoughts. By the time winter hit, she couldn't read his thoughts at all.

Without having to read either of their thoughts, Geordie could tell there was animosity between Seth and Matt. She knew they would never admit it, but it was apparent, as they weren't trying hard to hide it. They were cold and distant toward each other, even if they didn't realize it.

At the end of the day, none of their personal feelings mattered. They had the same goal and were on the same team. All three of them were aligned together to get out of the Immortal Realm alive. If they held the same goal, nothing could drive them apart. Geordie tried to go to sleep with that final thought in her mind, in the hopes they would make it out of the situation alive.

MATT

It wasn't until Breena's fire had died down that Matt had finally felt he could sneak out of the cave. He wanted to be completely alone when he decided to read the scroll that he had stolen from the cockatrice. Something about it drew him to it, and ever since he had gotten paralyzed by the monster, he had a constant urge to read the contents of the scroll.

As Matt got up and stepped out of the cave, he noticed Breena was sitting atop a large rock at a distance with her silhouette illuminated by the light of the moon. It would be impossible to get past her without her noticing.

"Good evening, Matt." She spoke without having to look at him. Her eyes were closed shut, and she stood perfectly still. "Beautiful night, isn't it?"

"I have to use the bathroom." His voice was short and irritable. She gave him a slight chuckle in return as she turned to watch him for a short moment.

"No, you don't." She then turned her head back towards the moon and closed her eyes once more.

Unsure of how to respond, Matt left the cave in silence and walked in a random direction until he felt safe to pull out the scroll. As he nestled himself against a random rock, Matt began to unravel the scroll with anticipation. At first it was blank, and Matt was taken aback at what he found. After a few seconds of staring at it in bewilderment, small black letters began to form into a paragraph.

As they formed, he read aloud, "This series of ancestries belongs to Carola Daron, first of her kind, Kearan Hallow, first of his kind, and all their following descendants. This tree is followed by a Daron matriarchy and Hallow patriarchy. No new patriarchs have been born since the death of the patriarch Kearan Hallow. The information provided is based on the Anthropaemia Codex's information."

Below, a detailed tree began to form with tiny names written above each branch. The list of names went down to a single route with the name Carola Daron sketched beside it. As Matt read the tree, he soon became entranced by what he saw. Only a few of them he recognized: him, his mother, and Nick. They were all descendants of a woman this tree claimed to be the first ever born faery.

Matt knew that he and Nick were only half-brothers since they were five years apart, and neither of them had a father to speak of. Ever since Matt found out that he wasn't entirely human, he never had an opportunity to confront his brother about it. Everything was happening so incredibly fast he didn't have a chance to confront anyone about his heritage. He knew Geordie knew something more than what she was letting on, and if that was the case, then Sam especially was hiding something, and that angered Matt.

Ever since they got trapped in the Immortal Realm with Seth, Matt found himself irrationally angry at everything recently. He was especially angry at Seth's presence. At first, he didn't really have any opinions of Seth, but then the more time they spent together, the more Matt hated him. He didn't understand why; he knew Seth had never done him any wrong, and he was always helping Geordie whether Matt liked it or not. So why did he hate Seth so much?

Continuing to read the family tree, it seemed there were two major family members. The founding member, Carola Daron, was a faery listed under Dark Order. Three generations later the next significant family member was born, a faery named Kearan Hallow mixed with vampire and human. Matt didn't understand how that was possible. It looked like he married a lygoid woman named Lilian, but no other family was listed under her name, and she didn't have a surname which Matt found odd. From that point on, every descendent of Kearan was given the surname Hallow.

At the very bottom, the last generation listed was Matt and Nick, and as predicted they were not from the same fathers. But that wasn't what took Matt by surprise. Under his heritage, Matt was listed as a witch, faery, vampire, and lygoid. Nick was only listed as a witch and vampire. Did Nick know he was half vampire? What bothered Matt even more was that Matt's father was listed on the family tree, but not Nick's. After looking back again he noticed only certain names outside the Hallow family were listed. Each of the later generations closer to Matt bore only one child, and they were each listed as 'Potential'. Any generation that bore more than one child, the other child's parent wasn't listed if it wasn't a Hallow.

Circling back to the bottom of the scroll, Matt stared for a long time at the name next to his mother's to be his father. The name was Gerrold Victoire, and underneath his name there was one species: Vampire. When he read the name of his father, it sent a chill down his spine. He didn't know who this person was, and he didn't understand why he felt the way he did, but he could already tell that he was uncomfortable with this person.

Upon staring at the scroll for a long moment, Matt realized that nothing about his life was ever truly normal, and no one in his life was normal. All the people he thought he loved and loved him back turned out to be liars and deceivers. Sam, Naómi, Nick, and even Geordie lied to him about his life. He wondered if anyone ever told him the truth about his heritage. Matt wondered if there was any kind of truth to his life.

Matt put the scroll down. He finally had a name for the father who abandoned him. For his entire life, his mother avoided telling him any details of his or Nick's fathers. All she told them was that their fathers were good for nothing, and they were better off without them. Matt was never quite satisfied with those answers. He wanted to know more, and now that he knew his father's name, he wasn't sure anymore if he wanted to know the truth.

"You will find the truth soon." A woman's voice behind startled Matt into crumpling the scroll into a crinkled ball. An old woman with silver, long hair and wrinkled, pale skin approached Matt, gently taking the crumpled piece of paper from him. "This should be returned back to its home."

The woman held the paper out with two pinched fingers in front of her, watching it catch fire and disappear into ash. A gust of wind suddenly picked up and blew the ashes away; Matt watched the ashes disappear into the night in disappointment. When there was no longer a trace of the scroll in sight, Matt turned to the woman and asked, "Why did you do that?"

"The golden scrolls of ancestry are never meant to leave that room, let alone this world. It is clear to me, however, that *someone* wanted you to know the contents of the scroll. Perhaps it was the scroll itself." The woman stared off at the city that was completely shrouded in dark storm clouds.

"That's impossible. How can a scroll *want* me to know something?"

"Who knows? Maybe it wasn't the scroll." She shrugged.

"Then who? Who would want me to know my family history? It didn't even tell me who father truly is, I only have a name. And all I know is that a woman named Carola Daron started my family line, and there was some guy named Kearan Hallow in my family. Kearan was the first of the Hallow name."

"Very good, boy. Now, doesn't the name Kearan Hallow sound familiar?" The woman asked as she took a seat on the rock Matt had previously been lying against before she startled him.

"Not really… No."

"Search your memories." The woman smiled patiently. "It's in there."

He wasn't sure what made the woman think he heard the name Kearan Hallow before, but he tried to remember. Something about the name did sound familiar but all he could think of was the angel, Corál. "The angel who saved me from the prison, he said I was the descendent of Kearan Hallow and a true creature of darkness. Who is Kearan Hallow?"

"A great man, once. My great grandson, was a miracle child when he was born. And when he grew up, he became a powerful and benevolent leader. For a long time, mortals and demons were united in peace because of him. Kearan was both feared and loved for the marks he left in the world. He was the only mortal ever to create an essence that bound all the dark creatures together in harmony, to him. As long as he was alive, there was peace, and the creatures of darkness thrived."

"Your grandson? Wait…" Matt paused for a moment, thinking of all the endless possibilities. "If he was *your* grandson, then that means…"

"I am the founder of your family line, Carola Daron. I am the first of the faeries and your ancestor."

"But then that means I am a prince of dark creatures?" Matt stared at the woman claiming to be the first of his family. Nothing about this made any sense. It all sounded impossible.

"It doesn't work that way. Ask your friends what they know and why they kept it from you. I am sure they had good intentions" Carola approached Matt, taking one of his hands in both of hers, but he could not feel it for some reason. "Talk to them."

"I am afraid to." Matt pulled away, looking down in disappointment.

"Don't believe in fear, and it will not consume you." Carola kissed the top of Matt's forehead lightly, and he suddenly woke up in his bed of soft flowers.

The clouds were dark, giving the flower fields a gloomy feeling. Matt rose out of bed quickly to join Geordie and the others as they stared at the dark and thundering sky. The darkness had consumed the city and was now overtaking the outlands. Everything about it made Matt feel uncomfortable. There was nothing natural about this storm. Breena stared out on the horizon toward the city, "We must get Vexus as soon as possible. Only he is capable of handling angels and lygoids."

CHAPTER 18

SAM
SPRING

Over the next few days, Sam and Melandria spent their waking time in the library researching possible clues for the location of the stone. Melandria was insistent on not skipping any information regarding the mirrors and read every entry possible in the Anthropaemia Codex. The only problem was that she refused to let Sam read the book himself. It remained in her possession at all times, and he was only permitted to see what she showed him. This slowed the research process exponentially.

Amidst Melandria's reading activities, Sam took it upon himself to research the history behind the lygoids and Kearan Hallow's family line. There was nothing written in the books available about Quinn being related to the Daron sisters, however, it was mentioned many times throughout Sam's readings that Quinncey DeLavonte used his powers to create the lygoid species and that he was the only born lygoid in existence.

The first lygoid Quinn created was a woman named Lilian whom he treated as his own daughter. She would later become Kearan Hallow's wife and mother of his successors. None of those heirs, however, ever wrought naturally born lygoids.

At one point, Quinn even took a wife before his imprisonment, however, she and their baby died in childbirth shortly after his imprisonment. From that point forward he was permanently trapped within the Immortal Realm, and what few followers he had put forth efforts into expanding the lygoid race over the course of the following centuries.

Sam never found any indication of Quinn's family before he was born, or how he was born in the first place. Based on what he found, it seemed like Quinn was on a mission to further his family line naturally rather than creating more lygoids. In the readings, it appeared that Gerrold got the same inkling. A few years before Quinn's imprisonment, Gerrold filed a petition to the queens to have Quinn executed. This petition was denied, but authorization for imprisonment was provided. There was also a petition for the imprisonment of Lilian and her children which had been approved.

Kearan Hallow contested the persecution of his family to the point of threatening a war on the vampires. A compromise was then made in lieu of Kearan gaining protection over his family. He used his power as king of the Shadow Kingdom to help Gerrold track down Quinn and trap him for the rest of time. At some point, reports came back following the deaths of Quinn's wife and child. Nothing else was written in the lygoids' history with Quinn aside from the random spurts of increased numbers over the course of time to the present day.

It made sense why Quinn wanted to start a war with the vampires, but it didn't add up why he didn't try to escape sooner. Sam also wondered if Quinn ever knew about the death of his wife and child after his imprisonment.

Over at a nearby table, surrounded by piles of books, Melandria was reading with a fierce intensity unlike her normal level of intense personality. She called over Sam with a distracted voice. "Sam, get over here… I need to show you something."

"What is it?" Sam leaned over her shoulder. She was on a page that was written by Vexus. The chapter was about magical artifacts.

"…When Pandora and Persephone cast the spell of eternal life, they also created a gateway between the Immortal and Mortal Realms to travel between worlds and keep balance. They were not aware of the consequences that befell them when they created these spells.

"They took a magical slab of marble with two sides to it, a light and a dark side, and carved out three objects. The first two objects were a puzzle box to control darkness and a spherical hollow orb to control the light. With the remaining stone, a third object was carved: a mirror to act as a gateway between the realms of light and darkness, intended for the objects to travel through.

"Using ancient magic, the mirror was split between the realms, so the light side resided within the Immortal Realm, and the dark side resided within the Mortal Realm. The box and the orb were hidden safely in their opposite worlds to keep the sisters from the temptation of opening their object and throwing the world out of balance.

"If these objects were to ever be combined into one, it would create a portal with the potential to travel through time. It is not known if this is truly possible as it has not been done ever before. It is best to keep these objects separated far from the mirror, Dark Reflection.

"As a consequence of creating these objects, for one mortal lifespan during a millenium, the two sisters are placed in the bodies of mortals to find and protect their object with no bias. During that year, balance must be released into the world within their respected realm. Pandora's box should only be used in the Mortal Realm, and Persephone's orb only to be used in the Immortal Realm. Otherwise, the world will fall into chaos.

"After years of searching, I have finally found the shard from Dark Reflection along with the orb and box and have passed them on to Breena to store in her secret vault. I have told her not to tell me where the vault is. I just know it exists and protects objects that have the potential to do harm if they fell into the wrong hands."

"This is the key. We know now that Breena had the stone in her possession, and we know she has a vault!" Melandria proclaimed excitedly. "We need to get to her office to find hints about the location of her vault."

"That sounds like a solid plan. We should head there immediately." Sam agreed. For the first time in a while, he was beginning to feel hopeful that he was getting somewhere in their mission to save Geordie and Matt.

Thirteen hours later, they arrived at a private airport in Southern California where it was still daylight out and they had to cover themselves head to toe in thick dark cloaks until they got to the private SUV. From there a human drove them to the Ancient Artifacts Library where they were greeted by a faery who immediately asked for their identification clearances, not knowing she was addressing one of the vampire queens. Before Sam could say anything, Melandria flashed a shiny charm bracelet with three gemstones on it in a rose shaped metal setting. One gem was purple, one a light green, and the last a sky blue. It was widely known that the vampire queens favored symbolic jewelry as identification, and there were only two other bracelets completely identical to the one Melandria bore. For further confirmation that she was one of the three vampire queens, she wore a necklace with a matching pendant to the blue stone on her bracelet as a symbol of her vampire line.

"Take us up to Breena Vollner's office, please." Melandria politely demanded with a firm voice. The faery nodded silently and brought them up what felt like thousands of steps worth of stairs.

Sam had not been inside the Ancient Artifacts Library in many decades, but it remained the same regardless. It was bright and sunny on the inside and practically sparkled from the white and grey marble walls. Colonnades decorated the ground floor leading up to a grand staircase that curved, splitting to either side of the room. Every step echoed loudly amongst the hundreds of feet going from one place to another on the black and white checkered stone floors.

At the landing of the staircase, four elevators greeted them and to either side of the landing, the first floor was a balcony overlooking the ground floor entrance that wrapped the perimeter of the room. Instead of taking one of the elevators, the faery led Sam and Melandria around one of the corners of the balcony. He brought them down a narrow side hall that led to a new flight of stairs that was less grand than the front entrance ones.

One of Sam's favorite aspects of the building was the amount of natural lighting it received. All the windows were spelled by faeries to filter out the dangerous UV rays of the sun so that vampires could roam freely during the daytime. A part of that spell also kept humans from seeing what truly went on in the building. The commitment to not let vampire impediments affect the general architecture of their buildings was something Sam greatly appreciated being a turned vampire.

When they finally reached the top floor where Breena's office was located, yellow and black keep out tape blockaded the door, and a faery stopped them in their tracks before allowing them to pass. "I apologize for the inconvenience; the office is still a mess. We haven't been sure how to handle the situation since Mrs. Vollner's disappearance."

"Open the door." Melandria demanded.

The faery did so, and they were greeted by a completely disheveled office that was not up to the usual standard of cleanliness Breena usually held. Most of the books on her shelves were tossed about. One of the chairs from her desk was destroyed. There was shattered glass all over the grey carpet in front of a wall length window that faced the ocean. The desk looked as though it took a beating but remained intact for the most part. Even though it was dry, Sam could smell faery blood everywhere.

The fact that Breena's employees kept her office in such a disarray was insulting to her nature and position as the head librarian of the Ancient Artifacts Library. Sam viewed Breena

and Vexus as his family, and he hated seeing them
disrespected in such a fashion.

"You will have this cleaned up immediately upon our
departure. Anything that can be replaced, do so, otherwise we
will leave it to Breena to figure out what to do about the
irreplaceable." Melandria ordered them, scanning the room
carefully with her fierce green eyes. Everything about
Melandria's demeanor was constantly met with an intensity
that overwhelmed Sam.

"Yes, Your Grace." The faery nodded and left.

Melandria and Sam began their search for clues on the
location of the secret vault Breena kept. Knowing Breena,
Sam felt it would make the most sense for the vault to be
located somewhere in the library where she could easily keep
an eye on it.

Melandria sifted through the books that were strewn across
the floor as well as anything remaining on the shelves while
Sam rifled through Breena's desk drawers. There was very
little of consequence, except in one drawer, there were various
pictures tucked away safely in a green envelope. One of them
was of Vexus holding a baby with dark hair and golden skin.
Another was of Seth with his girlfriend Leia. The third picture
was of Breena and another woman who was the spitting image
of her, and a man with his arms wrapped around the other
woman's waist. The other woman was holding a baby as well,
also with dark hair and golden skin, but this baby was
wrapped in a pink blanket. The fourth picture Sam almost
missed. It was Lapetus Vollner and a woman who Sam

assumed to be his wife, Elizabeth. Between them was a very young Geordie. There was no way Sam wouldn't have recognized her. It was the same pale skin, silver eyes of determination, and black hair she sported today.

Sam quietly pocketed the last picture and continued his search. After a while, Sam began to feel frustrated and slumped down in the one functional chair he could find. They weren't getting anywhere, but looking over at Melandria, she was still determined to find something. "Why are you doing this?"

"You're going to have to be a little more specific than that, Samuel." She spoke without looking up from what she was doing.

"Why are you helping me? What is the point in all this? What if we never find the vault or the stone?" Sam couldn't help but lose his composure. He worried at the thought of never getting Matt or Geordie back.

She finally stopped and sat on her knees, taking a deep sigh before answering, "I am the second vampire ever born on this earth. I have seen a lot in my day, and a lot of it was not pretty. I grew up with Gerrold, did you know that?"

Sam shook his head. He knew Kathleena turned him, he didn't know they were childhood friends. It was hard for Sam to imagine Gerrold as a child. It almost made him laugh.

"He was a noble from a nearby town on our island. He often came to visit our villa which you have come to know as the castle on Daron Island. He was a few years older than us, but completely smitten with my sister, Kathleena. For a long time, we did not like any humans, including Gerrold, because they liked to take advantage of our advanced sciences and magic. Often, the humans would pretend to be our friends to get what they wanted from us, and we could see it.

"We allowed it to happen though because it meant we lived in peace with the humans. At that point in time, on our island, there were the humans, and then there was my family, and our natures were common knowledge amongst the humans. I don't think the term 'vampire' had been established yet, but they knew we were magical and different. Ultimately, for many years we allowed them what they wanted because it meant they left us alone to mind our own business.

"Gerrold's family did business with my father, and therefore he was at the villa quite often. One day, an accident happened that resulted in a possibly fatal injury for Gerrold and Kathleena as they were playing. We were not even teenagers at this point. Kathleena tried to comfort Gerrold from the pain his frail human body could not handle, and in the fray, her blood mixed with his, and suddenly he was healed. The four of us witnessed this and it was the first time we discovered that our blood had magical healing capabilities. From then on, Gerrold constantly was asking questions of what we were capable of. Into our adulthood, he and Kathleena ended up together as a couple officially, and he somehow convinced her to be as curious as he was. They began to work with my father on experiments to learn more about what my sisters and I were.

"One day, Gerrold tried to take the information he had learned to the public. He wanted the world to see how incredible we were, but my father wouldn't have it. In his rage he killed Gerrold, and Kathleena tried to save him. She didn't realize he was almost dead, but she fed him her blood as he died. When she realized Gerrold had died, she turned on our father and killed him. It wasn't until we were doing a burial hours later that Gerrold awoke. It shocked us all, but we then learned if we fed someone our blood during their dying breaths, they would awaken as a newly turned vampire.

"From that point on to now, his lust for knowledge on the vampire race has only grown and he has stopped at nothing to further his experiments. He does things for his own personal thirst for knowledge, and I firmly believe he is a problem for our race. He has done questionable things to complete his goals, and he has hurt my sister countless times to do so. If he is permitted to continue, he will be the downfall of our race. If you allow Geordie to fall under his grip, she will become his puppet and there will be nothing we can do to stop him, especially if he really is after Lizzie. Geordie cannot choose a side in this upcoming war. She needs to remain steadfast in her position as a vampire and as an angel. Maybe then she can help both races. And in all of this, I want to help you ensure Geordie discovers her destiny, and that Gerrold is stopped."

"I thought you said we could still stop this war from coming?" Sam processed everything Melandria told him. He wasn't surprised that Gerrold has been the same person since before his vampire days.

"Whether it's a war against the lygoids or the angels, I am unsure. I am beginning to lose faith, however, that a war between either of them is avoidable. There's something in the pit of my stomach that tells me something is coming, and we must be prepared to deal with it."

Sam fiddled with a chess board on Breena's desk that remained completely unscathed amongst the damage. He didn't want a war to start against the angels or lygoids. The vampires would be at a disadvantage regardless of who they were up against. The angels were vastly stronger and harder to kill than the vampires even though they outnumbered the angels. The lygoids held the vampires at a disadvantage being able to take possession of their bodies with no real form of protection against the lygoid's parasitic powers. The outcome, regardless of the enemy, was not likely in the vampires' favor.

Sam tried to move a black king piece, but it seemed like it was stuck to the board. Not wanting to risk breaking it, he moved on to a different chess piece and it too did not move from its position. It was odd. A chess board with no moveable pieces. Wiggling each of them, only one piece moved. A knight moved forward three spaces and when it did, a large black tile on the floor in front of the desk with a horse on it opened up.

"Is this the vault?" he asked, dumbfounded.

"You tell me." Melandria gestured for him to go down to where the steps underneath led. "Go find out what is down there but try not to touch anything that you don't need to."

"You want me to go down there by myself?" Sam gave her a shocked look.

"No offense, Sam, but I am a queen and you are a guardian. You're more expendable than I am if something were to happen down there." She laughed and gestured again for him to get going.

With a quick eye roll, he headed down the mysterious dark steps that awaited him. As he delved down into the vault, it got darker, and eventually torches on either side of the walls lit up as he went further down. At the bottom of the stairs, torches all along the perimeter of the floor dimly lit the room. On the opposite side of the room, a wall of boxes stood before him going from floor to ceiling with various symbols on the knobs of each box drawer. The floor before him was a giant chess board standing between him and the wall of what he assumed to be the vault he was looking for.

The room felt more like a graveyard and less like a chessboard as all the pieces except for three lay in rubble all around him. Guarding the vaults, the three remaining whole pieces were a bishop, a king, and a queen. The pieces had to have been at least ten feet tall as they towered over everything. In front of them each stood three women. One was a young girl standing in front of the queen piece. The second was an average adult woman, she stood in front of the king. And the last an old woman stood in front of the bishop.

"A guest."

"Has come."

"For the first time in centuries."

"Where is Breena, young vampire?" They all spoke at once.

"I don't know." Sam spoke quietly, not sure how to take the three women each speaking parts of a whole sentence.

They looked at each other with expressionless faces and shrugged. "That is unfortunate. We will address you then."

"Behind us is the vault you seek." Spoke the adult.

"There are three boxes." The child pointed at the wall.

"You may choose one." The old woman trembled.

"But you must pass a test in order to proceed past us."

"I didn't sign up for any tests. Just give me the stone to Dark Reflection." Sam demanded impatiently, taking a step forward. At the same time, they also took a step toward him.

"You signed up when you opened the vault upstairs."

"Seeking an object from the material of Dark Reflection, you must take a look at yourself."

"And your life around you."

"We are the moerae, faeries of the past, present, and future. You must look at your life and choose a path to go down." They each instantly turned into an illusion of another person. The little girl morphed into Lizzie, the adult morphed into Matt, but the last was confusing. He did not know the last one. The old lady shimmered into a young girl with black hair like Lizzie's and the same green eyes she and Sam both had. She looked very similar to Sam; it was like looking in a mirror.

"One of us you must choose to save."

"The other two shall be lost forever."

"Not choosing will destroy us all."

"Yourself included." They all spoke simultaneously.

Sam hated being given ultimatums, and this was the worst one possible. He was being forced to choose who to save. He didn't know what he was saving them from, and he certainly didn't know who the last person was that he should have been saving. "You wish to force me to choose to save someone I love, and let the other two die?"

They all nodded together silently. Then Matt approached, placing a hand affectionately on Sam's shoulder. "You helped watch over me for my entire human life. You're protecting me even now while I am in the Immortal Realm as you look for the stone. You know that we are brothers forever. Even in death we will be together."

"Yes… you are my brother. The only brother I ever had, that is why I cannot let you die. I will save you no matter what…"

"And what of my fate, my love?" Lizzie approached, her soft hand caressing his cheek. "I turned you; I taught you everything I knew. I have brought you up to be the guardian you are today, and from that we have led a beautiful life together that bore fruit. Does that not mean anything to you?"

She looked over at the mysterious girl Sam did not know. Although he was confused, he trusted Lizzie's words. Even if they were an illusion. "It means the world to me, everything you did. You saved me, and you gave me a new life to be grateful for. I could never give you up."

"And what of me? Doesn't my fate deserve to be saved?" The young girl approached, wrapping her arms around Sam's waist. "Oh, how I have longed to meet you and be a part of your life. It's so lonely where I am, I have no one, but not for long."

"I'm sorry, but I don't know you… who are you?" Tears crept down his cheeks. Sam couldn't help but feel affection for this girl he had never met. For some reason she reminded him so much of Lizzie both in looks and personality.

"You will. We will meet one day, and we will grow a deep bond. My name is Onyx. I was named after your favorite stone." She smiled. Each of the fates presented to Sam stared urgently at him, awaiting his decision on whom he would save.

He slowly pulled away from them all, backing away and shaking his head. "I cannot. I can't choose to hurt someone to protect another. I won't let you make me chose based on what you've given me."

"Be careful, Sam."

"Choosing not to choose, may result in your own demise."

"The death of your loved ones will destroy you."

With a sigh and a self-righteous laugh, Sam declared, "I would much rather be destroyed than to be the cause of my loved ones' deaths. You can take your ultimatum and shove it up each of your asses."

"Very well."

"So be it."

"That is your choice."

At once they all swarmed him. Faeries under the illusion of his friends attacking him viciously and clawing at his skin. He tried to tear them off of him without harming them, but they persisted nonetheless. Eventually, Sam grew fed up and began tearing into them. He snapped the neck of Lizzie violently. The illusion of Matt lunged at him at the sight of a dead child moerae and Sam plunged his fist into Matt's heart, killing the second moerae instantly. The girl, Onyx, finally lunged at him, and therefore he lunged at her, sinking his fangs into her neck and draining her of all her blood.

Surrounded by the bodies of the fae, Sam wiped the blood from his mouth and licked it off his hands like a cat until they were relatively clean. The lights around him slowly dimmed and dark blood pooled all around him.

"I am the only one who chooses my fate."

He then stepped over the bodies and proceeded toward the wall of vaults before him. Amongst the possibly thousands of vault boxes on the wall, only three were able to be opened. They were also the only three with symbols on the knobs that matched the remaining standing chess pieces behind him. He gently pulled out the box with the king's symbol. Inside lay a black stone of the same material as the mirror, Dark Reflection.

Before he removed the box from the wall, Sam decided to peek inside the other two boxes on either side of the king's piece. Inside the queen's piece there lay a white, translucent sphere and in the bishop's piece there was a cube with engravings. Without touching either of them, he closed the boxes and pushed them back into their slots. He then removed the box holding the stone from its slot and went back up the stairs where Melandria waited.

"You found it?" Melandria stared at the box excitedly before noticing the mess Sam was in. "You're covered in blood."

"My endeavors were not without complications." He handed her a box and she carefully looked inside, affirming the stone really was in there.

"This is great, Sam. We are going to get your friends back. I promise you." She smiled at him genuinely. "Before we head out, I need to cast a protection spell over the vault so no one else can grab whatever may be in there."

"Right, Melandria… there were only two other objects in there." Sam began to speak but she waved him silent.

"Don't tell me, Sam. I don't want to know the contents of that vault. Clearly you were meant to be the one to find that vault, so you were meant to know its contents. Keep that information to yourself for as long as you live. Now, let me cast this spell."

Sam nodded and motioned for her to get on with it as he sat down on the floor, leaning against Breena's desk. With a few waves of her hands and some low mumbling incantations, Sam witnessed a magic seal cover the black knight tile on the floor and it sealed shut. "How are you able to perform faery magic?"

"My sisters and I carry some faery magic in us as well." Melandria smiled as she offered a hand to pull Sam to his feet.

"Is there anything you cannot do?" He chuckled lightly as he offered her the office door and they left.

"There's plenty, but that is for me to know and for you to find out."

CHAPTER 19

MATT
THE IMMORTAL REALM

Matt, Geordie, Seth, and Breena all walked for hours in the outlands without any sign of Vexus around. At some point, the layout had changed from being a beautiful, flowery field with petals flying everywhere to a gloomy dust bowl full of sand in the darkness. Looking up at the sky, the moon was no longer bright; it gradually disappeared with the surrounding darkness that loomed above them. Even though it felt as though it were in the middle of the night, and Matt knew the desert was an illusion, it still felt hot like a normal desert. Matt found himself constantly wiping sweat off his brow and wishing he had water.

Breena stopped for a minute and materialized water for Matt to drink before they continued their search for Vexus. Breena claimed that she could sense Vexus' presence somewhere in the outlands, but he was nowhere to be found in the endless sea of desert. It was like walking around in a labyrinth but instead of large identical objects surrounding them, it was just desert for miles.

"This is bullshit." Matt mumbled under his breath, forgetting that half of the group had supernatural hearing.

"Excuse me?" Geordie stopped and turned around.

"You heard me!" Matt snapped. He no longer cared who he offended at this point. "This is absolute bullshit! Breena says that she can sense her husband in this never-ending dustbowl, but how do we know she isn't just leading us on some wild goose chase?"

"That's enough!" Seth approached Matt getting between him and Geordie. "You need to calm down. You're tired, hot, and the Immortal Realm isn't the place for a mere human to be roaming around in. It's understandable if your mind is unwinding a bit, just take a minute to collect yourself."

"Don't start your condescending bullshit with me! I know you think you're better than me, being a faery vampire hybrid! You look down on me for being human!" Matt yelled at Seth, barely shoving him back.

"Matt, what is wrong with you?" Geordie grasped his arm in both her hands, trying to pull him away from Seth. He then shoved her away, causing her to hit the ground hard.

"Hey!" Seth quickly came to Geordie's defense and shoved Matt back but was quickly greeted by a swing to the face by Matt, but Matt missed. Seth turned around and landed an uppercut punch right in Matt's gut sending him flying.

When he landed, he immediately coughed up blood and could see in the distance Seth comforting Geordie. This angered Matt even more and he pursued Seth further. Before he could get close to Seth, however, Matt was immediately blasted by Seth's powers as he performed an attack spell with a flick of his hand.

Matt went flying again but this time he could feel his entire world spinning as he could feel dark powers emanate from his body. Matt's eyes turned black as shadowy vines crawled down from his skin and stretched across the sand in pursuit of Seth.

Seth slammed a hand onto the sand and the ground began to rumble. Dark shadows burst through the eruption of cracks in the ground, knocking back Matt violently in the stomach. Blood spilled out of him as he coughed, gasping for air. Everything began to blur. He could hear the voices of Geordie and Breena, but nothing made any sense. "He's dying. You did too much!"

It didn't make sense. He didn't land a hit on Seth. How could he be dying? Matt wondered if he accidentally used his dark powers again without realizing. That didn't matter, he couldn't move. His body wasn't working. Why wasn't it working?

"I'm sorry, but he kept attacking me." Seth's voice came at a distance. After their altercation, Matt knew without a doubt he absolutely hated Seth. He wanted to kill him, but he didn't understand why. Seth never did anything to Matt except attack him.

"Geordie, don't worry, I'm going to heal him." Matt could hear Breena's calm, soothing voice as she approached him quickly. He wanted to rest his eyes for a bit. He needed a bit of rest.

As his mind faded, images of Matt's past pushed forward…
Not images, memories. The memories contained Sam again.
He wondered why all his missing memories were related to
Sam.

"So, have you decided which colleges you're going to?
You got into almost all the places you applied." An image of
Sam flashed into Matt's mind, but he was different this time.
He wasn't adorned in head-to-toe clothing covering all his
skin.

"Well, I always wanted to go to Boston, so Berklee is
probably what I'm going to end up going with." Matt
whispered, sitting across from Sam at a lowly lit table. They
were in a library.

Matt remembered he had a tutor throughout high school.
He went to one of the hardest high schools to pass in the
district and had been struggling in his studies since day one of
his freshman year. Matt had gotten paired with Sam for his
vast knowledge of various subjects. Sam was maybe in his
mid-twenties but always seemed so much smarter than he let
on. Matt had found it occasionally jarring or suspicious, but
he let it go.

"That's sort of ironic, leaving Berkeley to go to Berklee."
Sam smiled as he checked over Matt's history homework.
"What makes Boston so interesting?"

"Well… this is going to sound stupid…"

"I rather doubt that."

"But, of the few conversations I had with my mother, she told me my father was from Boston, and, I don't know, maybe it could be a really cool place." Matt had thought of the idea of finding his father on occasion but was never able to go through with it due to being a minor under his mother's control, despite her constant absence.

"Are you sure going to Boston isn't a means of pissing Naómi off? Didn't you say she's never spoken highly of your biological father?"

Matt burst out laughing, "Yeah, I guess you're right. If I did find my father, I'm sure it would give her an aneurysm."

When his mother did speak of Boston or Matt's father it was always met with a venomous level of disgust that never ceased to surprise Matt. Outside of abandoning her and Matt, he never knew what she had against his father. He always wondered what that man did to make her hate him so much.

"Regardless, Berklee is an amazing music school and I want to finally become a real musician. This will be a great opportunity for me." Becoming a classically trained musician and escaping California was all Matt ever thought about.

"As long as you're leaving for the right reasons, then I guess it doesn't matter." Sam finally set down his pen and pushed the assignment back toward Matt. "Fix these."

Matt stared at the assignment, dumbfounded. Sam had marked all over the assignment in a red pen and at that point the text looked more red than black. "You marked all over it. Again."

"And you did better this time, just rewrite it with those errors fixed."

"Jeez, I thought you were supposed to be my friend." Matt slid the assignment away and leaned back in his chair, relieving a huge sigh. He hated writing unless it was for music.

"I am your friend. But for now, I am your tutor trying to get you through the last semester of high school. You still need to graduate." Sam pushed the assignment back toward Matt and pulled the arm of the chair back forward, slamming it back down on all four of its feet. "Get through this now and you'll be in Boston in no time."

"You sound like my mother…" Matt grumbled under his breath.

Once they had finished Matt's homework assignments for the evening, they packed up and Sam drove Matt back to Kensington Hill Estate where he lived with his mother and kid brother. Neither of them was likely to be home, so Matt had the house to himself as always. Usually, Sam hung out with Matt for a couple of hours afterwards, but this time he had stopped outside the front door.

"I'm sorry, I can't tonight. I have some important things to sort out."

"*What* important things? You don't have 'important things.'" Matt laughed, beckoning Sam inside, but he remained unmoving. "What is this about?"

"I just have some things I need to get ready for. Plus, you don't need me anymore for this chapter of your life." Sam took a small step towards the porch light, his bright green eyes focused on Matt's. He couldn't look away from those striking eyes; he had remained transfixed by them. Something about the feeling of it seemed familiar to him but all he could think about were the words he was about to hear.

"Matt, you are my friend and my charge, but for now it is time for us to part ways and for you to forget all about me. One day I will see you again, and you may not recognize me or remember me, just always know in the back of your mind, I will always be a friend. Move to Boston. Go to Berklee. But do it for yourself, not because of your mother, and not because your father might be there. In fact, forget all about your father. He abandoned you and your mother; he means nothing to you. The only family that is worth anything is the family that remains present: your brother, Nick. When you do anything in life, do it for reasons you can be proud of."

When Matt thought of that night, he remembered getting home from the library and across the paths of the estate, he remembered seeing a shadowy figure in the distance heading towards the estate gates at the end of the expansive driveway. He always wondered why a lone figure would be walking the estate that late at night. He didn't think anything of it, but now waking up in the present day, Matt remembered, it was Sam he had seen. Based on the previous memories he experienced, Sam had always been there.

"Matt! Open your eyes! This is not the time to quit!"

With a sudden jolt, Matt woke up, heart racing as if he were jump started by a bolt of lightning. He looked around quickly, one hand steadying himself on the ground, and the other gripping his chest as his heart pounded violently. "What happened?"

"You got stupid, picked a fight with a supernatural creature, and nearly got killed." Geordie stared at the sand, refusing to look up at him. "What's going on with you? You haven't been acting normally since we got here. Is it because you're human? Is this place taking a toll on you? I will understand if it is…"

"Geordie let's not pretend that you're not keeping secrets from me. As soon as you're willing to tell me the truth about what you're keeping from me, I will start letting you back in. In the meantime," Matt stood up, "just leave me alone."

GEORDIE

Geordie watched as Matt walked away from her, still angry. Matt's demeanor since they arrived in the Immortal Realm concerned Geordie. The Immortal Realm was not meant for living mortals to reside in. It was supposed to be the afterlife of mortal creatures and where the angels resided. The faeries who were born in there were creatures of the light essence and could therefore live there comfortably. It was never meant for humans to enter alive so Geordie wasn't surprised that being in the Immortal Realm might have been tolling on Matt's mental wellbeing.

She knew they needed to get out of the Immortal Realm sooner rather than later, but they could only do that as soon as they found Vexus. They couldn't just leave him to die in the Immortal Realm. Geordie especially couldn't leave him behind knowing he was the last of her family. All she had for family was already surrounding her, and she had every intention of protecting them no matter what it took.

"Geordie." Breena gently tapped Geordie's elbow, stopping her at a distance from Seth and Matt as they walked the desolate desert. Ahead of them, Seth and Matt were keeping a wide berth between each other as they looked around for any sign of Vexus.

"What is it?"

"I have suspicions… Do you know of the Potentials?" she asked quietly.

"Yeah, it's the four people of human, vampire, faery, and lygoid descent that could rule as king over the factions." Geordie sighed, "Why?"

"That is a correct basic summarization, yes." Breena nodded, still watching Seth and Matt carefully. "I have a theory that both Matt and Seth are Potentials."

"Well, I knew Matt was, but why do you think Seth is?" Geordie was now also watching them carefully, in case another fight ensued.

"In my time I have seen a lot of mortal Potentials come and go. Every time they meet, they end up hating each other out of instinct, and seeing as how they are the only ones that can murder each other, I feel confident in my suspicions due to Seth almost killing Matt. When I healed Matt, he was on the brink of death, Geordie. He wasn't just losing consciousness."

"Oh my god…" Everything Breena said made sense. Especially when Geordie thought about what Sam had told her. Seth was a faery, Matt was a human, and when they were separated, Seth briefly mentioned he couldn't sense Matt at all. Potentials were invisible to each other. "Two people I care about, are doomed to try to kill each other?"

"If we are correct, yes, that is what that means." They slowly continued walking, but kept a safe hearing distance from Seth and Matt. "We need to keep them separated as best we can, and we need to keep an eye on them at all times."

"If we make it out of here alive, how are we going to handle them both being Potentials? Only one of them can be king of the Shadow Kingdom."

"I'm really sorry to do this to you, Geordie, but that is going to have to be a problem we address after we escape." Breena continued forward before Geordie could argue or respond. She knew Breena was right. They needed to focus on escaping the Immortal Realm first before they addressed the problem of Seth and Matt trying to kill each other.

As they were walking aimlessly throughout the desert, a gust of wind picked up, whipping sand all around them. A sandstorm grew around them violently, making it impossible to see anything beyond. Within a minute or two, however, it stopped. When the sand finally settled, a tall, narrow building stood before them.

The building sat on a foundation surrounded by flowers and grass and vaguely resembled a small hospital. It was a rectangular tower that reached up many floors and sat alone within the desert. There was something eerie about the building that made Geordie not want to enter it, but without hesitation, Breena ran towards it, "Vexus! He's in there! I can feel it!"

Before anybody could react, she was already entering the building. Geordie, Matt, and Seth all followed as fast as they could, entering the building with no idea what they were about to face. When they got inside, Breena was standing at the bottom of a set of stairs in what seemed like a mental hospital. The place was completely empty but looked like it could've been functional not too long ago.

In the entry way there were small tables with a few chairs around each of them placed along the perimeter of the walls surrounding the grand staircase. At the top of the stairs was a large window that looked out to the desert, but when they all looked out the window, it just appeared to be a flower field with a slight breeze going. Seth crept back down the stairs and opened the front door slightly, peeking his head outside. From the top of the stairs, Geordie could see the desert and no flowers. Whatever the building was, Geordie knew it was an illusion.

"We should split up into two groups to find Vexus." Breena called down to Seth as he closed the front door again.

"That's fine. What do you want to do?" Seth met them up on the landing. As soon as he came up, Matt made his way back down the stairs to the ground floor.

"You go with Geordie and explore the top floors. Start at the top and make your way back down. I will go with Matt, and we will make our way up. Let's meet somewhere in the middle." Everybody, including Matt, nodded in approval of Breena's plan and separated off into their respective groups.

Matt and Breena began by investigating the rooms on the lower floor, and Geordie and Seth decided to use their vampire speed to try to reach the top floor of the building. After climbing many flights of stairs, they kept coming to the landing of a new set of stairs and it didn't seem like it would ever end. "Geordie, wait."

Seth stopped her before she could head up another flight of stairs. He then took a moment, looking out the window beside the staircase. "What are we looking at?"

"Roughly about four flights up, the floors began to look identical I noticed." Seth stared out the window inquisitively. "Looking out here, I know it's an illusion, but it seems like we are no farther up than four stories up from the ground floor. This building is never ending. Even if we go up another flight of stairs, we will just end up in the same spot that we were last."

"What do you want to do in that case?" Geordie asked, looking up the flight of stairs before them.

"We should explore each floor and make our way back down. There's no point in trying to go back up."

They took each floor room by room, slowly. They came across various residential quarters; some were private with one bed with restraints attached. Others were large rooms filled with rows of metal bar hospital beds. In another large room there was a sort of community area with couches, chairs, and a television organized in a manner that suggested various activities were to take place there.

Although every room Geordie and Seth came across was empty, it didn't have the feeling of being abandoned. It felt the opposite to Geordie. It was as if it were a new hospital, being primed for its grand opening. Everything they found down to even the medical supplies were unopened and new. Even operating rooms looked unused, along with changing rooms and a lounge with lockers.

"What do you think this place is?" Geordie asked, peeking inside yet another empty private patient's room.

"I don't know, but it creeps me out." Seth shut the doors of a nearby wardrobe. "It's an illusion of some sort, I know that much. What I don't get is that it feels very real, like everything I touch is real."

"My only reassurance that none of this is real is that I know what we see out those windows isn't real." Geordie stared longingly out the barred window of the bedroom they were in.

"Exactly."

For a moment, they both sat in the room at a pause, visibly frustrated at the situation around them. They searched multiple floors already, and the infinite loop of floors was still in effect as they made their way down, and there was still no sign of Vexus or another being in the building.

"So, you *really* never met your parents before this?" Geordie asked, almost scared of the reaction she might get from asking such a personal question. Instead, he just smiled briefly and thought about her question.

"Not really, no. I had seen pictures and heard a lot about them, but they gave me up as a baby. I have some resentment towards them, but I try to be understanding of the position they were in at the time. There was a war, and werewolves were targeting my kind, half faery children. So, they gave me up. It sucks, especially the family I ended up with before the Lees took me in, but I have managed to deal with it."

"Why did you never pursue a relationship as an adult or while you were with the Lee family?" Geordie leaned against the frame of the window.

"It never interested me, and we all lead individual lives. I'm a guardian to a vampire princess, Vexus worked at procuring magical objects, and Breena runs the Ancient Artifacts Library. If Breena and Vexus can't see each other as often as they would like as a couple, how would it make sense for me to try to build a relationship with them?" Seth laughed.

"You guys could try after this, after we return to the Mortal Realm…" Geordie tried suggesting, but she figured he would shut it down.

"Hmm… maybe…" Seth thought about it. "What about you? What do you want out of this relationship with your newfound family?"

"I have only known the act of running from the angels for most of my life, and my parents died when I was thirteen. I want support and community. But as you said, everyone has busy schedules. I also don't entirely know how to form new relationships anymore since most of the people I usually meet end up dying, and I don't want any of you to die."

"Death is inevitable, Geordie, even for those presumably immortal."

"I guess you're right. I'm just too used to being alone these days."

"I understand that feeling, I spent most of my life thinking that way as well, but then I came to realize that I'm never truly alone. I'm always surrounded by people who support me in one way or another. For example, you may feel alone right now, but you have Matt, and you have myself. Back home, you even have Sam. We are never really alone, even in our darkest moments–"

At that moment, Seth had been pacing and running his hands on the railing of a bed. He gasped and suddenly his entire body seized up and he remained completely motionless for a solid minute. Eventually his body relaxed, and he finally managed to open his eyes and he let go of the railing of the bed.

"Are you okay?" Geordie gave him a concerned look.

"I had a vision."

"Is that normal for you?" She approached slowly, alarmed at the sight she witnessed. She was unsure if she should comfort him or leave it alone.

"Not for me. Most faeries who are of the Lucis Order have the ability to get visions." Seth rubbed his head with both hands at his temples. "I'm of Shadow, Früx, and Summus Orders. I shouldn't have the ability."

"Well clearly you had the vision for a reason. What did you see?"

"Vampires, in a hospital like this one. Or maybe it was this hospital? I don't know." He concentrated as he spoke. "They were being tortured and held comatose in hospital beds. They were hooked up to some sort of high-tech machines that I've never seen before."

"That doesn't make sense. How could someone make a vampire comatose?" Geordie thought about the vision Seth had. Faeries were known mostly for seeing glimpses of the future. If he saw machines he'd never recognized, then maybe they weren't invented yet. "It doesn't matter right now. We need to keep heading downstairs and find Vexus."

"SETH! GEORDIE! GET DOWN HERE!" Matt called up to them from what seemed like right downstairs one floor. They ran down as fast as they could, and around a corner in a padded cell with a singular bed, Vexus Vollner had been found chained to the bed writhing and lashing out at Matt and Breena who were attempting to keep a safe distance inside the confined room.

"Breena, Matt, get out of here, right now." Seth ordered quickly.

"*Don't* tell me what to do!" Matt barked back.

"Matt! Get out *now*!" Geordie screamed at him impatiently and shoved him out the door. She then turned to Breena before shutting the door, "Try to find any kind of objects for storing liquid, like a bowl or something. Matt is going to need to donate some blood."

Behind her, Seth was investigating Vexus' condition more closely. Since Matt and Breena left the room, Vexus calmed down significantly but was still acting ravenous. If Seth got too close, he would swipe at Seth violently. Geordie was surprised the bed was holding onto the chain that was around Vexus. A vampire at full strength should have been able to break them. She then noticed Vexus' eyes were dark and full of thirst, and every movement he made ended in a level of sluggishness that made her think he was exuding more energy to move. His breathing was raspy, and his cheeks were gaunt. Vexus wasn't at his full strength. He was desiccating.

Vexus' appearance was not what Geordie was expecting. He had a long body, but he was thinner than Seth was with very little muscle build. His hair was long and silver with black lowlights, and he was relatively young. Geordie would have placed him in his early thirties. His skin was a slightly pale color but not overtly bright. It was like a pale caramel color.

"These chains are heavily spelled." Behind Vexus, Seth ran his hands along the chain carefully, making sure to fully inspect it. After a moment the chain began to glow as Seth ran his hand over the chain back and forth. "This is not faery magic, it's stronger. It's angelic magic. It was spelled to keep him in place and it's draining his energy, hence why he's so ravenous. We need to get these chains off him."

"How do we do that?" Geordie asked, dumbfounded.

"We don't. You do." Seth looked up at her, still crouched down at the chains behind Vexus. "You're going to have to use your magic as an angel to set him free."

"I don't know how to do that." Geordie felt pressured to do something she'd never learned how to before. A part of her was afraid of trying to use her powers as an angel. She feared she would turn into someone like Frost, a power mad angel with no regard for life.

"You managed to get us into the Immortal Realm, and you used your sight as an angel to find that trap door." Seth approached her confidently, placing two large hands on her petite shoulders. "I know you will do anything to ensure we all get home safely; I know you can do it."

Geordie took a deep breath slowly and moved around Vexus carefully as he tried to take a swipe at her. His dark, bloodthirsty eyes followed her every move as she knelt behind him. She ran both her hands over thick chain that was fastened to the hospital bed and extended over to Vexus' ankle, cuffing him to the bed by one leg. Under normal circumstances, any vampire could've easily broken through something as trivial as a metal chain, but as Geordie felt the metal in her hands, she could also feel the magic emanating off it.

It was like a strong electrical vibration that pulsed into her fingertips as Geordie tried to focus on the magic inside the chains. She had no idea how angelic magic worked, so all she could do was try to feel it within her body, her fingertips, and within the chains themselves. She gracefully slid her hands up and down the chain links, feeling every part of the metal material, the coolness of it, the vibration of the magic within it, and how it felt within her hands. Soon enough she could feel the entire chain heat in her hands as if on fire. It burned to hold them, but she grasped tightly onto the chain links as the magic pulsed within her body like fire burning inside her.

She could feel her body shaking as the magic seeped from the chains, through her fingertips, up the palms of her hands, and through her arms. Geordie felt the spell course through her entire body, through every bone and muscle and in her heart as the magic left the chains holding down Vexus.

For that singular moment, she felt stronger than ever before. She felt truly powerful for the first time in her life, like nothing could stop her. For the first time in her life, she truly felt like an angel: powerful, weightless, and one with herself.

Looking over at Vexus, who was still watching her intently, she could already see the spell lifting. The muscle in his body began to regenerate, and his eyes began to relax. They were still dark, but Geordie could tell the magic that was destroying his body left. Vexus' visage changed from a thirsty rage to a soft look of relief as his mind finally cleared.

Seth then called Matt and Breena back into the room, and they came in with a small container full of what Geordie presumed to be Matt's blood. Without a word, Breena offered it to Vexus and he drank the entire thing without hesitation. Matt kept his distance in a far opposite corner, and Seth stayed on the opposite side of the room closer to the hospital bed.

Breena and Geordie, on either side of Vexus, watched him carefully as he drank the small container of blood. When he finished, he set it down softly, and wiped his lips clean with a hand. He then effortlessly yanked the chains on his leg, and they shattered like glass into pieces, truly freeing him. He then curled up sitting on his knees and rubbed his head as if just recovering from the longest hangover, elbows leaning into his thighs and his long, jaw length hair draping over his face.

When Vexus finally looked up again, he and his wife stared longingly at each other as Breena welled up in tears. They then embraced each other tightly. When they finished, he then turned to face Geordie. His eyes were now bright and silver, just like her father's, just like hers. "Thank you, for saving me."

"Of course." Geordie could now feel herself start to cry as she came to realize she was now faced with one of her last living blood relatives.

"Vexus, my love, this is Geordie Vollner, Lapetus' daughter." Breena smiled and so did Vexus.

"I would recognize that face anywhere. You are the spitting image of your parents. You have the best qualities of both." He then embraced her tightly and kissed her cheek fiercely.

"And this, my love," Breena then gestured toward Seth, "is our son, Seth."

Both Vexus and Breena looked up with teary eyes as Seth cautiously approached, clearly unsure how to act. He started to kneel to Vexus' level as well but before he could, Vexus quickly stood up and took Seth's hand in his. He then pulled Seth into a strong hug and Geordie could see Seth finally relax as he wrapped both arms around his father. "I guess we never did get to do formal introductions."

Vexus and Breena both laughed, and Geordie merely smiled as her family was finally reunited. It was hard to believe that she finally had a family again. As much as she wanted to rejoice in the thought, she knew this was not the end of their journey. They still had to escape from the Immortal Realm.

"And what is your name, young man?" Vexus then turned to Matt who was still standing in a corner, watching from a distance. It was clear to Geordie he felt disconnected from the group, and she felt terrible for it.

"Matt Hallow, sir." Matt shook Vexus' hand.

"Well, if you don't mind, everyone, I would greatly like to leave this room. I don't know how long I have been in here, but it feels like a century." Vexus smiled and they all left and made their way back down to the entrance of the illusionary hospital.

"Vexus, how did you allow yourself to get captured?" Breena asked as they walked ahead, hand in hand. Walking behind them, Geordie had to look up to see their heads at full height. They were both incredibly tall people, Vexus barely inches taller than Breena. From behind, they looked like an intense pair. Breena with her fiery red hair that curled in gentle waves to her hips. The way it shimmered in the light, it looked like a waterfall made of fire cascading down her back. It was gorgeous when paired with her golden caramel skin that practically shone like a warm summer afternoon. Vexus' silver hair barely brushed the back of his neck like Seth's, except his was black with a slight purple tint to it. All three of them were exquisitely beautiful creatures. It was hard to believe Geordie was related to them. She felt plain in comparison.

"I heard you were captured by Frost, and I began investigating ways to get into the Immortal Realm. I guess Pyre caught on to what I was doing and decided to extend me a personal invitation by force to the Immortal Realm." They finally reached the base of the first-floor grand staircase landing as Vexus spoke. Through the great windows behind them, the illusion of fields was still at work. "He brought me to this place after beating me to death and spelled those chains to keep me in place."

"Do you know what this place is?" Seth asked looking around with skeptical eyes.

"No idea. At the time, Pyre brought me to the outlands, and I think he was planning on just dumping me there. Suddenly this place appeared before us, and he seemed just as surprised about its appearance as I was." Moving away from the windows, they went down to the front doors.

With two hands, Seth pulled open the giant doors, immediately greeted by a blustering desert and the glow of a near rising dark sun. The area was dark around them, and off in the distance they could see Cinereo Civitatum, surrounded overhead by a cloud of darkness. It looked miles away but Geordie knew it wouldn't take them long to get to the city.

"So, what is the next step?" Matt asked, standing beside Geordie.

"We have to head home, and possibly face our enemies." As she spoke the words, they felt heavy in Geordie's chest. She could tell Matt could sense her uneasiness and he then took her hand gently, giving her a look of reassurance.

"No matter what we face in that city, we will face it together as a family." Vexus looked at all four of them, including Matt. "All of us as one family."

CHAPTER 20

SAM
SPRING

The next day, Sam and Melandria arrived back at Daron Academy and were immediately greeted by Naómi who demanded to see the stone. With a slight amused look, Melandria carefully opened the box Sam had pulled from the vault and unwrapped the stone from its velvety dark purple cloth that protected it. It was completely smooth with no jagged edges suggesting it was a broken piece from a bigger object. It was very beautiful, like black marble.

Once Naómi had her satisfaction, Melandria put the stone away and they all proceeded to the cavern containing the mirror, Dark Reflection. Once they arrived at the mirror, Melandria stopped them before taking the stone out of its box once more. "Before we do this, I have some conditions you both must agree to."

Naómi almost looked dumbfounded that she was being bossed around, which almost made Sam laugh, but he managed to keep his composure. They both listened intently, especially Sam, since this was the moment he had been waiting for months for. He had no desire to mess up the possibility of getting his friends back.

Melandria looked to both Sam and Naómi to ensure they were paying attention to her. "Once the gateways have been connected, there is an extremely high chance your friends won't be the only ones coming through. I can guarantee you, they will come through that portal, but other creatures will be different."

"How so?" Sam asked, almost afraid of the answer.

"Angels, faeries, and lygoids can jump between worlds at will, as long as the gateways are open; they will sense it and will come through from the Immortal Realm as they see fit. This will provide Quinn an opportunity to escape the Immortal Realm and cause an overdrive of chaos here."

Sam didn't like the way things sounded. If they opened the gateways to get Matt, Seth, and Geordie back, they would be allowing Quinn all the opportunity he needs to escape. As Melandria turned to unlock the box, Sam asked Naómi, "Are you sure you want to do this? What if the world gets immediately thrown into chaos?"

"I won't let that happen. Seth and Geordie will sense when the gateway is open. All we have to do is give them a short time." Naómi spoke with little assuredness. "I won't let anything happen to my son. Besides... Quinn is already throwing the Immortal Realm into chaos; the Mortal Realm is just next on his list. It seems almost inevitable."

"She's right, but the less time it takes to get Matt and the others the better. I just hope we can shut it down once they are all through." Melandria watched Naómi with visible concern as she took the stone out of its box for one final time. "Sam, it's your friends, and your charge, would you like to do the honors?"

Sam nodded and gently accepted the stone. It was heavy, and he could feel the power emanating off it as he approached the mirror with it. It was as if the two objects longed to be together once again. He briefly wondered how long it had been since Dark Reflection had been activated, probably not since Kearan Hallow's reign, hundreds of years ago.

As soon as the stone piece fused with the mirror, all the cracks in it sealed shut and formed one solid frame. The glass of the mirror crystallized and revealed a grey town square with water spewing everywhere. In the reflection Sam could see a swarm of both lygoids and angels surrounding the town square. At first, he couldn't see Matt or the others in the square, but then from a distance ahead, he spotted them running towards him from an alleyway. They were in slow motion, and he couldn't hear a word they were saying, but he could still see what was going on. It was as if he were watching a slow motion black and white silent movie.

"Matt!" Sam yelled out, slamming his hand against the frame of the mirror.

"They can't hear or see you, Sam." Melandria gently pulled him away from the mirror by the shoulder. "All we can do is wait for them to get a chance to come through. They know the gateway is open. It's probably best that you don't touch the mirror either. If you fall in, there's no telling where you will end up within the Immortal Realm."

Sam nodded, watching his friends' confrontation silently. He briefly looked over to Naómi who was in tears, watching the portal with extended arms as if she were trying to reach out for her son. It was a sad look to see on her, but Sam shared the same feeling as well. Back in January, he had experienced his failure in protecting Matt as a guardian.

From that moment forward, after Matt got home safely, Sam vowed to never leave his side again. Matt may not have been born in vampire royalty, but he was Sam's best friend and family, and he was the heir to the throne of the Shadow Kingdom. No matter what anyone else tried to tell him, Sam knew in his heart that he was Matt's guardian until the day either of them died. If Matt had asked him of it, Sam would drop everything in the world for his best friend, no matter the price.

It was then he decided he would devote his entire being to helping both Matt and Geordie. Because Matt loved her, Sam would protect her as well. All for the happiness of his best friend. And he would wait there, in the cave, for as long as it took for his friends to come through. Sam would take any consequence for having the gateways open if he got his best friend back in the end.

GEORDIE

All together now, Geordie, Matt, Seth, Vexus, and Breena ran from the outlands back to Cinereo Civitatum. Since they had been in the Immortal Realm, Geordie lost all sense of time. Once the heavy storm clouds had reached the outlands, Geordie knew it was only a matter of time until the world came crumbling down, so she found it lucky that someone opened the gateways just in time.

By the time they reached the center of the city, Ezra was already there along with both a swarm of angels and lygoids. She and another angel Geordie recognized as Corál were confronting the large group of lygoids. "Quinn, please don't do this! If you unleash all this darkness on the Mortal Realm, everything will be thrown off balance!"

"You have no power over me, woman." The man she addressed, clearly a powerful lygoid, growled at her. "Your family is responsible for locking me away for thousands of years. You are also responsible for the deaths of my family. The crumbling of your world and all you hold dear should be enough punishment for you, Ezra."

She then turned to Corál urgently, clinging to his chest desperately, "Please, you must allow me to close the gateways! Quinn must not be allowed to escape!"

"I'm sorry… I truly am, but I'm not in control of the gateways. Your sister allowed them to open, not I. As long as that gateway is open in the Mortal Realm, you'll have as much control over the gateways as I do." Corál spoke calmly before noticing Geordie and the others. "Geordie, you have arrived. Good."

For a moment Ezra looked stunned to see Geordie, but it wore off quickly and she asked, "Is this a product of your recent activities, Corál?"

"Yes, it is. Leave them be, Ezra. They have no place here yet. They belong in the Mortal Realm, and we need them there to fix the damage that we have done."

"I know. I understand, Corál." Ezra gave Geordie a brief
solemn look.

"Hello, Ezra, it's been quite a while since I have had the
luxury of stirring things up for you." Vexus approached her
slowly, placing himself between their group and the other two.
He then nodded toward the leader of the lygoids, "Quinn, it's
been some time as well."

"Vexus, you are a product of the one who trapped me in
this world for centuries. Your demise is also impending. All
of you vampires will be dead before long, and both worlds
will be rid of your parasitic natures!"

"You're one to talk; isn't your species known for hijacking
other people's bodies because your little minions cannot take
their own forms?" Vexus laughed. "And you, Ezra, you're no
better. Your people kidnapped my wife and me, all to get
your grubby hands on my niece!"

"I did what I had to do to ensure balance is maintained in
both worlds. More than one of the fallen may not exist at a
time! It's dangerous for us all! I apologize for my role in the
recent times, but it was for the good of us all; for the angels
and the vampires!"

"And what of the good of the lygoids, auntie? Where is our
place in the world? Clearly, we don't belong next to your
precious angels, or the high and mighty vampires, so I implore
you to tell me, where do we belong?" Quinn begged for her to
answer him in a condescending tone.

"Your place belongs in hell. You have no place in this world or any other, you filthy creature." Ezra turned back to Quinn quickly.

"See, it's that prejudice that poisons your heart. Your lack of a moral compass will be the end of you." Quinn hissed back.

"Ezra, I don't blame you for addressing a fear you know nothing of, but today, we must set aside our differences for a greater issue at hand. You are correct, Quinn being allowed to escape will mean the destruction of your world, and chaos being brought into ours. This cannot happen." Vexus then faced Quinn full on. They stood less than arm's length away, "Therefore, I will do everything in my power, including siding with the angels, to stop you from destroying both worlds."

"You think you can stop me?" Quinn shrieked with laughter, clenching his arms around his stomach as he curled up laughing. "I have already won! I can escape any time I want! As we speak, my powers are bathing this world in complete darkness, and lygoids everywhere are travelling to the Mortal Realm! There's no stopping it at this point!

"Dark Reflection has been restored. The gateways are open, there *is* no closing them now! I assured it! Now creatures of darkness will come and go as they please, using both realms as an oasis of power!

"The nice thing about the Mortal Realm is that with the human population alone, it was already a realm of darkness before the vampires got there! I guess that is something we do

have in common, Vexus. The humans make a great feast for
us higher creatures.

"I even have some of your angels joining my cause! Just
think about how much you're hated, Ezra! Your own
creatures of light are willing to join the darkness if it means
being rid of you and the vampires simultaneously. And it's all
thanks to Frost here. Your precious angels, Frost, and the rest
of my followers here are all leaving together, and there's
nothing you can do about it! How does it feel to be useless,
Ezra? Tell me!" Quinn shrieked maniacally; he was a
madman.

Frost approached Geordie menacingly, "Just know your
contract with Ezra is null and void as soon as you leave the
Immortal Realm. I will kill you, Geordie Vollner, no matter
where you think you might hide, or who you think can protect
you. The next time we meet will be in battle, and you will die
by my hands."

Corál launched himself between Frost and Geordie,
shoving Frost away violently and then wrapping Geordie in
his arms. Completely enveloped in his pitch-black wings, he
then launched Geordie into the arms of Matt before turning
back to Quinn who was mid dodging an attack from Vexus.
Corál and Vexus both moved with a level of grace that
Geordie had never witnessed before. They were swift and
agile in their attacks even though they never landed a single
hit on Quinn. Meanwhile, Quinn wore a wide toothy grin as
he laughed at Vexus and Corál's failed attempts at subduing
him. All his movements were chaotic and jumbled yet just as
agile and quick as his pursuers. Geordie could tell he was
confident in his abilities by the fact that every time they tried

to land a hit on Quinn, he jumped back effortlessly whilst his hands never left his pockets as if this were just a casual training session.

Eventually, he slammed an elbow into the back of Vexus' neck, knocking him down, and took Corál by both wings and swung him around, flinging him into the air, sending him flying. Corál's recovery time was remarkable as he quickly steadied himself before allowing himself to get too far from the fray.

Before she had time to react, Quinn was suddenly nose to nose with Geordie, wrapping a boney arm around her waist and painfully pulling her head back by the hair with his free hand. There was no way for her to escape his grip, and he was stronger than any creature she had ever faced, including Frost. "Now, my dear, I have wanted to have a few words with you for quite some time."

"What do you want with me?" Geordie groaned. Behind her she could hear Matt scream in fear, trying to come after her, and Breena stopping him.

"Oh, I don't want anything in particular *from* you, but you living long enough in the Mortal Realm is key to my plan. Unfortunately, I cannot allow Frost to kill you just yet. Even though I have a moral obligation to allow her to do so. I'm sure you'll understand, and in the long term, you'll be grateful I spared you from those who would do you harm, including myself."

Behind them, one of the angels on Quinn's side approached slowly with a look of hatred towards her. The moment Geordie and the angel locked eyes, she felt an intense hatred burning inside her towards the angel as well. Quinn peered out of the corner of his eye behind him, and his smile widened. "Oh no, you two are not allowed to meet just yet, or else none of us are getting out of this situation alive."

He then spun around quickly and went to stop the angel from launching at Geordie. She took the opportunity to try to attack the angel but was rapidly stopped by Corál grabbing her and pulling her away. As soon as they were at a safe distance, the urge to kill the angel calmed down, but she could still feel it like a slight tingling feeling in the back of her neck. She had no idea what had just come over her at that moment of seeing the angel. She had never felt that way towards anyone before.

"And now, that is my cue to bid you all adieu!" Quinn declared, waving a hand majestically and bowing before he and all his followers disappeared one by one from the town square.

As soon as Quinn and his followers were gone, Ezra turned to Geordie and her group with an annoyed look on her face. Behind her, the angels had a mixture of confusion and worry across their faces as everyone around came to the same conclusion that war had just been declared on both worlds by Quinn.

"And what of you? What am I supposed to do about your existence and our contract?" Ezra asked Geordie impatiently.

"I think my existence throwing off the realms is probably the least of your concerns right now since Quinn has stated he plans on actively throwing them both off into chaos and darkness." Geordie stated simply, also annoyed at the number of enemies she somehow managed to accumulate.

"I think you are correct. I promised my sisters I would release you and your family for the time being. But you *will* come back to me in one lifetime or another." Ezra stood back with her angels showing no signs of wanting to stop Geordie from leaving. "And you, Seth, I am intrigued by you. I would like you to come back as well, of your own volition."

They all watched Ezra carefully as she spoke while Breena comforted Vexus with her healing magic, and he finally got back on his feet. Geordie didn't understand why Ezra was letting her leave so easily, but she decided not to question it.

"How do you expect Geordie or Seth to come back to a world that is actively crumbling from the loss of balance?" Vexus groaned painfully as he leaned on Breena's shoulder.

"I have taken precautions in the prevention of my world being completely destroyed, but it will take me some time to mend what has already been broken. It will be hopefully back to normal by the time the war has ended, and if it isn't then it probably means we are all dead."

"And may we count on your allegiance in the battle to come against the lygoids?" he asked skeptically, but Ezra shook her head.

"No, I will not be participating in any battle to come. My world needs mending. Many people, including my angels, will die within the Mortal Realm. There must be a place for them to go in the afterlife if balance is to be restored eventually."

"Fair enough, I can't say that I am surprised, but it's a reasonable explanation for your lack of participation in the war to come." Vexus shrugged, and he and Breena took a step into the fountain portal known as Aquavitas.

Corál approached Geordie, offering her his hand, and gestured toward the large fountain, while also keeping an eye on Ezra's every movement. "Geordie, we will meet again, I promise you, and I will be able to better explain my role in your life and your heritage."

"How can you explain my heritage? Who are you?" Everything about this man confused Geordie and she felt this longing to know more.

"My name is Corál Levington. I am the second fallen to ever have been born. You and I share the same heritage, and I can teach you what it means to be a fallen." Without another word, he lifted her onto the edge of the fountain, and she took Matt's hand in hers.

"And what about Seth? Will I see him again, here?" Ezra called out urgently.

"Yes, if it pleases you, I will be back eventually. I make no promises as to when though." Seth finally spoke for the first time they arrived in the town square.

"That time has yet to come. Let him go, please." Corál urged Ezra to let Seth go, who looked freaked out by her sudden attention to him. Seth then jumped into the water, also disappearing like his parents.

Geordie gestured for Matt to go next but he did not move. Instead, he grabbed Geordie forcefully by the arm, leaned in close to her, and whispered, "You lied about knowing my heritage and family history."

"Your heritage and family history will not matter in the end. I will see you not too long from now." Ezra interjected, grabbing Matt by the arm, forcefully ripping his grip away from Geordie before letting him go.

And with just a look of anger, Matt stepped into the fountain's water and disappeared. Heart pounding intensely, Geordie also stepped into the fountain without looking back at Corál or Ezra. In her mind she had more important things to worry about. Things she couldn't begin to figure out how to explain to Matt. But she had to do it. She had to figure out a way to explain make him understand her side of the situation.

MATT
MID SPRING

"Matt!" As Matt walked through the portal into the Mortal Realm, he was hugged by his mother until he could barely breathe.

Nearby, he could see Sam too stunned to do anything more than cry silent tears. He felt an odd sense of relief seeing his mother and Sam, confirming they really were back home in the Mortal Realm, aside from the fact that everything was no longer grey for Matt.

At the sight of Breena, Sam asked with a concerned voice, "Breena, what happened? Are you okay?"

"Frost kidnapped me, and Pyre tortured me nearly to death along with Vexus. I just need some time to rest." Breena stumbled, pressing a hand to her forehead. Seth caught her protectively as she collapsed, and he set her down against a cavern wall.

When Sam finally tried to hug him, Matt pulled away harshly, giving Sam a look of resentment and walked back over to his mother who was still sobbing. Behind him, he saw Geordie approach Sam cautiously and they began talking too quietly for Matt to hear. They were probably keeping more secrets from him.

As usual in her panicked state, Naómi was babbling endlessly at a speed Matt found difficult to keep up with or even process. He just let her babble until finally she broke down in tears hugging him tightly again and finally was able to hear what Sam was saying, "We were almost beginning to think you would never make it back."

"What are you talking about?" Geordie asked, as she caught the attention of everyone else.

"We have been looking for a way to get you all back safely for months now." A brunette with an intimidating presence spoke with a serious tone as she addressed Geordie's question. "The portal opened over a few weeks ago, and I only wanted to keep it open for a few minutes, but Sam swore to me he would take responsibility over anything that may cause havoc upon escaping to our realm."

"So how long were we gone for exactly?" Seth stood up from taking care of his mother.

"When I watched you disappear, it was January at the abandoned warehouse near the piers. Tomorrow is Easter." Sam showed them the date on his watch. They had been gone for almost four months. "We thought that when we opened the gateways, you guys would immediately come through, but you didn't. Thankfully we should be able to close the gateways now."

"That's not going to be possible." Matt spoke quietly, thinking about Quinn's words about keeping the gateways open.

"What do you mean, young man?" The brunette asked sternly.

"There was a guy, a lygoid named Quinn, he said he made sure the gateways could never be closed again. He wants to cover both realms in darkness so that the lygoids can thrive anywhere they please." Matt explained, thinking about Quinn specifically. He knew almost nothing about this guy except that he hated him as much as he hated Seth and he wanted to kill them both. It was an urge Matt was struggling to control.

He didn't like this side of himself. He felt like he was losing sight of who he was as a person. Every time he was around particular people, he felt angry and violent. Matt wished he could get answers about what was wrong with him, but he knew there were bigger problems needing to be addressed.

"Is this true?" The woman whose name Matt didn't know turned to Vexus, who was also comforting Breena alongside Seth.

"Every word, my queen." He looked up at her with his silver vampire eyes. That was when both Matt and Geordie exchanged a look of sudden but equal panic, but she managed to get the words out before he could.

"Wait… You're –" Geordie stared wide eyed at the queen. "You're the queen?"

"Yes, well… One of three. I'm a middle child. I do apologize for not formally introducing myself earlier, my name is Melandria Daron. I control the military forces and oversee the faction of guardians within the vampires. The situation here is a bit dire." Melandria leaned her head over to stare at Vexus who straightened up quickly, ready to get down to business as always.

"I am *so* sorry, Your Majesty! I did not know!" Geordie knelt and bowed her head respectfully.

"Not to worry, young one. We have more pressing matters." Melandria quickly turned to Vexus and Seth, "Did you see Quinn escape with anyone? No one came through the mirror before you."

"All of Quinn's followers escaped with him, but we have no idea where they could have gone." Vexus stated with a frustrated tone. "I was going to put out search parties from every coven looking for them as soon as I got back to the Los Angeles coven house."

"Don't bother, finding lygoids and angels has always been next to impossible for us. I know Quinn better than most, and I know he desires companionship. He will try to gain a stronger following between now and whenever it is he decides to strike us. I fear there's a chance we are alone in this war."

"What makes you say that?" Sam asked.

"Quinn can be very charming, and he might try to lure the faery orders to his side if he can convince them that we don't have their best interest at heart. They've always been a neutral party amongst the ongoing conflicts between angels and vampires. He might try to push them to choose a side for once."

"Then we must convince our allies to stay by our side in times of war." Seth stated bluntly. "Breena and I can convince our faery friends to join our side."

"We can try but it might be fruitless if we can't convince them to join a war they want no part of. Quinn isn't declaring war on the faeries; he's declaring war on the vampires." Melandria paced the room as she spoke, clearly trying to formulate a solid plan.

"Here's what we will do. Vexus, you're not going back to Los Angeles right yet. I want you and Seth to escort me back to Daron Island where I will inform my sisters of the most recent events. We will come up with a better plan from there, but I want you to rally the faeries and vampires on the island and convince them to stay by our side. When you are finished with that, go to each of the covens, except for Massachusetts, and tell them all that you have learned. Your ties to the faery community through Breena will be your greatest asset in this endeavor. Be prepared to do a lot of travelling."

"I will be sure to contact Triana and make sure she is ready to meet me." Vexus nodded shortly before turning to his wife, "When I contact her, I will make sure she takes you safely back to Los Angeles and protects you in my absence."

"Of course," Breena smiled, "It will be lovely to see her again after so many years. Melandria, what will you have me do?"

"Talk to your faery keepers at the library; convince them as well. You are the matriarch of more than one order; you can influence them. While you're at it, Quinn will be looking for that one treasure I know you still have. Make sure you take extra precautions to hide it. Move it if you must, I don't care."

"Of course, my queen." Breena bowed her head respectfully.

"Melandria, if you don't mind me asking, why don't you want Vexus and Seth going to Massachusetts?" Matt asked, happy he wouldn't have to deal with Seth in the foreseeable future, but still curious about her tactics.

"Yeah, I was going to ask the same thing." Sam nodded and Geordie also perked her attention towards them now.

"Given the coven elders are corrupt, and we don't know what Gerrold is up to, we must assume that if Vexus and Seth end up in his vicinity, he will either try to acquire them by force or take them down. Gerrold is incredibly stronger than them both combined. He will see their presence in his coven house as a threat and nothing else. And because of this, removing the elders from a position of power will also prove to be difficult." Melandria approached Matt, Geordie, and Sam, focusing on them now. "Like I said before, I know Quinn better than most. When he finally launches an attack on the vampires, the first move he will make will be on the Massachusetts coven house. His greatest enemy is there, and all of you will be there. He will be drawn to all of you in hopes of killing you all in one fell swoop. The fewer of our strongest and most loyal congregated in one location, the better."

"Wait, are you planning on using us as bait?" Sam exclaimed loudly. This plan already worried Matt, but he decided to listen regardless.

"Based on all our findings, there is nothing that can convince me that Matt Hallow isn't the heir to the Shadow Kingdom and a Potential. By the looks of things, so is Seth, and I already knew Quinn was a Potential as well."

Everybody in the cave stopped in awe at Melandria's nonchalant announcement of Matt being an heir to the throne of the Shadow Kingdom. Matt watched both Sam and Geordie's mouths drop simultaneously. Seth's eyes widened for a moment, and then slowly narrowed on Matt and they both exchanged a look of hatred. Matt took a step backward, widening the space between them.

"I know I am violating a thousand rules about the Shadow Kingdom's Potentials, but I have stopped caring at this point. We have bigger problems. Matt, Seth, it is in all our best interests to keep you two separated. Hence why I am sending you with Vexus, Seth. As for Geordie, Matt, and Sam, Gerrold Victoire is one of the oldest vampires alive. He is also the head coven elder in Massachusetts. As a Potential and as a fallen, he will view you two as prizes to be won. Sam has already informed me that Gerrold wants you to join his coven. Therefore, I want you all to learn all that you can and help us find a way to stop both Gerrold and Quinn at the same time. Sam, I want you to protect them at all costs. Living in that house will prove dangerous for them; they will need you."

"Your Majesty! Are you really going up against our enemies using Geordie? She has no idea what she would be stepping into!" Vexus protested Melandria's request.

"If my memory serves me correctly, Gerrold highly respected your brother. Therefore, seeing Geordie as she is the spitting image of her father should bring some interest in his desire to have powerful vampires in his coven. He lost both you and your brother because of his antics, he will try to acquire her and protect her." Melandria turned to Vexus with a stern attitude. "I would greatly appreciate it if you did not question my methods in the future. Sam will be there to protect them, his dedication to Matt assures that. If I am going to bring Gerrold to court, I will need someone who is not corrupted by Gerrold's influence to tell the truth about the activity over there. Geordie and Matt are the perfect candidates. But I cannot force them if they do not want to. Personal agency should still mean something."

Everyone, including Sam, turned to Matt and Geordie expectantly to hear their answers. Geordie's eyes trailed between everyone's staring faces as she gave her answer, "I'll do it. But I do not know how I will convince him to let me join his coven."

"Don't worry about that. He already wants you; your presence alone will be enough." Melandria reassured her, and then turned to Matt, "What about you? You can't join a vampire coven right now, but it might be an opportunity to learn something about yourself.

"My father is Gerrold Victoire. If he is as evil of a man as everyone makes him out to be, then I want to help in taking him out. He abandoned me as a child."

"So be it." Melandria nodded. She then spoke to Breena and Naómi one final time. "Hopefully all of this will be over by the summer migration. If not…"

"What?" Naómi asked worriedly.

"We'll deal with that when it happens. I must take my leave now. Everyone has their assignments; let us get to it then."

Everyone left the cavern and went out to Daron Forest. Vexus and Seth followed Melandria down the mountain path without saying goodbye, and eventually disappeared into the darkness of the forest. For a long, awkward moment, it was just Breena, Naómi, Matt, Geordie, and Sam.

"I must get back to my classes now." Naómi kissed Matt on the cheek and gave him one final tight hug. "Please be careful with Gerrold. He's too dangerous to trifle with lightly. Don't let him use you in any way."

"I will be careful, mother, I promise." Matt squeezed his mother's hands affectionately and smiled, eventually letting her go. He wasn't sure why she kept so many secrets from him as a child regarding Gerrold, but he figured there had to be a good reason if he was as bad as everyone said he was.

"Yes, I should probably get going." Breena turned to Geordie, wrapping her arms warmly around her. "I will see you again soon. I promise. I'm sorry it took me so long to finally meet you."

"Thank you, for everything." Geordie hugged her back, and then Sam suddenly jumped excitedly as if he remembered something.

"Breena! Wait!" He pulled out a photograph from his pocket and handed it to Breena. "I found this in your drawer while we were looking for the stone. I was wondering if Geordie could have it."

Everyone looked at the photograph. It was a picture of Geordie at a very young age with two people who looked practically identical to her in their own ways. Her parents. "Ah yes. My sister sent me this picture. Yes, of course, please keep it, Geordie."

She handed the photo to Geordie who began to cry. "This was taken right before my parents died. What do you mean your sister gave it to you?"

"My sister was Lily Perkins. Her husband was Burke. They briefly spoke of you shortly after the fire of their cabin and you disappeared."

"Lily!" Geordie cried out. "What happened to her?"

"She died many years later. I will tell you more about it later. For now, keep that picture and know that I will answer all your questions at the right time."

Geordie nodded and smiled, still very much crying. Breena then hugged all three of them and took her leave as well. Then it was just Matt, Geordie, and Sam at last. Matt still had no words for how upset he was with them, but he figured he could at least be cordial in the meantime.

"You guys can stay with me in the loft again until we get formally invited to the coven." Sam spoke awkwardly, finally breaking the silence after what seemed like the longest five minutes of their lives. "Look, Matt, I understand that you are upset with Geordie and me, and you have every right to be, but I hope you can find the means of forgiving us one day as we need to work together for all of us to succeed in our mission. And at the end of the day, I will always be there to protect you, no matter how mad you are at me.

"Okay." Matt whispered, his voice harsh and strained as if he had a sore throat or was refraining from crying.

Matt knew in his heart that one day he was going to have to forgive Sam and Geordie, but today was not that day. He was still angry about all the secrets that were kept from him about his life, and he needed closure, he needed answers. In the meantime, he was willing to work with everyone because they all had the same goal, but for now he needed time and space to heal from the feeling of betrayal he felt when he looked at Sam and Geordie.

Tiara J. Vasquez discovered her love of writing through experiencing various medias of storytelling, whether it be reading, music, television shows, or movies. She loves all forms of storytelling and wishes to be able to evoke the same feelings in her readers that she's experienced from the stories she's experienced. She began writing Fallen Ribbon in 2009 at fourteen years old and has since then started many other projects including the continuation of The Dark Nursery Diaries Series.

After moving to Boston, she joined the 2012 Grubstreet Young Adult Writing Program. She wrote her first published piece in an anthology; One Day We Rise And We Are Everywhere, a short story titled The Fall, about a boy throwing a cello down a flight of stairs to avoid parental expectations. She now lives happily in the Boston North Shore where she spends a lot of her free time writing new story ideas.